HOLY MOLY

ALSO BY BEN REHDER

Gun Shy
Guilt Trip
Flat Crazy
Bone Dry
Buck Fever

HOLY MOLY

BEN REHDER

ST. MARTIN'S MINOTAUR/NEW YORK

www.minotaurbooks.com

Library of Congress Cataloging-in-Publication Data

Rehder, Ben.
    Holy moly / Ben Rehder.—1st ed.
      p. cm.
    ISBN-13: 978-0-312-35754-2
    ISBN-10: 0-312-35754-0
    1. Marlin, John (Fictitious character)—Fiction. 2. Game wardens—Fiction. 3. Fossils—Fiction. 4. Texas—Fiction. I. Title.
PS3618.E45H66 2008
813'.6—dc22

                            2008003153

First Edition: May 2008

10 9 8 7 6 5 4 3 2 1

For Cisco, Karen, and Victoria
and
for Donnie

ACKNOWLEDGMENTS

I ASK A LOT of dumb questions, but helpful people continue to answer them for me.

Special thanks to Lieutenant Tommy Blackwell (retired from the Travis County Sheriff's Office); Lampasas County Game Warden Jim Lindeman; Dr. Edward Theriot, director of the Texas Natural Science Center; and John Grace, assistant criminal district attorney, Civil Division, Lubbock County.

Much appreciation also to Martin Grantham, Trey Carpenter, Cisco Hobbs, Carol Blackwell, Jim Haught, Kerry Hilton, Lloyd Bridges, Rob Cordes, and Mike Smith.

I'm repeating myself, but thanks again to my early readers: Mary Summerall, Helen and Ed Fanick, and Stacia Hernstrom, and to my copy editor, India Cooper.

Jane Chelius, Marc Resnick, Lauren Manzella, Sarah Lumnah, Talia Ross, and the rest of the team: I appreciate everything you've done for the Blanco County series. I'd go poaching with you anytime.

All errors or distortions of reality are my own.

HOLY MOLY

1

FOUR DAYS BEFORE he died, a thirty-year-old backhoe operator named Hollis Farley drove thirty miles to the Wal-Mart Supercenter in Marble Falls, Texas, and purchased a four-thousand-dollar sixty-inch plasma television. It had a high-definition screen, of course, along with a built-in digital tuner, picture-in-picture, and, as the salesman put it, "a whole shitload of pixels." Whatever those were.

All Hollis Farley knew, standing in the store, was that Jessica Simpson was spilling out of her Daisy Duke shorts in a manner that made him proud she was a fellow Texan. He couldn't sign the receipt fast enough.

Back at home, Farley drank a six-pack to celebrate. Then he yanked his malfunctioning nineteen-incher loose from its moorings and heaved it directly out the back door, where it landed with a crash next to a rusting Hotpoint stove and a vermin-infested mattress with stains of dubious origin.

Next, he set about hanging and connecting the new unit, an undertaking that, in Farley's semi-inebriated state, consumed the better part of the afternoon. The tricky part was climbing onto the sagging roof of his mobile home to replace the cables to his satellite dish; raccoons had gnawed through the old ones. Once he had everything hooked up, Farley grabbed the remote control and prepared to enjoy more than three hundred channels of jumbo-sized American entertainment.

He thumbed the ON button with a child's sense of wonderment and anticipation. Everything worked perfectly, and even Farley, a tenth-grade dropout, recognized the irony when the first thing he saw was the smiling, progressively scanned visage of Peter Boothe.

Or, as he was better known, Pastor Pete.

Betty Jean Farley loved her little brother to pieces, even though he had half the sense of a cigar-store Indian, bless his heart. A good-looking boy, that's what all her friends said, but any dumber and you'd have to water him. That's why Betty Jean felt obliged to come over once or twice a month to check up on her only sibling and maybe do a little light cleaning, which wasn't a bad deal, since he usually mowed her lawn in return. Good thing she stopped in, too, because on this particular Sunday evening, she found that Hollis had completely lost his mind. There in one corner, under his prized ten-point mule deer, was a television the size of a picnic table.

"Sweet Jesus, Hollis, when did you get that thing?" she asked.

"This morning. Just finished hooking it up," he replied, distracted, his eyes glued to the set. He was lazing on the sofa, shirtless, wearing denim shorts and a CAT DIESEL cap, his unshaven face reflecting the blue light from the television. A sixteen-ounce Budweiser was tucked between his knees.

"You gone 'round the bend or what?" Betty Jean asked.

No reply. Hollis was watching a religious program, which should've set off warning bells. Betty Jean had only seen her brother pray once in his life, years back, during the Super Bowl, when Emmitt Smith was slow getting up from a tackle.

"Well, you're gonna have to take it back, that's all there is to it. I hope you saved the receipt."

No answer. He often ignored Betty Jean when she griped at him, but this was different. Like he was in another world.

She let out a sigh of impatience. "You hear me, Hollis? You can't afford it."

Still no reaction.

Betty Jean continued, saying, "Tell me you didn't put it on your credit card. You realize you're paying eighteen percent? *Per annum*." The words made her shudder with disgust. Eighteen percent was for suckers. People like Hollis, bless his heart.

But Hollis didn't appear concerned in the least. All he said was, "You know who that is?"

Betty Jean glanced at the TV, where a preacher in an expensive suit was addressing a massive audience, all of them dressed in their Sunday best. The preacher's face was aglow with passion.

It's true, friends! Only God can deliver the life of abundance you deserve! Remember: "Wealth and riches shall be in his house, and his righteousness endureth forever." That means you are worthy of God's most gracious blessing! All you have to do is open your eyes and watch for it!

Betty Jean shook her head in exasperation. Honestly, why did she even bother? Hollis was old enough to know better. On the other hand . . . she had to admit, the new TV had a heck of a picture.

Speaking of watching, don't forget that my latest DVD, Breaking Bread with Jesus, *is now available for the low introductory price of only $19.95!*

Betty Jean reluctantly perched on the edge of the sofa, which groaned under her significant weight. She knew she shouldn't let up on her lecture; after all, Hollis needed new tires, new work clothes, and a whole bunch of stuff more important than a television set. But wow, she felt like she was in the middle row of a movie theater. It was *that* good. She could only imagine watching *Grey's Anatomy* on that screen. The dramatic tension would be unbelievable. It'd be like having Dr. McDreamy right in her living room. Now that she thought about it, she remembered that most stores had a thirty-day return policy. She figured it wouldn't hurt to let Hollis keep his new toy for twenty-nine days.

But the religious program stumped her. Why wasn't he watching sports?

"That there's Peter Boothe," Hollis said quietly, as if he'd sensed her puzzlement.

Betty Jean recognized the name, all right. *Pastor Pete.* Everybody in Blanco County had been hearing it lately. Peter Boothe was tall and slender with a boyish face. A nice-looking man. Midforties. Big white teeth and curly brown hair. He had a twangy country accent and a soothing voice. Except . . . Betty Jean didn't know what it was, but there was something vaguely creepy about the man. Sort of a cross between Mr. Rogers and a used-car salesman. She glanced at Hollis and saw an expression of utter satisfaction on his face. She had to wonder: *Has Hollis found God?* Wouldn't that be a hoot? Little Hollis, born again.

But there are times when you must also be a giver in life! Because you have the power to help spread the sacred word of Jesus Christ!

The camera cut to an elderly woman in the audience, who was nodding vigorously.

You can give your time! You can give your talents!

Betty Jean suddenly had an uneasy feeling in her stomach. She knew what was coming next.

Or you can make a financial contribution that will help me reach out with God's message of eternal hope.

An address popped up on the screen, and Betty Jean said, "Hollis, you ain't planning to send this guy any money, are you?"

He seemed almost hypnotized.

"Hollis?"

Finally, he looked at her, and, to her relief, she saw the same old Hollis. Mischief in his eyes. This was the kid who'd turned a cow loose in the principal's office during his sophomore year. He grinned and said, "Hell, no. It's the other way around."

"What the heck's that mean?" she asked. Hollis had a strange sense of humor sometimes.

He made a face like he knew something she didn't, but he never answered. Which was a tragedy, because if he'd told her what was happening, or if Betty Jean had pressed a little harder, maybe things wouldn't have worked out the way they did. It wasn't but four days later that her baby brother—poor, overextended Hollis Farley—was gone. Died on his backhoe, just the way he'd have wanted it. Betty Jean hoped they didn't administer some kind of IQ test at the Pearly Gates, or Hollis would be stuck forever on the outside, looking in.

Bless his heart.

2

PHIL COLBY, CHEWING on a piece of sausage, said, "You realize, of course, there's gotta be a bachelor party."

John Marlin, the game warden in Blanco County for more than twenty years, grinned. "You think?"

"Hell, yeah," Colby said. "We're talking expensive dancing girls and cheap whiskey."

Marlin played along. "What if I'd rather have cheap girls and expensive whiskey?"

"Whatever you want, hoss. We'll do it up right. After all, how often is my best friend gonna get married?"

"Just this once," Marlin said, cutting into a slab of brisket. "Unless you get me in serious trouble."

They were having lunch, as they often did, at Ronnie's Ice

House & Barbeque in Johnson City. Outside, beyond the plate-glass windows, it was a beautiful late-May afternoon. The temperature was in the midseventies, and rainbows of wildflowers blanketed the rolling hills and highway medians of Central Texas: Indian paintbrushes and huisache daisies, winecups and black-eyed Susans. The bluebonnets were especially plentiful, thanks to the abundance of rain they'd received all spring.

"The problem," Colby said thoughtfully, "will be finding strippers who aren't young enough to be our daughters."

Marlin smiled again. "That could be a challenge."

When it came down to it, he knew Colby was blowing smoke. The party would consist of a big group of lifelong friends who'd spend the night on Colby's ranch, cooking over a campfire, telling stories they'd all heard a thousand times. They'd attempt to drink beer until sunrise, getting lucky if they made it past midnight. But there'd be no girls, and that suited Marlin just fine. He was exactly seven weeks away from marrying the only woman he needed.

"You realize we were sitting at this same table when you looked at diamond rings last summer?" Colby said. "Weird, huh?"

Colby's girlfriend owned a thriving jewelry store in Austin, and she'd sent some specimens home with him to show to Marlin.

"We *always* sit at this table," Marlin said.

"Yeah, but back then, there wasn't a hot blonde checking you out from across the room."

Marlin shook his head. Colby loved to be a wiseass. It was probably some elderly woman with astigmatism.

"I'm not kidding. Over by the newspaper racks."

Marlin didn't look right away. He took his time. But when he glanced to his left, sure enough, he locked eyes with an attractive young woman who was dining alone. She smiled, then looked down at her plate.

Marlin went back to his own lunch.

"Can't keep her eyes off you," Colby said.

"Shut up."

"I heard a theory once. Women know when a guy's getting married. Some kind of intuition. And boy, they love a man who can commit."

"You're full of crap, you know that?"

Colby shrugged, obviously enjoying himself. "Better get used to it. Once you put a ring on, they'll be throwing themselves at you, like some kind of cheesy Cinemax movie."

Marlin pushed his empty plate away and took a long drink of iced tea. He wouldn't look over at her again. It was silly. "Remember, a week from tomorrow, we're getting fitted for tuxes."

"I remember. We going with lavender?"

Marlin ignored him. There was still a lot to do. The tuxes, the invitations, the limo. Nicole was working on the menu for the reception and ironing out details with the florist. She was keeping it together pretty well, though her nerves showed through on occasion. She was tired almost every night. Part of it was her new job. Plenty of stress all around. But in seven weeks—or seven weeks and one day—she could finally take a breath. They both could.

"Baby blue is nice," Colby said.

Without even thinking about it, Marlin looked again and caught the young blond girl staring at him. This time, Marlin had to look away first.

"Damn," Colby said. "Wish I was getting married."

She caught him in the parking lot, just as he reached his truck.

"Mr. Marlin?"

He turned, and she was four feet away. Phil Colby was right. She was gorgeous. Couldn't have been older than twenty-seven, twenty-eight. Dressed in white linen slacks and a pale blue blouse that matched the color of her eyes. Tall, too. Marlin was a shade over six-two, and her forehead was even with his jaw.

"I'm sorry, I didn't want to disturb you during lunch," she said. "I'm Susan Kishner. Jason Wright's aunt."

Suddenly, it all made sense. She hadn't been leering at him at all. Marlin realized he was a little disappointed.

"Oh, right, nice to meet you," he said, shaking her hand. "How's Jason doing?"

She laughed. "Staying close to home, that's for sure."

The previous weekend, two nine-year-olds had gotten lost in Pedernales Falls State Park. Marlin had organized a search party and found them in about thirty minutes, less than a mile from their campsite. They had never been in much danger, because the park just wasn't that large. Nonetheless, it had made the news in Austin. Must have been a slow day.

"I just wanted to say thank you," Susan Kishner said. "For saving his life."

"Well, I appreciate that, but I wouldn't say I saved his—"

"Oh, you're being modest. They could've been eaten by coyotes!" she said.

She was putting him on. Maybe flirting? "Either that or polar bears," he said.

"Oh, I know!" she said. "The polar bears are horrible this time of year! Especially if you forget your repellent."

They both laughed, and Marlin said, "I was happy to help."

She reached out and touched his arm. "You certainly had an effect on Jason. He says he wants to be a game warden when he grows up. Isn't that the coolest thing?"

"Yeah, that's great. We can always use a good recruit."

Through his open window, Marlin heard Darrell, the dispatcher, *Blanco County to seventy-five-oh-eight . . .*

"Of course, he'll have to learn how to navigate in the woods," Susan Kishner said.

"Hell, I'm lost half the time myself," Marlin said.

She tilted her head to the side and studied him. "Somehow I doubt that. You look like you know your way around."

Marlin was starting to squirm. "Listen, I really need to take that radio call . . ."

She nodded. "Okay, I won't hold you up, I just wanted you to know we appreciate everything you did. You're a sweetheart."

Before he knew it, she stepped forward and kissed him. Right on the mouth.

"Take care, now," she said, and then she was walking to her car across the parking lot. Marlin's face suddenly felt hot. The scent of her perfume was lingering in the air.

The radio squawked his unit number again.

Marlin ducked into his state-issued Dodge Ram and grabbed the microphone. "Seventy-five-oh-eight, go ahead, County."

"What's your ten-twenty?"

"Ronnie's."

"Can you meet with Bobby?"

"When?"

"Right now."

"On my way."

He started his truck and backed out, wondering if anyone inside the restaurant had seen what happened.

On Saturday afternoon, television viewers were treated to a live interview of Pastor Peter Boothe. The piece was a segment on *America's Talkin' 'Bout It,* a lightweight feel-good news journal, and the interviewer was Barry Grubbman, a producer-turned-reporter who formerly worked for a show called *Hard News Tonight,* which was anything but.

Grubbman, like all of the "journalists" on the show, had a reputation for lobbing softball questions designed to do nothing more than further the interviewee's agenda. What the audience didn't know was that the network had recently been acquired by

a large Japanese conglomerate, and the new owners were determined to bring a trace of dignity back to American broadcasting.
They'd decided that *Talkin'*, in particular, needed a face-lift; it
needed to tackle important issues head-on, in the tradition of
Mike Wallace or, at the least, Geraldo Rivera. So the first question caught Peter Boothe, and 2.6 million viewers, off guard.

"Pastor, is it true you own a twenty-thousand-dollar desk?"

The slightest hint of a smile crossed Peter Boothe's face. He
opened his mouth, then closed it. Finally, he said, "Interesting
question."

"Thank you. You do own a desk like that?"

"Why, yes, I do."

"And the desk was built from St. Helena gumwood, which is
one of the most endangered trees in the world."

"Unfortunately, yes. I, uh, I didn't know that at the time. But
I must say, it makes a beautiful piece of furniture. Truly one of
God's most dazzling wonders. I'm praying the gumwood can
make a comeback."

"You also own a private jet."

"God has asked me to deliver His word, and I see no reason
to dally." Boothe grinned at his own levity.

"You own a second home in Carmel, California. Eight bed-
rooms. Nine thousand square feet. Right on the beach."

Boothe's smile broadened, but those who knew him well
might've detected a hint of nervousness. "It's where I write
some of my best sermons. A magnificent stretch of Creation."

"Your wife is a lovely woman."

The abrupt change in questioning seemed to leave Boothe
perplexed. "She most certainly is."

"Her long blond mane has become somewhat of a trade-
mark."

"Vanessa is a trendsetter, no doubt about that."

"I understand she spends eight hundred dollars to have her
hair cut and styled. Does that seem extravagant to you?"

Pastor Pete made a vague gesture with his hands. "Forgive me, but I have no idea what services like that typically cost."

Grubbman crossed his legs, as if settling in for the long haul. "I bring all this up because, to put it bluntly, you have many detractors. Some fundamentalists call you a 'pastorpreneur.' They say you preach the idea that good Christians are entitled to a life of financial well-being. They say your sermons are empty of scripture and heavy on cheerleading about securing a better station in life. Would you say that's accurate?"

Boothe appeared to consider his words carefully. "I believe that good things await those who follow the Lord."

"And by 'good things,' you mean wealth and prosperity? A higher-paying job. A promotion. A big Christmas bonus."

"His blessings take many forms."

"Frankly, Reverend, you appear to be very blessed yourself."

There was a pause, then Boothe said, "Affluence is nothing to be ashamed of, as I stress in my new book." The book, after all, was the intended topic of the interview. Only $32.95 in hardback.

Now it was Grubbman's turn to smile. "Yes, your book. I want to talk about that in depth, but first I'd like to ask you about your background."

Boothe shifted uncomfortably in his seat.

"You used to own a marketing firm," Grubbman said.

"Boy, you've done your homework. Many years ago, yes, I was in the field of advertising. It helped me hone my communication skills, which I now use to spread the gospel. Time well spent."

Grubbman scanned through a sheaf of papers in a notebook. "You once wrote a commercial for a juicing machine."

Boothe chuckled. "I remember that one. The SqueezeMaster Deluxe. A fine product. American made. Pulps a grapefruit in less than three seconds."

"Your commercials sold all sorts of unique items. Michael

Bolton albums. A Raggedy Ann pen-and-pencil set. A solar-powered dehydrator. And now one might say you're selling Jesus."

This time, Boothe did not chuckle. Instead, he said, "Mr. Grubbman, I must take issue with your wording. I am not 'selling Jesus' by any stretch of the imagination."

"Your Web site is so retail-oriented, it would make the folks at Amazon blush. It appears to be nothing more than an online store for your books, DVDs, CDs, and audiotapes. And I gotta say, the prices are pretty steep."

By now, many viewers were expecting Boothe to start looking for an exit. To his credit, he did not. "We feel those prices are reasonable. We have to cover administrative costs."

Grubbman checked his notebook. "Administrative costs? Like this six-hundred-dollar dinner at Chez Moufette in Beverly Hills?"

"Yes, well, in my new book, I mention the importance of treating oneself to small pleasures now and again."

Grubbman let that one slide. "Your church in Dallas is the largest in America. Thirty thousand congregants?"

Boothe nodded, happy, back on solid ground. "And growing every week, praise Jesus."

"*The Pastor Pete Hour* is broadcast in thirty countries."

Here came the chuckle again. "Fortunately, I don't have to write my sermon in thirty languages."

"And now you're building a second religious complex, on a sixteen-hundred-acre ranch in Blanco County, Texas."

"We're trying to," Boothe said. "The good Lord has blessed that area with a lot of rain lately. Things are moving slowly."

"Why Blanco County?"

Boothe steepled his fingers, thoughtful, full of altruism and sincerity. "We want to open our doors to the good people in Austin and San Antonio. The location in Blanco County will offer both of those communities access to a Sunday afternoon service."

"Yes, right. I understand you'll fly between the two sites. A sermon in the morning, another in the afternoon."

"Precisely. Perhaps now you can understand why a man of God might need a jet."

"Just two days ago, a construction worker died at the job site. What can you tell us about that?"

Boothe was suddenly solemn. "The poor man flipped his backhoe. A veritable tragedy."

"Do you believe in signs, Reverend Boothe?"

"Signs? How do you mean?"

"Perhaps this man's death is God's way of saying the Boothe empire has reached its limits. Maybe your new church isn't meant to be."

Boothe narrowed his eyes and made a scoffing noise deep in his throat. "You can choose to think of it that way if you wish. But it was an unfortunate accident, and nothing more."

3

"WHY CAN'T WE have a normal homicide around here?" Sheriff Bobby Garza asked. He was sitting at a conference table, with Marlin across from him and Chief Deputy Bill Tatum to his left.

"We get fake drownings," he continued, "fake hunting accidents. A man supposedly gets attacked by a chupacabra, only it turns out he was really stabbed in the neck with a screwdriver. Hell, in the big cities people just walk up and shoot each other. It's quick, it's efficient, and there's no question what happened. But no, out here, people gotta get weird."

"Not to point out the obvious, but you said homicide," Tatum said. He was average height, but he had a weightlifter's physique—a thick torso, and biceps that stretched the sleeves of his khaki uniform. He was a good man, highly intelligent, but, unlike the sheriff, Tatum was never much for banter. He had a pale yellow circle under his left eye—the last traces of a shiner—and it made him look like a barroom brawler.

"I did," Garza replied. "Lem hasn't made the final cut, but he was able to tell us that much from the prelim."

The sheriff was referring to the autopsy of a local man named Hollis Farley, a backhoe operator whose body had been found the previous morning. The initial theory was that Farley had been crushed by his own rig late on Thursday afternoon after it had hit a boulder and flipped. Marlin had heard all about it, including the fact that it had taken the deputies nine hours to find a crane that could lift the eight-ton backhoe off Farley's corpse.

"So what'd Lem find?" Marlin asked. His mind was racing ahead; he had some relevant information to share, though it was probably a long shot.

"Here, tell me what you think." Garza placed a photograph on the table. "I puzzled over this thing for about ten minutes before I figured it out. At least, I *think* I figured it out, and Lem seems to agree."

Marlin leaned forward to study the photo. What he saw was a close-up of a round puncture wound, maybe a third of an inch in diameter, which was bisected by two inch-long slits, one vertical, one horizontal, like the crosshairs in a rifle scope. Near the wound were the bumps of vertebrae running along Hollis Farley's spine. The wound could have been mistaken for some sort of injury inflicted by the flipping backhoe, but Marlin knew better.

"Shot in the back with an arrow," he said.

Garza whistled. "Now I feel stupid. What'd that take you? Five seconds?"

Tatum picked the photo up and continued to examine it, scowling. "I'm still feeling stupid. This was an arrow?"

Marlin nodded. "With a broadhead hunting point. I'm guessing it was one of the mechanical types—with blades that open on impact—because the conventional broadheads generally have a smaller diameter."

"That's right," Garza said. "I wouldn't have thought of that."

Tatum shook his head. "Well then, somebody pulled the arrow out, because there wasn't one in him."

The chief deputy was an experienced hunter, but Marlin knew he didn't use a bow. Like most people, the only image he had of a human getting hit by an arrow came from the movies; cowboys getting attacked by Indians, arrows sticking out of chests and legs. Archery technology had improved greatly since those days, of course. "With enough draw weight," Marlin said, "most arrows will go clean through."

"Even if they hit bone?" Tatum asked.

"Depends on the bone. They can usually bust through the rib cage pretty good."

"And that's what this one did," Garza said, placing another photo on the table, "because this is the exit."

The wound to Farley's chest wasn't as neat. The skin was torn and ragged, and a splinter of rib bone was protruding from the hole.

"That means the arrow's still out there, unless somebody picked it up," Marlin said.

"Crap," Tatum said. "We didn't even know to look for it."

"Let's get a couple deputies back to the scene," Garza said. "See if we can track it down. In the meantime, there are plenty of people we need to talk to. Family, friends. We need to find out if this was something personal, or maybe Farley got crossways with a poacher."

"I guess that's possible," Marlin said, "but it seems doubtful that a poacher would shoot him off his backhoe. Most poachers just run, if you give them a chance."

"Then there's the possibility that it was related to the construction," Garza said.

"If it was, this'll be a cinch," Tatum said. "There won't be any more than about nine thousand suspects."

He was alluding to the entire population of Blanco County. Very few residents had voiced support for the Reverend Peter Boothe's new church. Marlin was against it, too, especially after he'd learned how large the project was. It wasn't merely a church, it was a massive religious complex, complete with an auditorium that seated nearly fifteen thousand. The parking lot alone would cover sixty acres. The airstrip would swallow another ten. Worse yet, the construction site was adjacent to Pedernales Falls State Park, on the banks of the Pedernales River, and the pristine waters were at risk for pollution. Most of the locals were outraged that the site plan had ever been approved.

"And don't forget that conservation group," Tatum continued. "We'll need to check them out."

Garza laughed. "Well, yeah, I plan to. But I think I'd better speak to them myself. Considering."

Marlin had heard about that, too—how Tatum had gotten sucker-punched by an elderly woman who'd chained herself to a cottonwood. Just one member of a group of protestors from Austin who'd visited the construction site earlier in the week.

Tatum showed a rare moment of humor, saying, "Give me another shot, Bobby. I think I can take her."

Garza said, "I don't know, Bill. She sounds pretty tough. Better let me handle it. Besides, you're leaving town, when, Monday morning?"

"That's the plan, but I can postpone it."

"No, that's fine. You should go. Your kids would be crushed." He explained to Marlin: "Bill's taking the family to Disney World."

"Oh, yeah? That's the one in Florida?" Marlin asked.

"Yeah. Near Orlando," Tatum said.

"You flying?"

"Driving."

Tatum had a look on his face like he'd just as soon lose a finger to a power saw. Marlin could only imagine two solid days cooped up with children in a car.

"Well, uh, good luck with that."

Garza asked Marlin, "You got some time to spend on this?"

"You bet."

Garza often involved Marlin in larger investigations; after all, Texas game wardens were fully commissioned peace officers and could enforce any state law, not just those pertaining to hunting and fishing. For the sheriff, it was like having an extra deputy on hand, when needed. Marlin, Garza, and Tatum had known each other since childhood, and they worked well together.

"Good," Garza said. "If I remember right, you've had some trouble with Farley in the past."

"Just once. Caught him hunting without a license a couple of years ago."

"Didn't I see him in your office a few months back?"

"You did, but he was actually helping me out with something. I don't know if this will lead anywhere, but . . . do either of you know a deer breeder named Perry Grange?"

"I know of him," Tatum said. "That high-fenced ranch down on McCall Creek Road."

Garza said, "I thought his name was Harry."

Marlin said, "No, that's his brother. Remember a movie called *Hell Hole*, from six or seven years ago?"

"Yeah, something about kids trapped in a cave."

"A *haunted* cave," Marlin said. "Harry Grange directed it. Shot it out near Llano, where he and Perry are from originally. Low-budget stuff, but it ended up making a fortune. Kind of a cult classic for teenagers. So then he got a big deal with one of the studios, but his next movie bombed, and he's been making cheesy horror flicks ever since. From what I can tell, Harry set his brother up in the deer-breeding business, like a silent partner.

Harry, I think, put up the money to buy the original stock. Now Perry's got eight or nine good bucks out there, and he breeds them with decent does and sells the buck fawns."

"How does this tie in to Hollis Farley?" Tatum asked.

Marlin smiled. "Patience, Bill, patience. In January, Hollis Farley called me and asked if there was any kind of reward for turning in a breeder who wasn't following the rules. I said yeah, I might be able to dig something up, depending on what he had. So he said Perry Grange was selling more fawns than his herd could possibly produce. He figured Grange was trapping wild fawns and selling them as his own. Which means his customers weren't getting the trophy bloodlines they were paying for, and, obviously, Grange was able to sell a lot more deer than he normally would. We're talking about fawns that sell for five or six grand apiece."

Garza shook his head. "You work in a strange business."

"Getting stranger all the time. A few years ago, a couple of breeders paid nearly half a million dollars for the biggest captive buck in Texas."

"Jesus. What the hell are they gonna do with it?"

"Breed it. Make their money back, and then some. Assuming it doesn't die. Even then, they're probably insured."

"Was Farley right?" Tatum asked.

Marlin said, "I think so, in one case at least. The problem was, I didn't have enough to get a warrant for DNA tests. But I managed to find two of Grange's customers whose fawns had supposedly been sired by the same buck. We tested them, and those fawns weren't any more related than the three of us."

"What'd Grange say?"

"That it was a mix-up. That one of the fawns must've come from one of his other bucks. Both customers got a refund, and neither was willing to take it any further."

"At that point," Garza said, "you'd think all of his customers would be lining up for DNA tests."

"Just the opposite. I think there's an embarrassment factor.

Most of Grange's customers use the fawns to stock their own ranches for commercial hunting, and they don't want to admit they got taken."

"Like, what, it'd be bad PR?"

"Exactly. They don't want people thinking their deer are no different than the ones on the roadside. But I do know Grange's business suffered. He's having to sell a lot further from home."

"So," Garza said, "boiling it down, Grange had a pretty good reason to be pissed at Hollis Farley."

"But there's a hang-up. Everything Farley told me was confidential. Grange wouldn't know who ratted him out unless Farley opened his mouth."

"Did he get a reward?" Tatum asked.

"A thousand bucks."

"A guy like Farley might've bragged about it."

"Yeah, maybe."

"Tell me about Perry Grange," Garza said.

"An odd bird," Marlin said. "Maybe thirty-five years old, but he dresses like an old-time trapper or mountain man. Thinks the government should stay out of his business."

"Got a temper?"

"I didn't see one, but it never got confrontational."

Garza sat quietly for several moments, pondering the information. "Okay, Henry's processing Farley's truck right now. In the meantime, John, you drop in on Perry Grange, but don't tell him why. Just poke around and see how he reacts. Bill, before you leave town, work on Farley's coworkers and family members. I'll look into that environmental group, but first I'll grab Ernie and search Farley's place."

They agreed on the plan, and Marlin got up to leave.

Tatum was staring at the photos again. "The arrow didn't go all the way through in *Deliverance*."

Marlin smiled. "That's the movies for ya."

4

RED O'BRIEN WAS snoozing in his recliner, his belly full of tamales and Keystone beer, when he heard brakes squeal on the county road in front of his trailer. He'd been hearing that same annoying sound six days a week for two months now, because it had been that long since he'd had any paying work. It always came in the midafternoon, right when he was napping. The vehicle would slow, come to a stop, idle for a few seconds, then move a hundred yards down the road and repeat the process.

Neither rain, nor snow, nor poorly maintained brakes . . .

Red's best friend and housemate, a three-hundred-pounder named Billy Don Craddock, was lounging on the sofa, the TV remote resting on his chest. On the screen, a tight cluster of

cars, all plastered bumper to bumper with various corporate lo-
gos, was roaring around Texas Motor Speedway. The volume
was turned low, so all Red could hear was the faint droning of
the juiced-up engines. As far as racing went, Red could take it
or leave it, but it was a decent thing to watch on a lazy Saturday
afternoon, with the spring breeze wafting through the open
window. Truth was, it was damn near hypnotic, those cars going
in circles like that. Could put a man to sleep before the tenth
lap.

Red stretched and yawned. Then he said, "Hey, Billy Don,
why don't you run down and fetch the mail?"

Billy Don didn't budge, but Red could see his eyes moving.
Lap 63. Mike Garvey was leading, with Kyle Busch right on his
ass. Red always figured the drivers' names were fake. They were
too show-bizzy. Names like Tony Stewart and Ryan Newman.
You never heard about a racer called Cecil Strump or Percy
Wiggins.

Four more laps passed, and Red was getting heavy-lidded
again, not even expecting an answer, when Billy Don said, "Go
fetch it yourself. You ain't left the house in three days."

"Neither have you."

"Yeah, well, none of the mail's for me anyhow."

Which was true enough. In the five years Billy Don had lived
with Red, the big man had received exactly one piece of mail: a
jury summons that Billy Don promptly flushed down the toilet.

So Red pushed himself out of the chair, went out the front
door, made his way to the road, forty yards away, grabbed the
mail—just a couple of bills—and picked up the *Blanco County
Record* from the weeds next to the caliche driveway.

Red wasn't much for reading the news, but he'd gotten a free
newspaper subscription, along with a handful of cash, when he'd
installed an illegal septic system at the editor's house. On his
way up the driveway, Red unfolded the newspaper, scanned the
headline, and abruptly came to a halt. "Nuh-uh," he said out

loud. "No way." This couldn't be right. He read the short article, then hustled back inside and said, "You ain't gonna believe this shit."

"What?"

" 'Member when Hollis Farley talked about sneaking us onto that job site to hunt pigs? Well, it ain't gonna happen."

"Why not?"

" 'Cause he's dead, is why not." Red enjoyed making dramatic announcements.

Billy Don glanced over at him. "The hell're you talking about?"

Red thumped the newspaper. "Some kind of accident. His backhoe flipped on him. Day before yesterday."

Billy Don sat up. "Shit fire. We just saw him, what, Wednesday night?"

"That don't make him any less dead. Poor son of a bitch."

Billy Don scratched his head but didn't say anything. Red, too, was at a loss for words. The world was strange sometimes. You go drinking with a man one night, and he ends up flatter than roadkill the next day. Hollis had been in a hell of a mood, too, joking around, buying all the drinks, and he'd said something interesting to Red right at the end of the night . . .

What was it? Some kind of secret? Red's memory was hazy. Too much beer that night. He figured it didn't matter now.

"We sure coulda used the pork," Billy Don said.

Red glared at him. "Shit, the man's dead, and you're worrying about yourself? Show some respect."

Billy Don nodded somberly. "Yeah, you're right. Sorry."

"Okay, then," Red said, thinking, *We sure coulda used the pork.*

In his cluttered garage, Jerry Strand stepped back and surveyed the box he'd just placed on an upper shelf. A large brown cardboard box sealed with gray duct tape. Nothing to draw attention to it. Could be old clothes in there, or family mementos. No reason for anybody—say, a nosy wife—to take a peek.

He hoped.

He'd had the box in his truck for safekeeping. But now, well, he figured it might be wise to find a better spot.

He shook his head at the thought of Nadine happening upon the box and opening it up. That would not be good. It would, in fact, be a disaster. She had a curious streak, always poking around, asking questions, and it could ruin everything. So he rooted through his toolbox, found an old carpenter's pencil, then took the box down and scrawled HUNTING STUFF on the top of it. What would be less inviting to Nadine than a bunch of old wool socks and bottles of doe urine?

He put the box back on the shelf—but he still wasn't satisfied. So he tugged a wooden knob at the end of a dangling rope and lowered the folding staircase that led to the attic. Then he hoisted the box up into the hot, stuffy space and slid it across the plywood floor, into a corner with a bunch of other boxes. Minor problem: The old boxes were covered with dust, but the new box was fresh and clean. Oh, well. It would have to do.

He heard a car pull up in front of the house. Then a door closing. He froze, listening. The garage was separate from the house, with a breezeway in between, so he couldn't hear the doorbell. But thirty seconds later, he heard Nadine calling out, "Jerry? Where the heck *are* you?"

He quickly backed down the steps to the garage floor, folded the staircase, and swung it back into place, just as Nadine came through the door.

"Oh, there you are. What are you *doing* out here?"

"Just cleaning up. Putting some things away." He noticed that the rope handle for the staircase was swinging lightly. Nadine seemed to be watching it, scowling, and her eyes went to the ceiling. He needed to distract her. "We got company?"

Her eyes came back to his, the attic forgotten. After all, it turned out, she had bigger fish to fry. "There's a deputy in the kitchen. Wants to talk to you again about Hollis."

The previous November, while checking licenses at a deer camp, Marlin heard a grizzled old hunter remark that modern-day deer antlers weren't all that different from fake boobs. Once man started fiddling around with the situation, he said, there was really no limit to how large you could make them. "So what's the goddamn point of it?" he asked, plainly disgusted. Marlin laughed about it at the time, but he could appreciate the analogy, and he felt the same way himself.

The problem was, many hunters were as mesmerized by those preternatural crowns of bone as they were by breasts. The bigger the better, most would say. Especially the deer breeders, who were obsessed with size. Big racks meant big wealth, and that's why they raised their deer in the meticulous manner of a Kentucky aristocrat raising racehorses. Breeders weren't just ranchers anymore, they were part scientist and part geneticist.

The deer were typically kept in high-fenced pens, and matings were carefully considered and orchestrated. Many breeders employed the latest scientific techniques, selling straws of semen that were used by other breeders for artificial insemination. The deer received the highest-quality veterinary care, including vaccinations and dewormers. They were fed a high-protein diet and mineral supplements to promote antler growth. They had ID tags in their ears or microchips under their hides. The does usually remained nameless, but the bucks were called Big Daddy and El Diablo and Goliath. They were sold at auction, or on the Internet, or in handshake deals between wealthy men who'd forgotten what hunting truly meant. Some of the biggest bucks were destined to live long, pampered lives as studs. The others would be shot by business executives who'd fly in for a weekend, pull the trigger, and write an enormous check.

It was legal, unfortunately, but Marlin despised all of it. Sure, the breeders would argue that they were simply helping nature along, and giving the masses what they wanted. But Marlin longed for the old days, when all deer ran wild, back when there was still some mystery involved, because nobody really knew what sorts of behemoths might be roaming the woods. Back, too, when average Joes weren't getting squeezed out of the sport by high prices and high fences.

Marlin's job required him to set those personal feelings aside when he dealt with breeders, and that's what he tried to remember as he drove through the entrance to Perry Grange's ranch, past a small sign that read NO TRESPASSING! ARMED RESPONSE!

Grange owned six hundred acres, but no commercial hunting took place there. He considered himself a specialist, concentrating on a small segment of the market. He didn't sell mature bucks or does, nor did he turn them out for hunting. He didn't sell straws of semen. He sold nothing but buck fawns, supposedly from his herd's "champion bloodlines." It was nearly the perfect con, if Grange was in fact selling fawns he'd trapped in the wild. As long as Grange's herd remained safely tucked in their enclosures, Marlin had no way to gain a DNA sample legally.

Your time will come, he thought, as he navigated the curves and swells of Grange's long blacktopped driveway. Nearing the house—a big lodge-style sandstone structure with a metal roof—he caught the glint of sunlight off glass. To the east, near the deer pens, a truck was parked in the sunshine. A blue quad-cab GMC. Grange's vehicle. Marlin pulled up next to it, killed the engine, and stepped out.

"Hello?"

He didn't see anybody, but thirty yards away, behind an eight-foot fence, half a dozen trophy bucks were staring in his direction. They were bedded beneath an oak tree, simply watching, waiting to see if perhaps it was dinnertime. Their eyes had the same dull gaze as cattle's. No wariness. No fear. Nothing wild left in there at all. Their antlers, freshly sprouted and growing rapidly, were sheathed in velvet, which the animals would scrape off in the fall, prior to the rut. At that point, the antlers would be sawed off, and each buck would be kept in a separate pen, to prevent them from injuring one another.

"Well, well."

Marlin hadn't heard him approach, but Perry Grange was suddenly standing right behind him, looking like a character out of *Jeremiah Johnson*. He wore fringed buckskin pants, which were tucked into moccasins that rose to his knees. His low-crowned broad-brimmed hat was crudely stitched from some type of bleached hide. He was shirtless, and the muscles across his chest and abdomen were well defined. On one hip was a large fixed-blade hunting knife; on the other, incongruous with the outfit, was a nine-millimeter automatic in a nylon holster. No antique revolvers for this guy, not when it came to protecting his hoofed assets. Grange had a thick black beard, and his face was as flat and ugly as an old skillet.

"How you doing, Perry?"

"You come to run me in?" He had a smirk on his face. His voice was deep and raspy, that of a longtime smoker.

"What for?"

"Hell, I don't know. I figure anytime a warden shows up at your house, it can't be good. Thought maybe you was here to hassle me some more."

"Well, no, but I could make something up if you wanted."

A quick laugh. "Yeah, I bet." An edge to his tone.

The bucks in the pen rose to a standing position, as if they were hoping to see a fistfight.

"Actually," Marlin said, "I had a call about spotlighters on McCall Creek Road last night. Wondered if you'd seen anything."

"No, sir. Doesn't mean they wasn't out there. Long as they don't come on my land, I don't pay much heed."

Marlin caught the odor of alcohol on the breeze. Grange had been drinking, though he didn't appear intoxicated. Maybe he held it well. "So you haven't been having any trouble with poachers."

"No, sir. Have you? I mean, really?"

"Have I what?"

Grange removed his hat and wiped sweat off his forehead. His hair was a bird's nest, as if he'd cut it himself. "I'm wondering what really brings you out. I'm thinking you want a look at my herd. Maybe count my bred does."

Marlin laughed. "I think you're being a little paranoid."

"Maybe so, but whoever turned me in this winter, they was lying to you. I run an honest outfit. Ain't much of an operation anymore. Business has gone in the shitter."

That didn't take long, Marlin thought. *I'm here for two minutes, and already he's agitated.* "Sorry to hear that," Marlin said, even though he wasn't. He wanted to keep Grange talking.

"Thursday, I was hauling three yearlings up to Amarillo, but two of 'em died by the time I got there. Fifteen grand, right down the toilet."

"This Thursday?"

"Yeah, two days ago."

"What time of day?"

Grange glared at him. "What difference does that make?"

"Well, if it got hot in the trailer . . ."

"I left around noon, but it wasn't any goddamn heat that got 'em, it was shock. They couldn't handle getting trailered that far. But nobody 'round here wants my damn deer. Meanwhile, the state's giving me all kinds of bullshit about not renewing my license. Hell, if they want a battle, I'm gonna give 'em one. If that includes you, so be it."

Marlin decided to push him. "You could've let me run the DNA tests. Cleared your name. You still could."

Grange pointed a finger at him. "I wanna know what gives the government the right to invade my goddamn privacy. Since when is a man guilty until proven innocent?"

"You were never charged with anything."

Grange shook his head and waved his hands, as if he'd had enough of the discussion.

Marlin wanted to keep the conversation going. "Your bucks are looking good, Perry."

No reply.

"That one on the left is a monster," Marlin said.

Grange couldn't resist it. "Only three years old. Wait'll next year." Grange couldn't keep the pride out of his voice. Like most breeders, he enjoyed bragging about his accomplishments.

"What's it gonna score?"

"About two-twenty. I call him Bull of the Woods."

The woods, my ass, Marlin thought. *That deer has never been outside this pen. He'd eat out of my hand.*

"I been thinking about it, you know," Grange said.

"About what?"

"Letting you draw some blood. Prove I ain't lying."

"And?"

"Well, shit, it just ain't right. Can't you see that?"

When he got back to his office, Marlin called Garza's cell phone.

"You get anything?" the sheriff asked.

"He says he left town at noon on Thursday. Hauling some deer up to the Panhandle."

"That's a good eight hours up there."

"Yeah. If he's telling the truth, he's clear."

"Easy enough to check."

"Grange should've filed for a transport permit, which would list the customer in Amarillo. I'll look into it. How's it going over there?"

"Just getting started. I'll let you know."

5

IN DOWNTOWN DALLAS, in the sixteen-story high-rise that housed the currently quiet offices of Boothe Ministries, a man named Alex Pringle rode the elevator down to the eleventh floor, which was occupied by the executive fitness center. He bypassed the steam room, the indoor pool, and the racquetball court and entered the vast workout room, which offered every type of torture device ever invented. The facility was empty, except for the only staff member who used the center on a regular basis.

She was hard at work, assaulting some sort of stair-climbing machine, driving the cushioned foot pedals up and down, up and down, accompanied by a soft hydraulic *whoosh . . . whoosh*. A Sheryl Crow number was playing on the sound system.

The walls were mirrored, so the woman saw Pringle approaching, but she kept on with her regimen, gripping the
handrails, frowning with exertion. He took a seat on a nearby
weight bench, straightened his silk necktie, and simply watched.

As always, he marveled at how astoundingly beautiful she
was. Granted, today, in her flaming red Lycra shorts and exercise bra, she looked less like one of God's angels and more like
one of Charlie's Angels. Yet somehow—maybe it was the long
ponytail swinging to and fro with each step, or those big green
eyes—she maintained the wholesome air of a minister's wife.
This was, after all, the same woman who led the congregation in
prayer at the beginning of every broadcast. The same woman
who earnestly reminded female members that there was honor
in running an efficient household, in rearing children, and in
"recognizing that your husband has needs that come before
your own."

Her public persona aside, Alex Pringle wasn't surprised at all
when Vanessa Boothe said, "Barry Grubbman is a two-bit cocksucker."

Pringle chuckled. "So you saw the interview."

"Interview, hell, it was a goddamn ambush. Peter should've
walked out." She was particularly snippy today. More protective
of her husband lately. He could understand that.

"I thought he held up pretty well. Besides, the show was live.
How would that have looked?"

"Oh, I don't know. Like he had balls, maybe?"

Whoosh. Whoosh. The great thing about the stair-stepping
machine, Pringle noticed, was that it caused Vanessa to hike her
ass high in the air. And, oh, what an ass. As enticing as the
sweetest Fredericksburg peach, and just as firm. Amazing for a
woman of forty-one, even a former fashion model. No middle-
age spread on this gal. No sags or droops, just a body that could
make St. Paul commit a mortal sin.

"I think he handled the interview just right," Pringle said.

"We knew this would happen eventually. Hell, we *planned* for it. Better that shitty little show than *Dateline* or *60 Minutes*. Now the big boys won't hassle him, because they'd look like copycats."

Whoosh. Whoosh. Pringle watched a bead of perspiration trickle down her throat, between her clavicles, and down into her cleavage. He could feel an urgency in his loins.

"How are the latest sales figures?" Her breathing was labored but steady. The woman was a true specimen. The lungs of an Olympic athlete. Tremendous upper body strength. Hell, her thighs were impressive, too. Could probably deflate a basketball.

"Too early to tell on the DVD, but the hardback's still on top of the nonfiction lists. We've moved half a million CDs."

"Yeah, well, we might see a dip after this fiasco."

"Tut, tut. Always the cynic. 'Trust in the Lord, my dear, and lean not on your own understanding.'"

She glanced over long enough to glare at him but kept right on climbing the imaginary staircase. She hated when he quoted scripture.

"You know what might make you feel better?" he said. "If I were to take you into the dressing room and lick every drop of sweat from your body. Just for old time's sake."

The dressing room was a safe zone. No security cameras in there. A lock on the door. But he knew it wouldn't happen. Those days were long past. And she proved him right by ignoring the comment altogether. Fine. Damned if he was going to beg for it. He had more pride than that.

She broke the awkward silence by saying, "I wished they hadn't mentioned Farley."

Ah. So that was it. That explained her mood. The poor girl was worrying. "Me, too, but I don't think it's anything to get excited about."

"You don't *think*? We've got a dead guy at the job site and you don't *think* it's a problem?"

Sheryl Crow was replaced by another female singer. A song with a Latin feel to it. Shakira?

"The cops think it was an accident," Pringle said, "and we're not in a position to correct them."

Without breaking stride, she grabbed a water bottle from an attached cup holder and squirted a few ounces into her mouth, swished it around, then swallowed. But she didn't reply.

So Pringle said, "Accidents are an unfortunate by-product of the construction industry, you know. Nationwide, there are more than a thousand fatalities every year. That's fifteen point two deaths for every hundred thousand workers." If it sounded like he was paraphrasing from a press release, he was. He'd written one that very morning, after doing some extensive research. Best to go into this thing well prepared.

"Well," she reluctantly agreed, "I guess that's good news."

Pringle checked himself in a mirror, and he liked what he saw. Perfectly groomed mustache. Thick, dark hair slicked back from his forehead. Immaculate double-breasted suit. "I'll be driving down there later today," he announced. "Community relations and all that. I'll probably stay until this blows over. But I wanted to remind you that Peter has a meeting with Ted on Monday."

"What about?"

"The water project. Keep him focused, will you?"

"You want *me* to go to the meeting?"

"I think it wouldn't hurt. Be supportive. Like a good wife should." He loved gigging her with lines like that.

She glared again. "You're such an asshole."

He smiled at her. She wasn't going to ruin his mood. The Rangers had beaten the Twins last night, and he'd made a killing. More than most people earn in a year. Finally, some luck. It had been a while.

"I've never seen him this angry," she said.

"He'll forgive you. Eventually. Anyway, I'll be gone for three or four days. Maybe a week."

"Have a good trip," she said, staring straight ahead. Being coy. Fickle bitch.

He couldn't resist one last plea. "How about sending me off with a smile on my face?"

Whoosh. Whoosh.

She finally looked over, eyeing him up and down. "You know, it wouldn't hurt if you got some exercise yourself now and then. Builds endurance. Might make you a better lay."

Chief Deputy Bill Tatum took a seat at Jerry Strand's kitchen dinette. It was an older home, built in the fifties. Lots of yellows and avocado greens. Nothing fancy, but it was tidy and clean, smelling of pine trees and ammonia. The motif for the kitchen, obviously, was bears. A bear-shaped cookie jar over on the counter. Bears printed on the hand towels hanging beside the sink. Above the stove, a framed print of a bear riding a tricycle. Bears on every shelf and every surface.

"It's a damn shame, is what it is," Strand said for the second time, shaking his head to reinforce that notion. He was perhaps fifty years old, with a graying crew cut and ruddy skin. His torso was burly and powerful, his hands stubby and thick; he was, in fact, quite bearlike. Go figure. His wife, Nadine, was busy brewing a pot of coffee. "Hollis Farley was a good man," Strand was saying. "Knew how to run a backhoe."

Tatum wasn't sure what distinguished a good backhoe operator from a bad one. "You two were friends?"

"Well, not friends, with the age difference and all. But I liked him. Good kid. Reliable as the sunrise. Lot of guys, they don't show up regular. One gray cloud in the sky and they're taking a weather day. 'Course, with all the rain we've been getting, even

Hollis couldn't work every day. But if it was just a drizzle, he'd be out there moving earth. Even on the weekends."

Nadine Strand was rooting around in the refrigerator, probably looking for creamer, but Tatum had the sense she was hanging on every word. She proved it by saying, "He sure was popular with the girls around town, I can tell you that much."

"That so?"

"Well, sure. Good-looking boy like that."

Jerry Strand was rolling his eyes, but Tatum said, "Was he seeing anyone in particular?"

"I'm sure I wouldn't know that. I think he liked to, you know, play the field."

Tatum turned back to Jerry Strand. "Why was he working by himself out there?"

"Had to clear a road for us. See, we couldn't get the heavy equipment in there yet. Hollis was knocking down cedar trees, filling in some culverts. We couldn't do nothing else till he opened up a path. He was on schedule to be done by Friday, meaning yesterday, which is still behind schedule, but now . . . well, it don't even matter. Screw the schedule. Breaks my god-damn heart, what happened."

"Jerry, language," Nadine said quietly. She smiled apologetically at Tatum.

"Well, it *does,* Nadine." Then, to Tatum, "I've never lost a man before. Boy had a lot of good years ahead of him."

They sat in silence for a few moments, until Nadine Strand, cheerful, said, "Here we go," and came over with a full tray. She placed three mugs on the table—more bears—and filled them with coffee. "Cream and sugar?"

"Black's fine," Tatum said.

"You sure?"

"Yes, ma'am."

She was disappointed, no doubt, that Tatum wouldn't be availing himself of the Yogi Bear sugar bowl. She turned and placed the coffeepot on the warmer, then came back toward the table, preparing to sit down.

"Mrs. Strand," Tatum said, "do you suppose I could have a few words with Jerry alone?"

"Oh. Well. I—"

"Nadine, honey, let us talk."

She gave her husband a stern look, but he didn't see it or had learned to ignore it. "Okay. I have laundry to fold, anyway. There's more coffee right over there if y'all want it." She stood in place for a couple of seconds, maybe hoping Tatum would give her a reprieve, then exited through the swinging door.

The room was silent, except for the ticking of the circus-bear clock above the pantry. Strand was staring at the tabletop, both hands wrapped around his mug. "Least he didn't have a wife and kids," he said. "Let me tell you, this thing is eating me up, but if he'd had family . . ."

Tatum didn't know if the news he was about to share would make Strand feel better or worse. "What I came here to tell you," he said, "is that it wasn't an accident. Farley was murdered."

Strand's head snapped up immediately. "He was what?" Pure puzzlement in his eyes.

"It was a homicide, Mr. Strand."

"But I . . . I thought he was crushed by the backhoe. Yesterday, y'all said—"

"That was speculation. The autopsy proved us wrong."

"Jesus H. Christ. That can't be right."

"Trust me. There's no question."

Back to the head-shaking. Like he couldn't quite comprehend what was happening. "But why? How was he killed?"

"I can't share that with you right now." Tatum gave it a moment to sink in. Then he said, "What I'd like to ask you is, can you think of anyone who might've wanted to harm Hollis? He ever mention anyone being angry with him?"

"No, I . . ." Then Strand slapped a palm lightly on the table-top, as if something had just occurred to him. "Jesus, those god-damn conservationists!"

"The environmentalists?"

"Yeah, those people."

"Why do you think it was them?"

"You saw how they are. The dyke that punched you in the eye. Have you talked to her?"

Rhonda Himmelblau, Tatum thought. *Woman with a mean right hook.* "Did they come back to the site?"

"Hell, no. Not since you come out and arrested them. Hollis woulda called you. I told him to."

"So you don't have any special reason to think it was one of them?"

"Shit, she got violent with you. What else do you need? Those sonsabitches! It *had* to be them, don't you think?"

"We'll be talking to that group, but we need to check out all the possibilities. That's some prime hunting land out there. You have any trouble with poachers at the job site?"

Strand shook his head. "Hollis never said nothing. Doesn't mean it never happened. They coulda come at night."

"If Hollis had seen something like that, would he have called the game warden, or would he have tried to handle it himself?"

"Hell, I don't know. He probably woulda just run 'em off."

Tatum sat for a moment, drinking coffee.

"Those tree-huggers," Strand muttered. "Buncha nutballs."

Tatum thought it was somewhat strange. Almost like Strand *wanted* it to be the environmentalists.

6

DURING FOUR HOURS of thorough searching, the only thing Sheriff Bobby Garza learned of interest was that Hollis Farley had once appeared on an episode of the *Judge Judy* show. Three years earlier, he'd sued his cousin for ownership of a rebuilt Chevy small-block engine. Farley had saved the debacle on videotape, and the critical exchange went as follows:

> JUDGE JUDY: I don't see a valid claim here, Mr. Farley. It was your cousin's engine to begin with, and it appears he paid for all of the new parts.
> FARLEY: Yeah, but I provided most of the labor. I worked my butt off on that thing.

COUSIN: I reimbursed him for his butt, Your Honor.
(Audience laughter.)
JJ: Is that just a joke, or did you actually pay him?
COUSIN: Oh, I paid him.
JJ: How much?
COUSIN: Over the course of a month, maybe three cases.
JJ: Cases of what?
COUSIN: Old Milwaukee.
(Audience laughter.)
JJ: You paid him with beer?
COUSIN: Bought him a bunch of breakfast tacos, too.
FARLEY: That chorizo gave me the runs, Your Honor.

In the end, the ruling went in the cousin's favor.

Other than that, Garza and Deputy Ernie Turpin had found nothing out of the ordinary. The trailer contained the types of things Garza expected of a young, single construction worker: soiled clothes on the floor; trash from fast-food joints; a few overdue bills; a pair of skimpy red panties under the bed.

The only inch of the trailer left unexamined was the gun safe. They'd discovered it in the closet of the spare bedroom but hadn't as yet located a key. Just as Garza was considering taking a crowbar to it, Turpin walked into the living room holding something shiny. "Found it hanging on a nail under the bathroom sink."

Inside the safe they found six American-made hunting rifles in varying calibers, roughly three hundred rounds of ammunition, and a gun-cleaning kit. Nothing unexpected.

Except for six thousand dollars in cash.

The American pop-culture landscape is littered with the desiccated carcasses of televangelists who disgraced themselves in spectacular headline-grabbing fashion. Sometimes the scandals involved money. Sometimes they involved sex. All too frequently, they involved both.

Jim Bakker, cohost of the seminal show *The PTL Club,* made the mistake of marrying a woman who had the cosmetic sensibilities of a rodeo clown, then hiring a secretary who could've stepped from the pages of a topless auto-parts calendar. Alas, Bakker's flesh was weak, and he eventually engaged Jessica Hahn in a rousing game of bury-the-bishop. Meanwhile, Bakker's bookkeeping practices—including a tendency to divert money from his ministry to finance his own extravagant lifestyle—ultimately landed him in hot water. He and his wife drove matching Rolls-Royces. They owned a ten-thousand-square-foot condo in Florida, with sixty thousand dollars in gold fixtures. They'd once ordered a hundred dollars' worth of cinnamon rolls simply to imbue their hotel suite with the aroma. When these facts came to light, Bakker was convicted on twenty-four counts of fraud and conspiracy, and spent nearly five years in a federal prison.

Jimmy Swaggart—cousin to Jerry Lee Lewis and Mickey Gilley, two fine showmen in their own right—built his television empire into a $150-million-a-year cash cow before a private detective photographed him exiting a seedy Louisiana motel room with a known prostitute. Swaggart reluctantly admitted to church elders that he'd struggled with a lifelong addiction to pornography. He then made a tearful on-air confession, and later claimed that fellow evangelist Oral Roberts had, via a phone call, cast out Swaggart's demons, rendering him free of moral defect. Great news! He was right with God and back on the straight and narrow! A few years later, however, Swaggart was stopped by police for driving on the wrong side of the road. In the car with him? Another hooker. Seems the poor man had had a relapse. Swaggart's most recent controversy involved a heated rant against homosexuals, in which he said, "If one ever

looks at me like that, I'm gonna kill him and tell God he died."
Apparently, in Swaggart's view, a man should love his neighbors,
but not in a way that was icky.

The list was virtually endless. Peter Popoff was condemned
for performing faith healings that were, in reality, elaborate
stage shows. Robert Tilton was accused of trashing viewers'
prayer requests unread—after removing the enclosed donations, of course. More recently, Paul Crouch—founder of the
world's largest religious media outlet, the Trinity Broadcasting
Network—was alleged to have sexually assaulted a male employee at a remote mountain cabin, and later paid the man
$425,000 to keep quiet.

Yet, despite the scandal, the hypocrisy, and the sordid history of televangelism in general, if the attack dogs from *Dateline*
or *60 Minutes* had, in fact, taken it upon themselves to discredit
Pastor Peter Boothe, they would have had no more luck than
Barry Grubbman. Recent events notwithstanding. Prior to this
week's catastrophe, they would have learned that Pastor Pete
was exactly what he appeared to be: a religious phenomenon; a
charismatic, media-savvy clergyman with a trophy wife and
more material possessions than a Saudi prince. None of which
represented a real problem.

Perversely, Boothe's "prosperity gospel" predecessors had instilled in many viewers' minds the idea that a minister *should* be
an icon of financial success. Wealth was proof—was it not?—
that God rewards those who spread His word. By that logic,
who should be more blessed than the ubiquitous Boothe, who
was only slightly less recognizable than the pope?

So, no, the fact that the Boothes lived in luxury while some
of their contributors squeaked by on Social Security was not an
issue. Nor was Boothe's million-dollar salary, or the fact that
Boothe Ministries was sitting on a $100 million cash reserve
and didn't need to beat the fund-raising drums quite as relent-
lessly as they did. Viewers simply didn't care. There was nothing

illegal about any of it. No hookers or gay affairs were involved, praise Jesus, so go ahead and pass the collection plate!

Yes, if journalists had dug into Boothe's personal life, they would've been baffled. Confused. Maybe even pleasantly surprised. Here was a man who, despite being surrounded by a bevy of plump-breasted parishioners and long-legged assistants, had remained doggedly faithful to his wife. Boothe had not only refrained from extramarital dalliances, he had never so much as caressed a nipple or fondled a buttock, though many were adoringly proffered.

None of this, though, was of particular comfort to Boothe as he reread, for the final time, the handwritten note that had brought his world crashing down. Oh, the disgrace! The treason! And because of it, so many things had gone wrong so quickly. The Devil had reared his ugly head, and Boothe hadn't had the strength to resist. Now, the truth could ruin him. He was profoundly disappointed in himself. He wasn't proud of Alex Pringle, either. And he was especially ashamed of Vanessa.

Harlot! Jezebel!

All of his problems stemmed from Vanessa, and he was uncertain if he could forgive her. He had to wonder: *What happened to our storybook marriage? How did we drift so far apart? How did we allow temptation to gain the upper hand?* It was troubling, indeed.

And he was about to make it worse.

He took the note—a simple declaration of love—and set fire to it before he could change his mind. It blackened, curled with flame, and was quickly rendered to ashes.

Obfuscating the truth. Another sacrilege against the Lord. Boothe chuckled bitterly and thought, *What's one more?*

He studied the gold-plated lighter in his palm. A fine piece of craftsmanship, delicately engraved with the Lord's Prayer. Purchased in France for two thousand dollars. Yet Boothe would joyfully give it all up—everything from his Gucci slippers to the twice-yearly trips to St. Lucia—for a woman who would remain faithful. If he and Vanessa were to heal their union, she would have to repent, starting with a vow to keep her knees together.

"I got a domestic violence call south of Marble Falls about two hours ago," said former Blanco County deputy Nicole Brooks.

She was leaning against John Marlin's kitchen counter, sipping beer from a frosted mug, as he piled spaghetti and meat sauce onto two plates. He'd had dinner ready at six thirty, but she hadn't arrived until eight. He'd have to reheat it.

"When I get to the house," she said, "I see Rick and Danny standing on the front porch."

"Rick and Danny?"

"Burnet County deputies. I've mentioned them before."

Marlin nodded, but he was still thinking about Bobby Garza's call an hour earlier, during which the sheriff had dropped two bombshells. First, Hollis Farley had nearly six thousand dollars squirreled away in his gun safe. Second, Henry Jameson—the forensic technician who served a five-county area west of Austin—had found something in Farley's truck: a receipt for a package of broadhead hunting points. That put a new spin on things. It meant Farley owned a bow—and since it hadn't been found, perhaps it had been in his truck at the job site. Maybe the killer had used Farley's own bow and arrow on him, then carried it from the scene. Which meant the murder might not have been planned.

Nicole said, "So I walk up and ask what's happening. Danny grins and Rick shakes his head, so I know something weird is going on. Meanwhile, I can hear these sounds coming from the other side of the door, like someone moaning in pain. Finally, Rick whispers, 'The complainant and her boyfriend are sharing a personal moment.' Danny's laughing, and he says, 'They were right on the other side of the screen door. I closed the front door to give them a little privacy. They didn't even miss a beat.'"

"A personal moment? That's an interesting phrase for it," Marlin said, sliding one of the plates into the microwave. Geist, the pit bull, was lying on the linoleum, watching intently, hoping a loose noodle might drop to the floor.

"Rick is older and kind of conservative," Nicole explained. "Anyway, long story short, the woman and her boyfriend had been drinking, and they got into an argument. The boyfriend slapped her, so she called it in, and before Rick and Danny even got there, they'd made up and were doing it on the living room floor. Didn't seem to care who watched, either."

"They sound like a lovely couple. We must have them over for dinner sometime."

Nicole gave him a small smile, then went on with her story. "So then, a few minutes later, the woman comes out, still pulling her pants on, and—"

"She doesn't want to press charges."

"Of course not. See, it was all a big misunderstanding, and besides, the boyfriend was awfully sorry for what he did."

"And he promised not to do it again."

"Well, sure. So Rick tells her the law *requires* them to make an arrest and that they don't have any choice. So she goes nuts and starts throwing stuff. Tries to keep them from cuffing her boyfriend, so they end up arresting her, too. The woman needs counseling, all right, but not the kind I had in mind."

Counseling. Marlin was still having trouble thinking of Nicole as a counselor, not a deputy. Four months earlier, the victim services coordinator for Blanco County had retired, and Nicole had surprised Marlin by applying for the position. Granted, Nicole had the right mindset for the job; she'd been a victim herself several years back. But Nicole had quickly discovered that working in victim services could be as stressful—and maybe more so—as being a deputy. She was on call 24/7. Funding was practically nonexistent. She also ran into the occasional victim, like the woman tonight, who made Nicole wonder if her job was relevant at all.

What Marlin wanted to say was: Are you sure you're enjoying this new gig? Is it bringing you the satisfaction you thought it would? And—particularly right now—is it worth the stress, the extra hours, the aggravation? He wanted to tell her that if she changed her mind, if she decided she wasn't the woman for the job, nobody would hold it against her.

Instead, he said, "The weather's nice. Why don't we eat on the deck?"

7

THE YOUNG LADY'S name was Candie, and she had no idea what she was getting into when she agreed to the blind date.

"He's a trust-fund baby!" her friend, a secretary for a tax attorney, had said. "His parents died in a plane wreck. Isn't he lucky?"

"He's rich?" Candie asked.

"Very."

"Like comfortable rich or Bill Gates rich?"

"Somewhere in the middle."

"Wow. What does he do for a living?"

"He's got a fossil collection or something. But mostly he just lives off the money his parents left him. We do his taxes, and believe me, he doesn't need to work."

Candie hadn't had much luck with blind dates, but this one was sounding pretty good. "What's he look like?"

"Really cute. But he's a little . . . short."

"How short?"

"I dunno, maybe five-six."

Candie could live with that. She was only five-two. "How old is he?"

"Late twenties."

"Ever been married?"

"Nope. Undamaged goods. Hell, I'd be all over him if he wasn't a client. Looks like he'd be good in bed."

"Rich *and* good in bed?"

A devious smile. "*You'll* have to tell *me*."

So Candie had agreed, and Darwin Parker picked her up on Saturday night in his convertible Jaguar, which, Candie duly noted, had leather seats, surround sound, and a GPS navigation system. Right from the start, he seemed like a great guy. Funny. Smart. Sophisticated, but not snobby. Good conversationalist. And he *was* cute! Wavy brown hair and strong cheekbones. Blue eyes. A perfect nose.

They went to one of the most exclusive restaurants in Houston, where Candie ordered lobster and drank several generous glasses of Dom Perignon, even though champagne usually gave her the burps. After the entrée, Darwin encouraged her to order the Baked Alaska. She said it had too many calories, but he said, "Judging by the way you wear that dress, it's not like you have anything to worry about."

I think I'm in love, she thought.

Later, back in his car, Darwin said, "What now?"

"Whatever," Candie said. "I'm easy." She giggled. She hadn't meant it *that* way. Well, not really. Her head was a little fuzzy. *Burp.* Oh, my!

Darwin said, "I don't ask many people this, but would you like to see my museum?"

Candie was astounded. "You own a *museum?*" She hadn't been to a museum since a field trip in elementary school.

"Well, not a public one. It's at my house. A private collection. How about a personal tour?" There was something playful in his smile.

She assumed it was a corny come-on to get her into bed, and she thought, *What the hell.* "Sure. Let's go see your museum."

Beneath the high from the alcohol, she was nervous. It had been a *long* time. Zipping along on Memorial Drive, Candie tried to relax by picturing Darwin naked. He'd mentioned that he worked out regularly. Maybe she was in for a treat.

As it turned out, he really did own a museum. Sitting right next to his mansion in the River Oaks section of town. The entire "compound"—his word for it—was on two acres, surrounded by a tall wrought-iron fence. As they cruised through the entrance gate, past manicured lawns and an ornate fountain, she was thinking, *This guy isn't just rich, he's absolutely loaded.*

He parked in front of the museum, a sweeping limestone-and-glass structure. He seemed excited, like a kid about to show off his new bicycle on Christmas morning. They strolled to the front door, where he had to enter a lengthy code on an alarm keypad. He ushered her inside, switched on some lights, and . . .

And . . .

"Oh my God," she said.

She'd been expecting Monet or Van Gogh or even that soup-can guy. Regular artwork. Not . . . *this.* It was creepy.

"Impressive, isn't she?" Darwin said in a hushed voice.

"What *is* that?"

Towering above them, in the high-ceilinged foyer, was the skeleton of a dinosaur. An actual dinosaur.

"*Allosaurus,*" Darwin said. "The biggest carnivore in North America during the Jurassic period. I call her Alice. Not very creative, I know, but it seemed appropriate."

Candie didn't know what to say. Alice had a humongous

head, long serrated teeth, and ominous claws. In short, she was butt ugly. "She's . . . she's . . ."

Darwin laughed. "Yeah, I know. But there's more. A lot more. Follow me."

For twenty minutes, he gave her a detailed lesson in paleontology.

"That's a *Herrerasaurus*, from the Triassic period. Another carnivore . . .

"This is a hadrosaur from the Cretaceous period. A snack for the *T. rex* . . .

"Here's a pair of maiasaurs, sort of a big lizard, and each fossilized egg in that nest is worth more than my car."

He explained that he bought and sold specimens through his Web site, but, as she could tell, he kept the best stuff for himself.

Candie oohed and aahed, but she was, to be honest, bored silly. She didn't know anything about ancient history, nor did she care to. It was nothing but a bunch of bones. Besides, she'd mentally prepared herself for sex, and now she was having a tough time focusing on anything else. She wanted to do it before she lost her buzz. Time to take charge.

He was rambling on about some strange creature when she placed a finger across his lips, shushing him. Then she reached down and began to unbuckle his belt. "You like meat eaters, Darwin?"

Wow! She never would have said that sober.

"I, uh . . ." said Darwin.

"Why don't you take my dress off?" she asked.

He smiled. "Okay." He began to fumble with the zipper running down her spine. Meanwhile, she finished unbuttoning his pants, and soon discovered that he was only at half-mast. *The champagne is slowing him down,* she thought.

He finally managed the zipper, and her dress dropped to the floor. She was wearing a lacy black bra with a matching thong.

But still he wasn't quite ready.

"Give me a minute," he whispered into her ear.

She did give him a minute. Longer than a minute. Despite her gentle kisses and deft caresses, the situation didn't improve.

Then he said, "I have an idea . . ."

"Yeah?"

"You might think this is kinky . . ."

Candie was always open to new experiences, as long as they weren't dangerous or demeaning. "Let's hear it."

"Promise not to laugh?"

"I promise."

"Okay, then. Why don't we pretend . . . we're tyrannosaurs."

"Do *what?*"

"Here, like this." He eased her to the carpeted floor and got behind her. "They roar when they're mating. Try it."

Candie had to stifle a giggle. Was this guy for real? She'd be embarrassed if she weren't so tipsy. "You want me to roar?"

"If you don't mind. It would really help me out."

"Grrr," said Candie.

"Louder," Darwin urged. He was breathing heavily over her shoulder.

"Aaarrrr!" And she definitely felt . . . movement.

"Yes," said Darwin. "Oh . . . yes. That's my girl."

Alex Pringle wished he'd had a chance to search Hollis Farley's trailer on Thursday afternoon, immediately after the backhoe operator died, but that hadn't been possible. Besides, he'd needed time to think, to quell the panic and evaluate the damage.

Now he was in Farley's living room with a small flashlight— knowing the cops had already been there, hoping he might find something they'd missed, or make sense of something that appeared meaningless—when his cell phone rang. He checked his caller ID but didn't recognize the number. Someone local.

He answered and heard, "Mr. Pringle, this is Sheriff Bobby Garza in Blanco County."

"Yes, Sheriff Garza, what can I do for you?" He used his friendliest voice.

"You're a tough man to get hold of."

"I'm sorry, I've been traveling. I turn my phone off when I'm driving."

"You're not in Dallas?"

No, I'm on the other side of the door you sealed with a big orange sticker. "Actually, I'm in Austin right now, on my way out to Blanco County. All of us at Boothe Ministries feel that we should have a representative on location. Someone to help your community through this difficult time. Such a tragedy."

"I'm afraid I'm about to make it even worse."

"I don't mean to sound flip, Sheriff, but how can it get any worse?"

"Well, it turns out it wasn't an accident. Hollis Farley was murdered."

Pringle froze for a few seconds, turning things over in his head. In his mind's eye, he could see the arrow flying straight and true, zipping through Hollis Farley's body like through a burlap sack filled with pudding. But the backhoe just kept rolling forward . . .

"Mr. Pringle?"

He wondered what he should say. Finally, he settled on "I'm here. I'm . . . I'm having trouble believing what you just told me."

"I can understand that. I just wanted you to be aware of the situation."

"I appreciate that."

"You'll pass the word to Pastor Boothe?"

"I certainly will. He'll be heartbroken to hear it. This is devastating news."

"We'll need to keep the construction site closed down for at least a few more days. Maybe a week."

"Yes, of course. But how—can you tell me anything about it? Do you know who did it?"

"We're working on it."

"I'm sure you are. I'll be praying for God to guide you and your deputies. 'Blessed are they who maintain justice, who constantly do what is right.'"

"Uh, thank you, sir."

Pringle closed his phone and sat quietly for several moments, struggling to maintain his composure.

Butch, wearing jeans and a black T-shirt, came out from Farley's bedroom. The floorboards groaned under his weight. The flimsy back door of the ramshackle trailer had been no match for Butch's big right foot. "Trouble?" he asked.

Pringle thought about it for a few seconds. "Nothing I didn't expect."

When Red O'Brien woke up from his second nap of the day, Billy Don was snoring on the couch and Dennis Quaid was on the TV wearing a goofy hat. Sort of a Willie Wonka–looking thing. And check out those sideburns. All the way down to his jawbone. Some silly shit. Whatever movie this was, Red had never seen it. Something set in the olden days, judging from the way everybody looked. Either that, or they were all on their way to a costume party.

He reached for his beer on the end table. Warm as cow piss. Man, how long had he been sleeping? It was dark outside, so he knew it had been a good while. But it wasn't like he had a schedule to keep.

He pushed himself out of the recliner and went into the kitchen for a fresh Keystone. Popped the top and drank about half of it in one swig. Good and cold. Made his teeth hurt a little.

He went back into the living room and stood there a minute, thinking about dinner. Run into town and grab a burger? Or eat that fat squirrel he'd shot out of the pecan tree in his backyard yesterday afternoon? Maybe chicken-fry it, with some mashed potatoes on the side. That sounded pretty good.

Now here came Billy Bob Thornton, looking every bit as stupid as Dennis Quaid. Talking funny, too. Asking some Mexican soldier if that man over there was Santa Ana. The Mexican guy nodded, and now Billy Bob was saying, "I thought he'd be taller." Santa Ana. Okay, so this was that movie about the Alamo. Red had been meaning to watch that one. It was his duty as a Texan, because the Alamo was one of the most important . . .

Wait a second . . .

Holy shit! The Alamo!

It came back to him all at once, out of the blue, like when you're trying to recall the name of that slutty cheerleader back in high school, and it won't come to you, and suddenly, a few days later, it pops into your head. It was just like that.

The haze had lifted, and now Red remembered what Hollis Farley's secret was.

8

MARLIN WOKE TO a heated voice in another room. Nicole on the phone. He lay there listening, but he couldn't make out her words. He pulled on a pair of shorts and went into the living room, where Nicole was sitting on the couch, holding a piece of paper, the phone cradled to her ear. Geist, curled at Nicole's feet, shifted her eyes toward Marlin but stayed where she was.

"It's two *hundred* chairs," Nicole was saying. "Two zero zero. Not two thousand." She looked at Marlin and rolled her eyes in frustration. "I understand that, but every time you send me a copy of the contract, there's a mistake in it. This is the third time. Last time it was the tables."

Marlin smelled fresh coffee. He went into the kitchen and

found a pot on the burner. He poured a mug, added milk and sugar, and took a seat on a stool at the bar.

"I'm not trying to be a bitch about this, Randy, I'm really not. I just don't want to show up and find two thousand chairs waiting for us. We're not *that* popular."

Marlin figured Randy was regretting that he'd answered.

"Okay, that's fine. Yes, to the same address. I'll look for it. Thanks, Randy." She hung up and said, "Aaaaa!"

Marlin grinned at her. She was wearing a sheer blue robe, loosely tied at the waist. Her auburn hair was pulled back in a ponytail, and her face was free of makeup. She was so beautiful as to look out of place in Marlin's simple living room, like osso buco on a paper plate. "I won't even ask," he said.

"Please don't. And no Bridezilla jokes."

"Who, me?" He slid off the bar stool and came to sit beside her on the couch. "Everything'll work out fine. Even if it doesn't turn out perfect, it—"

"But, see, there's no reason why it shouldn't be perfect. If these people would just pull their heads out of their butts."

"To you, it's the biggest day of your life. To them, it's just another day at the office."

"Yeah, and *that's* the problem. They're acting like I'm ordering office supplies or some damn thing."

Marlin put a hand on the back of her neck and began to massage. She was tense. "Maybe we should chuck it all and elope," she said. "The invitations haven't gone out yet."

"Is that what you want?"

"No, I'm kidding. Is that what *you* want?"

Oops. Shaky ground. "Of course not. Just remember, if you want me to help, all you have to do is ask. You know I'll do it." And he knew she wouldn't delegate anything, because, ultimately, she didn't want to. Like all the brides Marlin had ever seen, Nicole wanted to handle every detail. When it came to the wedding plans, she was downright possessive.

He used both hands now, kneading her shoulders, and her muscles finally began to relax. "God, that feels nice."

He started working on her back.

"Don't you want it to be perfect?" she asked.

"Honestly? As long as we don't end up on one of those home-video shows, I'll be happy."

She groaned. "Oh, crap. The videographer. I was supposed to call him yesterday."

"Shhh. Relax. Let me handle that one thing, okay? I'll call him later today. There's one less thing to worry about."

She nodded, but he could tell that her mind was still buzzing, running through a mental to-do list. He could practically hear the gears turning.

"What you need," he said, "is a round of Dr. Marlin's patented stress-reduction therapy."

She laughed. "Does it feel as good as what you're doing right now?"

"It comes with a money-back guarantee. One hundred per-cent satisfaction or you don't pay a dime."

She let him rub for a few more minutes, letting out the occasional appreciative moan. Then she stood, facing him, slipped the robe from her shoulders, and let it fall to the floor.

Somehow, after two years, nothing had changed. He still felt an electric surge through his body. His heart still swelled with a joy he couldn't imagine. *How did I get so damn lucky?*

She ran a hand through his hair, then pulled him close, holding his head between her breasts. "I love you, John."

"Alex Pringle, my man. Rough break on the game last night, cuz."

Pringle was in his motel room, fresh out of the shower, a towel around his waist, cell phone to his ear. The voice with the urban patter belonged to a bookie named Omar. Omar wasn't a one-man operation; he was backed by an outfit in Vegas—a group of men whose names ended in *i*'s and *o*'s.

"Goddamn bullpen choked," Pringle said. "You see it?" He'd felt so good about the fifty grand he'd won on Friday night, he'd doubled up on Saturday's game. Amateur move. Stupid. It reeked of desperation.

Omar laughed, but it wasn't good-natured; there was something condescending about it. "How long me and you been doing bidness?"

"I don't know. Four years?"

"Tha's right. And in that time, I ain't seen nobody—I mean nobody—piss away as much money as you."

"Well, gee, thanks, Omar. That's really encouraging."

"Man, I'm only saying. You ain't got the touch. You should move on to somethin' else. But first, we gotta settle up."

"What, really? Just like that?"

"Wasn't my call, but there it is. Certain gentleman getting nervous about your account. See, the last few bets, you been playin' on credit, so the rules change a little."

"Well, shit, give me a chance here, Omar. Let me put fifty on Wednesday's game."

"No can do, dog. Not till you wipe the slate clean. Like, tomorrow."

"All of it?"

"Hell, yeah, all of it. We ain't runnin' no soup kitchen."

"What's the, um, how much is the total?"

"Ninety-six."

Ninety-six thousand dollars. There had been a time when Alex Pringle could've written a check for that amount and hardly felt the sting. "Uh, tomorrow's gonna be a problem," he said.

Omar made a *tut-tut* sound. "Don't tell me that, Alex Pringle. Do *not* tell me that. You sayin' you ain't got it?"

"No, see, it's not that," Pringle lied. "It's just that I'm out of town. I won't be home for several days."

"Where ya at?"

"Johnson City."

"Johnson who?"

"It's a little town west of Austin."

"Shit, that ain't no big thang. My boy don't mind driving down. Where ya staying?"

At nine, they were still in bed. Nicole was sleeping soundly, and Marlin was thinking about his conversation with Perry Grange, when the phone rang.

Bill Tatum said, "We just got a break. Can you come in?"

"Yeah, sure. What's going on? You find the arrow?"

"No, better than that. We got a guy coming over from Austin who can fill in some of the blanks. It's, uh, well, it's too bizarre to explain over the phone. Let's hope he isn't a nutjob."

Dr. Scott Underwood had the bearing of a college professor, which made sense, because that's what he was. A small man. Slender, bordering on frail. Maybe five-five, early forties, with thinning blond hair and wire-framed glasses. Most people would say Underwood looked "bookish." He wore a plain gold wedding band on his left hand and, farther up, a Fossil wristwatch, which perhaps showed a sense of humor. He taught paleontology for the Department of Geological Sciences at the University of Texas in Austin; Marlin had learned that tidbit, but not much more, from the brief introductions.

Seated at the conference table to Underwood's left was Kate Wallace, who was his RA, or research assistant. She looked to be in her midtwenties, petite, with shoulder-length honey-colored hair and big green eyes. Cute, but in a reserved sort of way. Very little makeup. Wearing a conservative green blouse, buttoned at the neck, over a linen skirt and sandals.

Marlin and Bill Tatum were seated on the opposite side, and Bobby Garza was at the head of the table. The sheriff said, "Dr. Underwood, you told me you met Hollis Farley about a week ago."

"Both of us did. That's why we're here."

"And we're glad you called. You already gave me the high points on the phone, but if you don't mind repeating yourself . . ."

Underwood nodded, then said, "Kate, why don't you start?"

She looked a little surprised by the request. "Sure, okay. Nine days ago—I remember, because it was a Friday—Hollis Farley came to see Dr. Underwood in his office. Well, at that point, we didn't know who he was. He never gave his name. I was about to take off for the weekend when he showed up in the doorway."

"This was on campus?" Tatum asked.

"Yeah, the outer office. That's the one I use. You have to go through my office to get to his. It was about three fifteen, and I was getting ready to meet Victor for a beer."

"Who's Victor?" Garza asked.

"Victor Klein. Dr. Underwood's RA from last semester. He gave me some pointers when I took over, and we became friends."

"But he wasn't in your office that afternoon?"

"No, I was meeting him at the student union. The bar there."

Garza nodded for her to continue.

"Okay, so this man showed up and asked if this was Dr. Underwood's office, and I said it was. Then he asked if he could speak to him for a minute. I knew he wasn't a student, because he was filthy from head to toe. My first thought was that he worked for the maintenance department. He was wearing work clothes, and he was covered with dust and dirt. They're doing some road repairs along Speedway and in some of the parking lots. I thought maybe they needed us to move our cars or something."

"What happened next?" Tatum asked.

"I asked what it was regarding, and he said he'd rather speak to Dr. Underwood directly. That's when Scott poked his head out."

"The door between our offices was open," Underwood said. "I'd heard the conversation. So I asked him to come in and have a seat. He did, and I was sitting behind my desk, and it was peculiar the way he just sat there for a few seconds, looking around my office. He seemed nervous. Hell, he was making *me* nervous, the way he was fidgeting. He asked if we could close the door, and I said I prefer it open because it gets awfully hot in there with it closed. Then he just blurted it out."

"Blurted what out?" Tatum asked.

"What I told the sheriff earlier. This man, Hollis Farley, said he was pretty sure he'd found a dinosaur fossil."

Marlin stopped with a cup of coffee halfway to his mouth. A dinosaur fossil? He hadn't known what to expect from Scott Underwood, but it wasn't this.

"I was skeptical," Underwood continued. "People find fossils all the time, or think they do. But it usually ends up being a bone from a horse or a cow or a pig. Occasionally, it's something more interesting. A few years ago, a woman unearthed the better part of a giraffe skeleton on her ranch near Elgin. She thought she'd made this big, important discovery. It turned out the man who'd owned the property in the thirties had imported various species of African wildlife. He was attempting to start a zoo, but it never took off. But those bones were seventy years old, not seventy million. You have to understand, dinosaur fossils have never been found in Central Texas, at least not officially."

"But there *were* dinosaurs around here, right?" Marlin asked. "I've seen the tracks on the Blanco River."

"Yes, we've found plenty of trackways, but no fossils. All the species in this area lived during the Late Cretaceous period, when the ocean was receding and there were very few opportunities for deposition of bone. Not that it couldn't happen, but you'd have to have a situation where an animal died a natural death, without any scavengers nearby, followed by a very quick and sudden burial, most likely during a flood."

"So finding a bone around here would be a fairly big deal," Tatum said.

"Well, yeah. How big a deal would depend on what kind of fossil was found and what type of species it came from. Farley said he found a skull."

"Did he bring it with him?" Garza asked. Apparently, they'd already gone beyond the limits of their earlier conversation.

Underwood smiled. "Thankfully, no. In the one-in-a-million chance that he'd found an actual dinosaur fossil, it would've been risky for him to dig it up. He might've damaged it, and we could've lost the geological context."

"Couldn't he have found it on the ground?" Marlin asked.

Underwood nodded, as he might when a student asked a reasonable but naive question. "Chances are, if someone found a fossil, they'd find it partially exposed, probably after a rain, along a riverbank, most likely. Maybe along an oxbow, where sediment built up millions of years ago and there was some cross-bedding. There'd be a fairly small window of time when the fossil would be salvageable, but after that, it would start to deteriorate pretty quickly if it was left unprotected. A skull would be especially delicate, and the plates would start to separate. Eventually it would all just crumble or wash away."

"Okay, good," Garza said. "So let's come back to the present. Back to your office . . ."

"Well, I told him the same thing I just told you: that it probably wasn't a dinosaur fossil. I mean, I was friendly and everything, but I was probably a little dismissive. Then he showed me six or seven photos he'd taken." Underwood shook his head. "What I saw . . . I wondered if it was a put-on, maybe some of my colleagues having a little fun at my expense."

"So the skull looked good?" Garza asked.

Underwood opened his mouth but didn't speak right away. Then he said, "Yeah, it looked good. Amazing, really. So good that I called Kate in to look at the photos. She's doing her master's thesis on sauropods, somewhat of an expert on them by now, so I wanted to get her opinion. Farley didn't like that. He wanted to keep it confidential, between him and me. I assured him that he could trust Kate."

Kate Wallace nodded, saying, "He was pretty uptight about it. But he finally gave in, and I looked at the photos, and Dr. Underwood was right, it was a sauropod. There was only one species in North America during that period, and nobody has ever found a skull before. Not just here, but anywhere. They've found other fossils, but not a skull. And the other thing is, this sauropod has never been documented in Central Texas. It would be a major discovery. Not that this species didn't live here—maybe it did—it's just that we don't have any proof of it. This skull would sort of fill in some of the blanks."

"How big was the skull?" Marlin asked.

"Maybe twenty-four inches long," Underwood said. "Not as large as you'd think."

"The reason I ask—if Farley found the skull where we think he did, the previous landowner had some exotic animals out there. Various types of antelope, some elk, even a few zebra."

Underwood was shaking his head. "Believe me, Kate and I can tell the difference between a dinosaur skull and the skulls of those species. That'd be like—well, you're a game warden; do you ever get cows and deer mixed up?"

Marlin smiled. "Good point. I didn't mean any offense."

"None taken."

"So what'd you tell him?" Garza asked.

Underwood laughed. "The first thing I asked him—trying to be nonchalant—was where he found it. He wouldn't answer, and that worried me. I figured he was trying to make up his mind."

"About what?"

"Whether to share his find with the scientific community or to sell it on the open market."

"You can sell dinosaur bones?" Marlin asked.

"Ridiculous, isn't it? But yes. If the fossils are found on private property, the owner can do whatever he wants with them. Sell them, keep them, even destroy them. Anything he wants."

"What would something like this skull be worth?" Garza asked, cutting right to it.

"Oh, jeez, that's a tough question. See, I have nothing to compare it to. All I could do is guess."

"Please do."

"Okay, if the skull was authentic and in good condition—this is just a ballpark figure, but I imagine it would bring somewhere between five hundred thousand and a million dollars."

Garza let out a sigh of surprise. Nobody spoke for several seconds. A million bucks. Marlin hadn't expected *that*, either.

"I know that sounds like a lot," Underwood said, "but a *T. rex* named Sue sold for eight million dollars in '97. And remember, this would be the only *Alamosaurus* skull known to man."

"A whatasaurus?" Garza asked.

"*Alamosaurus*," Kate Wallace said. "That's what this species of sauropod is called."

9

DARWIN PARKER HAD been predestined, one might say, to develop a special fondness for dinosaurs. Both of his parents, after all, had been scientists—Dad an award-winning anthropologist, Mom a well-published archaeologist.

From an early age, Darwin had been surrounded by possessions intended to pique his interest in prehistoric times. *Tyrannosaurus rex* bedsheets. A Neanderthal Man lunchbox. Wallpaper featuring *Mammuthus primigenius* (the woolly mammoth) and *Smilodon fatalis* (a saber-toothed cat). Instead of a Bible, little Darwin had a copy of *The Origin of Species* in his nightstand. Both his parents were big fans of the author, of course; hence the goofy name they'd saddled him with.

But his sexual proclivities were cast in stone, no doubt, during his freshman year in college, when he went to a Halloween party dressed as Barney and got laid by a comely sorority girl dressed as Dino from the Flintstones.

When Darwin hooked up with the same girl a week later at his apartment, he realized, with a degree of concern, that he was disappointed that she hadn't brought her costume. He managed to consummate the act anyway, but it was a letdown. His heart simply wasn't in it. It didn't have the same zest, the same zing, the same primordial randiness.

After that, his propensities only deepened. No matter how attractive his partner, Darwin felt compelled to close his eyes and fuel his libido with elaborate fantasies. A heavy-breasted cocktail waitress, in Darwin's agile imagination, became a lusty *Gigantosaurus* cruising for a suitable mate. A tall, slender swimsuit model was transformed into a coquettish *Diplodocus*. A petite, spirited cheerleader took on the characteristics of a playful, nymph-like *Technosaurus*.

On the occasions when Darwin opened up and shared his predilections, he was usually met with a confused stare or, worse, a snort of disgust followed by a slamming door. Now and then, his more adventurous dates—like Candie from the previous evening—would play along. But those ladies, unfortunately, were few and far between, and they typically tired quickly of Darwin's colorful bedroom requirements.

There was, however, one segment of the female population that didn't give a damn either way.

"A what?" the young lady with bleached blond hair asked, plainly a little puzzled. Not judgmental, just puzzled. She'd called herself Tiffany, but Darwin assumed it was a fake name. Besides, her name didn't matter. Nor did her pink halter top, her Lycra pants, or her stiletto heels. For the next hour, Tiffany wasn't an escort living in modern-day North America, she was . . .

"A *Shuvosaurus*," said Darwin. "A small omnivorous thecodont from the late Triassic period." He was hoping she might show even the faintest glimmer of interest or curiosity. Wouldn't it be fantastic if he could finally meet a woman who shared his interests? A soulmate who understood that dinosaurs were the most intriguing creatures to ever roam the earth? Perhaps someday he'd find her. But not today.

"Whatever you want, sugar," Tiffany said. "I gotta do something special?" She was smacking gum. It was annoying. Darwin would have to pretend she was masticating plant materials.

"Can you squeal? You know, like a frightened rabbit?" The research on dinosaur vocalizations was limited; Darwin was free to fill in the blanks with his own preferences.

Tiffany shrugged and said, "EEEEEeeee!"

"Excellent! Can you stretch it out a little, and maybe go for a slightly deeper tone at the end?"

"EEEEEEEEeeeeeeeAAAAAA!"

"Perfect!"

He had his pants around his ankles when the phone rang. Damn! He'd forgotten to turn it off. Stupid! A few minutes later and it would have totally ruined the mood. There were no phones in the Mesozoic era! He answered brusquely and, following a pause, was greeted by a voice he hadn't heard in a long time. Darwin was glad he'd taken the call. He'd been waiting for it.

"The first fossils from this species were found in New Mexico near a cottonwood tree," Kate Wallace explained.

"And 'cottonwood,' in Spanish, is *alamo*," Garza said.

"Right. Has nothing to do with the mission in San Antonio."

Alamosaurus, Marlin thought. Strange. How come he'd never heard of it? "How would a person go about selling a fossil like that?" he asked. "I'm guessing you don't run an ad in the paper."

"No, no," Underwood said. "Typically, a fossil of that caliber would be sold through an auction house. Sotheby's. Butterfield's. Occasionally Christie's. Sometimes fossils are passed from collector to collector. And, of course, there's the Internet. Many dealers have their own Web sites nowadays. For less than a thousand bucks, you can get yourself a genuine *Apatosaurus* vertebra, or maybe a *Camarasaurus* tibia. Put it on your mantel and impress your friends. Be a big man."

"I'm guessing that pisses some scientists off," Garza said.

"It does. Most of us think fossils should be protected by law. They should belong to all of us collectively. Private individuals shouldn't be able to own them."

"Did you share those views with Farley?" Garza asked.

"Well, I wasn't going to lecture him," Underwood said. "Besides, I'd be pointing out that there *were* private collectors who'd be interested in his find. At that point, I don't think he even knew. So I told him I could understand why he felt the need for secrecy, but the scientific community would be grateful if he'd allow us access to the site."

"What'd he say?"

"Nothing. He thanked me for my time and left. He was courteous and everything, just tight-lipped."

"How long was he there?" Tatum asked.

"Maybe fifteen minutes."

"Any idea why he chose you?"

"None. I assume he simply asked a student who he should talk to about a dinosaur bone."

"How do you know this man was Hollis Farley?"

Underwood gave a sheepish grin. "Serendipity. You know all those goofy middle-aged guys who ride Harleys on the weekends, acting like genuine bikers? I'll confess that I'm one of them. I came out for an early ride this morning and stopped for breakfast at the Kountry Kitchen. I grabbed the local newspaper, and there was a picture of Farley, saying he was a murder victim, and I was pretty sure it was the same guy. So I called Kate, she met me at the diner, and we both agreed Farley was the guy from my office."

Kate Wallace nodded. "It was definitely the same man, no question about it."

Underwood said, "I kept thinking, well, it's a coincidence, it doesn't have anything to do with the fossil. But I couldn't help wondering if somebody might've, you know, actually killed him for it. So we called you, and here we are."

"And we appreciate it," Garza said. "You've been very helpful. I have one more question. How are your drawing skills?"

Riding along in Red's ancient Ford truck, over in the passenger seat, with his elbow hanging out the window, Billy Don said, "This don't feel right, Red."

There he was, being a downer again. Red was thinking, *If only I had a dime for every time I've heard him say that . . .*

It was always such a struggle to get the big man to go along with any of Red's ideas. The problem was, Billy Don wasn't the type to take chances, or to put forth any real effort to improve his life. His favorite saying was: Hard work pays off eventually, but laziness pays off right now. Billy Don was just fine with the way things were. Didn't mind eating day-old bread or the cheapest cut of steak. He was satisfied with discount clothes and four-dollar haircuts. Hell, the man didn't even play the lottery, and that right there was a sure sign that Billy Don had no ambition at all. Come on, the lottery! You plunk down a single dollar and, in return, you just might wind up with three million, four million, maybe even ten million. What kind of fool would pass up a chance like that?

Red, on the other hand, was willing to dream. In fact, he spent a good part of his day, every day, trying to think of ways to get ahead. Some of his ideas were a little out there, he'd admit that. Billy Don often referred to them as "get-rich-quick schemes" or, sometimes, "felonies." But that's what it took—big thinking—to mold yourself into an American success story. Besides, what was wrong with picturing a life of new cars and houses that didn't have wheels, of prime rib and name-brand beer? What was the harm in it? Well, there was the occasional letdown when things didn't pan out. Maybe even a little legal trouble here and there. But Red knew one thing for sure: A man without dreams was like a ship without a rudder. Or was it a train without an engine? Something like that. He'd seen it written on a fancy poster once, in an important man's office, when Red was applying for a job he didn't get.

In any case, Red wasn't going to let Billy Don's skepticism and pansy-ass attitude hold him back. The Lord had been kind enough to lay this opportunity right at Red's feet, and he was going to take full advantage of such a blessing, even if it meant breaking into a dead friend's trailer.

Red knew right away that something wasn't quite right, because there was a big orange sticker on the front door. When he and Billy Don got up on the porch, they saw that it was a notice from the sheriff's department, and it basically said to keep the hell out, only in nicer words.

"Guess that takes care of that," Billy Don said, obviously pleased with the situation.

Red wasn't so sure. Right now, he was wondering why the cops would be so worried about keeping people out of Hollis Farley's trailer. Didn't make sense. He stepped over to a window, peeked between the miniblinds, and got his second clue that something strange was going on. Furniture was turned upside down. Papers were scattered here and there. The place was a wreck. "Looks like they searched it," he said. "And they sure left a goddamn mess." If Hollis Farley had really found a valuable dinosaur bone—the big secret that Red had finally remembered—it was long gone. Red's plan was dead before it had even gotten started.

Billy Don edged up next to the window and pressed his nose to the glass, cupping his hands on either side of his face. "Red, why would they—"

"I don't know."

"But if Hollis died the way—"

"I don't know."

Fifteen minutes later, when he got back home and read the morning newspaper, he found out.

After Scott Underwood and Kate Wallace left, Bobby Garza said, "You think he even realized he was giving us all kinds of reasons to check him out?"

"He'd have to be an idiot not to," Tatum said. "But if he was involved, why would he come forward?"

"He pretty much had to, because the girl, Kate, would've seen the news eventually and called us. He knew it'd look better if he made the first move." They sat quietly for several moments. Then Garza said, "Maybe Underwood went out there to talk some sense into Farley, they got into an argument, and Underwood used Farley's own bow on him. Then he ditched the bow and the arrow afterward."

"But Farley supposedly didn't give his name, and Kate backed that up. So how would Underwood know how to find him?"

"Yeah, it's a stretch."

"He seemed okay to me," Tatum said. "Didn't seem rattled."

"And I have to wonder about something else," Marlin said. "Either of y'all ever shot a bow? A hunting bow?"

Neither of them had.

Marlin said, "Most guys, when they first start bow hunting, they're surprised how hard it is to draw the string back. Underwood's a tiny guy, and if Farley was hunting pigs out there, he probably had his bow set pretty tight."

Garza said, "Good point. Still, we need to give him a good look." He smiled. "Maybe he crossed to the dark side. Gotta make sure he's not selling a million-dollar fossil on eBay."

"If what he said is right, that skull is still somewhere on the job site," Tatum said. "Probably along the riverbank."

Garza said. "That's why I had Underwood sketch the skull. We got any reserve deputies available?"

"A couple."

"Give them copies and start 'em looking. But first, stress very firmly that word of the dinosaur bone is not to leave this department. Make that crystal clear. Otherwise we'll have treasure hunters trespassing all over that place."

"You know what I keep thinking about?" Tatum said. "Those panties in Farley's trailer."

"Yeah, I bet," Garza said, but Tatum didn't offer much of a smile in return.

He said, "Farley was sleeping with someone, and that could mean a jealous husband or boyfriend. Problem is, nobody I talked to mentioned Farley seeing anyone in particular—especially not lately, because he'd been working so much."

"Those panties could've been under his bed for weeks, or even months," Garza said.

"Betty Jean kept his place fairly clean."

"Sure, but how often did she check under the bed?"

Tatum didn't appear convinced.

Something else had been bouncing around in Marlin's head, so he decided to bring it up. "Y'all remember a ballplayer a while back who didn't believe in dinosaurs? Said they never existed? It was in a *Sports Illustrated* article."

"Yeah, that rings a bell," Garza said, nodding his head slowly. "Carl Everett. Played with the Rangers for a while."

Marlin chose his next words carefully, knowing that Garza

and Tatum were churchgoers. "If I remember right, Everett was a religious man. And I got the sense that dinosaurs didn't fit in real well with his view of Creation. I mean, if you take the Bible literally and you agree that the earth is maybe six thousand years old, but scientists say dinosaurs were here millions of years ago . . ."

"Oh, man, you're making me nervous just talking about that kind of stuff," Garza said. "I'm a good Catholic boy."

Tatum said, "Some people think dinosaurs were created on the sixth day, along with the other creatures. That man and dinosaurs lived at the same time."

To Marlin, that made as little sense as denying that dinosaurs had ever existed, but he didn't say anything.

Garza shook his head, grinning at Marlin. "Where're you going with this? You pointing the finger at Pastor Pete?"

"No, no, I'm just saying, if you were building a big religious complex, wouldn't it be kind of awkward, and even bad publicity, if somebody found a dinosaur bone? It's a no-win situation. If you kept it a secret, or destroyed it, you'd look like a bad guy if it ever leaked out. Like you're hiding something. But if you tell everyone what you found, then you've gotta do the right thing and open the place up for study. If you're Boothe, and you're saying, 'Sure, it's a bone, but it's only six thousand years old,' but the scientists on your land are trumpeting the discovery of a seventy-million-year-old fossil, wouldn't that put a damper on the festivities? Boothe'd have to rebut everything the experts said. The media would love it."

Nobody spoke for several moments, and Marlin noticed that Garza wasn't smiling anymore. He was thinking. Finally, he said, "I wonder how long it takes scientists to complete a dig. The project was already behind schedule because of the rain. If I were Boothe, I'd be worried about that, too. Not just the bone itself, but the delay a dig might cause."

"Good point," Marlin said.

Tatum said, "Now I'm wondering about the cash in Farley's gun safe."

"Think it was hush money?" Marlin asked.

Garza said, "Pastor Pete could afford it, that's for sure."

10

AFTER VANESSA SAID the opening prayer and the forty-voice chorus finished an upbeat gospel number, Pastor Pete walked onto the stage, his image magnified on several immense screens behind him, and welcomed his flock. He gave Camera #1 his best side and said, "Friends, I want to start with an amusing story this morning."

Boothe's smiling congregants waited in hushed anticipation. They were a sea of flannel and linen, floral print dresses and colorful blouses. Thirty thousand happy, trusting souls, stretching high into the mezzanine. Millions more were watching the broadcast around the globe.

Boothe was wearing a gray Domenico Vacca suit and a red

silk tie, with a microphone clipped to his lapel. He said, "A young man was living a life of despair and hopelessness, and Satan was whispering into his ear, so he decided to resort to burglary. He broke into a darkened home one night, and the first thing he heard was a voice saying, 'Jesus is watching you!' Well, the poor boy was frightened to death, so he said, 'Who said that?' He waited . . . but nobody answered. Our troubled young man decided it was only his guilty conscience talking to him. So he began to collect valuables and stick them into his bag. Then, once again, a voice, clear as a bell, said, 'Jesus is watching you!' The young man nearly jumped out of his skin with fear. He turned on his flashlight and saw a parrot staring back at him. 'Did you say that?' he asked. And the parrot said, 'Yep.'"

Audience members were starting to giggle.

"The burglar said, 'What's your name?' and the parrot said, 'Moses.'"

More chuckles.

"And the burglar said, 'Moses? What sort of people would name a bird Moses?' And the parrot said, 'The same people who'd name a rottweiler Jesus.'"

A wave of hearty laughter surged through the audience.

"The point is, every moment of every day, Jesus—the *real* Jesus—*is* watching you. Most of you, I'm sure, find that a comfort. What could be more glorious than having the Son of God at your side? What could be more divine than knowing He is there to help you make difficult decisions and navigate troubled waters?"

Boothe paused for a moment, letting that sink in.

"But He's there at other times, too. When you tell the police officer you didn't realize you were speeding, Jesus is riding along, knowing it's a fib. When a cashier gives you too much change and you don't give it back, He's right there, shaking His head, wondering how you can behave in such a manner. When you fudge on your taxes or tithe less than ten percent of your income, when you lie to your boss or stray from your spouse"— now Boothe was turning, and he locked eyes with Vanessa, who was sitting in her padded chair, legs crossed, hands primly on her knees, an enigmatic smile on her face—"Jesus is watching it all."

Vanessa looked away.

The folks back home thought it was an interesting story, the way Butch Theriot wound up working for a preacher's assistant.

Butch was born in the piney woods of East Texas, in Polk County, where he held an unofficial high school football record—not for rushing yardage or touchdowns or interceptions, but for the number of opponents he'd sent off the field on a stretcher. Every Friday night in autumn, under the vapor lights, Butch's drunk and extremely vocal fans—most of them cousins—would root wildly for a broken femur, facial lacerations, or maybe, if things went really well, a ruptured kidney. Butch rarely disappointed. In fact, his mayhem wasn't confined to opposing players; his long list of victims included a radio announcer who, during the playoffs, intentionally called Butch's hometown "Dullardsville" instead of Dallardsville.

After two years as a standout linebacker at a mediocre junior college, Butch moved to Dallas with the hopes of making it onto the Cowboy roster as a walk-on. But in a steroid frenzy one afternoon, he slugged a smart-mouthed equipment manager, and wound up driving a tow truck instead. He did that for several years, until two Jamaicans attacked him with broken beer bottles as he attempted to repossess their Yugo. Butch came away with a nasty scar on his cheek and a tendency to get hostile when he heard reggae music.

After that, Butch did all sorts of work. Roofer. Furniture mover. Mason's assistant. Garbage collector. He was twenty-eight years old when he finally landed the kind of cushy job he'd always dreamed of: security specialist at a gentleman's club. Also known as a bouncer at a titty bar. Between the drugs, the rampant sex, and the luxury of cracking skulls in air-conditioned comfort, Butch was in heaven.

Six months into it, he accidentally fell in love with a dancer named Chardonnay, whose claim to fame was a well-placed birthmark that bore a resemblance to Richard Nixon. They got married two months later, on center stage, with the bridesmaids—Chardonnay's fellow dancers—wearing matching leather teddies.

Things went swimmingly for eleven months. Marriage was a snap when neither mate expected the other to remain faithful, or to even come home at night. But as they neared their one-year anniversary, Butch noticed something troublesome: Bills were stacking up. He and Chardonnay were bringing in plenty of undeclared cash, but she was in charge of their finances, and Butch had to wonder where the money was going. He found out one afternoon when he got a call from a woman who sounded like she'd taken a handful of happy pills. Something about a bounced check.

"We've waived the service fee," the woman announced cheerfully, "because y'all have been such generous contributors in the past."

"The fuck you talkin' about?" Butch asked. "Contributors to what?"

"To the church, sir."

"Who the hell is this?"

The woman stammered. "I'm calling on behalf of Peter Boothe Ministries."

Butch had heard that name before. "This some kinda got-damn joke? Ain't he that faggot preacher on TV?"

She got huffy. "Sir, I would appreciate it if—"

"Call back and I'll set your tits on fire," Butch said, and hung up on her. Then he went to see Chardonnay at the club. He found her in the dressing room, in front of a mirror, getting ready for her set. She played dumb at first, but it didn't take long to get the truth out of her. Chardonnay explained that she had been feeling empty inside for the past few months. Lonely. She needed some direction in life. She said she felt like a lost soul, living a selfish and meaningless existence. But Pastor Pete was changing all that.

Those ain't her own words, Butch thought. *Sumbitches have done brainwashed her!*

"Bottom line, Chardonnay," he said. "How much've you sent these bozos?"

The answer knocked the breath out of him. "About seven thousand dollars," she said.

He heard a low moan of anguish, and he realized he'd made the sound himself. He wanted to punch somebody right in the throat. He wanted to eat someone's spleen. "They conned you, baby," he said, trying to keep the anger out of his voice.

Her lower lip was quivering. "I don't think so."

"Use your head, would ya? How come them preachers is always talking about the way God wants you to have all this cool stuff, then they ask *you* to send money to *them*? Doesn't that seem a little backwards?"

"But it's an investment in our future!" Chardonnay insisted, grabbing him by the hand. "Don't you see? We have to *give* to *receive*. That's what Jesus wants. It's like being a farmer. We have to plant a few seeds before we can expect a harvest. It's the only way we can reach our full potential!"

He couldn't believe what he was hearing. This wasn't Chardonnay talking! This was some kind of Bible-thumping imposter, masquerading in a feather boa and a silk G-string.

"Are you angry?" she asked. "Please don't be angry."

Butch wasn't listening. He was too busy wondering if the address for Peter Boothe Ministries was listed in the phone book.

Alex Pringle happened to be in the lobby that day eight months ago, waiting for the elevator. He heard raised voices, an argument, then a crash. Peering around the corner to the glass-walled reception area, Pringle saw a fierce-looking man in a stained T-shirt standing over Tony, the security guard. Tony was on the ground, out cold. Amy, the receptionist, was cowering behind her desk.

The man in the T-shirt—Christ, he was really big—glared at Pringle and said, "You work here?"

Pringle was tempted to whip out his cell phone and dial 9-1-1, but calling the cops meant bad press. So he took a tentative step forward and said, "Is there a problem?"

"Got-damn right there's a problem," the man said as he approached Pringle, pointing a finger. "You cocksuckers took seven grand from my wife and I want it back."

Pringle understood the situation immediately. What wasn't to understand? He held his hands up in a gesture of appeasement. "Sir, if your wife made a contribution to the church, I'm afraid we—"

The man grabbed Pringle by the lapels of his Armani suit. He smiled, and his breath smelled like pickled eggs. "You don't cough up seven grand right now, I'm fixin' to take it outta your ass. *Comprende?*"

Unfortunately, Pringle had been in this situation before, confronted by an angry spouse or relative demanding a refund. *You took Grandma's Social Security check!* they'd scream. Or *You suckered my wife outta next month's rent!* Such whiners. But usually they called on the phone, or, if the stakes were high enough, they made contact through their attorney. Seldom did they have the balls to come down to the office like this man and make a scene. It was impressive. He seemed to have no fear at all. Pringle realized this guy would be perfect for handling, well, other people just like him. So, three minutes later, Pringle wrote the burly stranger a check. Then he went one better.

He offered him a job. *No telling what this ox might be good for,* Pringle thought at the time.

When Nadine Strand decided to make omelets for brunch, just about anything was liable to wind up in the mix. She'd raid the fridge for leftovers, giving them the sniff test to make sure they hadn't turned, then toss them in the skillet. This morning it was scraps of grilled chicken, bits of home-fried potatoes, and pinto beans, all dumped on top of farm-fresh eggs. With some cheddar grated over everything, of course.

She'd just flipped the first omelet when she heard a car coming up their long gravel driveway. A moment later, she heard a door close. Then another one. "More comp'ny," she crowed. "Place is like Grand Central lately."

Jerry Strand looked up from the newspaper he was reading at the kitchen table. "What, the cops again?"

Nadine parted the curtains for a better look. "I don't think so." She saw two men in dark suits. The passenger had a thick mustache and hair slicked back over his skull. Nice-looking man, from what she could tell. Moved with confidence. The way he whipped his sunglasses off and stared at the house, it reminded Nadine of that red-haired fellow from *CSI: Miami*. Kind of cocky. Sure of himself. The driver, on the other hand, looked like he could lift a refrigerator straight over his head. Tall, and his suit seemed too small, like his arms might rip the seams. Narrow waist. Ugly face, with small eyes and a lumpy nose. Then she noticed that each man had something in his hand. Looked like they were carrying Bibles.

Jerry had moved up next to Nadine for a peek, and now he let out a low groan. "Oh, great."

"Who is it?"

"Some of Peter Boothe's people. Tell 'em I'm not here."

"But your truck is—"

"Then tell 'em I'm sleeping," Jerry snapped, moving toward the kitchen door, headed for the hallway that led to the master bedroom. "I need some peace and quiet today."

"Don't take that tone with me," she called after him, "or I'm gonna feed 'em your damn breakfast." Then she muttered to herself, "Nadine, language."

Nicole Brooks's first real date, more than twenty years ago, was with a hyper-hormonal fifteen-year-old who tried to feel her up during a matinee showing of *The Breakfast Club*. Sammy was his name, if she remembered right. Gangly and pimple-faced. The following Monday morning, at school, he told his nerdy freshman buddies she'd given him a hand job in his car on the way home. When the lie got back to her, she tracked him down in the cafeteria and dumped a bowl of chocolate pudding on his head.

Her first actual boyfriend, when she was a sophomore, was a football-playing senior. As big as a tackling dummy, and just as smart. He wasn't sophisticated or clever or particularly handsome, but he had a kind heart, and he could shotgun a sixteen-ounce beer in less than four seconds, which made him a popular man at parties. He graduated, went off to A&M on scholarship, and the romance fizzled. Nicole felt nothing but relief.

Her first experience with true love came during her second year at Southwest Texas State University, when she was pursuing a degree in criminal justice. The object of her affection? A liberal arts major named Chester. He looked like an underwear model. Good abs and pretty eyes. Drove a restored Mustang. Lived in an expensive condo. Wore designer clothes. Always seemed to have plenty of cash on hand—because he was dealing

Ecstasy. And pot. And sleeping with some of his customers. Male and female. Turned out he wasn't even enrolled.

There'd been other men, of course, in the seventeen years since then. A musician who still lived with his parents. A boat salesman who proposed on the first date. A city councilman who wanted her to be his mistress. An attorney with an Oedipus complex. An advertising executive with a Napoleon complex. A real estate agent with a Peter Pan complex. Sometimes Nicole wondered if she should've studied psychology instead. It would've come in handy, particularly six years earlier, when a man she'd been dating held a gun to her head. Never expected *that* one. The guy had a lot of problems, drinking being one of them, so she decided to end it. He didn't take it well. When he pulled the trigger on an empty chamber, she shattered his nose with the palm of her hand. She didn't like to think about it. That episode, understandably, rocked her trust in men in general.

No more mistakes, she said to herself. No more neurotics or psychotics or loose cannons. No more mama's boys or head cases or macho jerks.

Then, two years ago, she moved to Blanco County and met John Marlin.

Okay. Hold on a minute. This guy was intelligent and nice-looking and oddly . . . normal. Seemed to get along with everybody. Had a lot of friends. But wait, there had to be something wrong with him, right? Yeah, there was, and not what she expected. The problem was, he didn't seem to like her. Never said much. Didn't tell jokes or make small talk with her, like he did with the other deputies. Wasn't rude, but wasn't friendly, either. *Maybe he's a sexist,* she thought. *Doesn't like the idea of a female deputy.* A lot of small-town men felt that way.

Boy, was that off base. He finally admitted, during an awkward conversation, that he had a crush on her. So he got quiet when she was around. A crush. It was so darn cute she could hardly stand it. Long story short, they started dating, and John

Marlin turned out to be the best man she'd ever met. She went into it with a cautious heart and a level head, and she was in love in about a month. How could she not love this man? He was everything she'd ever hoped for.

But the phone call she received that morning, while John was at the sheriff's office, threatened everything.

11

"IS THIS NICOLE Brooks?"

"Yes, it is."

She was at home, in a bubble bath, taking John's advice, trying to relax. But she'd kept the phone in arm's reach, on the rim of the tub, because she was expecting too many important calls. Caterer. Florist. Photographer.

"Look, I . . . uh, are you alone right now?"

Nicole could feel her spine stiffening. *Obscene call?* "Who is this?"

She heard a sound, the caller making a noise, like he'd goofed up. "Jesus, I'm sorry, I shouldn't have asked you that. Forgive me, I'm nervous. I'm not handling this well."

The vibe was getting weirder by the second. "Who is this?" she asked again.

"My name is Michael Kishner. You don't know me, but . . . well, I asked if you were alone because I need to tell you something very sensitive."

"About what?"

"I live in Austin. My wife and I own a small ranch near Round Mountain, and I do some hunting out there. That's how we met the game warden. John Marlin."

He paused, and Nicole heard nothing but droplets falling from her elbow, hitting the bathwater. "What's this about? If you need to speak to John—"

"No, that's not it." His voice sounded emotional. The man was on the verge of tears. "I'd ask you to meet me somewhere, so I could explain everything, but I've already screwed this up. So I'll just tell you." Another pause, then: "I've learned that my wife, Susan, is having an affair with John Marlin. I thought you'd want to know. I understand he's your fiancé."

"Mr. Marlin?"

"Yes, sir?"

"This is Tom Daniels. You called me yesterday. I've been out of town and just now got your message."

"Thanks for calling me back. I'm following up on some paperwork for some deer you bought from a breeder down here in Blanco County. Perry Grange?"

"Yeah, I dealt with him, but two of 'em was DOA. I only got the one yearling. He tried to charge me for the others, but I ain't buying no dead stock."

"Grange came to your place this past Thursday?"

"That's right."

"What time did he get there?"

" 'Bout six o'clock. He in trouble for something?"

Doesn't look that way, Marlin thought.

"Beautiful place you have here," the handsome one named Alex Pringle said. "Must be nice to live out in the country."

Nadine Strand said, "It ain't so bad. It can get lonely when Jerry's not here, but I keep busy with my crochet work."

She and the two men from Boothe Ministries were gathered around the kitchen table, drinking coffee. She'd invited them in, of course, because it would've been rude not to.

"What've you got?" Alex asked. "Twenty acres?"

He was a city fellow. Didn't know it was rude to ask someone about their landholdings. She forgave him, because he was awfully charming otherwise. "Twenty-six."

Alex cocked an ear, listening. Then he smiled. "So quiet."

"It is that," Nadine said. "Too quiet, sometimes. Like to drive me crazy." Then she changed the subject. "Listen, I know Jerry would wanna talk to y'all, but I better let him sleep. He's just been so upset. Tossing and turning all night."

"That's exactly why we're here," Alex said. "To help people like Jerry cope with this tragedy."

"And he needs it, too," she said, nodding. "I hate the way he's holding it in."

"In a time like this, we can find comfort in the Lord's embrace."

"Ain't that the truth." Nadine was tempted to go back there and drag Jerry out of the bedroom. It'd serve him right for getting snippy. Besides, it might do him good to talk things over with a man like Alex Pringle. But Jerry would be angry as a hornet if she did. "I just hope they catch the man who done it," she said, making conversation, enjoying the moment. Such an attractive man, this Alex. "I happen to believe in an eye for an eye, just like the Good Book says."

"That's completely understandable, Nadine," Alex Pringle said. "But remember Jeremiah, 'Be strong, do not fear; your God will come, he will come with vengeance; with divine retribution he will come to save you.'"

Nadine nodded in agreement, but she was confused. Wasn't that from Isaiah? Granted, it had been a while since she'd given her Bible the attention it deserved, but she was pretty sure Alex was mistaken.

The big man, Butch—which was a strange name for a man who worked for a preacher—picked up the sugar bowl and studied it. Nadine was worried that he might drop it. His hands didn't look delicate at all. Matter of fact, neither did Butch. He had a big scar across one cheek, and Nadine could see that his nose had been broken at least once. "This Yogi Bear?" Butch asked. The first words he'd spoken.

"It is," she said, "and it's very fragile."

He didn't take the hint. Just kept looking at the bowl, turning it this way and that. "You got a matching one with Boo Boo on it?"

Nadine decided Butch was having fun at her expense. She tried to smile. Something about him made her nervous. Maybe he was one of those convicts you hear about that finally find God. She made a show of checking her watch. "I don't mean to run y'all off, but my daughter's working this afternoon and I gotta go watch my grandkids in Austin."

Alex did a slow head-bob kind of thing, like something the pope would do as commoners passed before him. "We can speak to Jerry at another time."

"I know he'd like that," Nadine lied, smiling brightly.

"The fuck're you doing asking her about Yogi Bear?" Pringle said when they were back in the car.

"What? I was just making small talk."

"You were making fun of her, plain as day. That seem like something a Christian would do? Fuckin' Boo Boo."

Butch started the car and said, "Where to?"

Pringle loosened his tie. "Back to the motel. We'll come back later."

Darwin Parker had attended school with a boy named Kevin Sawyer, but most of the students at the Wellington Academy had called him Snake—partly because he'd been tall and skinny, and partly because of a rather large organ that had made him the envy of all his classmates.

Snake was an enthusiastic pot smoker who could usually be found in his dorm room listening to Pink Floyd and assembling model airplanes. But if marijuana stole your ambition, you couldn't tell it by Snake. He was quite the entrepreneur—the go-to guy for just about anything a growing prep schooler might want. Booze. Weed. Various illicit pharmaceuticals. The answers to upcoming tests. Even jewelry or flatware, if you wanted a nice gift for your girlfriend or mother. At the time, nobody knew how Snake came by his copious inventory of contraband, but everyone assumed it had something to do with the rash of burglaries that plagued the neighborhood around the school. It was a logical deduction. Snake's father owned a large home-security firm, and rumor had it that Snake could get past every alarm system ever manufactured.

Darwin Parker had decided his old classmate's skills might come in handy. Which was why Snake Sawyer was currently sitting in Darwin's den, wondering, no doubt, about the "business proposition" Darwin had mentioned on the phone. The two men hadn't spoken since graduation, but, one month earlier, Darwin had heard all kinds of gossip about Snake, information that was now proving useful. To wit: At the age of twenty, a thoroughly stoned Snake had successfully broken into an electronics superstore, but he got arrested when the sales manager came in the next morning and found him sleeping in the stereo department. He served fourteen months. Three months out, and he got busted for burglary again, this time in a jewelry store. He'd been on his way to remove the videotape from the surveillance system when he got distracted by a plate of day-old muffins in the employee break room. Major munchies. He forgot all about the tape. Two more years in the slam. After that, he was arrested, but not convicted, for some type of Internet hacking scheme. Snake, with his high-tech background, had made the progression into the world of cyberburglary.

The word was, Snake's family had disowned him, and now he was jobless, with no reportable income. He did a little computer "consulting" on the side, which meant hacking. He might have an addiction, something harder than pot, but it was hard to tell, because Snake had never been that eloquent to begin with.

He was still tall, of course—maybe even taller—but he was no longer skinny. He'd filled out, and not necessarily in a good way. He wasn't so much fat as oddly proportioned. Narrow shoulders and big hips. *Like a bowling pin,* Darwin thought. Hairline starting to recede. He certainly didn't appear capable of burgling anything.

"You ever see any of the guys?" Snake asked in that lazy stoner voice he'd had back in school.

Darwin nodded. "At the reunion in April."

"Reunion?"

"The class reunion."

"It's in April?"

"It *was* in April. The ten-year reunion was last month."

"Ten years? Shit, dude, it's been ten years already? Time flies, huh?" Snake's hair was greasy and unkempt. His jeans were torn, his shirt rumpled. His eyes were glassy and bloodshot. *Still a pothead,* Darwin thought.

"We were all wondering why you didn't show," he said.

Snake was studying a *Deinonychus* femur on the bookshelf. He seemed entranced by it. Or maybe he was just zoning out.

"I said we were all wondering why you didn't show."

Snake looked at Darwin. "Didn't show?"

"At the reunion."

"Oh, right. Yeah, I moved around a lot in the last couple years. Hard to track me down. I never got nothing in the mail."

Darwin was starting to get concerned. The old Snake was no Rhodes scholar, but now he was completely fried. Maybe this was a bad idea. The problem was, Darwin couldn't think of anyone else to call. He simply didn't run with that sort of crowd. And he didn't know anyone who did. So he proceeded with caution.

"I need your help with something, Snake. There's some money in it for you, if you're interested."

Snake grinned. "I could use a few bucks. Is this, like, what, a job? What line of work are you in, anyway?"

"No, this is a onetime . . . project."

"Yeah? What sort of project?"

Darwin noticed that Snake's lips were chapped. He found himself trying to see into Snake's mouth, but he couldn't. "I have this hobby I play around with. I collect dinosaur fossils."

"Hey, that's cool. Like *T. rex* and stuff?"

Why, Darwin wondered, *is it always T. rex?* "More or less."

Snake's face suddenly lit up. "Whoa, dude, did you see *Jurassic Park*?"

"Yeah, I—"

"Wasn't that awesome?"

Unrealistic, Darwin thought. *Silly. Banal.* "Yeah, it sure was. Outstanding film."

"They made two more after that. They weren't as good."

"The sequels rarely are. Anyway, a man e-mailed me a week ago about a particular fossil. He wanted to sell it, and he sent a photo. This was a great specimen, from what I could tell, and

I—well, I wanted it. I really wanted it. So we exchanged a few more e-mails, and we agreed on a price, pending authentication—"

Snake frowned.

"Meaning," Darwin said, "if the bone checked out, I'd buy it. I thought everything was all set. But I haven't heard from him since. He hasn't responded to any of my e-mails."

Snake looked like he was trying to solve a tough calculus problem in his head. "So who was this guy?"

Darwin's patience was wearing thin. "I have no idea. And the problem is, I'm worried that he might've found a higher bidder, and I want to talk to him again before he sells. But I don't know his name, or where he lives, or anything about him. So I need to find out where the e-mails came from."

"This is a really weird situation, bro. Sounds like the plot for another movie. Hey, maybe it's *Jurassic Park IV*! We could write a screenplay together!"

Darwin stared at him. It was hopeless.

Snake continued, saying, "The movie could have, like, some geeked-out computer jockey who traces the e-mails for you. It wouldn't be that hard, you know."

"It wouldn't?"

"Naw, man, not usually. He coulda done a few things to cover his tracks, but you can usually get past those."

Okay, maybe I was a little hasty. Maybe Snake is the right man for the job. "How would someone go about tracking this guy down?"

"Start with the simple stuff, man. Do a search for that address. If you're lucky, the guy's posted to a newsgroup or bulletin board somewhere and you can learn something about him that way. If that doesn't work, you pull the originating IP address off the Internet header and do a reverse DNS lookup, which'll give you the hostname. From there, you—"

Darwin cut him off with a raised hand, because it was all gibberish anyway. "Are you good at that sort of thing?"

"Oh, shit yeah, man. I can track just about anybody, at least to a point, assuming they don't work for, like, the CIA or something. I steer clear of those guys. Major bad news."

Darwin's spirits were starting to rise. "What would something like that cost me?"

Snake waved his hand. "For an old bud like you, man, let's say five hundred bucks. Wouldn't take me long."

Darwin opened a desk drawer and removed an envelope. Inside was five hundred in cash. There were several other envelopes in the drawer, all with varying amounts, ranging from one thousand to ten thousand. He'd planned ahead, so he'd be prepared for whatever amount Snake might request. Plus a little extra, for incentive. "Let's say a thousand bucks. Half now, half later. That seems fair, doesn't it?"

Snake was smiling and nodding. "I'm not gonna argue."

"But I need you to do it as soon as possible. This has to take precedence over anything else on your schedule."

Darwin felt a little foolish saying that. What else could Snake possibly have on his schedule, other than bong hits? This guy wasn't taking part in corporate mergers or leveraged buyouts.

"I'm pretty wide open right now," Snake said, nodding seriously. "I can get right on it."

Darwin decided to hold off on describing the second part of the plan: how Snake might have to put his burglary skills to use once the e-mailer had been identified. One hurdle at a time.

Darwin caught himself staring at Snake's chapped lips again, and Snake seemed to notice. He pointed at Darwin, laughing. "Dude, I remember now. You were always asking me to show off at parties. You were, like, my biggest fan. Wanna see it?"

Darwin nodded. He couldn't help himself.

Snake opened his mouth, and out it came. The freakishly

long slab of meat that had earned him his nickname. He tried to say *See?* but it came out as "Thee?"

Darwin smiled casually, trying to mask his envy. *My God, what a tongue.* It was nothing short of reptilian.

Snake flicked it up and down, back and forth, giggling all the while. Darwin was mesmerized. It was like looking at a modern-day *Panoplosaurus*. Remarkable. And it was totally wasted, so to speak, on this aimless pothead. Darwin would've given every last dollar in his desk drawer for a tongue like that.

Back in his '95 Mazda, Snake grabbed a plastic bag that was stuffed between the front seats, next to the emergency brake. Four solid hours he'd gone straight, wanting to have his shit together for his meeting with Darwin Parker, figuring there was some money involved. Good thing, too, because he'd been right. But it had been a hard four hours.

He reached behind the seat and found a spray can of Pam that had been rolling around on the floorboard. Man, he loved that smell. He opened the bag and shot a healthy blast of Pam inside, until he had a small pool of liquid at the bottom. His hands were tingling with anticipation.

He held the bag up to his face, forming a good seal around his cheeks and mouth, and inhaled deeply. Oh, yeah. Good stuff. He could feel it immediately. Pure mellowness. He giggled. Giddiness was setting in. So familiar and warm. Pam was even better than model airplane glue. Pam was for special occasions.

Pam. Pam. Pam. What a great name. Short and to the point.

The car seemed to be swaying gently, even though he knew it was not. He watched a bird on a branch on a nearby tree. It was purple and pink.

Snake decided that if he had a girlfriend, he'd name her Pam. He might even call her Pammy. Or Miss Pam. Pamarama. Pamalot. Pamalamadingdong.

He chanted it as fast as he could, ten times, because, for reasons he didn't understand, it had become a ritual.

Pam, Pam, Pam, Pam, Pam, Pam, Pam, Pam, Pam.

Excellent. Wait, that was only nine.

Pam.

12

AFTER LUNCH, JOHN Marlin spent a few hours doing research. He had a computer in his office, and he used it to write reports and to find things on the Internet occasionally. He wasn't an expert at surfing the Web, nor did he fully understand the technology, but he could get around.

The search engine called Google was handy, and Nicole had taught Marlin a few tricks. For instance, he understood that a search for *Peter Boothe* was likely to return millions of hits, including any page with "Peter" or "Boothe" on it. But if he hyphenated the name, as he did now, and searched for *Peter-Boothe*, the results would only include pages with those words side by side. The first hit listed was the official site for Boothe Ministries.

It wasn't what Marlin expected. No dour paintings of Jesus on the cross. No Bible verses. In fact, at first glance, you might not know the site had anything to do with religion at all. The page was slickly designed, filled with vibrant colors and graphics that pulsed and flowed. It was heavy on the retailing of Peter Boothe, to say the least. Click here to buy Pastor Pete's best-selling book, DVD, videocassette, or CD. Click over there to watch his highly rated television show online, or to access a broadcast schedule. Fill in these blanks to sign up for his daily inspirational newsletter. You could donate to the church, send a prayer request, or listen to a podcast, whatever that was.

Marlin had to wonder, *Is this guy a minister or a motivational speaker?* There were no fewer than nine photos of Peter Boothe's smiling mug scattered throughout the home page. The man was definitely not camera shy.

Neither was his wife, Vanessa; there was a shot of her at a groundbreaking ceremony for the new religious complex in March. It was one of those corny publicity photos, but instead of holding a shovel or cutting a ribbon, she was seated on a backhoe. Probably Hollis Farley's backhoe. Marlin couldn't help noticing that Vanessa Boothe was damned sexy, even wearing a hard hat.

Marlin saw a button that said WHAT WE BELIEVE, so he clicked on it. The next page featured a bulleted list of seven or eight statements, all of which began with *We believe . . .*

The first one gave Marlin exactly what he was looking for. It said, *We believe . . . the Holy Bible is the word of God, literal and inerrant, and we accept it as the rule of our faith and practice.*

Aha. "Literal and inerrant." No room for maneuvering there. If Genesis said the universe was created in six days, well, that meant six days. And "days" wasn't some ambiguous word meaning "eons" or "epochs." A day, literally, was a day, and nothing more or less, right? Garza and Tatum had already left the office, so Marlin pasted the text from that page into an e-mail and sent it to both of them—along with a note that Perry Grange's alibi had checked out.

He poked around on some other Web sites, and he found, as he suspected, that the issue of dinosaurs and Christianity was, for Bible literalists, a delicate one. A few sites claimed that dinosaurs never existed, and one of those sites theorized that dinosaur bones had been planted by Satan as a means to shake man's faith.

Many more sites insisted that man and dinosaurs coexisted about six thousand years ago, because it was all spelled out in Genesis. The creation of dinosaurs, they said, was implied by "every thing that creepeth upon the earth." Further, scientists and educators who claimed that dinosaurs were millions of years old were simply mistaken because they relied on junk science, or perhaps they had a hidden agenda.

Then there were the nonliteralists—the more mainstream majority, it appeared—who felt that the language of the Bible could be interpreted symbolically, and evolution, therefore, fit sensibly within the framework of Christianity. The "sixth day," for example, could encompass an era of a billion years, couldn't it? So dinosaurs might have roamed the earth, and then perished, and then man came along—all on the same "day."

It's easy to understand, Marlin thought, *why atheists always sound so cocksure of themselves. At least they all believe, or disbelieve, the same thing.*

"You know, I just realized something," Red said. "We're forgetting about somebody."

They were back in their usual spots—Red in the recliner, Billy Don on the sofa, facing the TV. The Rangers were losing to the Mariners, but Red wasn't really watching. He was thinking about the creature known as the *Alamosaurus*. He couldn't let it go. Not if it was worth as much money as Hollis had said.

"Hey, Billy Don."

"What, goddamn it?" The big man was stuffing his face with some questionable beef jerky he'd bought at the wholesale club. Red had tried it, and it tasted like imitation meat.

"You listening to me?"

"I got a choice?"

"Know who we're forgetting?"

"Britney Spears?"

Just the kind of smart-ass answer Red had come to expect. Billy Don had a mouth on him, but there wasn't much Red could do about it. Except be persistent. He was good at that. Which would be helpful right now, because Billy Don would play an important role in the idea that was brewing in Red's head. So he said, "We're forgetting about Betty Jean."

Billy Don didn't reply.

"Hollis Farley's sister," Red said. "Works at the diner."

"No shit, Red. I know who she is."

Mike Morse smacked a single up the middle. Almost took the pitcher's head off.

"What I'm thinking is, she might know what Hollis done with the bone. I mean, hell, he told *me* about it, right? So you can bet he probably told his own sister."

Billy Don had a mouthful, but that didn't stop him from saying, "Yeah, and if she knows something, why would she tell us?"

Excellent. Red had been hoping Billy Don would ask that very question. He said, "It ain't no secret she's got the hots for you, Billy Don. 'Member last week when she gave you that free piece of pie? The way she kept hanging around, batting her eyes at you? Leaning over the counter?"

Red saw Billy Don's mouth twitch, like he wanted to smile but was holding it back.

"I ain't no expert in love," Red said, "but I do believe she thinks you're one fine hunk of man. She'd probably serve you a lot more than pie if you'd ask."

"You're a moron," Billy Don said, but he actually seemed to be blushing.

The thing was, what Red was saying was true. He didn't understand it, because Billy Don wasn't much to look at, so he didn't have a lot of luck with the ladies. But Betty Jean Farley, for whatever reason, maybe her vision was poor, seemed to find Billy Don attractive. Maybe it was because they were both large people. Maybe Betty Jean kept an eye out for men who were bigger than she was. And that narrowed the possibilities down quite a bit, especially in a town the size of Johnson City.

Red kept pressing. "Wouldn't hurt to ask her out, would it? Take her dancing. Get a few beers in her and see what happens. Even if she didn't know nothin', you two kids could go and have a good time. You might even get lucky."

Billy Don didn't say anything, just sat gnawing his jerky. When he finally spoke, he said, "Ain't got no vehicle."

Red was prepared for that. "You can borrow my truck. We'll clean the beer cans out and do something about the smell. Man alive, you'll sweep that gal right off her feet."

But you'd better bring a king-size broom, he thought.

Rhonda Himmelblau was from an older generation of strong-willed, straight-shooting Texas women, the kind who managed to make a stinging rebuke come across as an affectionate scolding.

When Bobby Garza had phoned her the previous day, asking if she could come to Johnson City to talk about Hollis Farley, she'd said, "Last week y'all ran me outta the county. Now you want me to drive out for a chat? Well, you can kiss my German ass, mister." Somehow, it was colorful rather than offensive, like it was a joke they were sharing together. Himmelblau didn't sound like an environmentalist; she sounded like a tough old gal who should be banging a gavel in a county courtroom.

Garza immediately liked her. And that feeling grew when he met her in person.

The offices of the organization she led, Greener Texas, were in the heart of Austin, a short walk from the capitol. Like a lot of professionals in the area—attorneys, dentists, consultants of every stripe—Greener Texas had converted a forties-era two-story home into office space. It was a cozy environment, with hardwood floors, wainscoted walls, and rooms filled with carefully selected secondhand furniture. Everything in the foyer, which served as the reception area, was neat and orderly. Rhonda Himmelblau's office, on the other hand, was chaos. Materials stacked on every surface. Magazines and newspapers. Loose documents. Binders. One bound study had a title on the spine: *The Prevalence of Perchlorate Pollution in Texas Groundwater.* Fun, fun, fun, and alliterative, too.

Himmelblau herself had an unkempt manner about her. Not sloppy, but unconcerned. Like she'd applied her makeup, what little there was, in the car. She was dressed in cream-colored slacks and a simple white blouse. She appeared to be well into her seventies—hair thoroughly gray, plenty of wrinkles around the eyes and mouth—but she had a regal, youthful bearing.

She moved a large stack of manila folders from a chair so Garza could sit down. She didn't offer coffee.

"You're gonna have to talk fast," she said, taking a seat behind her desk. "I've got a conference call with a state senator in eight minutes."

"On a Sunday?"

"Yeah, he says he has to go to church to work up the nerve to deal with me. I'm trying to change his vote on an upcoming wetlands-preservation bill. Personally, I'd rather have sex with Rush Limbaugh than talk to this blowhard, because at least I'd know up front I'm getting screwed. But you don't want to hear all that crap. You're here about Hollis Farley."

"Yes, ma'am."

"I understand he was killed on Thursday afternoon."

"Thereabouts, yes, and—"

"And you have to question me about it because I'm a nut. My whole group is a bunch of left-wing wackos, and there's no telling what any of us might do." There was a gleam in her eyes.

"You did punch one of my deputies," Garza reminded her.

"It was an elbow," she said. "He tickled me when he was frisking me. Accidental, I'm sure, unless he's got a fetish for old ladies. But I jerked backward and caught him with an elbow. Didn't mean to. My lawyer's gonna chew me a new one for even telling you that. We were saving it for the deposition."

"Deputy Tatum said it was your right hand."

Rhonda Himmelblau paused for a moment, considering something. Then she said, "Sheriff, have you ever heard of von Willebrand disease?"

"Yes, ma'am. My mother-in-law has it."

"Then you know it causes serious bruising from even a light blow." She was rolling up her sleeve, and now she showed him her elbow, which was thoroughly purpled. Her hand, Garza noticed, was unmarked. Good evidence, but it didn't really matter, and he told her why.

"Sorry you were injured. I can tell you that the prosecutor has no intention of taking the case to trial."

She grinned. "Well, that's good to hear. He woulda got his butt whupped."

"Looks that way. But since I only have six minutes left—"

"Five," Himmelblau said, glancing at a clock on the wall. "But don't let me rush you."

"Can we talk about Hollis Farley?"

"I was in Houston," she said. "Drove over there on Wednesday morning. Came back on Friday evening. That means this ol' granny has an alibi."

Garza wasn't thinking of her as a suspect. "Frankly, what I want is a list of your employees and members."

"And what I want is a night alone with George Clooney."

He smiled. "You won't share the list with me?"

She stared at him for a long moment. "I suppose if I don't, you'll be back in my hair tomorrow with a court order."

"Absolutely. More likely this afternoon."

"Okay, fine. I'll pull it together and e-mail it to you. Y'all got e-mail out there in the sticks?"

"We do. And running water. When can you send it?"

"Tomorrow?"

"I'd rather have it today."

"You don't ask for much, do you? Okay, I'll do my best, but no promises. I'm stacked with meetings."

"I would appreciate it," he said.

"All right, but let me mention two things," she said. "First, that list includes about two thousand people—everyone who's ever given our organization one tax-deductible dollar."

"I'll wade through it. What's the second thing?"

"It's a waste of time. The kind of person who joins Greener Texas ain't gonna go out and murder a man, especially a backhoe operator. Hollis Farley was just working for a living. He wasn't the one who decided to build a monstrosity on the banks of the Pedernales River. Our members would know that."

"Well," Garza said, "if it's a waste of time, I'm willing to handle the disappointment."

Himmelblau smiled brightly. "I'm not talking about wasting *your* time, darlin', I'm talking about wasting *mine*."

13

JERRY STRAND WAS well into a fifth of Wild Turkey—attempting to calm himself down, and succeeding—when he heard the car doors again. He parted the curtains and saw Alex Pringle and that other guy from earlier. Stout son of a bitch. Tall. Mean-looking, too, though Strand wasn't feeling particularly intimidated at the moment. Not like earlier.

Might as well get this over with, he thought.

He opened the door just as the men crested the porch. "I gave at the office," he said, and laughed, because the last word came out as "offish." Bourbon always did wonders for his sense of humor. And his confidence.

"You doing all right, Jerry?" Pringle asked, raising an eyebrow, an amused expression on his face.

"Better'n Hollis Farley, that's for sure." It occurred to Strand that he still had a highball glass in his hand, so he took a long drink. Boy, it was going down easy now. Then he wiped his mouth and said, "I figure that's why y'all are here, right? 'Cause of Farley?"

"Can we come inside and talk about it?" Pringle asked. "Maybe join you for a cocktail?"

Strand suddenly wondered why Pringle had rattled his nerves on previous occasions. He was just another overbearing guy in an expensive suit. So Strand made a sweeping motion with his arm, gesturing toward the interior of his house, saying, "*Mi casa es su casa*. Come on in and take a load off."

The two men filed through the kitchen, into the living room, and Strand followed behind them. He grabbed two highball glasses from the bar, turned, and said, "Bourbon okay?"

"That'll be fine," Pringle said, still standing.

Strand poured a couple of inches into each glass and handed one to Pringle and one to the stranger. "You don't talk much, do ya, bud?" Strand asked him.

The stranger stared down at him without speaking. He had a long scar across his cheek. Strand wondered if this guy was a murderer. He sure looked like one.

It was as if Pringle read his mind, because he said, "Awful sad what happened to Farley."

Strand nodded. Despite the liquor, he felt his courage slip a notch or two. "One of those damn environmentalists. That's who done it." He truly wanted to believe that.

"Think so?"

"That's what I told the deputy."

Pringle was staring at him. "I have to confess something, Jerry. I know it's crazy, but it's crossed my mind that it might've been you. Maybe you killed Farley."

"You're shittin' me."

"Greed is a powerful motivator. We'd be splitting it two ways instead of three. Sounds pretty good, doesn't it?"

He's playing head games, because he knows I've been thinking the same thing about him. "Hell, no, wasn't me. Are you crazy?"

"Okay, good," Pringle said. "Nice to have that out of the way. On the other hand, if you didn't do it, you've probably been wondering if I did." Pringle downed his bourbon in one swallow, made a face, like it wasn't up to his standards, and set the glass down on an end table. "I'll put your mind at ease. I didn't. Nor did I have it done."

"Never crossed my mind," Strand lied.

"Fine. So neither of us did it. Now I have to ask you something important. Where's the bone, Jerry?"

Strand frowned. He'd been expecting that question and considering how he should react to it. Confusion seemed to be the best option. "The bone? How should I know? Hollis had it."

"You said you were gonna take it from him for safekeeping."

"Yeah, I tried, but he wouldn't go for it."

Pringle lowered himself into an easy chair and crossed his legs, making himself right at home. The man with the scar remained standing. "This isn't making a lot of sense," Pringle said. "If Hollis had the bone, the cops would've found it, and they would've said something to me about it by now. But they haven't." Pringle grinned again. "You sure you haven't got it tucked away somewhere? Maybe you're just holding on to it, waiting for this mess to blow over. Just being cautious?"

"I'm telling you, I ain't got it. Got no idea where it is."

Pringle gazed at him for a long moment. Strand couldn't hold his gaze, so he went to the bar for more bourbon. While he was pouring, Pringle said, "Then you won't mind if Butch here looks around a little. Since you're not hiding anything."

Strand turned with his full glass, smiling, shaking his head, sort of an I-can't-believe-you-don't-believe-me gesture. "Be my guest. Search the whole damn place. Just don't break nothing. Believe me, you don't want to upset Nadine. Woman's a hellcat about her stuff."

Nobody moved. Nobody spoke. Finally, Pringle said, "I don't think that's necessary. But I do have another question for you. Did you tell anyone about the bone? Maybe Nadine?"

"No. No way. That woulda been stupid. I didn't tell nobody. Especially her. Damn woman would be on the phone blabbin' in two minutes."

"What about Farley? Had he found a buyer yet?"

Two million bucks, Strand thought. *All to myself if I keep my mouth shut. That, and track down the buyer. Or find a new one.* "I don't think so. If he did, he didn't tell me. No, definitely not, 'cause he woulda said something. Hollis wasn't the type could handle something like this by hisself."

"Had he contacted anybody?"

"He didn't have time. He was still doing research, trying to figure out what it was worth."

"Doing what kind of research? Calling people?"

"No, he was using the Internet. Taking it slow, because we wanted to get a good price."

Strand was getting nervous again. All these questions.

"So Farley had a computer?" Pringle asked.

"No, he was using the ones at the library."

Another long pause. Pringle was obviously thinking things through, maybe wondering if the cops could trace things back to them. "That professor," he said, "you sure Farley didn't give him his name?"

"Absolutely not. I mean yes, I'm sure, he didn't give his name. I told him not to. He always listened to me. Good kid."

"So nobody but us knows where that bone came from."

It wasn't a question, it was a statement, but Strand corrected him. "Just us and the Boothes."

"That's perfect, Jerry. Just perfect."

Something strange was going on. Pringle was removing a handkerchief from his suit pocket, picking up the glass he'd been using, wiping it off. What the hell? Strand glanced to his right, to see what Butch was doing, but he wasn't there. Then, in a fraction of an instant, Strand knew. He knew, and he didn't have time to react, and then he felt an arm like a steel cable wrap around his neck. Strand was strong, but not strong enough.

I'm so stupid, he thought. *So goddamn stupid.*

Marlin called Nicole at home and said, "I ran off without that videographer's phone number. You got it handy?"

"Hold on a sec." She came back half a minute later and read it to him. Then she didn't say anything.

"We still on for dinner?" he asked.

"I don't know if I'm up to it."

"Everything all right?"

"Oh, I've got a massive headache. Took some aspirin and I was lying down."

"So . . . no dinner then?"

"I'd rather not." She was abrupt.

"You sure everything's okay?"

"I just told you, I have a headache. This conversation is making it worse."

"You don't have to snap at me."

She didn't reply.

"Okay, I'll see you tomorrow," he said.

She hung up.

Hell of a headache, Marlin thought.

Red and Billy Don walked into the Kountry Kitchen at ten after six. There wasn't much of a crowd, so they took a booth along the front windows. Billy Don was wearing overalls, looking like a hayseed, but at least he'd shaved and run a comb through his hair. He'd even put on some cologne from a free sample he'd found in *Modern Ammo* magazine. Smelled like Hoppe's gun oil.

Billy Don was holding a menu, but his eyes were darting around the room. "Don't see her," he said quietly.

"Maybe she's in the kitchen."

"Didn't see her truck out front."

Aha. Red smiled. "She drives a truck?"

Now Billy Don looked down at the menu. "Seen her around town, that's all."

Red knew better. It meant Billy Don had had his eye on Betty Jean for quite some time. But Red let it go. If he razzed Billy Don about it, the big man might just get huffy and scrap the entire plan. "If she ain't working the floor," Red said, "you'll have to wing it. Maybe stop at the counter and offer your condolences. That sort of thing."

"I know, Red. We already went through this."

"I'm just saying."

Suddenly there was a waitress at Red's elbow. Not Betty Jean. A skinny thing, no more than twenty, twenty-two. One of those young gals who'd rather be anywhere else but here. Trish, according to her name tag. Trish had an earring through her eyebrow, of all the damn places.

"Y'all know what you want?" she asked, sounding bored.

"Chicken-fried steak, green beans, and fried okra," Red said.

She was scribbling on her pad. "To drink?"

"Iced tea." Red would've preferred a cold beer, but the diner didn't have a liquor license.

She looked at Billy Don.

"Chicken strips. Double order. Mashed taters with lots of gravy. Gravy on the chicken, too, come to think of it. Pinto beans, cole slaw, and fried okra. Some of them cornbread muffins, too. Oh, and bring me a side of catfish nuggets with plenty of tartar."

"That all?"

Red realized Trish was being a sass-mouth, but Billy Don didn't pick up on it. "Lemonade," he said, handing her his menu.

When she was gone, they sat quietly for several minutes. Then Billy Don said, "Red, I been thinking."

There's a first time for everything, Red thought.

Billy Don said, "With Hollis being murdered and all, don'tcha think it's got something to do with the dinosaur bone?"

Red had been wondering that same thing himself, of course, ever since he'd seen the morning newspaper. He figured it was a pretty good guess. But he hadn't mentioned it, because Billy Don would've wanted to run to the sheriff and spill the beans. Red didn't want anybody else knowing about the fossil. Besides, there were other possibilities. "Not necessarily," he said. "Coulda been somebody who was mad about the church being built."

Billy Don made a face, like, *Hmm, I hadn't thought of that.*

Red still hadn't seen Betty Jean. And a woman like her wasn't easy to miss.

Five minutes later, the waitress returned with their food. Most of it, anyway. She had to make two trips. When she set the last plate down, Red said, "Betty Jean working tonight?"

She looked at Red like he was a complete idiot. He'd seen that expression before. "'Course not," she said. "Her brother's funeral is tomorrow afternoon."

That's right, the funeral. Red hadn't planned on going, because Hollis Farley hadn't been much more than an occasional hunting buddy. Funerals were a hassle, too, because people got all dressed up, and the women got all weepy, and the preacher quoted a bunch of Bible stuff that Red never quite understood.

But now that he thought about it . . . Betty Jean would need some comforting. It'd be best if Billy Don was right there, waiting in the wings, ready to dry her tears.

14

ALEX PRINGLE POSSESSED a love of money so pro-
found, he could only assume it stemmed from the fact that he'd
once had none.

He grew up in a shabby home in a marginal Dallas neighborhood surrounded by industrial complexes. Not far away, on a
busy street, women wearing short shorts and high heels called
out to passing cars.

Alex often heard his parents arguing about finances or dis-
cussing creative ways to juggle overdue bills. They shopped in
secondhand stores, drank generic beer, and smoked discount
cigarettes. Sometimes Alex contemplated running away, as
much for their sake as for his own.

Then, when he was twelve, he spotted an ad in the back of a comic book:

WANT EXTRA SPENDING MONEY? LOTS OF IT?

We'll tell you how! Easier than a paper route! Impress your friends! For details, send three dollars (cash, no checks or money orders) to P.O. Box . . .

Alex was intrigued. This was exactly what his family needed—some easy money—and all it would cost was three dollars. So he sent three grubby one-dollar bills—money he'd earned mowing his neighbor's lawn—and waited eagerly for the response. Soon the secret to success would be his! Two months later, an envelope arrived from a company called Advanced Marketing Concepts.

Inside was a typewritten note that appeared to be a photocopy of a photocopy of a photocopy:

HERE IT IS! THE MONEY-MAKING SYSTEM
YOU'VE BEEN WAITING FOR!

Dear Friend,

As you know, there are thousands of publications across America—magazines, newspapers, periodicals, newsletters, comic books. The people who read those pulbications—smart people like you—are always interested in new oportunities to earn money. So here's the secret . . . All you have to do is place ads just like the one you responded to, then send your customers a reply like the one you're now reading. That's all there is to it! Thank you for your interest. Good luck with your new business!

Alex felt the heat rise in his face. His hands trembled. He'd been conned. Swindled. Duped. Just plain outsmarted. He was angry and embarrassed—and more than a little impressed. Yes, they'd suckered him out of three dollars, but Alex Pringle learned a valuable lesson that day.

Mowing lawns was for the birds. If you wanted someone's money, the solution was simple: All you had to do was take it.

Alex soon discovered that he was a natural at it, and he quickly developed a few cons that got him through his teenage years. Stealing pets and "finding" them later for the reward money. Collecting "donations" for underprivileged children during the holidays. Well, shit—he was underprivileged, wasn't he?

It was all so gloriously simple! The average schmuck was ready to believe just about anything you told him.

Fast-forward two decades and Alex Pringle was worth a cool two million. His career had consisted of a series of frenetic forays into a broad range of ventures, some more legitimate than others, but none that would earn him any merit badges. Multilevel marketing programs. Questionable real estate deals. Junk bonds. Elaborate Ponzi schemes. Telemarketing swindles. A bogus African diamond mine. He'd owned a home-improvement company that cut corners like a drunken seamstress, a financial-consulting firm designed to part senior citizens from their money, and a literary agency that charged exorbitant reading fees but never sold a single book.

Along the way, not surprisingly, Pringle attracted plenty of unwanted attention from law enforcement. Then it happened. After seven indictments, a conviction. One count of mail-order fraud. A twenty-thousand-dollar fine and ten years of probation. The next time, the judge warned him, he'd do jail time.

So Alex Pringle decided, finally, to go straight—more or less. He began looking for new opportunities. What he wanted was something immensely profitable—but with an air of legitimacy that placed him above reproach. Perhaps a charity or nonprofit foundation, arenas in which a clever CEO could skim an enormous salary.

As it turned out, he didn't have to go looking for his next big moneymaker, because it landed right in his lap. Literally. He was taking Southwest Airlines to Austin and he happened to open the in-flight magazine. Right there, on page fourteen was an interview with an up-and-coming pastor in Houston. WHEN PROSPERITY KNOCKS, the headline said, THIS MINISTER OPENS THE DOOR.

Pringle was riveted. Not because the pastor had a congregation of "six thousand and growing, and a beautiful new church." Not because he preached that God wanted all of His followers to be wealthy and successful. Pringle was mesmerized because he immediately recognized the man. Four or five years earlier, when Pringle had been selling a worthless line of foreign-made kitchen gadgets via an 800 number, he'd hired an ad agency to create some television commercials.

This man—this pastor—had been the copywriter on Pringle's account. His name, of course, was Peter Boothe.

Pastor Pete.

Bobby Garza called at five fifteen the next morning.

"I thought game wardens never slept."

"Been up for an hour," Marlin said. The croak in his voice gave him away.

"How come you don't have any lights on?"

"I use candles. They conserve energy. Please tell me you're not in my driveway at this ungodly hour."

"No, of course not. I'm standing on your front porch. Hell of a watchdog you got."

Geist was still curled on her dog pillow beside the bed. She had one eye open, watching Marlin.

"Why are you bothering me this early?"

"Beause Bill's gone to Florida and that leaves you. Can I tell you something interesting?"

"That's debatable."

"Jerry Strand is missing."

Marlin swung his feet onto the floor. "Since when?"

"How about you make some coffee and I tell you the story?"

"Nadine Strand called me about two hours ago," Garza said. He was sitting at Marlin's kitchen table, dressed in jeans, an untucked flannel shirt, and tennis shoes. Marlin was leaning against the counter, wearing shorts and a T-shirt, waiting for the coffeemaker to finish doing its thing. "She'd been gone most of the day yesterday, got home at around ten last night and Jerry wasn't there. His truck was still at the house, so she figured he'd gone off with one of his friends and maybe got to drinking some beer. She went to bed, woke up at two thirty and he still wasn't home. So she started calling around, waking people up. Nobody knew where he was. So she waited till she couldn't stand it anymore and called me. I just came from her house."

"And?"

"And nothing. He's gone and I don't know where he is."

"No wonder you're a revered lawman."

Garza ignored him. "There was no sign of a struggle, no indication that he took anything with him. I don't know, it's probably too early to get worked up about it. He's probably sleeping one off somewhere."

Marlin poured two mugs of coffee and handed one to Garza. "Obviously you think there's more to it than that."

Garza blew on his coffee and took a sip. "First Hollis Farley, now this. Can't be a coincidence."

"Where was Nadine Strand yesterday?"

"Watching her grandkids in Austin from noon till nine."

"Did she talk to Jerry anytime during the day?"

"She called once, but he didn't answer. She left a message."

Marlin sat down at the table and tried to think things through. "You figure it has to do with the dinosaur bone."

"I'd say that's almost certain."

"So the question is, who did Farley tell about the bone?"

"Strand didn't mention it to Bill. I guess there's a chance Strand didn't know, but . . ."

"If you're Farley, and you discover something like that at a job site, the first person you tell is the boss."

"Exactly. I really doubt Farley even knew the significance of what he'd found. Or that the bone had any value."

"Okay, if we make that assumption—that Farley went to Strand—what next? Did Strand tell his client?"

"Meaning Peter Boothe."

"Or one of his underlings."

Garza smiled. "Interesting that you say that. There's a guy named Alex Pringle—Boothe's executive director. He and another guy dropped by Strand's house yesterday morning, an hour or so before Nadine Strand left the house. I talked to Pringle two nights ago, and he said he was coming to town to"— Garza made quotation marks with his hands—"help our community get through this difficult time."

"What does that mean?"

"Hell if I know, but Nadine said Jerry didn't want to see him. He made Nadine tell them he was sleeping. Said he just wanted some peace and quiet. But she said there was something weird about it. Jerry seemed upset."

Marlin's mind was going in several different directions. "I see so many possibilities, I'm not even sure where to start."

"Throw one at me."

"Okay. What if Farley, Strand, and Pringle planned to sell the dinosaur bone and split the cash three ways. But Pringle gets greedy and kills them both."

"Interesting, but remember that Farley's murder doesn't look like it was planned. If the killer used Farley's own bow, it was likely a spur-of-the-moment thing."

"Okay, probably, but maybe not. Think about this. If Farley

was doing a little hunting after work on the church property,
Strand probably knew about it. He would've known the bow
was there. Maybe Pringle is clean and everything is Strand's doing. Maybe Strand and Farley had a two-man partnership, then
Strand killed Farley, and Bill's visit scared him, so Strand took
off with the bone."

Garza sat quietly, thinking it over.

Marlin said, "Those reserve deputies find the skull yet?"

"Nope. They'll be out there again today."

"Wasting their time if someone dug it up."

Marlin could hear a neighbor's rooster crowing in the distance. Then Garza changed the subject for a moment, saying,
"Listen, I should probably mention something about Bill. I
know we could use him right now, but he and Lydia are having
some problems. I think he needs some time with his family."

"I've been wondering. He seems kind of tense lately. But I'm
surprised he told you about it."

"Yeah, he's not known for opening up, is he? What happened
was, I heard him talking to her on the phone, and he knew I
heard, so we talked about it. Briefly. He said Lydia brought up
the idea of a divorce."

"I wouldn't have guessed. Bill is so . . . I don't even know the
right word. Self-contained, I guess."

"Maybe that's part of the problem." Garza drained the last of
his coffee, then said, "Well, since I can't talk to Strand, and
since I've already talked to Rhonda Himmelblau, I guess I'll talk
to Alex Pringle."

"As well you should."

"You keep doing what you're doing."

"Drinking coffee?"

"Actually, why don't you have a follow-up conversation with
Scott Underwood. We still need to check him out."

15

"WELL, FUCK ME," Alex Pringle muttered to himself. He was lying on his bed at the Best Western, his back against the headboard, reading Hollis Farley's funeral notice in the local newspaper. It told him something he hadn't known before. He grabbed the phone and dialed the room next door.

Butch answered by saying, "Nothing yet."

"I'm not calling about that," Pringle said. "I'm calling because Hollis Farley had a sister."

"Yeah? What about it?"

"How did we not know that? How did you miss that?"

"Hey, hold on. You asked if he had a family. I thought you meant, like, a wife and kids."

Pringle took a deep breath, then spoke slowly. "No, I asked if he had *family* in the area. I didn't ask if he had *a* family. There's a difference." Pringle wanted to call Butch a dumbshit, but he never quite had the balls to go that far. Butch seemed like a man who wouldn't put up with it.

"Okay, so he has a sister. So what?" He sounded defensive. He didn't like getting blamed for things.

Pringle shook his head, amazed at Butch's stupidity. "Don't you think I should talk to her? Don't you think I wish I'd known that before now?"

Ted Finley, the pudgy, middle-aged vice president of product development for Peter Boothe Ministries, raised a piece of black presentation board off the tabletop, revealing a brand name and a slogan on the reverse side. He stretched one hand toward the horizon, like an explorer inviting a king to envision a far-off land, and gave voice to the words: "Prosperity Water!" He went on proudly, "Quenching your thirst for a better life!"

Peter Boothe, across the table, sat quietly. He didn't appear to be paying attention. Finley waited eagerly for a response, trying to look as if he had no doubts about the project at all. He pasted an expression on his face that said: *What do you think? Isn't it brilliant?* Flanking him were three of his subordinates, well-groomed young men in expensive suits.

"What happened to Miracle Water?" Vanessa Boothe asked pointedly, just as Finley had known she would. "I thought we were calling it Miracle Water." She sounded irritated. She was on Peter Boothe's side of the table, wearing a form-fitting V-neck magenta top, with a short black leather skirt and matching boots.

Finley immediately began nodding appeasingly. "Yes, we were, but the guys in legal felt that name might be . . . problematic."

Vanessa frowned. "How so?"

Finley made a vague gesture with his hands. "Well, you know, if the water doesn't actually, uh, perform miracles."

"That's asinine," Vanessa said. "Miracle Whip doesn't perform any miracles."

Finley tried to smile. "Well, see, nobody expects it to. But this is different. When you consider the context within which our water would be marketed—since we're a church, and since every bottle would be blessed by Peter himself—people might, um, think it actually performs miracles."

"Why would they think that?" Vanessa asked.

Finley wanted to sigh deeply. "Because we'd be implying that it does. That would have to be part of the marketing plan, of course. Otherwise, uh, why would anyone buy it? Especially at five dollars a liter." He was choosing his words carefully, trying to avoid sounding critical or pessimistic, because the entire bottled-water concept—really more of a scheme—was Vanessa's idea.

"I think you're overreacting," Vanessa said. "It's just a stupid name. Victoria's Secret has the Miracle Bra, and the women who buy it don't expect to grow brand-new tits."

Finley chuckled nervously. "Well, yes, point well taken." Finley was, of course, a pious man—a man with a quiet, homely wife and three bookish kids—and it disturbed him when Vanessa Boothe used such crass language. It disturbed him because he found it somehow arousing, and it made him wonder what Vanessa would look like bare-ass naked on the couch in his office. He was certain she had fantastic breasts. *Tits,* he allowed himself to think. *Titties.*

He pushed those thoughts from his head and said, "I think we need to look at this realistically. If we go ahead with the launch, it will mark our entry into a whole new product category. Books are one thing, and DVDs and audiocassettes. Those items provide a tangible benefit. But bottled water . . . we have to be very careful how we position it. After all, we all know it takes more than mere water to bring about a change in a person's life. It takes guidance from our Lord Jesus Christ."

Vanessa waved a hand dismissively. "Yeah, but if a person *believes* the water will help them, then it becomes a powerful spiritual tool. It can help them reach their goals and achieve their dreams. It's about *faith,* Ted, you should know that."

Finley couldn't believe he was being lectured by Vanessa Boothe. Pastor Pete still hadn't spoken a word.

Finley said, "To a point, I agree, but—"

"It's like those sports drinks implying they can make you a better athlete," Vanessa said. "The same principles apply here. If you have faith, who's to say that this water *won't* perform an authentic miracle?"

She looked pleased with herself. She had an amused smirk on her face that seemed to say, *Sure, I know it's a crock, and you do, too, but it'll be our little secret, right?* It made Finley feel conspiratorial. It made him feel unclean. It made him want to grope Vanessa's firm buttocks, and maybe give them a hard spank, because she was impudent and needed discipline. Still, he needed to outline the potential problems. Like lawsuits. Like charges of consumer fraud. "Vanessa, I—"

"I don't see how the new name is any better. Prosperity Water? That still makes a promise. Drink this and you'll be prosperous. That's what it says."

"Well, our thinking is that prosperity is a less . . . grandiose . . . expectation than a miracle. Prosperity can mean many things. It could mean that—"

"What do you think, Peter?" Vanessa asked her husband.

All eyes went to the Reverend Peter Boothe.

"I think," he said slowly, "you should keep your mouth shut for ten damn seconds and let the poor man talk."

Thank you! Finley thought. *Oh, God bless you!*

Vanessa looked as if she'd been slapped. She opened her mouth, then closed it. Her face turned a bright red. She crossed her arms and glared at the tabletop, pouting. There was an awkward silence for several seconds.

Then Peter Boothe said, "Ted. You were saying?"

Finley cleared his throat and said, "Listen, to be perfectly frank, I have concerns about this product, no matter what we call it. But *especially* if we call it Miracle Water."

Peter Boothe nodded encouragingly. "And those concerns are?"

Finley pressed his hands together, a subconscious imitation of prayer. This was intimidating. Neither of the Boothes had ever encouraged his input before. Not like this. Sure, they routinely wanted his insight on market trends, sales projections, hurdle rates, demographics, psychographics, ethnographics, overseas manufacturing, pricing strategies, alpha testing, beta testing, concept optimization, and all the other buzzwords that made up Finley's daily existence. But his *opinion*? His big-picture, this-is-what-we-should-do opinion? Never. He seized the moment, and he was surprised by how passionately he spoke.

Avoiding eye contact with Vanessa, he said, "Let's say I'm a little old lady with gout, and it gets so painful that there are days when I can barely get out of bed to watch your show, even though I'm a loyal viewer. Then one day you tell me about Miracle Water, and lo and behold, it sounds like the answer to my prayers. So I order three liters—which would have to be the minimum sale to make this feasible—and I drink those three bottles and . . . nothing happens. My gout is no better, and in fact it might be worse, because I've quit taking my medicine. So I place another order, this time for six liters. It's bound to work sooner or later, I say to myself, because Peter Boothe said it would, right there on my television. So I keep drinking it, glass after glass, day after day, but it doesn't work. Now, if I'm that little old lady, one of two things might occur to me. I might think that the Lord doesn't intend to cure my gout. I'm stuck with it, and that is how He wants it, so there's nothing I can do. *Or . . . or . . .* I might think that Peter Boothe misled me. I might think that Miracle Water is nothing but . . . water. And suddenly my image of Peter Boothe is tarnished. That's what it's all about. Image. I think selling a product like this could make you look like a two-bit huckster. Possibly even a con man."

Finley's testicles were in his throat. He'd spoken the gospel truth, and now he fully expected all hell to break loose. He'd gone against Vanessa, and everybody knew that Vanessa, when it came down to it, really ran things. But that's not what happened.

Peter Boothe reached across the table for the blackboard and slid it in front of him. He studied the words thereon for a great while. Then he said, "I think you are absolutely correct, Ted. And I appreciate your willingness to be so blunt. I see no need to even discuss it further. Let's shelve this concept."

It was more than Vanessa could handle. "But, honey, the profit potential in bottled water—"

He held up a hand, silencing her. "It's not always about profit, *honey,* can't you understand that? Sometimes it's about trust. Can you imagine trusting someone and then having that trust abused? Can you imagine how empty you'd feel? Can you imagine the anger and bitterness that might grow out of that?"

Finley noticed a strange look pass between the Boothes. He had the feeling they weren't talking about bottled water anymore.

Vanessa said, "If we were to offer a guarantee, maybe a refund if—"

"Enough!" Peter Boothe shouted, and everyone around the table jumped. "I will not have you turn me into some circus-tent faith healer hawking snake oil! It's ridiculous." Boothe shook his head and muttered, "I feel ridiculous enough already."

Finley had no idea what *that* meant.

Nicole was sitting in a booth at Nutty Brown Café, a popular spot on Highway 290 between Austin and Johnson City. The restaurant had a large beer garden, where live music drew enthusiastic crowds on weekends. But right now, on a Monday, during lunchtime, all was fairly quiet. Nicole had chosen to sit inside, where she could see the front door.

For the hundredth time, she tried to think of a plausible explanation. Maybe Michael Kishner was delusional. Maybe he was a psychotic who'd gone off his meds. Paranoid. It could happen. He'd seemed awfully rational on the phone, though.

Maybe he was flat mistaken. A mix-up of some sort. What if some other game warden was sleeping with Kishner's wife? If the couple liked to rendezvous in Blanco County, and if Kishner had called the sheriff's office to ask who the game warden in Blanco County was . . .

That buoyed her spirits a little. That scenario was entirely possible, wasn't it? She held on to that thought, because the alternative made her heart feel like a stone.

She checked her watch. He was five minutes late.

She pegged him as soon as he came through the door two minutes later. Just an average-looking guy in an average looking suit. Medium height and build. Black hair. Maybe thirty years old. He took off his sunglasses and looked around. Saw her looking and came right to her.

"Nicole?"

"You're Michael Kishner." Her voice sounded hoarse.

He nodded, then slipped into the booth across from her. They didn't shake hands. Neither of them was smiling.

"Thanks for meeting me," he said.

Before she could reply, the waiter was there. "Something to drink?"

"Iced tea would be fine."

After the waiter left, Kishner said, "Well . . ."

Nicole was feeling light-headed. She could feel her pulse in her wrists, her temples.

Kishner said, "I've been trying to think of an easy way to do this . . . but I don't think there is one. So . . ."

He reached into his jacket and came out with a photograph, which he laid on the table in front of her. She didn't want to look at it, but finally she did, and there was John, standing next to his truck, and a beautiful blond woman in white linen slacks and a pale blue blouse was kissing him on the lips.

"I thought you said you had an iron," Billy Don called from the small utility room at the far end of Red's mobile home.

"I think so," Red hollered back. "Somewhere in there. Look in those cabinets."

"I *am* looking."

"Well, look some more."

Red had an ex-wife in his past—or maybe she wasn't his ex, since they'd never gotten an official divorce, or maybe she'd never even been his wife, because there were bigamy laws to consider. In any case, this woman, named Loretta, had used an iron once or twice, if he remembered right. This was several years back. And she hadn't taken it with her, that's for sure, because she'd left in such a hurry. That was because Billy Don—a stranger to Red at the time—had shown up and revealed that Loretta was married to him, too, and while he and Red were arguing about who was really Loretta's husband, she'd hotfooted it in Billy Don's Honda.

Ah, memories.

But he didn't have time for that sentimental crap right now. He was in his bedroom, digging through a dusty box of neckties, trying to decide whether he should wear one or not. Billy Don, too. It was, after all, a funeral. The problem was, some of the ties were pretty strange-looking. Red had inherited them ages ago from his dad, who'd been a world-renowned rodeo clown, or as renowned as rodeo clowns can get, and the styles were so outdated, it was tough to tell which ties were authentic and which were for clowning. Plus, Red didn't own a suit, much less a sport coat, and he didn't know if you were supposed to wear a tie without a jacket. Red figured he could take a tie with him, and if there were other guys wearing ties with no jackets, he could just clip one on real quick. Problem solved.

16

A HOUSEWIFE NAMED Marian Peters was enjoying a quiet day as a volunteer at the Johnson City Visitor Center on Highway 281 when she heard a rhythmic thumping that grew progressively louder. A moment later, a gigantic vehicle—one of those Hummers—pulled up and parked by the front doors. The thumping, she realized, was coming from the Hummer. Was that supposed to be music? How could anyone listen to that? And so loud.

The music stopped abruptly, the door to the Hummer swung open, and a young African American gentleman stepped out. He swaggered to the glass doors of the visitor center and went inside. His baggy shorts hung to his knees. His sneakers were large and unlaced. His fingers glistened with an assortment of

bejeweled rings, and a medallion hanging from a chain identified him as B-DOG.

"May I help you?" Marian asked, smiling pertly. She suddenly
felt self-conscious wearing a straw cowboy hat and a gingham
neckerchief—her official outfit as a volunteer.

"Yeah, I'm trying to find the Holiday Inn."

"The what?"

"Holiday Inn."

"Uh, well, Johnson City doesn't have a Holiday Inn."

The man stared at her. "No Holiday Inn?"

"No, sir. We do have a Best Western."

"Yeah, I seen that one, but I'm s'pose to meet a dude at the
Holiday Inn."

Marian Peters didn't know what to say. She shrugged. "I . . ."

The young man gestured to the south. "What's that other
town that way?"

"Blanco?"

"Yeah. They got a Holiday Inn?"

"I'm afraid not. There's no Holiday Inn in Blanco County."

He stood there a moment longer, not smiling, not frowning,
just thinking. "You know a dude named Alex Pringle?"

"No, sorry."

"Awright. Thank you."

Marlin parked in a faculty spot, figuring the campus cops
wouldn't ticket a state vehicle. Two minutes later, he was in the
lobby of a nine-story brick building, waiting for an elevator,
feeling hopelessly old and out of date. The foot traffic on campus was light, but the students he'd seen so far—young adults,
but God, they looked like children—were all so hip and cool. Or
whatever adjectives people used nowadays. The weather was
balmy, so there was plenty of exposed skin, revealing a creative
array of tattoos and piercings.

When the elevator door opened on the sixth floor, which had a deserted feel to it, there stood a kid with short black hair sort of swept upward in the center, like the bristles down a dog's back. He had eyeglasses with thick black frames, and a diamond stud in each earlobe. He looked like a cartoon version of Buddy Holly.

Marlin tried not to smile and went in search of Kate Wallace's office, which he found at the end of an L-shaped hallway. The door was open, and her eyes opened wide when she saw him. "Oh, wow, is it two o'clock already? Dr. Underwood isn't back yet. His last class is probably running late."

"No hurry," Marlin said. "I didn't give him much notice." He'd called that morning to schedule the meeting.

Kate came from around her desk to clear some papers off the sole visitor's chair. "Here, have a seat. Sorry about the mess. It gets like this at the end of the semester."

He gestured toward the hallway. "If you've got things to do, I could wait—"

"No, that's okay. I'm sure Dr. Underwood'll be here any minute. You won't bother me. I've been grading papers, and believe me, I could use a break."

So he sat down. As Kate retreated behind her desk, Marlin couldn't help noticing her trim figure. Like the other students, she was dressed in casual campus attire: sandals; a sleeveless blouse; well-fitting faded jeans with worn spots at the knees and black stains, like shoe polish, on the inside of the left cuff. Apparently it was trendy to be ragged and unlaundered.

"Dr. Underwood tends to lose track of time when he's lecturing," she said, sitting down. "Until his students start to fidget."

"He must enjoy what he does."

She nodded. "Oh, he's very passionate about his work. I'm lucky to be his assistant. I've learned a lot from him." Marlin could tell she was wearing more makeup today. She looked good. Sexy, rather than cute. Her arms were tan.

"Is the campus always this quiet?" he asked.

"A lot of the kids have already finished their finals."

He looked around the windowless office. Fluorescent lighting. Low ceiling. Not much floor space. Lots of books jammed onto plain wooden shelves. Some might call it snug or cozy. Others might say cramped or dreary.

He was planning to sit quietly, let Kate Wallace get back to work, but she was looking at him with a curious expression. She said, "You know, my uncle was a hunter, and . . . I thought game wardens went after poachers. People who shot deer on the side of the road. Things like that."

"And you're wondering why I'm working on a homicide case."

"Well, yeah. It seems kinda strange."

He shrugged. "Sometimes the sheriff asks for help."

"And you can do that?"

"Makes you wonder about our legal system, doesn't it?"

She opened her mouth, then smiled when she realized he was pulling her leg. "I didn't mean it to sound that way. I'm sure you're more than qualified."

He grinned. "Yep. Got a gun and a badge and everything."

She was about to reply when Marlin heard footsteps in the hall. Then Scott Underwood bustled through the doorway, a leather satchel in his hand, shaking his head. "Ah, you're already here. Sorry I'm late."

"Not a problem."

Marlin rose to shake his hand.

"Been waiting long?" Underwood asked. He was dressed in khaki trousers, a blue knit shirt, and leather deck shoes.

"Just a few minutes."

"Kate keep you entertained?"

"She offered to play 'Foggy Mountain Breakdown' on the harmonica."

Underwood laughed. "A cop with a sense of humor. I like

that. Come on in." He led the way into his office—which was a bit larger and better organized than Kate's—and closed the door. He had two windows that provided a sweeping view of the side of the brick building next door. The perks of professorship.

Underwood placed the satchel on his desktop, sat down, and absentmindedly picked up a handful of pink telephone message slips. "Just let me get my bearings for one second, make sure there aren't any major catastrophes"—he sorted quickly through the slips—"and there aren't." He settled back into his chair and looked at Marlin. "Okay. What can I do for you today?"

Marlin was wondering what sort of catastrophe might occur in a paleontologist's world. He said, "Just a few more questions."

"Shoot."

"Let's say Hollis Farley did find an *Alamosaurus* skull."

"Okay, let's say that."

"And let's say the owner of the property invited some scientists to dig it up."

"With you so far."

"How long would that take?"

"Oh, God. That's like asking how long it takes to build a house. Or how long a song is. It can vary enormously, depending on the geology of the area, the weather, the accessibility of the site, and a bunch of other factors."

"Okay, can you give me a range? Doesn't have to be exact."

Underwood was drumming his fingers on the desk, rocking his head to and fro, weighing the question. "It could be as brief as a week or two. If we found the skull, but no evidence of anything else, it could be quite short. That's if everything went as planned, and it usually doesn't."

"And the worst case?"

Underwood smiled. "By 'worst case,' I assume you mean a longer dig, and that would actually be the best case. Means we found more stuff. In that event, it could drag out for a while."

"Like what? A month?"

So far, Underwood seemed nothing but poised and composed.

"Probably longer," he said, "if the landowner agreed to it."

"Three months? Six?"

"A couple of months, most likely, but six months is feasible. Especially if there were weather delays. I know a guy—what we call a site preparator—who literally camped out on the banks of Shoal Creek prior to a dig. They'd found the remains of a plesiosaur down there, and he had to protect it from rain."

"Shoal Creek here in Austin?"

"Right."

"I thought there hadn't been any dinosaur bones found in Central Texas."

"Good memory. The plesiosaur was a Mesozoic-era reptile, but it wasn't actually a dinosaur. For the layman, it's semantics."

"Okay, so the bottom line, a dig could take several months."

"Yeah, that's a fair statement."

"Would the media be interested?"

Underwood smiled again. "In an *Alamosaurus* skull? Well, the scientific journals, sure, they'd be all over it. Magazines for geeks like me. *Newsweek* or some other national pub might do a short piece. But if you mean local media, it's the kind of thing that'd get about twelve column inches on page five of the metro section, or thirty seconds on the ten o'clock news."

Underwood, of course, didn't know—or didn't appear to know—that the skull had been found on the site for Peter Boothe's religious complex. That would add a major hook to the story. Reporters loved irony.

"Let's talk about Farley's visit again," Marlin said. "What time did he get here?"

"A little after three, wasn't it? I'm bad with time. Kate could tell you for sure."

"How long was he here?"

"No longer than fifteen minutes."

"How many photos did he show you?"

"Maybe half a dozen."

"He didn't happen to leave those with you?"

"No, he put them right back in the envelope he'd brought them in. Didn't we cover all of this yesterday?"

Marlin smiled. "We did, yes, but sometimes a second go-round can jog the memory. Even a minor detail could be significant."

"By all means, then, go right ahead."

"You said that Farley never gave his name?"

"No, when I introduced myself, he didn't return the favor. At first I thought he was just socially awkward, but later I realized he was being discreet. He didn't *want* to give his name."

Marlin was looking for inconsistencies in Underwood's recounting of events. There were none. So he said, "You know, if I were you, I would've been tempted to follow Farley out to his car. Maybe try to see if he really did have the skull with him, and beg him for a look at it. Or at least copy down his license plate number, as a way to find him later." He smiled. "And if you did that, I could understand why you didn't want to tell us about it yesterday morning."

Total confusion on Underwood's face. He seemed to have no idea what Marlin was implying. Then he got it, and he began a slow, amused nod. "Okay, I see what's happening. You have to make sure I'm clear, right? You have to rule me out, as they say on the cop shows." He chuckled. "This is really pretty funny. The mild-mannered paleontology professor is a suspect in a homicide investigation. I can't wait to tell some of my colleagues. They'll think that's pretty cool."

"I wouldn't say you're a suspect," Marlin said.

Underwood appeared almost crestfallen. "No?"

Marlin grinned. "You didn't kill Hollis Farley, did you?"

"I'm afraid not."

"Do you know who did?"

"Not a clue."

"Just for fun, why don't you tell me where you were on Thursday afternoon and evening."

"No problem. Let's see, Thursday afternoon. I was here at the office until about six. Met with several of my students, so they can confirm it. That evening . . . ooh, this won't look good. I was home alone. My wife was at a convention in San Diego all week. She's a sales manager for Dell, so she travels a lot."

"Do you have any kids?"

"Nope. Wanted to keep our lives simple."

"I can understand that. What's your wife's name?"

"Monica."

"When did Monica get back from San Diego?"

"Late Saturday evening."

Marlin was bothered by something. "Last time we talked, you said you went for a motorcycle ride yesterday morning."

"I ride every Sunday morning."

"By yourself?"

"Sometimes I meet some other riders, but this time I was alone."

"Where'd you go?"

"Made a loop through the park, then went out past Enchanted Rock. I don't understand why this is relevant."

"By 'the park,' you mean Pedernales Falls?"

"Yeah, it's beautiful this time of year. But you know that."

"Does your wife ever ride with you?"

"Oh, God, no. She thinks I have a death wish. That I'm going to get squished by an eighteen-wheeler."

"Did it bother her that you went for a ride yesterday morning?"

Underwood scowled. "Why would it?"

"Well, she'd just gotten back from a long trip. I'd think you'd want to hang around and spend some time with her."

Underwood's jovial mood seemed to have stiffened. "This is getting awfully personal," he said.

Marlin waited.

"I guess there's no harm in telling you this," Underwood said. "My wife and I are contemplating a divorce."

"I'm sorry to hear that."

"Good thing we never had kids, I guess."

"Maybe so."

Underwood tried to smile. "This has been fun, but I really have a lot to do this afternoon. Are we about done?"

17

THE FUNERAL HOME was a wide, low metal building with as much charm as an airplane hangar. Right in front, off to one side, was a garage door, from which the hearse presumably entered and exited. So much for discretion and decorum.

In the foyer, Alex Pringle found an astounding assortment of hicks, hayseeds, bumpkins, yokels, rednecks, and rubes—most of them dressed as if they were auditioning for *Hee Haw* right after the services. Men stood around awkwardly, wearing stained jeans and scuffed boots, holding cowboy hats in their hands, while women in outdated dresses spoke in hushed tones. *Such a shame. He was so young. Have they figured out who done it?* Organ music—recorded, not live—gave the proceedings all the dignity of a minor-league baseball game.

Pringle tried to appear appropriately somber as he signed the guest book then made his way toward a middle-aged man in a cheap suit standing near the double doors leading to the chapel. Pringle had him figured for an usher because of the expression of forced sincerity on the guy's face. *Takes one to know one,* Pringle thought.

"Excuse me," he said in a low voice, touching the man lightly on the elbow. "Could you point out Betty Jean Farley for me?"

"Yes, of course," the usher said, turning toward the open chapel doors, through which Pringle could see a fair number of mourners waiting for the services to begin. "That's her at the casket. Wearing the flowered muumuu."

"Thank you."

Pringle strolled up the center aisle, and as he got closer, he saw that Betty Jean Farley wouldn't win any beauty pageants, though she might earn a blue ribbon at a livestock show. She was standing alone, one hand on the casket, the other mourners giving her a moment alone with her brother. Perfect.

Pringle would introduce himself, express his deepest sympathies, and let her know that Peter Boothe Ministries was fully prepared to help her handle her grief. That included paying for the funeral, naturally. Reverend Boothe felt it was the least he could do, seeing as how Hollis Farley had made the ultimate sacrifice in the name of Jesus Christ. There would be a few papers to sign, of course, and if Pringle could just stop by Betty Jean's house later, they could get it all worked out.

That's the way it would've gone, except, when Pringle was three steps away, another man approached from Betty Jean Farley's right. A big man. Huge. Much larger than Butch. Dressed in overalls and a necktie that would've made Picasso uneasy.

"Betty Jean?" the big man said.

She turned. "Billy Don! How nice of you to come."

"I figured you might need some, uh, comforting and such."

"Well, bless your heart."

"They were sent from the Johnson City Library," Snake said, obviously proud of himself. "It's in a little town called Johnson City."

"I sorta figured that last part out," Darwin Parker replied, cradling the phone with one shoulder, speaking in a low voice to prevent Tiffany and Steve from eavesdropping. "But who *sent* the e-mails?" Tiffany had returned to Darwin's house, and she was now standing in the middle of his living room in a push-up bra and a thong, her arms stretched horizontally to either side. She appeared bored. Steve, Darwin's tailor, was carefully assessing various parts of her anatomy. He did not appear bored.

"Uh, that's where it gets tricky," Snake said. "I was hoping just knowing they came from the library would be good enough."

Darwin took a calming breath. They were getting closer. Now was not a good time to lose his patience. No sense in worrying about Snake's slurred voice, or the fact that he sounded like he'd had a recent brain injury. "Snake, I need to know who specifically sent the e-mails."

Steve was measuring Tiffany's bustline. He'd already measured it twice, but apparently several go-rounds were necessary to get it right. Darwin figured Steve knew what he was doing. Darwin got all of his suits from Steve's little shop on Westheimer. Three grand a pop, but they fit like a second skin. Which was why Steve was going to create a special suit for Tiffany. Darwin was paying extra for overnight service—and discretion.

"I tried, man, I really did," Snake whined. "The firewall was a breeze, so I was able to get into the server, but all that got me was the guy's password. I was hoping they kept a database of users, and that his password was linked to his library card, and then I'd have his name, but, man, there was nothing there."

"I need that name!" Darwin said.

"Hey, bro, take it easy. I'm just trying to explain the situation. You don't have to bite my head off."

Speaking of biting heads off, Darwin had decided that Tiffany, with her nubile body, would look splendid as a coelurosaur, a small, fast-moving predator that preyed on early lizards. Darwin knew it was somewhat overzealous to make such an investment on a professional escort, but who else would wear a suit like that without complaint or judgment?

"Besides," Snake continued, still defending himself, "if you wanna get technical, you never told me you needed to know *who* sent the e-mails. You said you needed to know where they *came* from. I remember, man. That's what you said. I've got a good memory for stuff like that."

You can barely remember your own name, Darwin thought, gritting his teeth. "Okay, what now? Surely there are other things you can try."

"Yeah, there might be another way, if they've got blocking software."

"What's that?"

"You know, like CyberNanny or PC Tattletale or one of those."

"No idea what you're talking about."

"See, it's software, man. It blocks access to specific sites, but it also keeps a log of the Web sites users go to and records e-mails and chat conversations. I could see every keystroke, man."

"How would that help us? Sounds like we'd end up with copies of the e-mails I already have."

"Yeah, we would, but if this guy sent any other e-mails, we'd get them, too. Like, if he sent an e-mail to you, then sent one to a friend one minute later from the same computer, that might help us. Or we might be able to figure it out from the sites he visited, especially if he filled out any forms with his name on them."

Darwin had no idea whether a library would use software like that, but he decided it was a distinct possibility. "How would you access this software? Hack in?"

"Naw, man, I'd have to go down there."

"Then do it. Go down to Johnson City and visit the library. But let me be clear this time. I want to know *who* those e-mails came from. Not *where,* or what goddamn *domain,* or what fucking *IP address.* Got it?"

"Yeah, man, yeah. But don't we need to talk about, you know, more money? I gotta travel, so there's gonna be expenses."

Darwin thought of the *Alamosaurus* skull, and what a fantastic addition it would be to his collection. "How much?"

"Another thousand?"

Chicken feed. "Deal." He heard a prolonged hissing sound through the phone. "What's that noise?"

"Uh, just a can of Raid, bro. I got a big ol' wasp flying around in here."

Billy Don was flattered when Betty Jean asked him to keep her company at the funeral home, and even more so when she asked if he'd escort her to the cemetery, but when they were sitting graveside, the preacher rambling on about all of Hollis's good qualities, and Betty Jean reached over and took Billy Don's hand in her own, his heart lurched with the sheer surprise of it. He couldn't remember the last time he'd held hands with a woman.

It felt nice, and he was hoping his hand wasn't sweaty. Or trembling, neither, because the truth was he was kind of nervous. He'd never been very smooth with women, except hookers and strippers, but it didn't take much more than a handful of dollars to impress them. Around ordinary women, though, Billy

Don never knew quite what to say or how to act. He usually just kept his mouth shut, if he was sober.

He was trying to be cool about the whole hand-holding thing, but he couldn't resist peeking sideways over at Betty Jean, and when he did, she caught him at it and gave him a sly smile. Then she squeezed his hand. Twice. Like she was sending some sort of secret message, just for him.

There went his heart again, thumpity-thump.

Billy Don turned his gaze forward again, looking out across the top of the raised casket, and there was Red in a group of mourners on the other side, grinning at him. Before Billy Don could look away, Red winked at him, like he was saying, *You're doing great, bud.* Just that quick, Billy Don began to feel ashamed.

What the hell was he doing? He liked Betty Jean. Always had, ever since she'd served him that first double order of pecan pie at the diner. Gave him a free scoop of vanilla ice cream on top, and he hadn't even asked for it. Now Red had talked him into cozying up to Betty Jean under what they call false pretenses. At her brother's funeral, no less. Was that any way to treat a good-hearted woman?

Butch didn't know shit about dinosaur bones, and he couldn't imagine why someone would pay a hundred grand for a skull. But if Pringle was willing to part with half for Butch's help, Butch was willing to do just about any damn thing to make the sale happen.

He was, however, getting bored fucking silly in the motel room. Plenty of channels to watch—the basic cable package—but it was all crap on a weekday morning. Talk shows. Reruns of *Seinfeld* and *Friends*. And another one Butch had never seen called *Holy Roller*, which was about a nun who roller-skated down the boardwalks in Venice, California, trying to save souls. Who thought this shit up?

There were a couple of baseball games on the sports channels, but Butch thought baseball was, in general, for pussies. Like Pringle. Sure, you might get the occasional collision at home plate, where a base runner might lose a tooth, but other than that, it was a fag sport. Didn't use to be, not when guys like Nolan Ryan were playing. Ryan, with the fastball that could take your head off at the shoulders. Butch remembered, back when he was a teenager, the time Ryan nailed Robin Ventura, and Ventura decided to rush the mound. Big mistake. Ryan—old enough to be Ventura's daddy—got Ventura in a headlock and proceeded to thrash him like a misbehaving stepchild. *That* was good baseball. Nowadays, you had steroid freaks who thought they were movie stars. Bunch of freaking assholes.

So Butch turned the set off and eyeballed Jerry Strand, who was firmly duct-taped to a chair. He'd wet himself long ago, because Butch wasn't about to unwrap an entire roll of tape to let the man use the toilet proper. Besides, it showed Strand that Butch was serious. He wasn't here to play patty-cake.

"You 'member where you hid that bone at yet?" Butch asked.

Strand made a feeble grunting sound, because of the tape across his mouth. He was shaking his head, like he had more to say than just no.

Butch chuckled. "Well, when you get your memory back, I'm right here waiting on ya."

Pringle had told Butch to "refrain from getting physical," but Butch figured it was only a matter of time. Actions, he knew very well, spoke louder than words.

Finally, thankfully, the services came to an end, and Alex Pringle was the first to head for his car. The humidity was unbearable. His Ike Behar shirt was soaked through, sticking to his skin, and his mood was equally damp.

This whole thing had been a waste of time. The big hillbilly had remained by Betty Jean Farley's side like a goddamn Siamese twin. So Pringle had decided to approach her at the wake, early on, before they busted out the fiddles or whatever these types of people did to mourn a loved one. He wanted a chance to speak to her alone, if he could manage it.

Pringle had just opened the door to his Cadillac roadster, which was like a frigging oven inside, when he heard, "Mr. Pringle?"

He turned, and there was a uniformed deputy. A clean-shaven Hispanic man with a square jaw, maybe forty years old. Pringle read the man's name tag and realized he wasn't just a deputy. "You must be Sheriff Garza," Pringle said with his friendliest smile.

They shook hands as Garza said, "Yes, sir. Good to meet you, finally. I figured I might find you here."

"Oh? Have you been looking for me?"

"Well, I just came to pay my respects, but I do need to ask you something."

"Certainly." Pringle already knew what was coming.

"I understand you dropped by Jerry Strand's place yesterday."

"I did indeed. Myself and one of my colleagues. Spoke to Nadine, a lovely woman, but Jerry was sleeping."

"About what time was that?"

"Around eleven." Pringle frowned. "Is something wrong?"

Garza had a look on his face that seemed to say, *Okay, I'll share this with you, but let's keep it between us.* What he actually said was, "Mrs. Strand left the house shortly after your visit, and nobody's seen Jerry since then. He wasn't there when she got home last night."

Pringle gave it an appropriate pause, as if he were confused. Then he said, "My gosh. You mean he's missing?"

Mourners were passing by, all of them oblivious to the conversation Pringle was having, but the sheriff kept his voice low anyway. "Not officially, no, but his wife is plenty worried. She says it's not like Jerry to just up and go. Not without letting her know. We're hoping there's a simple explanation."

"That's very disconcerting," Pringle said, wondering if the sheriff even knew what that word meant. "First Hollis Farley and now this."

"You didn't happen to come back to Strand's house later in the day, did you?"

There it was. The key question. Pringle had to make a decision. Admit that they had returned, and face an onslaught of additional questions. Or deny it. If there were witnesses—perhaps a little old lady on her front porch who had nothing better to do than watch cars pass all day—it could be a problem. He decided to chance it. "No, just the one time." Pringle gave the sheriff a self-deprecating grin. "To be honest, I got the impression that Mr. Strand wasn't actually sleeping. More like he was avoiding us, which has been known to happen from time to time. Not everyone prefers to seek solace from the holy scripture. I wouldn't force my presence on anyone. I leave that to the Jehovah's Witnesses."

Garza gave him a weak smile. "So you never spoke to Jerry Strand yesterday?"

"No, sir."

The sheriff nodded at the Cadillac. "This the vehicle you drove to his house?"

"It is." Pringle could feel a tension in his chest. Maybe someone *had* seen his car on the second trip to Strand's house.

"Nice. Surprised you don't have the top down."

"Force of habit," Pringle said. "If I left it unlocked in Dallas, it'd be gone in seconds. Guess you don't have that sort of crime around here."

Garza didn't reply to that; he was simply gazing out over the flat, lush landscape of the cemetery. "Did you visit Betty Jean Farley yesterday?"

Whoa. Change of course. What's this about? "No, I didn't."

"Seems odd," Garza said. "Since you're here to comfort the bereaved, I'd think your first stop would be Betty Jean's house."

Pringle did his best to rebound. "I knew I'd be seeing her today. I've found it's best to let the family have a bit of solitude before the services."

"Very thoughtful," Garza said, though Pringle had the sense that the sheriff was being sarcastic. It was hard to tell. "How's she holding up?"

Pringle said, "I still haven't spoken to her. I understand there's to be a wake at her cousin's house. I plan to stop by and offer my condolences, and any type of support she might require."

The sheriff nodded. "Okay, I appreciate your help."

They shook hands again.

"Anytime," Pringle said. The tension in his chest was beginning to drain away. "You have my cell phone number."

"You gonna be in town a while?"

"At least until tomorrow, I would imagine."

"Good deal. Maybe I'll see you around town."

Pringle brought out the warm smile again. "I hope so."

The sheriff turned to leave, then stopped and said, "Oh, hey, one last question."

Great, Pringle thought. *The Texas version of Columbo.*

"This colleague of yours," Garza said. "The man who was with you yesterday morning. What's his name?"

18

BETTY JEAN HAD an uncle named Buzz, who'd driven his El Camino down from Little Rock, and he sidled up to Billy Don late in the evening with a jelly jar full of whiskey in each hand. "Made it myself," he said proudly. "Corn mash. My grand-daddy ran the biggest damn still in northwest Arkansas, back in the day." He shoved a jar into Billy Don's hand. "G'won now, give it a sip."

Billy Don didn't need to be told twice. He loved whiskey. He took a large gulp and regretted it immediately. His throat burned, his eyes watered.

"'Zat something, or what?" Buzz asked.

Billy Don had a feeling that if he tried to speak, the whiskey might come back up, so he nodded vigorously instead. Betty

Jean, meanwhile, was across the room, having a conversation with a man Billy Don didn't recognize. He was dressed in a suit, which ruled him out as being a member of the Farley clan. Now Betty Jean was actually hugging the man, looking real happy about something. Billy Don felt a strange pang in his belly, and he realized he was jealous.

Buzz nodded in that direction. "Don't think I haven't noticed. You got your eye on her, don'tcha?"

"Well, I—"

"Oh, sure ya do. You can tell me."

Billy Don was feeling awkward. "She's a real sweet gal."

Buzz cackled. "I thought so! You got that puppy dog look. You gotta take it easy on her, though. Last boy she went with done broke her heart. You might know the SOB. Perry Grange?"

Billy Don had heard the name but didn't know the man personally, and he sure didn't feel like talking about Betty Jean's old boyfriends, so he shook his head and took another drink of the whiskey just to keep his mouth occupied. It tasted a little better the second time around.

"You better slow down a little, son," Buzz said.

On the phone, Bobby Garza said, "And how'd it go?"

"I can't get a handle on the guy," Marlin replied. It was eight thirty, and he'd just finished supper. Then he'd tried to call Nicole, but she didn't answer. He'd left a message. Now he was talking to the sheriff about Scott Underwood. "He seemed composed, I guess—didn't contradict himself—although he did get touchy when the subject of his wife came up."

"Any idea why?"

"He said they're talking about a divorce—and maybe that's the full story, but I've got a theory. I think he's sleeping with his assistant, Kate Wallace."

"Oh, yeah?"

"Maybe this is a stretch, but she had a stain, like motor oil or grease, on the inside cuff of her jeans. The kind you might get from riding a motorcycle."

"That's right, Underwood's got a Harley."

"You think I'm grabbing at straws?"

"Hey, when there's nothing else to grab at . . ."

"I'm even wondering about yesterday morning, when they came in for the interview. Maybe she didn't drive out from Austin. Maybe she was already with him."

"Underwood uses his rides as an excuse to hook up with her?"

"Could be. On the other hand, even if she does ride with him now and then, that doesn't mean they're sleeping together."

"Not necessarily, no."

"And even if they are, what's that got to do with Hollis Farley?" Marlin said.

"It could mean she'd be willing to lie for him."

"About what?"

"About whether Farley ever gave his name. Or whether he told them where he'd found the fossil. Or just about anything else."

Marlin thought it over. "Yeah, could be. I'll dig around." Marlin switched the phone to his other ear. "Any word from the reserves yet?"

"They've been up and down that riverbank half a dozen times, and so far, nada. Tomorrow I'll have them widen it out. There's a creek that feeds into the river. They'll need to check there."

"We're assuming Farley found the skull along a waterway," Marlin said.

"Didn't Underwood say that was the most likely scenario?"

"He did, but he didn't say it was an absolute. If Farley was wandering around hunting pigs, that skull could be anywhere."

"Man, I hope not. If we have to search that whole place, I'd say we're pretty much screwed. What is it, sixteen hundred acres?"

"Yep, which is about two and a half square miles."

"Like I said, we're screwed."

"How'd you do with Alex Pringle?"

Garza made the type of frustrated groan a grade school teacher makes at the end of a long day. "Guys like him give religion a bad name. There's something slimy under there. You remember that kid from *Leave It to Beaver*? Eddie Haskell?"

"The insincere little punk. Thinks he's fooling everyone."

"Exactly. Alex Pringle is Eddie Haskell all grown up."

"What do you expect? He works for Peter Boothe."

"Yeah, cut from the same cloth. Plus he's got this guy named Butch Theriot running around with him. I checked Theriot's record and he's an overachiever, including a couple of agg assaults. Bar fights, that sort of thing. He once held a man's face against a hot motorcycle muffler. The victim was a member of the Hells Angels. Theriot put two of them in the hospital."

"And he's still walking around?"

"You mean he should be in prison, or he should be dead?"

"Take your pick," Marlin said.

"Maybe he's born again. Struck up a relationship with Jesus and became a new person."

Marlin laughed. "Hey, I thought I was the cynical one."

"You're rubbing off on me. Then again, I'm probably wrong, because he has a warrant on him for an unpaid speeding ticket. Petty stuff, but good Christians pay their fines."

"A good Christian wouldn't get a ticket to begin with."

"Hey, Christians aren't perfect, just forgiven. Saw that on a bumper sticker."

At nine thirty, the phone rang again.

"Hey there, Johnny," she said.

Which was a clue. Nicole only called him Johnny when she was being silly, or when she'd had a drink, although the two were sometimes linked.

"Hey, there. What's going on?"

"Not so much. Fixin' to hit the hay."

"Having a glass of wine?"

"I am. Needed somethin' to relax."

"Where were you earlier?"

"Workin' late."

"On what?"

"Oh, you know. Stuff. What is this, twenty questions?" She laughed. Nicole was not a big drinker. One glass of wine was enough to make her downright tipsy. Two glasses could put her out cold. Right now, she sounded like she'd had a glass and a half.

"I wanted to see you tonight," Marlin said.

"Yeah, I know. Sorry."

"Haven't seen you much lately."

"Funny how a new job and planning a wedding'll do that, huh? Busy, busy. Speaking of which, d'you call the videographer?"

Oh, crap. He felt like an ass. He'd totally forgotten. "Not yet," he said. "First thing tomorrow, I promise."

"You said you'd do it."

"I'm know, and I'm sorry. I'm making a note to myself right now." Which he was.

"Do you wanna marry me, John?"

"What, are you kidding me? Of course I do. More than anything. Where is this coming from?" He couldn't tell if she was joking around or not.

"Never hurts to check. Wouldn't want you making a mistake."

"My only mistake was not asking you earlier. Sounds like you're the one with cold feet."

"Not me. No, sir. My feet are just fine. Toasty."

"Good."

"You'll be a good husband, won't you, John?" Her tone was playful, like a mock interrogation. He went along with it.

"Damn right I will."

"Faithful and all that good stuff?"

"Absolutely. Loyal as a hound dog. Or a Boy Scout."

"Won't run off with some tall blond floozy?"

"Not a chance. You're the only floozy I need."

"That's what I thought. Okay, I'm going to bed now. You can forget this conservation ever took place."

He couldn't help grinning. *Conservation.*

"Hey, Nicole?"

"Yeah?"

"There's nothing to worry about, okay? It's gonna be great."

"Yeah, I know. Just had to ask, though. Full steam ahead."

Alex Pringle returned to his motel room and changed out of his sweaty clothes.

Omar, his bookie, had called six times today. Six calls, and Pringle, of course, hadn't answered any of them. He hadn't even had the guts to check his voice mail. His nerves were rattled enough already, so why make it worse?

How the hell am I going to get out of this? If he had known this thing with the fossil would turn into such a giant clusterfuck, he never would have gotten greedy. It had seemed like easy money, and that should've been a clue right there.

It had all started eleven days earlier with a phone call.

"Mr. Pringle, this is Jerry Strand. The construction supervisor?" The connection was poor. A cell phone out in the boonies.

"Yeah, Jerry."

"Sorry to bother you, but we've got sort of a weird situation out here at the job site."

Pringle wasn't in the mood for anything "weird." They'd

already had enough problems with the freakishly wet weather. Plus, the day before, Pringle had received a call from a woman in Austin who led a group of environmentalists. She was worried about pollution to the river and had threatened to stage a protest—a sit-in or some shit—if the construction plans weren't modified. Pringle had warned the old biddy to stay off the property. Had she ignored him?

"What now?" Pringle asked.

Strand surprised him by saying, "Hollis found a bone. Or I guess it's really a fossil, to get technical. 'Member Hollis? Runs the backhoe for me?"

"I remember him. He found a fossil?"

"Yes, sir."

"Yeah, so what's the problem? People find fossils all the time."

He could tell that Strand was covering the phone, talking to someone else, probably Hollis, who was a certified shit-for-brains. Pringle waited impatiently and was on the verge of hanging up when Strand said, "This ain't no ordinary fossil, sir. I'm no expert, but I think it's from a dinosaur. It ain't like nothing I ever seen."

"Did you say a dinosaur?"

"Yes, sir."

"You're joking."

"No, sir."

Well, hell. This was not good. Pringle didn't even have to waste time pondering the implications. "I think that's highly unlikely," he replied. And it was, wasn't it? Weren't dinosaur bones found mostly in Africa and the Middle East and places like that? Or was that caveman bones?

More muffled conversation. Then Strand said, "You really oughta come down and take a look for yourself."

"I don't need to take a look, Jerry. Whatever it is, I want you to bury it."

" 'Scuse me?"

"I said bury it."

A long pause, then, "That legal?"

"Well, of course it's legal," Pringle said, having no idea whether it was or not. "It's on church property. Peter Boothe owns the damn thing. So get rid of it."

"You sure about that? This thing looks like a—"

"Look, you want to get your crew working as soon as possible, right? If we called in some experts—which we are *not* required to do—we're looking at more delays. We'll have a bunch of eggheads playing around in the dirt while your guys sit around with their thumbs up their butts. You want to pay for all that downtime?"

Strand was suddenly more agreeable. "Jeez, yeah. That's a hell of a point. I hadn't thought of that."

"So bury it. And keep this thing under your hat. Both of you. We clear on that?"

"Not a problem. I'll take care of it."

Pringle figured that ended it. Until the next day, and another call. Strand said Hollis was being stubborn, that he didn't feel right burying something as important as a dinosaur fossil. Pringle couldn't believe the gall of this redneck.

Strand said, "Hollis took some pictures up to a geology teacher at the university in Austin and—"

"Oh, you've got to be kidding me. I said to keep this damn thing quiet!"

"I know, I know, but he didn't give his name or nothin'. Problem is, this teacher said this was a really significant discovery. That's the word he used. 'Significant.' "

"I don't care if he said it was proof of life on Mars, that bone is the property of Peter Boothe and I want it destroyed!"

Strand was quiet for a moment or two, then said, "See, Hollis has kind of an ornery streak in him. He don't like people telling him what to do. I been thinking, things might work out best if you offered him some kind of, uh, bonus for keeping quiet. Matter of fact, since we're talking about it, I could use one myself. Know what I mean?"

Pringle knew exactly what he meant. They wanted money for their silence. Pringle could respect that. It was a reasonable request. But now he'd have to bring the Boothes into the loop. So he scheduled an emergency meeting and explained the situation. The Boothes agreed it was a sensitive issue, one that could result in some unwanted press, and it needed to be handled properly.

"How much will it take?" Vanessa asked, always pragmatic.

"I'm thinking ten grand apiece," Pringle said. "For that, they bury the bone and keep their mouths shut. Like the bone was never there."

Vanessa nodded. "I think that's more than generous."

They both looked at Peter Boothe, who said, "You're certain we won't be breaking any laws?"

"Not a one," Pringle said, though he still hadn't checked.

Boothe hesitated.

"Look," Pringle said. "That bone is yours. You own it. You're not obligated to alert anyone about it."

Boothe mulled it over for a few seconds. "Then do it."

Which Pringle did. He FedExed the cash that very afternoon. *Now* he thought everything was taken care of. Then came the third phone call.

"Mr. Pringle, it's Jerry Strand again. Sorry to bother you."

Pringle lost his temper. "What the fuck is it now?"

"It's about the fossil."

"That damn thing better be under ten feet of dirt by now."

"Well, not yet, but when you hear why, I think you're gonna be real happy about it."

Pringle was ready to drive down to Blanco and strangle the

idiot. Hollis Farley, too. "What in the name of Jesus H. Christ are you babbling about?"

"Well, see, Hollis was still having second thoughts, you know? I mean, we appreciate the cash, but he went and done some research about dinosaur bones. What he come to find out is that there's a good chance that bone's worth some money. I'm talking a shitload of money, pardon my French. Seems crazy to just bury it. And from what Hollis says, when you sell a fossil, ain't nobody has to know exactly where it come from. So I was thinking the three of us could work something out. Like a partnership. Know what I mean?"

Again, Pringle knew exactly what he meant. And he couldn't help thinking, *This seems like a much better gamble than baseball.*

Pringle went next door to Butch's room. Strand was still taped to the chair. His chin was on his chest, and he was snoring.

"You talk to her?" Butch asked. He was on the bed, leaning against the headboard, a bottle of beer in his hand. There were seven empties on the nightstand. He was watching television with the sound turned low.

"Where'd you get the beer?" Pringle said. He couldn't keep the irritation out of his voice.

"Little store next door. Ain't no big deal. Grab yourself a cold one." Butch pointed to the trash can at Pringle's feet. Four plastic bottles of beer floated in ice water.

"Jesus, you left him here alone?" *What kind of moron would do that?*

Butch snickered. "Where's he gonna go? Took five minutes."

Pringle didn't feel like arguing—what was the point?—so he opened a beer and drank deeply. Then he said, "I spent the entire day with a bunch of shitkickers for nothing. When I finally got her alone and told her Boothe Ministries was going to pay for the funeral, the tub of lard hugged me. She started crying, for God's sake. You know what that means?"

Butch appeared puzzled.

Pringle said, "It means she's hard up for money, and *that* means she doesn't have the fossil."

"Well, shit," Butch said.

"Well put," Pringle said. He gazed at the television screen for a few seconds. "What the hell is that?"

"*Dancing with the Stars.* I'm waiting for someone to pull a groin. Plus, get a load of what that gal's wearing."

Pringle shook his head. What the hell was the world coming to? He looked at Strand. Honestly, Pringle had no idea what to do now.

Betty Jean Farley didn't have the fossil. The cops hadn't mentioned it. The sheriff would've brought it up, right? *Mr. Pringle, were you aware that Hollis Farley found a dinosaur fossil at the construction site?* But no, not a word. So where was it?

Could it be true that Strand really didn't know where it was? When they'd grabbed him, that possibility had never even occurred to Pringle, and it was a major problem. Not just for him, but for Jerry Strand.

Now they'd kept him hostage for far too long, and Pringle had no viable exit strategy. If Strand really didn't have the fossil, there was only one way, really, that this could end. Pringle didn't like it, but he couldn't come up with an alternative.

He got up to leave the motel room. "Wake him up and keep after him all night. Don't let him sleep. If he talks, call me."

Two in the morning, and a blue 1995 Mazda hatchback was heading westbound—more or less—on Highway 290 between Austin and Blanco County.

If a highway patrolman or a sheriff's deputy or even a game

warden had happened down that stretch of highway at that particular moment, the driver would have been pulled over and arrested on the spot.

His hands were occupied, holding a plastic bag to his face, so he was steering with his knees, weaving wildly from lane to lane, attempting to find his way to Johnson City.

Pam. Pam. Pam. Pam . . .

19

PETER BOOTHE WOULD agree that the Lord does, indeed, work in mysterious ways. After all, he'd become a world-renowned minister and cultural icon because a housewife in Dallas had been mortally injured by a contraption designed to increase breast size.

He could vividly remember the day, eight years earlier, when his partner had come into his office and said, "You working on the script for the BustBuilder 3000?"

"Yeah?"

"Well, stop. It's been pulled from the market."

"What happened?"

"Doorknob came loose and cracked some broad in the forehead. Major lawsuit coming."

"You're kidding. Is she okay?"

His partner chuckled. "Not unless you think dead is okay."

Boothe was incredulous. "She *died*?"

"Yeah, and we'll be lucky if we don't get caught up in the crossfire. The family's suing everybody involved. The designer, the manufacturer, the investors."

Boothe felt a sudden pang of guilt. He knew that his infomercials touted a variety of products that were, at best, ineffective and shoddily constructed. But fatal? Who would've guessed that a cheap set of bungee cords and an aluminum pulley could create that amount of pent-up energy?

He went home that evening and tried to shake it off, but all he could think about was that poor nameless woman who had dared to dream of a larger cup size. He could picture her looping the BustBuilder 3000's anchor strap over a doorknob, as instructed, kneeling on the floor, grasping the padded handles, and giving her pectorals "a vigorous, bust-enhancing workout." He could imagine her surprise—if there was time for it—when the doorknob came loose and rocketed toward her face.

Boothe tried to console himself with the notion that all products—including those that were expertly designed and rigorously tested—were a crapshoot. Until a product hit the marketplace, you never knew exactly what was going to happen.

But the BustBuilder 3000 had never even been tested. The manufacturer had falsified the numbers. Boothe and his partner had been willing to overlook that omission because, well, their firm was making a fortune. Besides, testing wasn't their responsibility. They were just the marketing guys.

Boothe recognized that for the rationalization it was.

It's greed, he admitted to himself. *The problem is greed. Nobody cares about anything except the bottom line. Including me.*

In the weeks that followed, Boothe's posh lifestyle crumbled around him. As his partner predicted, the lawsuit expanded to include their direct-response ad agency. Boothe lost his home, his Mercedes, his thirty-six-foot sailboat. His girlfriend—a hottie named Vanessa, whom Boothe had met during a video shoot for a diet supplement called Flab-Be-Gone—said it might be best if they took a break while he tried to get his shit together.

Boothe spent his days dodging creditors, until the phone was disconnected. He applied for jobs that he didn't get. The weeks dragged into months, Boothe slipped into depression, and one Sunday morning he woke to find an eviction notice tacked to the door of his squalid apartment.

His neighbor, a black divorcée named Anita, knocked an hour later.

"You got the notice from the Man, huh?"

"Yeah."

"What you gonna do?"

"Honestly, Anita, I have no idea."

"Come on down to the church with me. It'll do ya good."

Boothe considered himself a Christian, even though he hadn't been to church in years. "Thanks, Anita, but I don't—"

"Go on and get yourself cleaned up." She put her hands on her hips. "Don't make me drag you down, 'cause I will."

The church was a modest building overflowing with a mixed group of blacks and whites, all well dressed, smiling, friendly. When the service began, the congregation sang hymns that soared to the rafters, and they prayed with a passion that left Boothe mystified. How could anyone be so certain?

The minister—Pastor Jeb—was a distinguished middle-aged white man who said he was going to speak today of a loving and benevolent God. Boothe anticipated a fairly routine sermon, and that's how it began—but he soon began to notice certain words and phrases that seemed oddly out of place.

"Prosperity . . ."

"Abundance . . ."

"Our Lord's generous blessings . . ."

"God wants you to enjoy the good life."

Is it just me, Boothe wondered, *or have things changed a lot since I last went to church? Is this guy talking about money? Is he saying that being a Christian leads to material rewards?* Boothe decided he must be misinterpreting the pastor's words.

In the middle of the service, however, Pastor Jeb called for testimony from his flock. One by one, members made their way to the pulpit and shared their tales of victory, and if the pastor's message was subtle, the congregants' proclamations were not.

"I got a nice raise this week," one man said, "and I want to give thanks to Jesus!"

Amen!

"God found me a new job with better pay!" another man shouted. "With shorter hours!"

Amen!

"The Lord blessed me this week," a giddy woman shrieked, holding aloft a stub of paper, "and I won five thousand dollars on a scratch-off ticket!"

Amen and praise the Lord!

Boothe was stunned. Not only were these churchgoers as fond of money as he was, they showed no shame about it whatsoever. He'd never seen anything like it. He began to wonder: *Is it possible that greed isn't a character flaw after all? Is it possible that the housewife in Des Moines wasn't killed by negligence but by bad luck and a loose doorknob?*

At that very moment, Boothe experienced what could only be described as an epiphany. He felt his spirits lift, and his crippling guilt began to evaporate. He was a new man!

I was wrong! God doesn't smite His followers for being wealthy. In fact, He favors it!

Oh, the liberation!

Moments later, the collection plate began to make the rounds, and Pastor Jeb pointed out that when you give to others, that's when your own needs will be met. "Live to give!" he said. "And your generosity will be returned many times over. Only by giving can you experience the wondrous rewards God has in store for you!"

In his former life, that statement would have struck Peter Boothe as contradictory and nonsensical. But now, in his rapturous condition, he happily parted with a ten-dollar bill, a sum of money that he couldn't afford to squander at the moment. But investing in his future as a Christian—that wasn't squandering, was it? No, sir! He was purchasing a one-way ticket to a life of fulfillment and happiness—and he would be led there by none other than the Reverend Jebediah Wimple.

He thought.

Boothe was at the service one week later when, during an informative sermon that touched on tax shelters and oft-overlooked deductions, Pastor Jeb dropped dead from an intercranial aneurysm.

The congregation, of course, was devastated, and as the ambulance departed, mournful wails could be heard throughout the parking lot.

But Peter Boothe wasn't about to let his newfound spirituality be so easily derailed. He could still remember what Pastor Jeb had said only seven days earlier:

When the Lord lays an opportunity at your feet, you have to open your eyes . . . open your mind . . . open your heart . . . and fully receive His blessings!

Without a moment's hesitation, Peter Boothe hoisted himself into the bed of a Chevrolet pickup, stood tall, and began to address the crowd. He had no idea where it came from or whether he could ever repeat it, but what spilled from him that glorious day was the most compelling and inspirational sermon ever delivered in the history of the Holy Nondenominational Church of God's Redemptive Embrace.

Boothe was, it seems, a natural.

The rest, as they say, is history.

20

"MR. MARLIN? I took the chance that you were an early riser. Hope you don't mind the hour."

Seven forty-five. The caller was using a speakerphone. Marlin hated speakerphones. "Who am I talking to?"

"This is Harry Grange. Perry's brother." He had a deep voice with a mild Texas accent, and he spoke as if he were an old acquaintance from the country club. *John, you old rascal! Ever cure that slice? Damn good to see you again. My best to the missus.* A schmoozer.

"What can I do for you, Mr. Grange?"

There was a moment of silence. Then Harry Grange said, "Listen, I think you and me need to talk. Perry says you came out to see him again on Saturday."

"I did."

"Yeah, and it has him sorta worked up. He and I both thought we'd put that business from January behind us. He's working hard, trying to rebuild his name, and the last thing he needs is a warden after his ass all the time."

"I'm not 'after his ass.' I went out there to ask him about spotlighters."

"Uh-huh." Sarcastic.

"You need something in particular, Harry? Otherwise . . ."

"Just think about giving Perry a break, okay? Think about what you've put him through in the past six months."

"You can't blame me for Perry's circumstances."

"I feel that I can."

"Then there's no reason for this conversation to continue."

"Well, fuck you," Harry Grange said and abruptly hung up.

Apparently, he and Marlin were no longer golfing buddies.

Butch Theriot learned something critical about the fine art of abduction on Tuesday morning: If you decide to release the abductee, inform him of that fact *before* you cut him loose. You'll encounter far fewer problems that way. Something to keep in mind should he ever pull a dumb-ass stunt like this again.

Pringle, dressed in a suit as usual, finally knocked on Butch's motel-room door at eight thirty, during an episode of *Green Acres*. Jerry Strand was safely tucked away in the bathroom. Butch had dragged him in there—chair and all—at six in the morning, because Strand had crapped his pants and the stench was just too much.

Pringle didn't ask why Butch wasn't questioning Strand; he just turned the TV up to cover their voices and said, "We're running out of options. Make one last run at him. This time, get physical."

Butch nodded. *Finally!* "He'll talk, believe me."

"Good, because if he doesn't, there's only one alternative."

"Turn him loose and skip town?"

Pringle hesitated. "Not exactly."

"What, then?"

"In that case, we're going to have to figure out . . . a permanent solution."

Butch didn't like the way that sounded. *A permanent solution?* "You mean . . . what do you mean?"

"Listen, I've been thinking about this all night. We don't have any other choice. If he doesn't have the fossil, we can't let him go. And we can't just keep him tied up forever."

"You're talking about . . . getting rid of the guy?"

Butch didn't know if he could do it. It was one thing to shatter a guy's kneecap or to bite half his ear off—things Butch had done on the football field—but it was something else to flat-out murder a guy. Yeah, maybe he could kill a dude in a bar fight or something, but a man taped to a chair? That didn't seem right.

Pringle took a deep breath, then said, "You know what the punishment for kidnapping is? You want to go to prison?"

"Hell, no, but—"

"If we turn him loose, he'll go straight to the cops. He has no reason not to."

"But then he'd have to tell 'em about the fossil."

"So what? If he doesn't have it, he has nothing to lose."

"But they'll wonder why he didn't mention it earlier."

"He'll just say he didn't think it was important. He'll say he didn't know the fossil was valuable, or that anyone would kill Farley for it."

Butch was getting confused. "How is anything different if he *does* have the fossil?"

"Then he'll have a reason to keep quiet, because I'll offer him a cut."

"Okay, but what will he tell the cops? They'll wonder where he's been for the past two days."

"He'll just come up with something."

"Like what?"

"I don't know, maybe an out-of-town girlfriend. Doesn't matter. Hell, he wouldn't even have to answer them. He could just say it's his own damn business where he was."

Butch was angry for getting himself into this fucked-up situation. "Are you making this up as you go along, or what?"

Surprisingly, Pringle didn't have a smart-aleck answer. "I never planned on this, no. I figured he had the fossil. I still think he does. But we need him to talk."

"Oh, he'll talk," Butch said, hoping it was true. "If he knows anything, he'll talk."

"Okay, then," Pringle said, grabbing the key card for the room off the credenza. "I'm going next door for some coffee. Do what you need to do, but keep it quiet. Last thing we need is some wetback maid getting an earful."

Jerry Strand could hear them talking in low voices out there. Deciding his fate, no doubt. Were they going to kill him? Would they go that far? Strand had to decide just how long he was willing to keep up his bluff. The fossil wouldn't do him any good if he was dead. But it was damn tempting to think he could keep it all for himself.

Pringle, that double-crossing son of a bitch. Triple-crossing, if he was the one who killed Hollis Farley, which seemed like a no-brainer.

Strand had had plenty of time to contemplate his situation. If he told Pringle where the skull was, would they let him go? Probably not. Strand was a big loose end, and he knew too much.

He was willing to bet they wouldn't kill him in the motel room. No, they'd take him out in the woods somewhere, which meant they'd first have to get him into the car. If they moved him now, in broad daylight, they couldn't exactly carry him out taped to the chair. He'd have to walk out. They'd have to cut him loose—at least his feet. That's when he might have a fighting chance. That's when he'd—

The talking in the motel room stopped.

He heard the front door of the room open and close.

Then the bathroom doorknob turned.

Butch tilted Strand backward—Christ, the smell—and dragged him roughly out of the bathroom, the chair legs leaving furrows in the cheap motel carpet.

Then, without even asking a question, Butch grabbed the index finger of Strand's right hand and bent it sideways until the bone gave with a satisfying snap. Strand grunted with pain, his eyes bulged, but the tape across his mouth held tight.

Butch got right in his face. "You ready to tell me where that fossil is?"

Strand grunted again, a full sentence. It sounded like "I don't know." Sweat was building on his forehead.

So Butch grabbed the next finger over, the middle one, and snapped it, too. Going sideways like that not only broke the bone, it tore the ligaments to shit. Butch knew that from personal experience.

"How 'bout now? I'll do all ten of 'em if I have to. And that'll just be a warm-up."

Strand was moaning now, with tears leaking from the corners of his eyes.

"Where's that got-damn fossil?"

Strand shook his head and grunted the same sentence again. Snot was running out of his nose.

Butch had fully intended to work Strand over until he passed out, but he found that he had no patience for it. He grabbed his Ruger .22 automatic off the dresser and aimed it at Strand's forehead.

"I've already checked," he said. "Ain't nobody in the rooms to either side of us or the one above us. And this piece here is plenty quiet. Nobody'll hear a thing. So listen up. This is your last chance, understand? Tell me where that fossil is or I'll blow your got-damn brains out."

Butch thought it all sounded like corny dialogue from an old gangster movie, but Strand was obviously terrified. He was trying to say something, but Butch couldn't make it out.

"You ready to talk?"

Strand said, "Ooommph."

"All right. You scream or pull any shit and you're a dead man. Then I'll go have a little chat with your wife, and you don't want that. You hear me?"

Strand nodded obediently.

Keeping the muzzle of the gun against Strand's forehead, Butch yanked the tape off, and Strand immediately started babbling: "I really don't know where it is and I'm not lying you gotta believe me 'cause I woulda told you by now please don't kill me I swear to God I'd tell you if I knew."

Damn it to hell! Despite his earlier reservations, Butch was so frustrated now that he really considered shooting the guy. Just pop a slug into his brainpan and let it bounce around. Dump the body somewhere and be done with it.

He said, "Look, buddy, you're putting yourself in a bad spot here. You gotta tell me where it is. If you don't, he wants me to kill you, you understand? But if you talk, we're gonna let you go. That's how it works."

"But I don't know where it is!" Strand whined.

"You're signing your own death warrant, you realize that?"

Strand didn't say anything.

"I'm warning you. Talk!"

Nothing.

Butch kept the gun in place, his finger on the trigger, and he slowly began to squeeze. Then he stopped. He lowered the pistol. Hell, no. He couldn't do it. Not for Alex Pringle. Not because of some damn dinosaur bone. He had to let the son of a bitch go. Butch'd do prison time if he had to, though he imagined he could get a lesser sentence if he narked on Pringle.

Butch stood up again and removed a small hunting knife from his pocket. He popped the blade open and went behind Strand, who started to whimper.

"Jesus, quit your crying. Fuckin' pathetic." Butch began to cut through the duct tape, freeing Strand's legs, then his arms. Strand was trembling. Butch gestured toward the bathroom. "You smell like a damn outhouse. Go clean yourself up. You can't walk outta here like that."

Strand had been bound for so long, it was hard to stand upright. His muscles ached and his joints burned as he began to use them again. The pain from his broken fingers was extraordinary. He limped into the bathroom and closed the door. His mind was racing. He turned the shower on, but cleaning up was the farthest thing from his mind. He needed a weapon. But what? All he had was towels, washcloths, and a roll of toilet paper. Maybe the rod suspending the shower curtain would work. No, it was too flimsy, and Butch would hear him taking it down.

Then he figured it out. Yeah, that could work.

Now he just needed some time to regain his strength—and to forget about his mangled hand.

The shower had been running for ten minutes.

"You ain't cleaning up for a damn beauty pageant," Butch called through the door. "Let's get a move on." Now that everything had fallen apart, Butch was anxious to get the hell out of town. First, he'd warn Strand to keep his mouth shut—tell him he was lucky to get out of this alive. Then Butch would head for home, lie low, and hope the cops didn't come looking.

The water kept running. Butch stepped over to the bathroom door and said, "Shake a leg in there."

Strand didn't reply. Butch grabbed the knob and swung the door open.

And Jerry Strand brought the lid from the toilet tank crashing down onto Butch's head.

She'd heard it so many times as a deputy: Oh, Joe or Scott or Dave would never do that, not in a million years. He's just not that kind of guy. No way. I'd stake my life on it. He wouldn't beat his wife. He wouldn't wag his willie at kids on a playground. He wouldn't shoot anyone. Hell, he wouldn't even run a red light. The suspect's friends or coworkers would look at Nicole like she was crazy, or scoff at her inability to recognize an innocent man.

Then the evidence would be presented—usually a mountain of it, sometimes topped with a confession—and it became obvious that good ol' Joe or Scott or Dave had fooled everybody. *I'm shocked,* they'd say. *I thought I knew him.* They'd shake their heads and grimace and wonder how they could've been so wrong. Or, worse, they'd say, *You know, I always wondered about that guy.* Like they knew all along. Yeah, right.

Now Nicole was wondering, of course, if she was making the same mistake. Because, no matter what she'd seen in that photo, she refused to believe it. *He wouldn't do that. Never. Not John.* But what was the explanation for it?

Could Michael Kishner be holding a grudge? Maybe John had written him up for an offense, and this was Kishner's way of getting even. That thought had occurred to her when she woke up, and she couldn't shake it, so she'd called in sick to stay at home and do a little snooping.

What she'd found out so far:

There was indeed a man named Michael Allen Kishner who lived in Austin with a wife named Susan. Nicole learned that tidbit courtesy of the Web site for the Travis County clerk's office. The Kishners had been married for six years. So that part was true.

Nicole hopped over to the county tax assessor's site and learned that the Kishners owned a home in South Austin. They'd bought it six years earlier. Less than twelve hundred square feet, built in 1955, but Austin was a boom market and it was valued at $187,000. The lot was worth twice as much as the structure. She could picture it: a modest, aging frame house on a tiny lot. But a good starter home for a young couple.

Then she visited the sister site for Blanco County. Again, Kishner wasn't lying. He and Susan owned fifty-two acres near Round Mountain, deeded to Michael in 1995. Probably an inheritance. The Kishners received an agricultural exemption, which meant they probably ran a few goats or cattle.

This information was all fairly useless. So she decided to dig deeper.

If she'd still been a deputy, she would've been tempted to run a criminal history on Kishner through the department's computers, even though that would've been against policy, since she wasn't officially investigating him. But there was another way to access that information. For a fee of three dollars plus tax, she could search the Texas Department of Public Safety database. So she created an account, then purchased two search credits — one for Kishner and one for his wife, just in case.

She was grateful that Kishner had an unusual last name; a name like Michael Smith or Jones likely would've returned several pages of offenders to sort through.

So she typed in his full name, his sex, and his race, and when the results came back, she immediately saw that it had been a waste of time. The name Michael Kishner came up empty. Same thing for Susan Kishner. No record for either of them. Was that a good thing or a bad thing?

She logged off.

21

THE IMPACT WAS staggering. Large shards of broken porcelain flew everywhere. Butch's legs buckled and he fell to his knees. *My damn skull is cracked plumb in two,* he thought. He could feel the shock wave of the blow clean down to his toes. Blood cascaded down his face, into his eyes, his mouth. His vision was hazy. He braced his hands against each side of the doorjamb, supporting himself, but also preventing Strand from getting by.

Strand tried anyway. He attempted to bull his way past Butch's outstretched arms, but Butch wrapped him up around the thighs, like he was bringing down a hefty running back. Strand toppled to the floor, with Butch holding on for dear life. His face was directly in Strand's soiled backside. Strand writhed and squirmed but couldn't get loose. They were like two wrestlers locked in a death match. Butch knew he couldn't keep this up for long. He was too weak.

He remembered his gun on the dresser. If he could just get to it, he could stop this craziness. Did Strand know where it was? Apparently he did, because he was using his left hand to claw his way toward the dresser.

Butch used one hand to grab Strand's belt, trying to halt his progress. Strand struggled over onto his back to fend Butch off. Butch grabbed the front of Strand's shirt—and a handful of chest hair underneath—and began to twist. Strand yelped, but then he brought a knee up and caught Butch square in the jaw, slamming his teeth together with a resounding clack. Butch tried to punch Strand in the stomach, but his arms were like wet noodles. Strand had one leg free now, and he stomped Butch on the top of the head, right on his open wound. The pain was excruciating.

I'm getting my ass kicked by a geezer, Butch thought. *I'm Robin Ventura.*

He took another flailing shot at Strand's midsection, but there was stout muscle under that thick belly. The punch had no effect at all. So Butch aimed lower. He gathered all his strength and slammed his fist into Strand's crotch. He heard a grunt of pain. So Butch hit him in the balls again. And again. And again.

And that ended it. Strand was going fetal, moaning, guarding his privates. The fight had gone out of him.

Butch rose clumsily to his feet, swaying, blood dripping from his head like water from a poorly maintained faucet. "Son of a bitch," he said. "You're fuckin' history." His breathing was harsh and labored. He lurched to the dresser and grabbed the pistol. *What I get for having a heart,* he thought angrily. *Pringle was right. Gotta kill the guy.*

Strand saw him coming. He forgot about his balls and covered his face with his hands, cowering like a little girl. Butch held the pistol at arm's length. He began to squeeze the trigger, felt it starting to give, and Strand said, "Wait! I'll tell you where it is!"

At this point, Butch didn't even realize what Strand was saying. He was too angry—and embarrassed that an old guy had nearly gotten the best of him.

Strand must have seen the fury on Butch's face, because he said, "I'll give you half! A million bucks, just don't shoot!"

Butch eased off the trigger but kept the gun extended. His ears were ringing. What the fuck? "A million . . . what the hell're you talking about?"

Strand apparently saw a ray of hope, and he couldn't talk fast enough. "You and me, we'll split it! Fuck Pringle! We'll each take a million!"

Butch lowered the gun. It had to be a trick, right? Pringle had said it was worth a hundred grand. But Pringle was apparently a piece of shit. "You're saying that dinosaur bone is worth two million bucks?"

"Yeah, yeah, I swear to God. We got a buyer!"

Martha Crain was seventy-four years old, with blue eyes that complemented her blue hair. In spite of her age, her posture was impeccable—her spine ramrod straight, her shoulders squared, her head held high. She spoke with masterful diction and no recognizable accent. She could smile, and she proved it by actually doing so several times a year. She had never married, nor had there ever been a proper suitor to whom she would have felt comfortable making such a commitment.

Martha's father had been a combat veteran—an air force colonel during World War I, a stern man, a disciplinarian—and he had instilled in Martha a solemn demeanor. There was no time or place for what her father called "grab-ass." As a result, Martha Crain believed in an adherence to proper protocol and a stringent code of personal and professional conduct. She brooked no nonsense or fiddle-faddle. Life, after all, was serious business, not a wintertime sleigh ride.

Martha Crain was the head librarian in Johnson City.

To say that she ruled over her domain with an iron fist would, in her opinion, be unfair. She merely brought a structured order to the place, and she insisted that others follow it fervently, to the letter, at all times, with no exceptions.

Books, videotapes, and DVDs were to be returned by the due date. Period. Procrastinators incurred a late fee of twenty-five cents per day, and their borrowing privileges were revoked until such time as all monies had been remitted.

The Xerox machine was not to be abused or mishandled, nor to be used in a manner in violation of federal copyright laws. Duplicating an article from the most recent *People* magazine — Britney's latest misadventure, for example — was strictly out of the question, and Martha could often be found lingering nearby, keeping a watchful eye on those who availed themselves of the machine.

The twin Internet terminals were of particular concern to Martha because, as she understood it, there was all manner of vile adult content to be found in "cyberspace." The young man who had installed the terminals had assured Martha that a software program — a filter of some sort — would keep smut from youthful eyes. The technology was beyond her grasp, so she was forced, in this instance, to relinquish a small bit of control. But she insisted that patrons who wanted to use the computers sign in at the circulation desk, and that eased her mind a bit.

All in all, Martha Crain ran a tight ship, and she was proud of her accomplishments. Thanks to an aggressive fund-raising program, the library was a modern, well-equipped facility, worthy of a much larger and more sophisticated community. She only wished she could get the locals more interested in reading. It seemed so few people appreciated literature—or even genre fiction—these days. Nine thousand residents in the county and only three hundred and twelve were card-carrying library patrons. Sad, really. On any given day, the library might have ten or twelve visitors, most of them retirees who browsed aimlessly through the magazines and newspapers. The truth was, nobody was beating down the library door to put its full resources to use.

Which was why, on Tuesday morning, as Martha Crain parked her meticulously maintained Ford Focus in her reserved spot—arriving thirty minutes early, as always—she was pleasantly surprised to see a young man, perhaps a teenager, seated on the bench on the front patio, patiently waiting for the library to open. This was a first. What an unexpected delight! How refreshing!

Martha grabbed her handbag and her sack lunch, locked her car securely, and headed up the stone walkway toward the front door. As she neared the man on the bench, she realized with amusement that he was sleeping. The poor lad had dozed off while he was waiting. Never mind. She could forgive that in a person who was so eager to expand his mind and broaden his horizons.

Upon closer inspection, however, Martha began to have doubts. This fellow was a bit rough around the edges: cheeks unshaven, hair matted, clothes wrinkled and stained. Was he perhaps a homeless person? A drifter? A wino? Had he slept overnight in this very spot? Good heavens. This sort of thing was a rarity in Blanco County. Martha was considering calling the authorities, but no, no—now she spotted an aging Mazda in the far corner of the parking lot, and judging by the vehicle's dented fender and unwashed exterior, it almost certainly belonged to this man.

Martha cleared her throat. The man—not so young, now that

she got a good look—was snoring softly. A generous string of drool was dangling from his mouth to his chest.

Martha cleared her throat again. The man didn't so much as budge. She shook his shoulder gently, then firmly. Finally, he twitched. A lazy hand rose and pawed at the drool on his face. His eyes opened—glassy and red—and he blinked several times. He glanced left and right slowly, frowning, as if confused by his whereabouts. Then he looked back at Martha, smiled, and said, "Hey there. You the library lady?"

The library lady. Indeed. Such impertinence.

"I'm the librarian, yes."

"Cool," the man said, standing, stretching, yawning, scratching various body parts. "Been waiting on ya."

Martha couldn't place it, but the man carried a familiar odor about him, a scent that somehow reminded her of baking cookies.

She turned toward the library entrance, keys in hand, and the man began to follow behind her. As she unlocked the door, she said sternly, "The library opens in"—she checked her wristwatch, which was set to military time—"twenty-seven minutes."

The man snorted. "You're kidding, right?"

"Kidding?" Martha said. "About what?"

"I really gotta wait?"

"No, sir, you don't *gotta* wait. You're free to leave if you wish. But as for the library, it opens in twenty-seven minutes."

With that, Martha entered, let the door swing shut behind her, and locked the dead bolt with a crisp flick of her wrist. She heard a muffled voice from outside: "Well, jeez, what'd ya go and wake me up for, then?"

Marlin had put Geist into the backyard and filled her bowl with kibble, and he was walking out the front door, keys in

hand, when he remembered and turned back to call the videographer.

When Billy Don came to, he couldn't move his left arm. He
smelled room deodorizer or toilet cleaner or something with a
flowery scent to it, and that puzzled him, because his bedroom
usually smelled like pork rinds or bean dip.

He lay still for a few moments, trying to get his bearings.
What the hell had happened? His head ached a little, and his
mouth was bone dry, but his condition wasn't as bad as he expected, considering that he couldn't remember much of anything
after talking to Buzz Farley. Had he made a fool of himself? Said
anything stupid? He hoped to God he hadn't wrecked Red's
truck on the way home. *That damn moonshine.*

Then he heard the low murmur of people talking in another
room, and he detected the aroma of bacon and coffee, and it occurred to Billy Don for the first time that he might not *be* at
home. And if he wasn't at home, where the hell was he?

He tried to open his eyes, but they were crusted shut from
sleeping so hard. He finally managed to wiggle them loose, and
boy, did his lids open wide when he saw that his arm was pinned to
the mattress by Betty Jean Farley's head. That's where the flowery
smell was coming from—her hairspray. She was lying right beside
him—on his arm, in fact—on a strange bed, in a bedroom he'd
never seen before. The blanket was pulled up to her chin. Her big
brown eyes were looking up at him, like she'd been waiting for
him to wake up, and she said, "Good morning, sleepyhead." She
smiled like she'd just won a blue ribbon in a pie contest.

"Mornin'."

"I thought you was gonna sleep all day."

He attempted to smile back at her, but he wasn't sure it
worked. He was trying not to exhale in her direction, just out of
pure courtesy, because he figured his breath had a funk to it.

"But since we were up so late," she said, "I wouldn't blame you if you did." She snuggled in closer.

Up so late? Jesus, doing what?

Billy Don attempted to sort through his memory banks and come up with a clue—just a tiny shred or snippet to let him know what had happened in this bedroom last night—but it was like trying to thread a fishing line in the dark while wearing oven mitts. Had he and Betty Jean fooled around, and now he couldn't even remember it? If so, well, that wasn't quite the way he had hoped things would happen. Betty Jean deserved better. Hell, they both did. So he eased into the discussion by saying, "Boy, your uncle's whiskey sure has a mean kick to it."

"Yeah, I warned you, didn't I?"

Had she? He had no memory of it.

She said, "You gotta be careful with that stuff, or it'll make you crazier than an outhouse rat. You got a hangover?"

"A little one," he said. "Nothing a couple aspirin can't handle."

"Want me to get you some?"

Which would mean she'd have to get out of bed, and she'd probably be stone naked, and wouldn't that be sort of awkward in the bright light of day?

"Thanks, but not right now. Let's just lay here a minute."

"Fine with me," she said. "I could use a few minutes of peace and quiet, to be honest with you, after the past few days. This is nice, ain't it?"

"You bet it is."

He was trying to decide what questions he should ask, because it was a tricky situation. He knew it'd be a mistake to sleep with a woman, then let on that he couldn't remember it. He figured that wouldn't go over real well. He had to be clever, and being clever wasn't one of his strong points. He found himself wondering what Red would say. Red had a knack for using words in just the right way. Then Billy Don got an idea.

"What time did we finally come to bed?" he asked, trying to sound casual.

" 'Bout three o'clock."

"That late, huh?"

"Thereabouts."

"And what time did we get to sleep?"

"Do what?"

"I was just wondering what time we fell asleep."

She raised her head and looked at him, puzzled. Then she began to grin. "Oh, this is a hoot," she said. "You don't remember anything, do ya?"

As usual, he hadn't been clever enough. But the good thing was, Betty Jean didn't seem angry. "Things are a tad foggy," he admitted.

"And now, seeing as how we're in bed together, you're wonderin' if we done the deed last night. Ain't that right?"

"Well, see, I—"

"Billy Don, you're too much." She had a teasing tone in her voice, like at the diner, when she'd be clearing the plates and she'd ask if he'd managed to fill his hollow leg. And now, without any warning, she tossed back the covers.

They were both fully dressed. Well, no shoes, but Billy Don was still wearing the overalls and tie he'd worn for the funeral. Betty Jean had changed into jeans and a big T-shirt somewhere along the way. Billy Don didn't know whether to feel relieved or disappointed.

"What kind of girl you think I am?" she asked, teasing. "Think I'd hop into bed right after my brother's funeral?"

" 'Course not, and I didn't mean to say—"

"Now, the day *after* the funeral—that's something else."

She batted her eyelashes at him, and he found it awfully darn cute. He wasn't sure what he was supposed to do. Kiss her? Fondle something important?

Before he could decide, she said, "Guess you don't recall all the nice things you said to me, huh?"

"Come on, now. 'Course I do."

She jabbed him lightly with an elbow. "Okay, then, Mr. Smooth Talker, what'd you say?"

Billy Don was enjoying himself. She was razzing him good and hard, and he liked it. *Mr. Smooth Talker.* Him? "You just want to hear it all over again," he said.

"You can't blame a girl for that. Boy, you went on and on. Guess it was the liquor talking."

She looked at him, and suddenly things seemed more serious, like her feelings might get hurt if he wasn't careful.

"I meant every word," he said. And he was certain he probably did, whatever it was he'd said.

"You remember what we planned for tonight? Dinner at my house?"

"I'll be there," he said. "You can count on it."

"Good. I've got a big surprise for you."

"Oh yeah? I like surprises."

"Something Hollis left behind. I think you'll like it."

There it was, just like that.

Something Hollis left behind.

Billy Don had a real good idea what that something was, and now he felt another wave of guilt wash over him, just like at the funeral. He wanted to come clean, to tell her why he'd gotten cozy with her in the first place. He'd point out that it was all Red's stupid idea, and besides, now that they'd spent some time together, Billy Don didn't care about any old dinosaur bone. He cared about *her*.

But he was afraid that he'd mess it up and that she wouldn't understand. So all he said was, "Think they got any extra bacon in there?"

22

THE KOUNTRY KITCHEN was world famous for its chicken-fried steak, or so the ads said, and the manager, Clarence, had eaten his fair share. He had to weigh two-forty, thick all over, with a bright red face and a buzz cut.

"I wasn't here myself—that's my day off—but since it was a Sunday morning, I woulda had four girls on the floor," Clarence said. "To handle the after-church crowd."

"You remember who was working?" Marlin asked.

"Hang on a sec." Clarence left the small space behind the cash-register counter and disappeared into his office.

Marlin looked around.

Nearly nine on a Tuesday morning and the diner was fairly empty. Mostly older folks, locals, lingering over coffee and pastries. He recognized most of them. There was one guy in a suit, hair slicked back, a mustache. Probably a businessman passing through.

Clarence came back holding a sheet of paper in his hand. A work schedule, apparently, because he said, "Dorothy, Irma, Liz, and Trish. They all worked six to one, 'cept for Trish, who worked all day."

"I saw Irma when I came in. Any of the others here?"

"Trish should be in any minute. Running late."

Two out of four. A fifty-fifty shot.

When Martha unlocked the library door at precisely nine o'clock, the man was back on the bench, sleeping again. Fine. He could snooze the day away for all she cared. Martha went to the circulation desk and busied herself with paperwork—a handful of stern late notices to delinquent borrowers.

A few minutes later, however, the front door swung open and here he came. He strode to the center of the room before he apparently realized he didn't know where he was going. He stopped, looked here and there, then walked resolutely toward the back of the room. Toward the computers.

"Excuse me!" Martha called out. "Excuse me! Sir!"

The man stopped again. "Me?"

Well, yes, you, Martha thought. *Who else is here?*

She said, "Are you planning to surf the Internet?" She still felt peculiar when she used that phrase.

"I was, yeah."

"Very well. You'll need to sign in." Martha placed a clipboard on the counter.

He gestured vaguely toward the back of the room. "I don't sign in electronically? On the computer?"

She tapped a pen on the clipboard. "No, no. Right here."

"Oh." Then, for some reason, his face seemed to light up. He approached the desk, picked up the pen, and gazed at the blue form. He appeared to be puzzled by it, and his smile vanished as quickly as it had appeared. He lifted the sheet—the only sheet—and looked underneath it. Then he looked at the front again and said, "Wow. That's a lotta rules. Takes up the whole page."

Martha didn't answer. If he didn't want to abide by the rules, he could go elsewhere. It was that simple.

"You use a different form for every person that signs in?"

"We most certainly do."

"Seems like it would be more, like, efficient and stuff if you had one sign-in sheet per day. Or week. Or whatever. Depending on how many people use the computers. Everyone could just sign in on one sheet."

"That's not how we do things," she said briskly. "Now, if we're done with the small talk, you simply sign at the bottom, indicating your willingness to comply with the user guidelines, and I'll give you a temporary password. That will give you access to a computer for one hour, or longer if nobody is waiting."

The young man raised the pen, then stopped.

"Is there a problem?" Martha asked.

"There's a space here for my patron number."

"Yes, there is. You'll find it in the upper left-hand corner of your library card."

"I, uh, don't have one."

"You don't have what? A library card?"

"No, ma'am."

"Are you a resident of Blanco County?"

"No, ma'am."

"Oh, well, that simply won't do," Martha said as she slid the clipboard away from him. "That won't do at all."

Now his smile returned. He dropped the pen onto the countertop and said, "That's okay, I don't really need to use the computers anyway. I can get what I want."

With no further words, he was gone. Out the door, as if he'd never been here at all. *Peculiar,* Martha thought. *Very peculiar.*

Irma was in her fifties, with brown hair and a few fine lines around her eyes. She was slim, maybe naturally, or from scurrying around the diner all day.

Marlin ordered coffee, and when she returned with it, he told her why he was there and placed a photo on the tabletop. Scott Underwood's driver's license photo.

Irma pulled a pair of glasses from her apron and slipped them on. She picked up the photo, squinted at it for a few seconds, and said, "Yeah, I think so. He looks familiar. Don't think I waited on him, though. I think Trish had him."

Less than one month after Alex Pringle signed on as executive director for Boothe Ministries—on an evening when Peter Boothe was out of town—Vanessa invited Pringle over for a "get-acquainted dinner" and promptly screwed his socks off.

Which didn't surprise Pringle at all. He'd noticed the lingering looks she'd given him. The absence of affection between her and Peter.

That first night, Vanessa Boothe was a tremendously athletic and adventurous lover—and Pringle got the sense he was nothing but a tool for her pleasure. He did his best to oblige, but after the third go-round—punctuated by Vanessa's moans, grunts, and yelps—he was a spent shell of his former self.

"Not bad for a guy your age," she said.

He was still panting on the sweat-soaked sheets. "Thank you." Experience had taught him what to do next, if he hoped to be a visitor in her bed again. So he caressed her cheek with the back of his hand. "This has been like a dream. I think you are the sweetest, most wonderful woman I have—"

She started laughing. He didn't know what to think. It was embarrassing. When she finally stopped, she said, "Get over yourself, okay? You got laid. Don't make anything out of it. Now get dressed. It's two o'clock and I need to get some sleep."

Fine. Now he knew the ground rules, and he readily played by them for five years. It became a routine; when Peter left town, which was nearly a weekly occurrence, Pringle would get a voice mail, an e-mail, a note in his in-box. They'd rendezvous at the Boothe estate or at the Four Seasons or, in a pinch, in the back of her Mercedes SUV.

Pringle didn't know what Vanessa's idea of heaven was, but he'd found his own sacred ground. He explored the contours of her sculpted body with the enthusiasm of a Spanish conquistador.

But then—as abruptly as it started—it stopped. It happened two months ago; suddenly, inexplicably, Pringle lost his fuck-buddy. He made overtures, only to have them snubbed. His calls went unreturned. His e-mails went unanswered. If he scheduled a meeting, she skipped it.

The odd thing was, Vanessa had also begun to travel regularly. To Blanco County.

Here she was, a woman accustomed to jetting off to Paris or Milan when the mood struck her, and suddenly she was spending days at a time in Bumfuck, Texas. It didn't make sense, but she claimed an interest in the construction of the new church.

Someone needs to meet with the land planner. Vanessa was happy to volunteer.

The architects have a first draft of the blueprints. Vanessa would arrange a meeting.

The zoning commission has some questions. Vanessa would drive down for a chat.

Then, at a moment when Pringle's former lover wasn't even on his mind, he happened across the publicity photos from the groundbreaking ceremony. As he started to file them away, one caught his eye. And the truth jumped out at him.

Oh my God, she's fucking the backhoe driver.

He never would have believed it, but looking at the stills, it was obvious. The photographer had shot an entire roll of Vanessa up on the backhoe, wearing a hard hat, and Hollis Farley was in several of them. Pringle saw the two of them laughing, smiling at each other, some intangible message passing back and forth. It was plain as day. The mutual attraction was there, no doubt, and Vanessa Boothe wasn't one to shy away from it.

Now—as Pringle sat in the diner next to the motel, wondering if he'd given Butch enough time with Strand—he had to smile about it all. Vanessa behaved like . . . well, she behaved like a man. He'd confronted her about his suspicions, of course, and she'd denied it. She'd denied it right up to the end, until Peter Boothe found an incriminating note and realized exactly what his wife was doing. Or *who* his wife was doing.

Pringle was jarred out of his thoughts when he noticed a man in uniform a couple of tables away. Had a round badge on his shirt. Some kind of cop, but not a regular one. Maybe a park ranger, or a game warden. But still a cop.

Pringle thought about what Butch was doing right now, just a few hundred yards away.

He threw a few dollars on his table and sauntered out of the diner. Crossed the parking lot and proceeded to the rear of the motel. It was quieter back here, with just a handful of cars parked here and there. Something seemed odd, but Pringle couldn't pin it down.

He stopped in front of Butch's room and listened. Nothing except the TV. Good. Pringle didn't want to interrupt something that might turn his stomach. He was the first to admit that he was squeamish about certain things, which was why he'd chosen to skip the interrogation.

Pringle checked left and right—didn't see anybody—then he inserted the key card into the slot, got a green light, and opened the door slowly. The room was empty. The lights were out.

Standing on the threshold, Pringle reached out and flicked the switch.

He didn't like what he saw.

"You need me for something?"

Trish was cute, maybe twenty, and if she'd been wearing trendier clothing, rather than the official diner apron, she could've fit right in with the students Marlin had encountered the day before. She had that detached demeanor so many kids seemed to have today. And, of course, a small hoop earring through her eyebrow. Marlin was surprised that Clarence let her keep it on at work. Blanco County, after all, was not the UT campus.

He held the photo up. "Do you remember waiting on this man Sunday morning?"

She looked at the photo, then at the badge on Marlin's chest. "What's this about? You a cop?"

"A game warden. I'm investigating a case. I'd appreciate your help."

She eyed the photo again but didn't reach for it. "Yeah, I remember him. Picky about his food. Said his eggs were too runny. I was like, whatever."

"Do you know what time he came in?"

"I don't know. Pretty early. Maybe eight or so."

Which meshed with Underwood's account.

"Was he alone?"

"At first, yeah, but later there was two of them."

Again, just like Underwood had stated. He'd seen Farley's photo in the newspaper, then called Kate Wallace, and she'd joined him at the diner. Then they'd come to the sheriff's office together. But Marlin wanted to verify it.

"What did she look like?"

"Who?"

"The woman who joined him."

Trish's answer threw him completely. "Wasn't a woman."

"Pardon?"

"It was a younger guy, like maybe his son or something. A few years older than me."

Marlin was getting excited. He gestured toward the chair across from him. "Do me a favor and have a seat for a minute."

Trish glanced over her shoulder.

"It's okay," he said. "Clarence knows I need to talk to you. It won't take long."

She pulled the chair out and sat down. She crossed her arms, a little reluctant now, probably wondering what she'd gotten herself into. It was totally uncool, no doubt, to talk to a cop, or to anyone over the age of thirty.

"Please start from the beginning," Marlin said. "From when he first came in."

"Which one? The young one or the older guy?" Her tone said it was all a terrible bother and she'd just as soon be doing something else. Like waiting tables. Or getting a root canal.

"The older one."

"Okay. He came in and ordered. He was by himself. I brought his breakfast to him, and he complained about the eggs, but he ate them anyway. Then the younger guy came in and sat down. He was only here a few minutes."

"Did he order anything?"

"No." She stared at him. "Was he supposed to?"

Marlin ignored her smart mouth. "What happened next?"

"He left, and then the older guy left a few minutes later."

"Did a woman ever join the older guy?"

She scowled and shook her head impatiently. "Why do you keep talking about a woman? I never saw a woman."

"Did you ever see him reading a newspaper?"

"Not that I remember."

"What did the young guy look like?"

Trish shrugged. "Kinda cute, I guess. Wore glasses. But he had a faux-hawk, which is getting so old."

"A fohawk?"

She rolled her eyes. Marlin was a lost cause. "Yeah, like a fake Mohawk, you know? You spike your hair up with gel in the center. Like Ryan Seacrest used to do."

Marlin wasn't sure who Ryan Seacrest was, but that didn't matter. He could picture a faux-hawk, because he had seen one recently. Just the day before, in fact. "It wasn't shaved on the sides, right?"

"Uh-uh. That's a real Mohawk. Nobody does that anymore."

Now the slam dunk. "You said he had glasses?"

She snorted. "Yeah, with thick black frames. Lame, if you ask me. Like, trying to be retro or something."

Retro is right, Marlin thought. *Just like Buddy Holly.*

Betty Jean Farley had an unlisted phone number, and Red thought that was one of the silliest things he'd ever heard. An unlisted number? Come on. Like men would be calling her up night and day if she was in the phone book. On the other hand, that unlisted shit worked, because when Red tried to sweet-talk the number out of the operator, she wouldn't give it up.

So Red was seriously considering hiking the four miles over to Betty Jean's place—he'd even gone so far as to pull some comfortable boots on—and that's when he finally heard a vehicle chugging up the driveway. He knew it was his truck, because he recognized the familiar hole-in-the-muffler sound.

Red stepped out onto the front porch into the cool morning air just as Billy Don rounded some cedar trees and pulled up in front of the trailer. The big man cut the engine, sat for a few seconds, then climbed out. Weird. He wasn't smiling like a man who'd just gotten laid. In fact, he looked like hell. Red-eyed and tuckered out.

"About goddamn time," Red said, leaning against a porch post.

Billy Don shook his head in a you-don't-want-to-know kind of way. But he still wasn't smiling. He clambered up the steps, and as he passed, Red caught a familiar whiff.

"Jesus. Y'all dip into the tequila last night?"

"Moonshine," Billy Don muttered. "Too much moonshine. I need a Alka-Seltzer. Then I'm goin' to bed."

"Hey, hold on a second." Red followed him through the front door into the living room. "Ain't ya gonna tell me what happened? Where you been all night?"

"With Betty Jean."

Red chuckled. "It musta been one hell of a night if you're just now—"

Billy Don wheeled and pointed a sausage-like finger at him. "You better be careful what you say. She's a sweet gal."

Red held his hands up, palms outward. "Okay, take it easy. I wasn't gonna say nothin' smart. Just wondering if you learned anything."

"About what?"

"Well, Christ, Billy Don. You kiddin' me? About the dinosaur fossil. That's what this is all about, remember?"

Billy Don shook his head. "She don't know nothin' about it."

Red was dejected. "You sure?"

"I'm sure."

"So you asked her?"

"Yeah, I asked her."

Something wasn't quite right. Red wondered why Billy Don was giving such short answers. "How'd you go about it?"

"Whattaya mean, how'd I go about it?"

"I mean, did you flat-out ask if Hollis had a dinosaur bone, or were you a little more subtle about it?"

Billy Don let out a sigh. "All I know is she don't have it, okay? And she don't know where it is. End of story. Now leave me alone. I gotta sleep. Eatin' dinner with Betty Jean later on."

And with that, he turned and trundled down the narrow hallway to his bedroom. The door closed with a loud thud.

Red didn't know what to think. Billy Don had been Red's best friend, poaching partner, and housemate for more than five years, so Red knew the big man inside out. Red knew, for instance, that Billy Don preferred chocolate-covered doughnuts instead of glazed. He knew that Billy Don slept with a night-light. He knew that Billy Don had enough hair on his back to weave a rug.

And he knew when Billy Don was telling the truth and when he was bending it a little. Or a lot. Like now.

The chair Strand had been taped to was vacant. Strips of used duct tape were scattered all over the floor. But what concerned Pringle more was the large drops of blood on the carpet. And what the hell were those white things? Shards of porcelain? Pieces of a toilet?

"Hey, Butch?"

No reply.

Pringle wished he had a gun. He'd never carried one, but he could understand why men like Butch did.

"Butch?"

Still nothing. Pringle quickly stepped inside, closed the door, and locked it behind him. The bathroom door was open about four inches. Was Butch in there? Why wasn't he answering?

"Everything okay? Butch?"

Pringle took a step forward and grabbed the remote control off the bedspread. He turned the TV off and listened. All quiet. Moving slowly, he approached the bathroom door and slowly swung it open. Nobody. The lid was missing from the toilet tank.

Where was Butch? Had Strand gotten loose? Was he on his way to the cops right this minute?

Then a different—and much more likely—scenario crossed Pringle's mind: *Butch got rough. Strand talked. And now they're both gone. Together.*

It was one of two things: Butch wanted the fossil for himself, or Butch and Strand had partnered up.

Pringle quickly returned to the front of the room and parted the curtains. Now he realized what he'd overlooked a moment ago.

His Cadillac was gone.

23

"HE WON'T REPORT the car stolen?" Jerry Strand asked. He'd lowered the tinted windows a few inches because he was still carrying a reek about him. He was wearing a pair of Butch's pants, but he hadn't had time to clean himself up.

Butch was holding a towel filled with ice cubes to the top of his head. Strand had a similar ice pack wrapped around his hand.

"Maybe later, but not right away," Butch said. "Think about it. He don't want the cops talking to us, right? Shit, he'd get charged with kidnapping. No, what'll happen is, he'll figure you and me partnered up, so he'll either come after us hisself—which, if you ask me, he ain't got the 'nads—or he'll just let it go."

They were backed into a parking space at a rest stop along

Highway 281, six miles south of Johnson City. A hundred yards away, Highway 290 broke from 281 and ran east into Austin.

Strand had been holding off on telling Butch the entire truth, but he'd have to eventually, and he decided now was as good a time as any.

"There's one thing I need to tell you," he said slowly.

Butch looked at him. The ice in the towel was melting and water was running down his temples.

Strand said, "Okay, now, like I said, Hollis had a buyer, and this guy was willing to pay two million bucks in cash, or wire the money to our offshore accounts, or whatever we wanted—as soon as the fossil was authenticated."

"Yeah? And?"

Strand was on a roller coaster of emotions: scared to death of Butch for two days, and now they were partners. But the fear was still there, because there was a fair chance Butch might shoot him smack in the face for what he was about to say.

"Well, it shouldn't be a problem—we can probably figure it out right quick—but I don't know exactly who the guy is."

Butch looked perplexed—and a bit angry. "Which guy?"

"The buyer. I don't know his name."

Butch lowered the ice pack. Yep, he was angry, all right. "Listen, you stupid fuck, if you're trying to pull a fast one—"

Strand spoke fast. "I'm not, I swear. Hollis never told me the man's name. He found him on the Internet, and they was sending e-mails back and forth. The deal was almost set, and then Hollis died. We'll find him, I promise. I mean, how many fossil collectors can there be in Houston?"

Strand had inadvertently shared a piece of the puzzle. He'd have preferred to keep that part secret, because he didn't trust Butch entirely. Or at all, really.

"He's in Houston?"

Strand nodded. "That's what Hollis said. One of the few things he told me."

Butch had an amused smirk on his face now, and Strand took that as a good sign. Butch said, "That's funny. Farley didn't trust you enough to give you the man's name."

"I never asked for it," Strand said defensively. "And you can't blame him for keeping it to himself. I mean, you just never know who's gonna stick a knife in your back."

It was a snide remark, alluding to Strand's treatment over the past two days, but Butch didn't care. He tossed the soggy towel into the backseat. His mood seemed to change suddenly, like he was losing patience, and he said, "Okay, enough of all this bullshit. We need to come up with a plan. How we gonna get that damn bone outta your house?"

Earlier, Strand had said the fossil was in his bedroom closet, rather than in the attic above the garage. Being cautious. In case Butch got any ideas.

"Well, let's think about it. It shouldn't be too hard."

"Were you being straight up about your wife? She don't know about the bone?"

"Hell, no. She'd blab to everyone."

"Even with a million bucks on the line?"

"She'd never go for that. She'd say it wasn't our fossil and we got no right to it. Damn woman's got principles out the wazoo."

Butch nodded, as if he'd known troublesome females like that. "Then we just wait till she goes out somewheres."

"If I know Nadine," Strand said, "she's staying put. You couldn't get her outta that house with a forklift, because a good wife would be waiting by the phone, and she wouldn't want anyone thinking she wasn't a good wife."

What's more, Strand figured Nadine was loving every minute of this drama, being the center of attention, worrying about her poor missing husband. Enjoying sympathy calls from friends, neighbors, and relatives. She probably had the Bible out on the credenza, to impress any visitors who dropped by.

"Well, hell," Butch said. "We might have to take more of a long-term approach."

"Long-term?"

"Yeah. You go back home with some sorta story. Like, you say you got a girlfriend on the side, which'll explain why you was gone. The cops'll want to talk to you, but you stick to your story until it blows over."

Jerry Strand didn't like that approach at all. During this ordeal, he had fully expected to die, and now that he had another shot at life, it made him realize something: For years, he hadn't been a happy man. He wasn't just unhappy, he was miserable, and when it came down to it, he figured Nadine was to blame. So damn bossy. Always telling him what to do and how to do it. Nagging. Cold, too. They hadn't had marital relations in five months, and when they did do it, she was always patting him on the back, hurrying him along, like she had errands to run. And the bears. All those goddamn bears. He hated every one of them. He simply couldn't stomach the thought of going home. In fact, now that he mulled it over, he'd just as soon never see Nadine's fat, ugly face again. If he had a million dollars, he wouldn't have to.

"Absolutely not," he said.

"What?"

"No way. Not a chance. Nadine'd kill me."

"Well, shit, between you and me, from the things you've been saying, sounds like you'd be better off without her."

"Forget about that, because it wouldn't work anyway. The cops would ask for this imaginary girlfriend's name and where she lives and all that kinda crap, and they'd figure it out in about two seconds. We need something better."

The kid with the faux-hawk and thick glasses — the same person Marlin had seen waiting on the elevator near Underwood's office—could have been any of the professor's students, past or present. But Marlin had a hunch. Kate Wallace had mentioned one student in particular who visited the office on a regular basis—Underwood's previous research assistant.

Victor Klein.

Marlin returned to the sheriff's department and asked Darrell to pull a driver's license photo and a criminal history, if Klein had one. Then he went to his desk and put in another call to Kevin Masch, the videographer, who answered on the third ring.

"Yeah, I got your message earlier. A wedding, right?"

Masch sounded sleepy. And young. Lately, everybody seemed younger than Marlin. "That's right."

"What was your name again?"

"Marlin. John Marlin."

"And you were a referral?"

"Yes, one of your former clients gave us your name. She's a friend of my fiancée's."

"And her name is?"

"Nicole Brooks."

A pause. Paper rustling. "Hmm. I don't remember a client named Nicole Brooks."

"No, my fiancée is named Nicole Brooks. Your client's name is Missy Burns."

"Oh, okay. Now we're getting somewhere. I know Missy. Sure. So what date was that?"

I left all of these details on your machine, Marlin thought. *Don't you write these things down?* "July twelfth."

Marlin waited as Masch consulted his calendar. "Ooh, that's gonna be tough. What time?"

"The ceremony starts at seven, with the reception to follow. All at the same location."

"Which is where?"

I mentioned that, too. Marlin was starting to get irritated. "In

Blanco County, at a ranch off Miller Creek Road. It's about an hour west of downtown Austin."

"Okay, I remember now. Geez, I'm wide open the following weekend. Sure you don't want to do it then?"

Marlin waited a beat, then said, "You're kidding, right?"

"Man, I really don't think I could be there before about eight or so. I've got a family reunion earlier that day. They booked it four months ago. You're kinda late on this, you know? Seven weeks' notice is—"

"So you can't do it?"

"Hold on a sec. Are you going Gold, Silver, or Bronze?"

"I don't know what that means."

"You gotta pick a package—Gold, Silver, or Bronze. It's all on my Web site."

The last thing Marlin wanted was a bunch of choices, but he didn't see any way around it. "Why don't you give me the highlights of each package."

"Okay, the Bronze is one manned camera during the ceremony and the reception, for up to seven hours. Silver is two cameras—one manned and one fixed during the ceremony, then one manned during the reception—for seven hours. Gold is two manned cameras during both the ceremony and the reception, up to nine hours."

Marlin was a hypocrite. He hadn't written any of that down. "What are the prices?"

"Bronze is six hundred, Silver is seven fifty, and Gold is twelve hundred. Costs go up when you have a second videographer."

Twelve hundred dollars? Marlin had bought his first car for less than that. "What I'm wondering is, how does my choice affect whether or not you'll be available at seven o'clock?"

Marlin heard the tone of an e-mail arriving on his computer.

"Well, if you go Gold," Masch said vaguely, "I could probably juggle some things around. We could probably make it work."

"I don't need 'probably.' I'd want you there by seven."

"Listen, if you go Gold, I'll be there at six thirty."

"Okay, fine," he said. "We'll go with Gold."

He saw that Darrell had sent him an e-mail, with an attachment. He clicked on it.

"You won't be disappointed, my man. It'll be beautiful. Now, all I need is a deposit. It's half down and half on delivery of the final DVDs."

"Can I mail you a check?"

"I'd prefer a credit card through my Web site."

Darrell's note read: *Attached is Victor Klein's TDL photo, which is recent. He renewed in January. No record.*

"You there?" Masch asked.

Marlin double-clicked the file, and a photo appeared on his desktop. Victor Klein. He didn't have a faux-hawk. He didn't wear glasses. It wasn't the same guy.

24

DARWIN PARKER'S APPRECIATION for the human female form hadn't abandoned him entirely; indeed, there were times when the sight of Raquel Welch in a loincloth bikini appealed to him as greatly as the prehistoric creatures who pursued her. But at the moment, neither stimulus was working for him.

Instead, he was filled with a listless, crawling angst.

He hated waiting—he was typically a man of action—but things were out of his control. He'd called Snake's cell phone but received no answer. Poor service in Blanco County? Or was Snake stoned? Difficult to know, but Darwin did know this: With each tick of the clock, the *Alamosaurus* slipped farther from his grasp. The pessimist in him said it was likely sold by now.

In trying to allay his trepidation, Darwin had settled into his media room and cued up the DVD of *One Million Years B.C.* Ridiculous film, really. Other than Miss Welch's two estimable assets, the picture was a joke. Anachronisms all over the place, ludicrous story line, poor production values. Darwin had it in his library nonetheless. In fact, he owned virtually every movie ever made, good or bad, that featured dinosaurs. Hundreds of them.

Adventures In Dinosaur City.

Valley of the Dinosaurs.

Attack of the Super Monsters.

The Land That Time Forgot.

Yes, even the *Jurassic Park* trio, because, plot blunders aside, the special effects were astounding.

Then there was the granddaddy of them all: *Gojira.* The original Japanese version of *Godzilla,* shot in 1954. Darwin decided a viewing would cheer him up. He had the DVD in his hand when—thank God—the phone rang.

"You won't believe this," Snake said, "but they keep it all on paper. It's like the Stone Age down here."

"They keep what on paper?"

"When someone wants to use a computer. I figured each library member had a unique password, you know? And you'd enter that password on-screen to use the computer, so all the records'd be electronic. But no. There's an old hag running the place, and she keeps it all on paper. Is that a kick, or what?"

Which meant that somewhere in the library there was a completed form with the name of the person who had contacted Darwin. This was fantastic news.

"Where does she keep the forms?" Darwin asked. "Can you get to them?"

Snake laughed. "Well, yeah, I could. But it would require an after-hours visit, if you catch my drift."

Darwin didn't hesitate. "Then do it. Do it tonight."

There was a long pause. Then Snake said, "Dude, I'm not

trying to nickel and dime you, but that's gonna cost a lot more, you know? If I get caught, I'm up shit creek."

"Whatever it takes, Snake—you got me? If you can nail the name down for me—an actual name—there's ten thousand bucks in it for you. How does that sound?"

No pause this time. "Ten thousand? That's fair. But what if I get caught?"

"You won't. You said it's like the Stone Age down there."

"Yeah, but if I do, I'm gonna need a heavy lawyer, and ten K won't cover it, man. Not for a third strike. I'd end up with some court-appointed loser."

Darwin was ready to pull his hair out. He was being manipulated, quite shrewdly, by a burnout. But what was the alternative? "Okay, here's the deal. If you get caught—and I know you won't—I'll get you a lawyer. But only if you agree that you'll never mention my name. Not to the cops, not to the prosecutor, not to your own fucking grandmother. Understood?"

"Yeah, man. I'm nothing if not discreet."

Nicole cruised slowly past the house on Sacramento Drive in South Austin. There was an SUV in the open garage.

Am I taking this too far? Should I tell John and see how he reacts? Or just forget the whole thing?

She reached an intersection, hung a right, and circled the block. This time around, she pulled into the driveway and parked.

No reason to be nervous.

She stepped from her car and walked with false confidence to the front door. It was a beautiful day. She rang the bell. No more than ten seconds later, the door swung open and Nicole was face-to-face with a young, slender, sandy-haired woman. Not the woman in the photo, but that didn't mean anything. Could be a sister, a nanny, a housekeeper. There was one way to find out.

"Hi. Are you Susan Kishner?"

"I am. May I help you?"

Nicole was trying to keep a straight face, but she couldn't hold back a smile. She didn't know who the blond woman in the photo was, but it was obvious that Michael Kishner was lying.

But now what?

"I'm with the *Austin American-Statesman*," Nicole said. "We've had some delivery problems in this neighborhood, and we wanted to apologize if your paper has been delayed."

Susan Kishner was giving Nicole an odd look, and who could blame her? Nicole was grinning like an idiot. "We don't take the *Statesman*. I read it online."

"Oh, my mistake. Sorry to bother you."

Rodney Bauer was filling his crew-cab Chevy with gas, wondering why we didn't just bomb the shit out of the Middle Easterners for jacking up the price of oil, when a man with a suit jacket slung over his shoulder suddenly appeared beside him.

"I'll give you a hundred bucks for a ride to the airport in Austin," the man said.

"Pardon?"

"My car broke down. I need a ride. I'll give you a hundred bucks. Cash."

Car trouble. That explained the pissed-off look on the man's face. Rodney mulled it over. Fifty miles to the airport. No cabs in Johnson City. No buses. The man was in a bind.

"I got a buncha shit to do this morning," Rodney said. "But if you make it two hundred, I bet I can rearrange my schedule."

The man reached for his wallet.

Marlin called Kate Wallace and told her he needed to meet with Dr. Underwood again, preferably that afternoon.

"He's in meetings most of the day," she said, "but he's free at five. Does that work? Or is it urgent?"

"No, that'll be fine. I'll be there at five."

Depression. Anxiety. Hopelessness. Bitter despair. Vengefulness. Rage. In the past five days, the Reverend Peter Boothe had experienced all of these and more.

Oh, and paranoia. Can't forget paranoia. Every time Boothe's cell phone rang, his heart rose into his throat. It would be Alex Pringle calling with bad news, he just knew it. *The cops figured it all out,* Pringle would say.

But it hadn't happened yet. Might never happen.

The funny thing was, there were times when Boothe wished it *would* happen, because this entire charade could be drawn to a conclusion. It would be a relief, of sorts. Then he could stop feeling like a sinner and an imposter, because that's what he felt like right now, standing before a small girl in a wheelchair.

"This is Kelsey," Donna Jones said. "She's from Brenham."

It was early afternoon, and Peter Boothe was in the cancer ward at the Texas Children's Medical Center in Houston.

"I have Ewing's sarcoma in my leg," Kelsey said brightly. "But I'm doing okay." She couldn't have been more than eleven years old. Other than the hospital gown, she appeared to be a happy, healthy preteen.

Boothe knelt at the girl's side. "You're a brave girl, Kelsey. God will reward your courage."

"I hope so. Wanna play a video game?"

Boothe smiled. "You know, I'd love to, but I have to say hello to the other children."

A camera flashed as Boothe placed his hand on Kelsey's forehead and said a quick prayer. Then the small group moved on.

Boothe Ministries made contributions averaging a thousand dollars per month to the facility. Less than Boothe's car payment, but he'd always considered it a reasonable amount. Today's visit, however, wasn't about money. No, Boothe dropped in a few times every year just to chat with the children and buoy their spirits. It was all about the kids. Of course, Boothe was trailed by one of his staff photographers, who might opt to post one or two of the photos on the ministry's Web site. But that was simply a way to reassure Boothe's followers that the millions of dollars they donated every quarter were helping to support a worthwhile cause.

Today, as usual, Boothe was accompanied by several members of the hospital staff, including Donna Jones, the vice president of fund-raising. Jones was an efficient woman in her sixties, but she had an aloof demeanor about her; Boothe always suspected that Jones wasn't entirely satisfied with the size of his donations. But what was he to do? Sell his home and go back to living in a crummy apartment? Trade in his Bentley and buy a lesser car? How would that look? Could he speak with conviction about God's generosity and a life of abundance while driving a Hyundai? Ironically, without the trappings of success, Boothe might lose his charisma, his power to gently goad Christians into opening their pocketbooks and giving, giving, and giving some more. Skeptics like Donna Jones couldn't understand that.

They stopped in the room next to Kelsey's, and Donna Jones said, "This is Orion Davaur."

Aw, Jesus. He was no more than eight. He did not look well. He was sitting up in bed. Some sort of robot toy was lying forgotten on the bedspread.

"How're you, Orion? That's a cool name."

Orion shrugged. "You're the man on the television."

"I sure am. Have you watched my program?"

"My parents watch it."

Boothe chuckled. "Well, God bless your parents, then."

"They've been sending you money so I'll get better. They say you pray for me every night. Is that true?"

Donna Jones gave him a smug look.

In a way, it *was* true. No, Boothe didn't pray for Orion specif-ically, but collectively, yes, Orion was included. That wasn't too much of a stretch, was it? "I pray for all the sick children in the world," Boothe said simply. He felt like an evasive politician. It seemed awfully hot in this small room.

"My brother was here this morning," Orion said. "He's thir-teen. He'll be in high school next year."

Boothe's legs were shaky, and he couldn't seem to get enough air into his lungs. He sat on the edge of Orion's bed. "I'm glad . . . you got to visit with your brother. What's his name?"

"Trent." Then Orion said something that was like a blow to Boothe's solar plexus. "My daddy sent six hundred dollars to you last week, but I still feel bad. Does that mean God hates me?"

Donna Jones made a slight move, as if she were going to step forward and console the small boy, but she stopped herself and remained in place.

"Of course not," Boothe said, trying to give Orion a comfort-ing smile. "He just . . . He . . ."

Boothe was dizzy now, there was no doubt about that, and he felt a hot tear slide down his cheek. Orion was fidgeting with his toy, paying no mind to Boothe or the incomplete answer he'd given, because what could it matter to an eight-year-old who would likely pass away before year's end?

There was a hand on Boothe's shoulder. Donna Jones leaned in and said, "Perhaps we should take a break in my office."

She said something about an anxiety attack and gave him a pa-per bag. He breathed into it for several minutes, and that seemed to help. She was watching him closely. They were alone; they'd left the entourage in the hallway.

"Better?" she asked.

He nodded. He wanted to say something.

"Seeing these kids can be very stressful," she said.

It wasn't the children, he thought, but he wasn't entirely sure that was the truth. Maybe it was. He didn't know what to think. He wanted to say something, but if he did, he couldn't take it back. Once the words were out there, that was it, he couldn't change his mind.

"Are you on any medications?" Donna Jones asked. There was a framed certificate on her wall. She was a registered nurse.

He shook his head.

"Medical conditions I should know about?"

"No."

"Have you had one of these attacks before?"

"Never."

"But you're feeling okay now? No longer light-headed?"

"I feel . . . I do feel better."

"Good."

"Miss Jones, I—"

"Mrs."

She was wearing a wedding ring. He'd never noticed that before. "Mrs. Jones, I want to give the hospital one million dollars."

There. He'd said it. He was feeling odd again. But not in a bad way. *This,* he thought, *is the most exciting thing I've done in years.*

"Pardon?"

He reached into his suit pocket for his phone. "Actually, not one million dollars. Two million. I want to have a check cut and couriered over. Right now. You're trying to expand the chemotherapy ward, and this would give you a good start."

She appeared startled. "Are you sure? I mean, of course we'd be thrilled, but you might not be thinking clearly. I wouldn't want to take advantage of— "

"No, I feel fine," he said and began to dial. He realized how absurd it was; with a single phone call, he had the power to change lives. He had the power to make extraordinary things happen. How had that fact eluded him all this time?

"This is amazing," Donna Jones said. "I . . . well . . . thank you."

Boothe didn't know how to respond. He waited as his call was going through.

She said, "Should we, uh . . ." She was looking toward the closed door to her office. He knew what that meant. *Do you want your photographer in here for this?* she was asking. *Do you want to take photos and splash them all over the newspapers in a gaudy public display of your philanthropy?*

"Just one condition," he said. "This will be an anonymous donation. Are you okay with that?"

"I could use some lunch," Jerry Strand said.

Butch didn't reply.

It was well past the noon hour, and they still hadn't come up with a plan to get Nadine out of the house. They'd been tossing ideas back and forth, but nothing seemed to have any potential. There was always a flaw, and it usually involved a chance that Nadine would call the cops. Or that she might get hurt. Strand didn't want that. Only if they couldn't think of any other way.

Now they were parked in the main lot of Blanco State Park. Not much traffic here on a weekday. A good place to hide out, because Strand had to keep a low profile.

"You hear me?" he asked. "About lunch?"

"Just keep thinking," Butch said.

Strand was having a hard time concentrating, because he was so damn hungry. He was daydreaming about one of his wife's hamburgers. Say what you will about Nadine, but she could make a hell of a burger. Little pieces of onion and bell pepper in the patty. Strand was about to suggest a trip to the Dairy Queen drive-through when Butch leaned forward in his seat and his expression changed—like he'd had a breakthrough. "Okay. Okay. I think I got it. I got an idea. A good one."

"Yeah?"

"Hell, yeah. And we're doing this one, whether you like it or not."

25

NADINE STRAND COULDN'T help herself.

She knew she shouldn't be thinking of anything except her beloved husband of thirty-one years. She knew that she should be worried sick, and that she should be on her knees every spare minute of the day, imploring God for Jerry's safe return.

But . . .

She had to admit, having the house to herself was kind of nice. It was so peaceful. She didn't have to pack Jerry's lunch in the mornings or start dinner in the middle of Oprah. She didn't have to pick up his dirty socks or scrub the ring out of the bathtub. She didn't have to put the cap back on the toothpaste for him or lower the toilet seat or make a second pot of coffee because he liked his stronger.

All the same—despite the feeling that she could get used to this new lifestyle very quickly—when the phone rang and it was Jerry on the other end of the line, she was overcome by emotion. Relief, mostly, with only the slightest hint of disappointment.

She answered with an efficient "Strand residence," because it might be another newspaper reporter and she wanted to prove she could still put on a brave face.

What she heard in reply was, "Um . . . hello?"

She sprang up from the couch, where she'd been eating Chunky Monkey ice cream straight from the carton. "Oh my God! Jerry!"

"Who . . . who is this?"

"It's me, honey! Nadine! Where are you?"

"Nadine." He didn't sound quite right.

"Are you okay, Jerry? Are you in a hospital?"

"No. I don't think so. I don't know where I am."

Which seemed like an awfully peculiar response. But not half as strange as what he said next, which was:

"Uh, Nadine, this might sound like a stupid question, but . . . are you . . . are you my wife?"

For just an instant, Nadine was baffled. What kind of question was that? Was this a sick joke? If so, it was just plain sadistic! How could Jerry be so cruel at a time like—

Then it dawned on her. It was like Jack Snyder on *As the World Turns*. Or Michelle Bauer on *Guiding Light*. Or, going way back, Tad Martin on *All My Children*.

Jerry had amnesia!

"Jerry, honey, I need you to tell me where you are." For some reason, she was speaking very slowly.

"A pay phone."

"But where, exactly?"

"I think I'm in Blanco. That's where we live, right? Everything is so foggy."

Definitely amnesia. They didn't live in Blanco, they lived just outside Johnson City, thirteen miles to the north. But maybe he *was* in Johnson City and had the two towns confused.

"What do you see, Jerry? Any street signs?"

"I'm at a gas station. I was just walking near a river. There's a sign across the street. CJ'S PIZZA. Does that help?"

Blanco! He was in Blanco!

"You stay where you are. I'm going to call the police and—"

"No! Please. Don't call the police."

"But they've been looking for you."

"Nadine, I just want to come home. I don't remember much, but I think I remember our home, and I need to be there. Where I'll feel safe. Just for a little while. Let me have one night back home, then we can call the cops tomorrow."

He sounded so pitiful it just about broke Nadine's heart.

"Don't you move an inch," she said. "I'll come get you."

Jerry agreed, and with that, Nadine hustled outside to her car. It never occurred to her that, for a man who'd lost his memory, her husband hadn't had any trouble with his home phone number.

They'd decided to call from the Super S grocery store in Johnson City, because Nadine would drive right past it on her way to Blanco.

Before making the call, Strand had asked Butch to stop at a liquor store for a bottle of Wild Turkey, and he'd agreed. Maybe he wasn't such a bad guy after all. Strand was hoping the bourbon would calm his nerves, and it did, which gave him the guts to ask the question. Not *a* question, *the* question.

"Did Pringle kill Hollis?"

Strand thought it was strange the way it came out, nonchalant, like he was asking whether Butch thought it was going to rain later.

"Hell, no," Butch said. "Pringle's a pussy."

Strand remained quiet, just staring at Butch.

Butch finally looked over and got the message. "Hey, it wasn't me, either, if that's what you're thinking." He grabbed the bottle and took a big swig. Then he wiped his mouth and grinned. "Wasn't me. But I was there."

Strand was going to ask the next obvious question, of course, but right then Nadine drove past.

There were several methods by which to contribute money to Boothe Ministries, if one were so inclined. Credit card. Personal check. Money order. Western Union. PayPal. Of course, the ministry would happily accept more creative offerings: bearer bonds, stock certificates, bequests, trusts, you name it.

The bulk of the donations—a full eighty percent—came in via telephone or online transactions, but the remainder arrived from older viewers who still preferred the good old U.S. Postal Service, and a surprising number of them opted to send cash. Which was why Alex Pringle, as one of his first orders of business as executive director, had strictly limited access to the mailroom. Lest someone with a true heart be tempted, Pringle then installed a high-tech video monitoring system that would've made a Vegas blackjack dealer feel right at home. The cash—carefully counted, sorted, and banded—went directly into a safe each night, and the contents were whisked away to the bank by an armed guard on the last business day of the month.

In total, the combined donations to Boothe Ministries had topped an eye-popping $115 million annually for four years running. As a result, Boothe Ministries employed a veritable army of financial personnel—from common clerks and bean counters to battle-scarred investment analysts—to track, monitor, and manage its assets.

Every morning, these stern-faced men—they were all men— arrived at the high-rise in downtown Dallas and went straight to their cubes on the fourth floor. They wore charcoal suits over crisply starched white button-downs and sedate neckties. There was no jovial banter or watercooler gossip for these boys. They had serious work to tend to.

In short, these dedicated, loyal, hardworking employees were tasked with maximizing every cent that found its way into the Boothe coffers. After all, millions of dollars couldn't just lie around; it had to be *doing* something. And that something was earning even more money. There was a delicate balance to achieve, of course—one shouldn't put all his eggs in one basket— so the money tenders at Boothe Ministries parked cash in everything from short-term CDs to blue-chip stocks to high-yield bonds.

They were quite good at what they did, and, oh, how they loved to watch the money grow. It gave them a sense of purpose and accomplishment. It made them feel *alive*. Conversely, they were made quite uncomfortable when money flowed *outward*. Especially large sums of money. Especially when said money was simply given away. To charity.

The word alone—"charity"—was enough to give a Wharton MBA a premature ulcer. Which was why Alex Pringle—who had flown into Dallas's Love Field and was now waiting in line for a rental car—received a panicked phone call from T. Everett Farrell, the ministry's chief financial officer.

"I think Boothe's blown a gasket," Farrell said. "You need to talk to him ASAP."

"What's he doing?"

"Okay, get this. An hour ago, he called and wanted me to cut a check for two million dollars to the children's hospital. I tried to talk him out of it, or at least get him to reconsider the amount, but he insisted. So, okay, fine. It's a big chunk of change, but I figure we can get some national media play out of it. Dallas ministry saves sick children. That sort of thing. But then he tells me it's going to be an anonymous donation."

Jesus, one crisis after another, Pringle thought. *In the morning I'm cleaning a bloody motel room, in the afternoon my idiot boss is giving away the farm.* "Did he say—"

"Hold on, there's more. Just now, he calls me on his cell, riding back to the office, and says he wants me to cut a bunch of other checks. Half a mil to the homeless shelter. Half a mil to the battered women's center. A quarter million to some damn literacy program. This is a fucking catastrophe. He wants to teach people how to read!"

Pringle was suddenly very weary. How had everything gotten so fucked up so quickly? The Hollis Farley debacle. An angry bookie. A disappearing fossil. Getting screwed by Butch.

"You hear me, Alex?" Farrell asked.

"That's not good."

"Hell, no, not good! He can't just be giving money away left and right. Anonymous or not, word'll get around, and before you know it, we'll have a line out the front door—people sticking their greedy palms out. The Red Cross, Goodwill, PETA, Amnesty International. They'll be circling like vultures."

"Did he say why he was doing it?" Pringle asked, though he already had a theory forming in his head.

"Not a word. Just said he wants the checks to go out by the end of the day. You've got to do something. He listens to you. Can you talk some sense into him?"

Pringle sighed. "I can try. In the meantime, don't send a dime to anyone."

Butch steered the Cadillac up the driveway and slammed it into park behind Jerry Strand's truck, and they both quickly hopped out. They wouldn't have much time, because Nadine would almost certainly call the cops when she couldn't find Jerry.

Strand scurried up the walkway to the front door and, using

his good hand, reached into his pants pocket. And his heart dropped like a stone. "Oh, no. Oh, son of a bitch!"

"What?"

"My keys. I don't have my keys."

Butch had murder in his eyes. He also had a gun in his hand; not the .22, but a Glock nine-millimeter this time. Butch said, "Don't even joke—"

"These are your pants!"

"You idiot cocksucker. Are you sayin' your keys are in your pants in the motel room?"

"Don't blame it on me! We were in such a hurry—no, wait. Hold on. When you grabbed me on Sunday, I wouldn't have had them in my pocket."

"So where the fuck are they?"

Strand slammed his left palm against the door. He knew exactly where they were. Hanging on the Winnie-the-Pooh keyholder in the kitchen. "In the goddamn house."

Butch reached and tried the knob. It was locked. "We'll break a window."

"We've got an alarm system."

"Think she set it?"

Nadine had to be halfway to Blanco by now. "Fifty-fifty," Strand said. "She usually does, but today . . . maybe not, being in a hurry and everything."

Butch stepped into the yard and picked up a brick that was lining a flower bed.

"If the alarm goes off," Strand said, "the neighbors'll hear it. Plus, it dials the sheriff automatically. We won't have time to get in and get out."

"You got a better idea?"

Strand was sweating profusely. He couldn't come up with anything. He knew he never should've agreed to any of this.

"All right, then," Butch said. He stepped in front of a window and heaved the brick through.

Before the glass even hit the ground, the alarm began to drone.

"Well, fuck," Butch said. "Fuck! Fuck! Fuck!" He ran toward the Caddy.

Strand didn't move. He hadn't planned it, but now he realized he wasn't going anywhere. He'd had enough. No more lies, no more guns, no more dinosaur bones.

Butch looked back and saw him standing in place. "Come on!"

Strand shook his head. "I'm done."

Butch stopped. "You're *done?* The hell you are."

"You'd better go. Cops'll be here soon."

Butch raised the gun from fifteen yards away. "Let's go."

"No."

"Last warning. Get in the car. I fuckin' assure you I'm not kidding around."

Strand hung his head for a second, weighing his chances. "Okay," he said. "All right." He took a step, then another, then he wheeled and ran as fast as he could in the other direction. If he could just make the corner of the house, he'd be fine. Butch wouldn't chase him, not if he had any sense at all. Not with the cops on the way.

The corner of the house. That's all he needed.

Ten yards.

Five yards.

It was too far.

The bullet hit him in the back with the force of a sledgehammer, and down he went.

He heard a second shot, but he didn't feel it.

"Turns out Scott Underwood wasn't entirely forthcoming," Marlin said.

He was in Bobby Garza's office. The sheriff was at his desk, in the process of sorting through a long list of contributors to Greener Texas, a task that had consumed most of his time for the past twenty-four hours.

"Do tell," Garza said.

"Underwood was with someone else at the diner on Sunday morning, before Kate Wallace drove out to meet him, but he never mentioned it."

Garza put his pen down and leaned back in his chair. "That's interesting. Who was it?"

"Don't know yet. Younger guy. I'm guessing maybe a student. I got a description from one of the waitresses, and I'm fairly sure I saw the same kid outside Underwood's office yesterday afternoon. I had a hunch that it might be Underwood's assistant from last semester—this Victor Klein—but I pulled his photo and it wasn't him. So now I've got a five o'clock set up with Underwood, and I was wondering if you'd like to join me."

"Oh, yeah. Absolutely. You gotta wonder why Underwood left that part out. Good work."

"Could be nothing."

"Yeah, or maybe Underwood sent this kid after Hollis Farley."

"There's still the part about Underwood not knowing Farley's name. So how could he send anybody after him?"

"All we've got is Underwood's word on that. Maybe Farley did give his name, later, when they were alone in Underwood's office."

Marlin was willing to concede that point.

Garza said, "This young guy you saw—did he look strong enough to pull a bowstring back?"

"He was bigger than Underwood, that's for sure. And remember, when I said Underwood might not've been able to draw a bow, that was just a wild-ass guess."

Garza stayed quiet for several seconds, then said, "Your guesses are usually pretty sharp."

"Thanks."

"Okay, so we need to leave at about four?"

"Maybe a little earlier. Austin traffic."

"I'll be ready."

Marlin started to leave.

"How're the wedding plans going?" Garza asked.

Marlin shook his head. "It's gonna cost me twelve hundred for a wedding videographer."

Garza grinned. "Hell, I'll do it for half that and a case of beer."

"Little problem. You're in the wedding party, remember?"

At the Wal-Mart in Marble Falls, twenty minutes north of Johnson City, the man known as Snake approached a cashier and plopped several items on the counter.

Black shirt.

Black jeans.

Black sneakers.

Black socks.

Three cans of Pam.

"Wow," the cashier said. "You must really like black."

"It's what everybody's wearing this season," Snake replied. He'd come up with that line ahead of time.

Nicole was back in front of her computer, and this time she didn't go directly to a particular Web site. No, she wanted to cast a wider net and find out everything she could about Michael Kishner, something she should've done from the start. Again, it was fortunate that he had an unusual name, versus, say, David Miller.

She logged on to Google and typed: *michael-kishner.*

There were only forty-seven hits. The first two were unrelated:

one about a man who ran an auto-parts store in a small Kansas town, and the other, on one of those genealogy sites, about a man who died in 1896.

But the third hit, and the remaining forty-four, gave her what she was looking for.

Michael Kishner—the same man she'd met the day before, she was sure of it, because she was looking at a photo of him on her screen—was an actor. Not much of one—he certainly didn't make a living at it—but he'd had small parts in *Walker, Texas Ranger* and *Friday Night Lights*. Plus a couple of minor roles in B movies, including one called *Hell Hole*. The title rang a bell. Wasn't it filmed in Central Texas? Up near Llano?

She searched for *hell-hole movie*.

Everything fell into place when she saw who directed it.

26

BILLY DON HADN'T gotten out of bed by two o'clock, or by two thirty, or by three, and Red was going apeshit. He wanted another shot at the big man. Ask some more questions until he cracked, like a witness on one of those fancy lawyer shows.

Did you really ask Betty Jean if she had the bone?

You expect me to believe that? What are you leaving out?

Are you lying? Are you? Answer me!

Billy Don didn't have the smarts to stand up to Red's keen probing for long. Red would pick-pick-pick, like a vulture on a deer carcass, until he got the truth.

But first, he needed Billy Don to come out of the bedroom. Red had heard some moving around in there earlier—the bed frame creaking—like Billy Don was slowly waking up. Red wanted to speed the process along, and he had just the thing.

He went to the kitchen pantry and grabbed a pack of Orville Redenbacher's best stuff. He stuck it in the microwave, and three minutes later the trailer smelled like the lobby of a movie theater. Red dumped the fluffy, buttery popcorn into an empty KFC bucket he found on the counter, retreated to the living room, and sat in his La-Z-Boy. Then he waited. Wouldn't be long now.

It was, in fact, less than two minutes. Red heard Billy Don's bedroom door opening, then the sound of floorboards creaking, and here came Billy Don, like a bear drawn to fresh honey. He sat on the end of the couch closest to Red's chair. Glanced over at the popcorn but didn't say anything.

Some old comedy was on AMC. Had Jonathan Winters in it, plus Sid Caesar, Milton Berle, Spencer Tracy, Ethel Merman, Buddy Hackett, and Mickey Rooney. All of them chasing after a fortune they'd heard about from a dying thief. Strange how crazy these people got about money.

Red took a handful of popcorn and stuffed it in his mouth.

"I seen this one before," Billy Don said.

"Well, don't ruin it for me."

"He's fixin' to bust through that wall."

"I said don't ruin it." Another mouthful of popcorn.

Billy Don looked over at him. "Gonna share?"

"Thought you was eatin' dinner with Betty Jean."

"After a while."

"Ruin your appetite."

"I'll be all right."

Red handed him the bucket, and Billy Don dug in. Sure enough, Jonathan Winters smashed through the wall of a gas station. Left an outline of his body in the Sheetrock, like in a cartoon.

"Speaking of Betty Jean," Red said, "I was wondering if—"

"Don't wanna talk about it," Billy Don said sharply.

"But all I want to know is —"

"Can't you leave it alone? She don't know where the bone is, and that's that. End of story."

This wasn't working out too good. Billy Don wasn't fessing up, and Red was wondering what one of those tricky TV lawyers would do now. They always knew what to say next. Red finally asked, "Is that really the end of the story, or just the beginning? Hmm?"

Billy Don snorted. "I don't even know what that means."

"I don't think you're giving me all the facts."

"You think I'm lying?"

"You tell me."

"You think I'm trying to keep the bone for myself?"

"Is that what you're doing?"

Billy Don set the tub of popcorn aside, starting to get angry. "I can't believe you. Whyn't you let the poor woman grieve in peace? She lost her brother, in case you forgot."

Well, that sealed it. Billy Don wasn't fighting fair. Nothing Red could say now, not without looking like a grave robber. But he couldn't help noticing that Billy Don hadn't answered the question.

Bobby Garza reappeared in Marlin's doorway, looking dumbstruck.

"This is nuts. Ten minutes ago, we got an alarm call at Jerry Strand's house. So Ernie heads out, and not a minute later we get a call from Nadine Strand, who says her husband has amnesia and is wandering around in Blanco somewhere. And now Ernie just called, and Strand isn't in Blanco at all, he's lying in his front yard with a gunshot wound. Make sense out of all that for me."

"I wouldn't even know where to start."

"I've gotta get over there, so you're on your own with Underwood. Let me know what happens."

"How bad was Strand hurt?"

"He's not dead, that's all I know."

"And no idea who shot him?"

"Not a clue."

"That boy's name is Ojok, and he's from Zaire," Peter Boothe said, pointing at a photograph on his desk. "He has a cleft palate. A severe case. Not a pretty sight, is it?"

Not my problem, Alex Pringle thought. *And why, suddenly, is it yours?*

"There are thousands of kids like Ojok around the world," Boothe continued. "Can you imagine going through life with a disfigurement like that? Could you handle the embarrassment?"

The photograph had come from an elaborate portfolio that had been delivered to Boothe as a solicitation. The charity that sent it wanted a sizable donation, of course. Everybody wanted a donation. Boothe received dozens of such requests every week. He seldom paid them any heed.

"But we can help Ojok!" Boothe said. "Don't you see what we're capable of? All it takes is money, and, Praise God, we have plenty of it!" His eyes were actually glowing with passion.

He's coming unglued, Pringle thought. *His conscience is eating him alive.* Pringle couldn't understand the hypocrisy of it, the rationalization of right and wrong. Boothe's feelings of guilt were destroying him—so how had he managed to live like a king for all these years, without any apparent shame at all?

"May I say something?" Pringle asked.

Boothe wasn't listening. He was pointing at a second photo. "This little girl is Gabriela. Doesn't it break your heart?"

"You're overreacting," Pringle said. "Because of what happened in Blanco County."

That seemed to sink in. Boothe continued to sort through

the photos, but his demeanor changed. His head was lowered, almost as if in prayer.

"What's happening down there?" he asked cautiously.

Oh, well, there's a two-million-dollar dinosaur bone that I can't put my fucking hands on, Pringle thought. *Plus, Butch and I kidnapped Jerry Strand—hope you don't mind—and now I have no idea where either of them is.*

"I think everything's going to be fine," he said.

Peter Boothe nodded.

"Are you going to be okay?" Pringle asked.

Boothe nodded again.

Pringle was leaving when Boothe said, "I still want those checks to go out by the end of the day."

The EMTs had done what they could and were now preparing Jerry Strand for transport.

Garza kept his distance. You couldn't ask questions of a man whose eyes were rolled back in his head. Deputy Ernie Turpin was standing to Garza's left. There was a lone news van—KHIL stenciled on the side panel—parked on the county road. Those guys were always so damn fast.

"Was Strand conscious when you found him?" Garza asked.

Turpin shook his head. "He'd lost a lot of blood. They say he'll go straight into surgery."

"Where'd it hit him?"

"Below his left shoulder blade. Exited two inches below his left nipple."

Lung damage, probably, and Garza didn't know what else. Must've missed the heart, or Strand would be gone by now.

"Did you pass any vehicles on the way over here?" he asked.

"Not a one. They could've gone south. Could be way down the highway by now." Turpin pointed to a yellow evidence flag stuck into the soil five yards away. "I found brass from a nine-millimeter right over there. But the interesting thing is . . ." He pointed to another flag ten yards closer to the driveway. "There's another casing—also from a nine—right over there, along with several drops of blood."

Garza was puzzled for a second. "But no other blood between that flag and where Strand was lying?"

"Nope. I don't think he ran after he was hit. I think he fell straight down."

It was a big break. The shooter was wounded.

Marlin rode the elevator to the sixth floor, wondering if he might see Buddy Holly again, but he didn't. He walked down a hallway, turned left, and proceeded down a second hallway to Underwood's office.

Kate Wallace was behind her desk. "Oh, there you are. He just got back."

As if on cue, Scott Underwood appeared in his office doorway and waved Marlin in. He closed the door behind him and came around to his desk. They both sat down.

"Now what?" Underwood asked. "More questions about my storybook marriage?" He smiled thinly, but evidently he was still perturbed from their last conversation.

"Not this time, no. What I want to ask you is . . . when Kate drove out to Johnson City on Sunday morning, did she meet you inside the diner or out in the parking lot?"

"You came all the way over here to ask me that?"

"Just checking some details."

Underwood sighed deeply. "In the parking lot. I'd finished my breakfast, so I waited outside. It was a nice day."

"Where were you when you read the newspaper?"

He shook his head, frustrated. "Don't you people write anything down? We've gone over this. I've tried to be as accommodating as I can, but this is becoming a waste of time."

"I apologize for that. Please bear with me."

"I was in the diner, okay? Eating my breakfast. Where else? I certainly couldn't read it while I was riding my motorcycle."

Now Marlin dropped the bombshell. "Who was in the diner with you before Kate showed up?"

Underwood blinked several times. "Nobody. I don't know what you're talking about."

Marlin stared at him, but Underwood stared right back.

"A younger guy," Marlin said. "Wearing glasses with thick black frames. Styles his hair in something called a faux-hawk."

Now the professor was waving his hand back and forth, dismissing the statement altogether. "Ridiculous. I don't know where you got that information, but it's wrong."

"In fact," Marlin said, "I saw the same guy in this building yesterday morning. He was waiting for the elevator on this floor. I'm betting he had just come to see you."

Underwood was shaking his head, staring at his desktop.

"You lied to me, Professor Underwood. And that makes me wonder who this other guy is and whether he was involved. You don't have to tell me who he is, but it won't take me long to find out. In fact, I bet Kate knows. We could ask her."

"I . . . I don't . . ."

Marlin started to rise. "Let's call her in here."

"Okay," Underwood said softly. "Okay. Jesus. Enough."

Marlin sat back down and waited. He noticed that Underwood's face had turned a bright red.

"His name is Terry Stewart. He's a student of mine."

"A current student?"

"Yes."

"And why did he meet you at the diner?"

"It had nothing to do with Hollis Farley. Trust me. Can't we please leave it at that?"

"I'm afraid not."

"If I tell you, I'll be risking my career. My reputation."

Marlin suddenly knew what was coming, and it made him slightly uncomfortable. But he had to hear it. "If you haven't done anything illegal, I'll do my best to keep it between us. But you need to tell me the truth."

Underwood cupped his face in his hands and rubbed his forehead for a long time. When he put his hands down, he had the blank expression of a man who'd just walked away from a bad car wreck. "Terry and I have a personal relationship."

That was all he said.

"You sleep together."

The professor leaned his head back until it touched the back of his chair. "Yes, we sleep together. We're lovers."

"Why was he at the diner?"

"You're going to ruin me with this."

"Not if it's the truth."

"I've never done anything like this with a student before. Or any man."

"None of that matters to me. Why was he at the diner?" Marlin needed Underwood to commit to a story.

"We were at the Best Western next door," he said. "I saw the newspaper article and it freaked me out. So I called Kate while Terry was in the shower. When he got out, he could tell that something was wrong. So I told him everything . . . about Farley coming to see me. He advised me to keep my mouth shut and forget about it, because something like this would eventually happen. But I couldn't."

Marlin felt certain that Underwood was telling the truth. "You did the right thing," he said.

Underwood remained quiet for several moments, and Marlin didn't press him. When Underwood spoke again, his voice was filled with regret. "Terry was supposed to go home, but he came over to the diner because he had an idea. He said I should call in with an anonymous tip. I should've listened to him."

"Is there a university rule against . . . what you've done?"

"Not specifically, no. But this . . . they'll find a way to get rid of me."

"I'll try to—"

"Don't kid yourself. It'll get out, one way or another. When you catch who did it, I'll have to testify."

Underwood was right. The defense attorney might even point the finger at the professor in an effort to create reasonable doubt. In that case, Underwood's tryst would almost certainly become part of the court record. There wasn't anything Marlin could do to prevent it.

"I need you to take me to Terry Stewart."

"Now?"

Marlin nodded. If the story was a fabrication, Marlin couldn't give Underwood and Stewart a chance to confer. If Marlin left Underwood here, he'd be on the phone immediately.

"My wife's going to divorce me," he said.

Marlin didn't know what to say. He rose out of the chair.

Underwood stood, too, and came around the desk. Marlin opened the office door, and Kate Wallace looked up at him. He wondered if she'd overheard any of the conversation.

Underwood stopped at her desk. "I have to leave now. I won't be back until tomorrow morning."

Kate nodded but didn't say anything. She seemed to understand that something unusual was taking place.

Marlin moved out into the hallway. That was his only mistake, but it was a big one. He should've let Underwood lead the way. Because the professor stopped abruptly and said, "I forgot my wallet."

Before Marlin could react, Underwood quickly turned and went back into his office. He closed the door. And Marlin could hear the lock sliding into place.

He hurried to the door and banged on it. "Professor Underwood!"

He heard a noise. A window sliding upward.

Marlin backed up, raised his right foot, and slammed it against the door. It held fast.

He spun to face Kate, who had risen to her feet. "Do you have a key?"

She shook her head. Her face was tight with fear. "What's happening?"

Marlin raised his foot again. Drove it into the door. No luck. "Underwood! Don't do it!"

He kicked again, and again, and now he could hear wood splintering. The frame was finally starting to give.

Behind him, Kate was starting to wail.

"Underwood! Wait!"

He backed up, got some momentum, and slammed his shoulder into the door, which swung open and crashed against the wall.

The small office was empty.

And Marlin began to hear screams from six stories below.

27

THE SECOND SHOT had torn the better part of Butch Theriot's right ear off.

Talk about piss-poor luck.

He'd taken the shot at Strand because he simply couldn't help himself. It was pure reflex, like a dog chasing anything that runs. Strand bolted, and Butch hadn't had time to think, so he'd squeezed one off. Strand fell. Dead or alive? Who the fuck knows? Was he even hit? Sure looked like it.

That's when Butch decided it was time to get the hell out of Dodge. He turned to sprint for the car, tripped on the edge of the sidewalk, and—*boom!*—his ear was now a ragged pulp of tissue. A big chunk of it was hanging loose. Hurt like a son of a bitch, and it wouldn't quit bleeding.

When Butch had squealed away in the Cadillac, he'd immediately driven south, the opposite direction they'd come from earlier. Away from the cops. Then he began to worry about getting lost, because he didn't know these little county roads well enough to find the highway. The Caddy had a GPS navigation system, but he'd never learned how to use it, and now wasn't the time for a lesson.

Then he saw an old barn.

Abandoned, it looked like. Out in the middle of nowhere, like a goddamn oasis. Butch's ear was gushing, and he was still in panic mode, so he whipped a right turn through a gap in the fence and followed an overgrown caliche road to the barn. Hopped out and peeked inside. Plenty of room for the Caddy.

Now he was safely parked inside, and he figured he'd stay right here until . . . well, until what? Now he had some breathing room and he could think.

He couldn't hang around for long, could he? Not now, seeing as how he might've killed a guy. Problem was, he just didn't have enough information. It was possible that Strand was still alive, and that meant . . .

What the hell did that mean?

Well, if Butch was in Strand's shoes, he'd keep his damn mouth shut, or stick with the amnesia story. Because now, through pure dumb luck, Strand had the fossil all to himself again. He could cash in and kiss his wife good-bye.

On the other hand, what if Strand *was* dead? How would anybody know who'd done it? They wouldn't. The cops didn't know who'd kidnapped him, so they wouldn't know who killed him, either. Right?

So Butch had a choice to make. Did he have the *cojones* to stick around? When it came down to it, it was awfully hard to let the money go.

He turned the rearview mirror so he could get a better look at his ear.

"Aw, fuck me."

Looked like he'd gone several rounds with Mike Tyson.

It had been so long since Billy Don Craddock had gotten laid, whenever he tried to replay the last time in his head, it was like looking back at an old home movie. Things were sort of hazy, and he couldn't remember all the details.

But tonight, if he'd read the signals right, that was going to change. Tonight he was going to get lucky. Best of all, it was going to happen with a girl he cared about a lot.

In preparation, Billy Don had pulled out all the stops. For example, not only had he brushed his teeth, he'd actually flossed and gargled. Then he'd taken a good hot shower, scrubbing himself from head to toe, and he washed his hair twice.

After he toweled off, he put on a thick layer of roll-on deodorant, then shaved real close and slathered his face with some Old Spice aftershave that had been in the medicine cabinet for years.

I've got a big surprise for you, Betty Jean had said yesterday. *Something Hollis left behind. I think you're gonna like it.*

Billy Don didn't care about that anymore, even though it lingered in the back of his mind.

He'd considered shaving his back, but that would've required an extra set of hands, and he wasn't quite prepared to ask Red for that kind of help.

But he'd plucked some protruding nose hairs, and a few strays between his eyebrows, and a couple on his earlobes, and now he felt fairly presentable.

It had been a long time since he'd felt this way. Not since opening day of deer season. Oh, man, it was going to be great.

* * *

Or maybe it wasn't, because when he got to Betty Jean's house, she was crying. Just sitting on the porch swing, her eyes all red and puffy, dabbing at her face with a tissue.

When Billy Don came up the steps with a fistful of flowers he'd plucked from the highway median (why pay good money for a bouquet when Mother Nature was giving them away for free?), Betty Jean tried to smile, but she didn't do a very good job.

"You okay?" he asked.

She nodded and patted the seat of the swing beside her. He sat down, and the support chains gave a little groan in protest. He could only hope the chains were anchored in something sturdy.

Neither of them said anything for a while.

It was nice, sitting there without talking. He didn't know what to do—reach out and hold Betty Jean's hand?—but it wasn't awkward, it was comfortable, like old friends passing the time.

Finally, Betty Jean said, "I had everything ready in the kitchen, the roast in the oven, so I came out here to cool off. Then I started thinking about Hollis."

That made sense to Billy Don. Hollis had only been dead for five days, and it took longer than that to get over someone who'd passed away. Heck, Billy Don had grieved longer over a hunting dog he'd had in his younger days.

"He was a good man," he said softly.

Betty Jean sniffed. "Yeah, in his way, he really was. Not the smartest bull in the herd, but he had a good heart. He used to . . ." Betty Jean was getting choked up again. Her lower lip was quivering. "He used to come over and cut my grass. That was our deal. I cleaned his house, and he cut my grass."

Billy Don put an arm around Betty Jean's shoulders. The truth was, he was starting to get a little teary-eyed himself. "He's in a better place now," he said. He'd heard people express similar notions at the funeral.

Betty Jean laughed. "Lord, I hope so. Some of the things he done, you just never know. In fact . . ."

She shook her head. Whatever she'd been planning to say, she'd changed her mind.

"What?" Billy Don asked.

"Well . . ." She laughed again. "I shouldn't be telling you this, but do you know Perry Grange?"

Billy Don remembered the name. Her uncle, Buzz, had mentioned it. Betty Jean's previous boyfriend. "Heard of him," he said.

Betty Jean turned to face him, and she had a look on her face like she'd just heard a good joke. "See, Hollis was mad at Perry for reasons I won't even go into, and Perry runs one of them deer farms. He was selling a bunch of fawns—more than his herd could turn out, according to Hollis—so Hollis ended up calling the game warden on him."

Billy Don couldn't imagine such a thing. Calling the game warden? That was something city folks did when they heard shots in the suburbs. On the other hand, Buzz had said that Perry Grange had broken Betty Jean's heart. Something like that might make a brother seek revenge.

"But Hollis never knew for sure about the fawns?" he asked.

"Not for absolute certain, no."

"That's cold."

"Oh, I know—but Perry's a real asshole." She was giggling.

And he didn't blame her, because it *was* funny.

So he started laughing, too, and he thought they were having a fine old time, when suddenly Betty Jean started crying again. Was that confusing, or what? *Don't even try to figure a woman out,* Red had cautioned him once. *Won't do no good, and you'll only wind up with a headache.*

"I miss him," she said. "I miss him so much."

He assumed she was talking about Hollis, not Perry.

He pulled her closer, and she laid her head on his shoulder.

"He's in the arms of the Lord," he said. More stuff he'd heard at the funeral.

Her nose was all snotty, and she wiped at it. "I know."

"And you know what?" he said. "I'll come over and cut your grass for you. Tomorrow afternoon. I'd be happy to."

She pulled away and looked at him, and now she was positively beaming, but she was also blubbering and bawling at the same time. It was almost spooky. "You're an angel, Billy Don. Now come on inside. Remember when I said I had a surprise for you?"

"It had to've been amnesia," Nadine Strand said confidently. "He could hardly even remember who I was! What other explanation can there be?"

She doesn't get it, Bobby Garza thought. The phone call. The brick through the window. Jerry Strand had lured his wife away from their home, and Garza could think of only one reason he might do that. And Strand had had an accomplice or a captor, obviously, because he hadn't shot himself in the back.

So who was it? And how had the shooter gotten wounded? Henry Jameson was outside right now, processing the scene. A type test had confirmed that the blood droplets nearer the driveway had come from somebody other than Jerry Strand.

"Mrs. Strand, do you have caller ID?"

She frowned. "What on earth do we need that for? We just answer the phone like normal people."

They were sitting at the kitchen table, where she had already pointed out Jerry Strand's key ring hanging on a peg by the door. He hadn't had his keys; hence the need to break in.

Garza had an idea. He went to the phone on the counter and dialed *69. It rang seventeen times, and just as Garza was ready to give up, a man answered with a tentative "Hello?"

"This is Sheriff Bobby Garza with the Blanco County Sheriff's Department. Who am I speaking to, please?"

"Uh, Walt Conley."

"Okay, Walt, where are you right now?"

"Seriously?"

"Yes, please."

"The pay phone outside the Super S."

"The one in Johnson City?"

Had to be; *69 wouldn't work on long distance calls. Walt confirmed it. Garza thanked him and hung up.

"I really should get to the hospital," Nadine Strand said.

"One last question. Do you mind if we search your house?"

It wasn't what Billy Don expected. Not even close.

It was a television. One of those huge suckers they sell at the discount stores. It took up one full corner of Betty Jean's living room.

"Some of my cousins helped me move it a few days ago in my truck," Betty Jean explained. "Then, when you and me, uh, got together last night, I figured we'd have our own movie night, right here on my couch. It's got stereo sound and everything. I rented *True Grit*, because that was Hollis's favorite. Is that okay? You like John Wayne, don't you?"

She was looking at him expectantly. She was the sweetest woman he'd ever laid eyes on.

"That sounds great," he said.

She stood, took his hand, and led him inside. He left the flowers on the swing, but he didn't think it mattered.

A television. Not a valuable dinosaur fossil.

Billy Don was thrilled.

By nine o'clock, Garza had found nothing. He and Ernie Turpin had searched the Strand house thoroughly. No fossil. Garza had felt certain it would be in there somewhere, but it wasn't.

They were outside now, leaning against Garza's cruiser, drinking bottled water. The KHIL news guys had finally left after Garza had given them the barest of details. *One man shot, condition serious, assailant unknown.*

"What about the garage?" Turpin asked.

Garza had been thinking about that. But the garage was separate from the house, with a breezeway in between. If the fossil was in the garage, why would Strand break a window into the house? Didn't make sense. This case had been like chasing wisps of smoke, and he was tired of it.

"No, let's pack it in," he said.

The library didn't have an alarm system, and the lock on the door was a piece of crap, so Snake was inside in seconds. Guided by a small flashlight, he went straight to the circulation desk, rifled through the drawers, and found a folder filled with blue slips. Everything from the current month. Perfect. Too easy.

He was tempted to take the entire folder and haul ass, but his instincts told him that would be stupid. Why leave any indication that he'd been here? All he needed was a name, and all he had to do was compare the sign-in forms with the dates and times of the e-mails Darwin Parker had received.

So Snake started thumbing through the folder, and in less than two minutes, he had it. A cakewalk. Ten grand, baby! Now he could leave, maybe go somewhere and celebrate, but . . .

While he was here, shouldn't he go ahead and hack the computer the guy used? See if the library used blocking software? Snake figured he might learn something useful. Something Darwin Parker would pay more cash for. No reason not to. The whole town was already asleep. He had plenty of time.

*   *   *

The doorbell in Alex Pringle's three-thousand-square-foot condo rang at ten fifteen, and when he looked through the peephole, he saw Omar's giant, bald head.

Pringle stood perfectly still. He wished he hadn't turned the stereo on earlier. Then again, some people leave the stereo on when they're gone to ward off burglars.

The doorbell rang again.

Pringle was holding his breath. His heart was pounding. As far as Omar knew, Pringle was still out of town. Thank God his Cadillac wasn't in the parking garage.

It rang once more, then Omar spoke through the door: "Listen, motherfucker. You in there? I'm bein' civilized so far, you unnerstand? But when you tell me you stayin' at the Holiday Inn, then my boy drive all the way down there and see they *ain't* no Holiday Inn . . . shit, and you won't answer your cell . . . that seem like you duckin' me. That all right, I catch up with you *real* soon. Me and you gonna talk, Alex Pringle. You hear? We mos' definitely gonna talk."

After a few seconds, Pringle heard heavy footsteps receding down the hallway, then the ding of the elevator arriving. He went for a bottle of scotch, hands quaking as he poured.

There were questions, of course. Lots of them. For several hours, Marlin had to play the role of witness, not investigator.

He had to tell the story—the *entire* story, not just today's events—five times to different members of the university police and the Austin police. They'd taken him to a small brick building on the campus.

They questioned Kate Wallace, too, and they allowed Marlin to sit in. Then Underwood's wife showed up, looking distraught but in control. She didn't ask many questions of her own. They told her what had happened, but not why. In time, they would.

Eventually, they were done with Marlin. He'd hung around,

hoping they'd locate Terry Stewart, but they couldn't reach him. His roommate said he was out of town. Didn't know where. Maybe back home in Uvalde.

Marlin got home after midnight. Earlier, he'd called Nicole and told her what had happened. He'd said it would be a late night and she should go home and get some sleep—but she was waiting in his kitchen for him.

The first thing she said, after hugging him, was, "It's not your fault."

He shook his head. "Yeah, but I could've stopped him."

"It's hot in here," Tiffany whined, her voice muffled. "And I can't see anything. He forgot the eyeholes."

"Shh," Darwin Parker whispered. "Remember what I told you: Dinosaurs can't speak."

"Well, they must notta been able to breathe, neither."

Ventilation issues aside, the coelurosaur suit was a reasonable success. Parker was nude, and he had a raging erection. It was the perfect distraction—exactly what he needed. After all, it was two o'clock in the morning and he still hadn't heard from Snake.

"If you're gonna do me, could we get the show on the road?"

"This won't take long," Darwin said. He didn't mention that he was anticipating a second round. Possibly a third.

"Can't I at least take the head off? I could be, like, half woman and half lizard."

"A coelurosaur is *not* a lizard!" Darwin snapped. His erection waned a bit, though it was still impressive. "Now, do something. Move around a little. Act like you're pursuing a small mammal. Imagine that your very survival depends on capturing it."

She took one ungainly step forward and tripped over an ottoman.

COFFEE STAINS.

Martha Crain couldn't believe it. She'd taken Jeff Abbott's newest thriller home the previous evening, and she'd discovered coffee stains on the third page of chapter nine.

Someone had not only had the audacity to read and drink coffee at the same time—a disaster waiting to happen—but had returned the book as if it hadn't been damaged. The sneak! Well, she'd see about that, wouldn't she? It wouldn't be difficult to track down the most recent borrower.

She stormed into the library on Wednesday morning, switching on the lights as she went. She went straight to the circulation desk. That's where she'd find the name of the perpetrator. She'd send a stern reprimand, outlining the infraction and asking for remuneration to the tune of—

She saw something that brought her to an abrupt halt.

Her birdlike heart fluttered in her chest. Her anger melted, replaced by fear.

Somebody was in the library. An intruder!

He was right over there, at one of the reading tables. His head was resting on the tabletop, and he was snoring. Martha began to turn, with the intention of driving straight to the police station, less than a minute away.

But wait. She tilted her head. Was that who she thought it was? The wastrel who'd visited the library the day before? The one who'd wanted to use the computers but didn't have a library card? She took a few tentative steps closer for a better look, and yes, it was the same young man.

What in heaven's name was he doing here?

She knew she should leave, but she couldn't help herself. She stepped even closer. *I feel like Miss Marple,* she thought. *Investigating a mystery.*

There were dozens of blue forms scattered across the table. Computer sign-in forms. What did he want with those?

Stranger still, near the man's cheek was a glue stick, which Martha used to attach date-due slips inside the front covers of books. The slips were available in a self-adhesive version, but Martha preferred doing it the old-fashioned way.

The man's eyes popped open. He was looking right at her.

Martha's knees began to buckle.

He raised his head. A blue sheet was stuck to his face.

For the second morning in a row, Billy Don Craddock woke up fully clothed. And it didn't bother him a bit.

He and Betty Jean had eaten dinner, then watched the movie, then talked—yeah, just talked—far into the night. About all kinds of stuff. Not just bullshit, like the conversations he had with Red, but *real* stuff, like their jobs, and where they'd grown up, and dreams they had for the future. It got late, and both of them started yawning, and the next thing Billy Don knew, he was waking up. Still on the couch, sunlight coming through the blinds, with Betty Jean snuggled up against him.

He had to pee something fierce, and he tried to get up without waking her, but it didn't work. She started moving around, and her eyes came open, and she stretched like a cat. She looked at him and smiled.

"You want breakfast?" she asked. "Ham and eggs?"

I could get used to this, he thought. *Real quick.*

Jerry Strand was having a conversation with Hollis Farley, or re-membering one, he wasn't sure which.

Farley said, "It looked like rain again, so I dug it up."

They'd talked about digging it up together, but Strand didn't make an issue of it. "How'd it go?"

"Smoother'n shit through a goose. The ground was good and soft. When I got it home, I took a little brush and removed all the dirt. It was like working on an old deer skull."

"Was the whole thing there?"

Part of the fossil had been buried, and they'd wondered if the bottom half was as flawless as the top half.

"It's perfect. Like something in a museum."

Strand didn't point out that Hollis had never been to a mu-seum in his life. "Where is it now?" he asked.

Hollis grinned. "Got it tucked away someplace safe."

Strand let a moment pass, then said, "I got a suggestion, okay? Let me keep it at my place. Your trailer ain't safe."

"Safe enough."

"Hollis, we're talking about *two million bucks.*"

Hollis Farley opened his mouth and a strange rhythmic

beeping sound came out. Hollis faded away, right before Strand's eyes.

Something smelled like vomit.

Pain. He was aware of pain.

And footsteps in a tiled hallway.

Butch.

Who was Butch? *Oh, Jesus, he's the guy who shot me.*

He opened his eyes—just a slit, because that's all he could manage—and there was Nadine. Sitting in a chair, reading a book. With bears on the cover.

He closed his eyes again, before she caught him looking.

He'd told a fib, and he had to remember what it was.

Butch Theriot had slept in jail cells that weren't as comfortable as the backseat of the Caddy. Of course, he'd had to sleep mostly on his left side, because of his right ear. Didn't want to roll over on it. The damn thing still throbbed, like when you smash your thumb with a framing hammer.

Other than that, things were looking up.

He'd been listening to a regional radio station overnight, and he'd learned that Jerry Strand wasn't dead. The first few reports mentioned an unnamed victim in critical condition. The most recent report, early this morning, gave Jerry Strand's name, saying he was stable after surgery.

The question was, had Strand ratted Butch out? If the cops knew Butch's identity, they would've warned the public, right? They hadn't, and that meant nobody was looking for him.

He decided to give it a few more hours, just in case.

Bobby Garza put his feet up on his desk, clasped his hands across his belly, and said, "Not your fault. Beat yourself up all you want, but it was Underwood's decision, not yours."

"Shoulda walked out behind him," Marlin said.

"What're you, a mind reader?"

"Apparently not."

Garza sat quietly and drank some coffee. They'd decided to work side by side until they had this case solved—or until it became obvious they couldn't solve it.

"This case sucks," Marlin announced.

"Come on, now. We're getting close."

"I feel completely lost."

"You have to be an optimist. The glass is half full."

"Yeah, of hemlock."

It was eight forty. They were waiting for nine o'clock.

"You think Underwood was telling the truth?" Garza asked.

"We won't know until we talk to Terry Stewart."

Garza crossed his arms and stared at the wall. "Okay, let's leave Underwood out of the mix for a minute. It's gotta be Strand, right? Him and whoever shot him. Let's say Hollis Farley found the bone, and he told Strand about it, then they both discovered how valuable it was. Strand killed Farley to keep the money for himself."

"So who shot Strand? How did a third party get involved?"

"If we're lucky, when Strand comes around, we'll get some answers. I'd also like to know how the shooter got wounded."

"You know," Marlin said, "Underwood said he didn't think Farley knew what the fossil was worth. Meaning he hadn't contacted any dealers or collectors."

"Yeah?"

"Well, Farley had six days to figure that out after he met with Underwood. What if he made contact with somebody in that time? Somebody who wanted the fossil but didn't have money."

"Good theory, but if that's what happened, we literally don't have a clue. He hadn't gone out of town recently, and we don't have any evidence of anyone coming to see him. We checked his phone records. Nothing there."

"Maybe he sent an e-mail."

"He didn't own a computer."

"Could've used someone else's. Does his sister have one?"

"Yeah, but she said Hollis hadn't been to her place in a couple of weeks. Look, I'm not saying you're wrong, I'm just saying that Strand—or whoever shot Strand—looks a lot more likely at this point than an anonymous killer."

Marlin nodded his agreement. Garza was right. You had to go where the evidence pointed you.

"Let's go on over," Garza said. "Maybe he's early."

When Michael Kishner exited his driveway, heading west, Nicole fell in behind him. He took a right on South First, and so did she. She was surprisingly calm. Eager, even. This was going to be fun. He stopped at the light at Oltorf, and she pulled up next to him. Honked the horn.

When he looked over, his expression was priceless. Total shock. His window was up, so she signaled with her hand.

Pull over.

"I spoke to your assistant manager about an hour ago," Bobby Garza said. "And he told me I need to talk to you."

Doyle Cook was the store manager. Fortyish, heavily freckled, with rust-colored hair. Wearing a blue-and-yellow tie. The official Super S colors.

"What can I help you with?"

They were in Cook's office—a musty, windowless space in the back of the store, tucked in a corner near the loading dock. It smelled like old bananas.

"You run security video here," Garza said. Marlin and Garza had noted two exterior cameras on their way inside.

"Yep."

"That includes the parking lot."

"Most of it."

"Do either of the cameras cover the pay phones?"

"I think so, yeah. One of them does. What's going on? Did something happen on our lot?"

"A man made a call from one of those phones yesterday at about two forty-five. I'd like to see the tape."

"Actually, it's not tape, it's digital. All on hard drive."

"That's fine," Garza said. "Can we see it?"

Cook looked like he wanted to ask questions, but he didn't. He said, "Sure, let's take a look," then swiveled his chair and faced his computer. "You said two forty-five?"

They parked side by side at a convenience store, and Nicole hopped into the passenger seat of Michael Kishner's car.

"Thanks for stopping."

He gave her a sheepish smile. "Nicole, wow, you really freaked me out back there. I wasn't expecting to see you."

Yeah, I bet.

"Sorry. I needed to talk to you, but I forgot to ask for your cell number yesterday, and I didn't feel comfortable calling your home number. In case your wife answered."

She could see it in his face—panic at the idea that she might call his house.

"I don't blame you," he said. "What, uh, what's going on? How did you know where I live?"

"Phone book."

"Oh, right."

He's the actor, but it's my turn to put on a show. "Look, this is tough, but I've got some bad news for you."

He frowned. "Okay."

"After we talked yesterday, it occurred to me that my fiancé was in Austin right that very minute. He said he had a meeting at headquarters, but I started to wonder if he was hooking up with your wife. So I looked up your address, then I went over to your house, and I did the same thing I did this morning. I sat and watched."

She was taking a chance. If Kishner had gone home after their lunchtime meeting, her ruse wouldn't work. But she was betting that his so-called acting career didn't pay the bills and he had a nine-to-five job somewhere. He didn't reply.

Nicole said, "Eventually, your wife came out, and it really threw me at first, because her hair was a little darker than the photo you showed me. She must use highlights, huh?"

Nicole had to act like she couldn't distinguish between the real Susan Kishner and the woman in the photo. He nodded.

"Anyway," Nicole said, "I don't want to sound like a psycho or anything, but I followed her."

Kishner had gone pale. "You followed her?"

"Yep. Right to the La Quinta at Ben White and I-35."

He was shaking his head slightly now, totally confused. Nicole was loving it.

"Here's the hard part," she said. "She met someone . . . but it wasn't John. It wasn't my fiancé. Get what I'm saying? I hate to tell you this, but it looks like your wife is cheating on you with two different men."

His face was a mask of disbelief. "No way. No . . . I—"

"She went into a room, and I waited a few minutes, then I snuck up to the window and peeked between the curtains. It was some short guy with gray hair and a mustache. I couldn't see him clearly, because your wife, well, she was on top, and—"

"No! You're wrong!"

She acted like she was taken aback. "I know it hurts," she said, "but I'm a little confused. I mean, come on. You knew she was cheating on you with one man, so it shouldn't come as a surprise there's a second."

Kishner was moaning now, rubbing his forehead with one hand. "I can't fucking believe this. I married a slut."

Nicole was tempted to let the charade continue. Let him go home, make false accusations, and leave his marriage in tatters. But she stuck with the plan. She still had her car keys in her hand. Attached to the key ring was a can of pepper spray. Good to have, because who knew how he'd react to the truth?

She said, "Fortunately for you, I'm lying."

A pause. Then he looked at her as if she'd just flown in from Jupiter. "Do what?"

"It's a lie. Like the one you told me yesterday."

His reaction could've made the highlight reel from one of those hidden-camera shows. His mouth fell open. His eyes bugged. He made strange sounds but couldn't seem to form complete words. Then it finally sank in, and he tilted his head back against the headrest, muttering, "Oh my God, oh my God, oh my God . . ."

"Now you know how it feels."

"Oh my God."

"Makes you want to curl up and die, doesn't it?"

He didn't respond. She gave him some time.

He finally brought his head down, but he wouldn't look at her. He was breathing noisily through his nose. "What now?"

"Simple. You're going to tell me the full story, starting with Harry Grange."

29

"THERE HE IS," Bobby Garza said.

Jerry Strand had just walked up to the pay phones. He was alone, wearing sunglasses and a ball cap pulled low. The time code read 2:51 P.M. The view also revealed a small wedge of the parking lot.

The three men watched silently.

On-screen, Strand removed the receiver, put some coins into the slot, and punched in a number. He was using one hand exclusively, because, as they'd learned, several fingers on his right hand were broken. A few seconds after dialing, Strand was having a conversation. A woman walked past with two kids in tow. Strand turned his back toward them. Being cautious.

Near the end of the call, Strand shook his head. Marlin figured that was in response to his wife saying she was going to call the police.

Then Strand hung up and quickly walked out of the frame.

That was it.

"Does that help?" Cook asked.

"It does," Garza said. "Can we check the other camera?"

"I don't think it covers the pay phones."

"That's okay. I want to see more of the lot, to see if he arrived in a vehicle."

"Gotcha." Cook scrolled through a menu, did some typing, and a new window popped up. Now they were seeing from the second camera's perspective. It was aimed diagonally across the parking lot. The time code read 2:50 P.M.

Less than a minute later, a long black car eased along the far side of the lot and stopped in a space near the pay phones. It would've been just out of the first camera's range.

"Sure looks like a Cadillac roadster to me," Garza said with apparent satisfaction.

He knows whose car it is, Marlin thought. *But he won't say in front of Doyle Cook.* Marlin could feel the excitement building inside his chest. Garza was right. They were getting close.

The glare of sunlight on the windshield concealed the interior of the vehicle, but the passenger door opened and Jerry Strand stepped out. He hurried toward the pay phones, out of camera range. The car sat. A short time later, Strand came back and climbed into the car.

Nothing happened. The car didn't move.

They're waiting for Nadine Strand to drive past.

Nobody said anything. After two minutes, Doyle Cook said, "You want me to fast-forward it a little?"

"As long as we can see the action," Garza said.

"No problem. This program has all the bells and whistles." Cook punched a single key; the car remained motionless, but Marlin noticed that people coming and going from the store were moving quickly, in herky-jerky fashion. "This is three times faster than normal," Cook said.

Finally, at 3:03, the car appeared to squeal out of its parking spot, right toward the camera, then it was gone.

"I'll back it up," Cook said. He punched another button, and the car came back into the frame in reverse. Then another button, and the car moved forward normally.

"Can you freeze it?" Garza asked. "Right there."

The moment had passed, and now all you could see was the Cadillac's roof, but Cook did his magic and the car went backward again, one video frame at a time.

"There," Garza said again.

The glare on the glass still hid the driver, but the license plate number was easy to make out.

It wasn't very complicated. Harry Grange had told Michael Kishner that John Marlin was corrupt.

"Harry said a competing breeder paid your fiancé to hassle Perry. It ruined Perry's business."

Total bullshit, but how would Kishner know that?

"And Harry wanted revenge."

"Yeah."

"So he thought, 'Hey, I know a bunch of actors. I can use that to my advantage.'"

Michael Kishner was staring at his dashboard. Remorseful. Or maybe he was just acting again. He nodded.

"And you knew Harry Grange from *Hell Hole,*" Nicole said.

"Actually, I knew him before that. We went to high school together. We're not close friends, but we've kept in touch."

"You know Perry, too?"

"Vaguely. He was a couple years older than Harry and me. Haven't seen him in years."

"Was Perry involved in this?"

"Not as far as I know. I don't think so."

"What did Harry offer you?"

"Huh?"

"Why'd you do it? Don't tell me you did it for nothing."

Kishner sighed heavily. "A decent role in his next film."

Nicole tapped the photo Kishner had shown her yesterday. It had been in his glove compartment. "Who's this woman?"

"No idea. Probably some actress."

Nicole could guess how it had happened. The blonde had found John in town somewhere. Approached him, struck up a conversation, maybe flirted a little. John wouldn't flirt back, but he'd be too gentlemanly to rebuff her completely. Maybe she concocted a story—a reason to speak to him. Then, quite suddenly, she kissed him. Someone was nearby with a camera. Maybe one of her friends.

Nicole studied the photo. Now that she knew the story, she realized there was a hint of surprise in John's eyes. The blonde was kissing him, but he wasn't kissing back. How had she missed that earlier?

Nicole said, "I could make your life hell, you know that?"

Kishner nodded.

"But I won't. With one condition."

"What?"

"Don't say a word to Harry Grange."

Darrell Bridges ran the plate, and it came back to Boothe Ministries, Inc., just as Bobby Garza had said it would.

"That's the same car I saw Alex Pringle driving at Farley's funeral," he said. He and Marlin had returned to Garza's office.

"You think Pringle was driving in that video? That he shot Jerry Strand?" Marlin asked.

"That, or he had Butch Theriot do it. All three of them could've been in that car."

"So Farley found the fossil, he told Jerry Strand, and Strand told Alex Pringle."

"Sounds about right—and who knows what happened after that? Maybe the three of them formed a partnership to sell it. Except somebody got greedy, or something went haywire. Maybe Farley wasn't playing ball, or he was trying to keep the fossil for himself. He probably didn't even realize what the fossil was worth until after he'd told Strand he'd found it."

"And either Strand or Pringle killed him."

"Considering what we saw on that video, and the likelihood that Pringle had something to do with Strand getting shot, I'd say he's good for Farley, too. Him or Theriot. Or both."

"Okay, then, what now?"

"We talk to Pringle and see what he has to say."

Garza was reaching for the phone when Marlin had a thought.

"Hold on a sec," he said. "There might be a better way."

Garza paused. "Yeah?"

"That Cadillac roadster Pringle's driving . . . what is that, an eighty-thousand-dollar car?"

"Hell if I know."

"I bet it has an onboard navigation system. With GPS."

Garza grinned and put the phone back in its cradle.

"I got good news and bad news," Snake said. "Which do you want first?"

"Jesus, Snake, I've been waiting all night. What the hell happened?"

Darwin Parker was still in bed, but he hadn't slept well. He'd sent Tiffany away at four in the morning, after it became obvious that she had neither the dramatic sensibilities nor the physical prowess to portray a realistic coelurosaur. Very discouraging.

"Good news or bad news?"

"Shit. The good news."

"It's done, man. I got the name, and a whole lot more. Libraries are great places for learning stuff, you know?"

Darwin Parker sat up straight in bed. This was the moment he'd been waiting for. "Let's hear it."

"The name?"

"Yes, the name!"

"Okay . . . drumroll, please . . . the name is Hollis Farley."

"Hollis Farley?"

"Yeah, man, Hollis Farley. You recognize it?"

"Farley. Hollis Farley. No, I don't think so."

"Good, 'cause he's dead."

"*What?*"

"He's dead, dude. Happened last Thursday, which explains why you quit hearing from him."

"I . . . what . . ."

"When I found the name, I googled it to see what I could learn about him. The first hit was a story in the local paper. At first the cops thought it was some sort of construction accident, but now they're saying it was murder."

Darwin Parker's heart sank like a sloth in a tar pit. "Oh, crap. You know what this means?"

"Not really."

"It means somebody else knew about the fossil, and they killed him for it. Now they've got it!"

"I don't think so, dude."

"Why not?"

" 'Cause I hacked into the computer and checked all the e-mails he sent. The only other person he contacted was his sister, but he must've typed her e-mail address wrong, because it bounced. Lucky for us, because it tells where the fossil is."

"Oh my God. It does? You know where the fossil is?"

"Yeah, man. That's what I'm sayin'."

Darwin Parker suddenly felt faint. The crown jewel of his collection was nearly within his grasp. "Where is it? Tell me!"

"Hold on, let me read this to you."

"Just tell me!"

"I'm trying to, dude, so listen." And Snake began to read: "Dear Sissy, first, promise me that you won't read the rest of this unless something bad has happened to me . . ."

Marlin's phone rang at ten fifteen.

"Is this the studly game warden I've been seeing around town?" Nicole asked.

Marlin smiled. "One and the same. What can I do for you?"

"You busy?"

"Actually, I'm writing an affidavit to get a court order to track a car with an onboard GPS."

"Cool. That sounds interesting."

"Yup. We're going high-tech here in Blanco County."

"Should I let you go?" Nicole asked.

"I can spare a minute or two for my fiancée."

There was a pause, then she said, "I'm sorry if I've been acting like a freak lately."

"I wouldn't say that."

"I just love you so much. I wanted you to know that. I can't wait to be your wife."

It had been several weeks since she'd spoken to him in that way. She sounded less stressed out, more like the old Nicole. "That's nice to hear," he said. "I love you, too. I talked to the videographer."

"You know what? I don't care if we even have a videographer. As long as the minister shows up, that's all that matters. Now write your affidavit. You can tell me all about it later."

* * *

Snake closed his cell phone and looked out the front door of the library. He'd placed a handwritten sign on the door that read CLOSED FOR INVENTORY. Did libraries count their books? He had no idea. In any case, nobody had knocked yet, but he knew it was only a matter of time.

He walked back to the circulation desk to check on the librarian. She was one pissed-off old lady. But she was also a little frightened, which was why she wasn't causing trouble. She hadn't budged from the chair she was sitting in. Hadn't touched the phone, either, which wouldn't have done her any good anyway, because Snake had the cord in his pocket.

"Okay, we need to talk," Snake said.

She was looking toward the rear of the room, her nose in the air, ignoring him. Refusing to cooperate.

Ever since he'd woken up with her gaping at him, he'd known his ass was in a crack. He'd stuck the note on the front door and tried to come up with a way out of this jam, but he wasn't exactly an idea man.

That's one of the reasons he'd called Darwin Parker. Parker was smart. He freaked a little when Snake told him the situation, but then he had a suggestion. A damn good one, if Snake could pull it off.

He said, "Look, Mrs. . . . uh . . . what's your name?"

The librarian gave him the silent treatment. The old bag.

"Okay, whatever your name is, I need to apologize, all right? I'm sorry I had to break in here, and I'm sorry if I scared you, but there's something you need to know."

No response. As far as she was concerned, he was invisible.

He plowed forward. "I'm with the Federal Internet Security Division. Fizz-dee, we call it. Basically, I'm a cop, understand? I'm investigating a crime. And I need your help."

She snuck a peek. She *was* listening.

"See," Snake said, encouraged, "a guy was killed out here in Blanco County last week. Did you hear about it? Seen the newspaper articles?"

Snake waited her out, and she finally spoke. "I only read the *New York Times*," she sniffed. Not friendly, but at least she was talking. "And I don't own a television," she added. "It poisons one's mind."

"Hey, I'm with you completely on that," Snake lied. "Now about this dude that was killed. There are, like, some big clues that he left in some e-mails and stuff. E-mails that he sent right from this very library. Normally, I woulda just come right out and told you what I needed, but it's all top secret. In fact, it has to do with national security, and I'm taking a big risk even telling you about it."

Now she had turned her head and was studying his black clothes carefully.

"This is my undercover outfit," Snake explained. "Everything about me—the way I dress, the way I talk—it's an act. I have to stay in character because it's good practice and stuff. But now I got a problem. I was supposed to get in here and get out without anybody knowing. But you caught me. You're too smart, I'll admit it. I think you even had me pegged yesterday, didn't you?"

There was pride in her voice when she said, "I had my suspicions."

"I bet you did." Snake grinned. "Clever lady like you. But what I need now—from you—is your promise not to tell anybody you caught me. Not only would you be helping me out, you'd be doing a service for your country. Whattaya say?"

She looked at him for a long time through her flimsy little glasses. Then she said, "I could do that. For my country."

30

AMY, THE RECEPTIONIST on the ground floor, buzzed and said, "Mr. Pringle, you have a visitor in the lobby."

Pringle was in his office with the door closed and the lights turned off. His head was pounding. "Who is it?"

"A gentleman named, uh, Mr. Omar."

Pringle rubbed his temples with his fingertips. If he hadn't still been a little drunk from the night before, he would have been in more of a panic. It was much easier to deal with Omar when he was twelve stories down, rather than on the other side of the door. "Tell him I'm not here."

"Well, I would, but, uh, he—"

"He heard you just now. He already knows I'm here."

"Exactly."

"Then tell him I'm in a meeting and I'll call him later."

"He said it's urgent."

"Tell him I understand completely and I will take care of the matter by five o'clock today. He'll know what that means."

Pringle hit the intercom button and cut her off before she could reply. His head felt like it was in a vise.

What were his options?

As executive director of Boothe Ministries, his annual salary was four hundred thousand a year, which meant, after taxes, he took home about twenty-six thousand a month. Not bad— plenty to play around with—unless you happened to hit the worst losing skid in the history of sports gambling. And if that skid stole nearly every dime you'd ever earned, stolen, or fucked somebody out of, what then?

If you were Alex Pringle, maybe you decided to move on. To get a fresh start. Reinvent yourself. He'd done it before. Just pick a new city and go. Or a new state. Hell, the way things were going, maybe a new country. It was worth considering.

Vanessa Boothe was in her walk-in closet—which was roughly the size of a room at the Ritz-Carlton—surrounded by dozens of her closest friends.

Vera Wang and Oscar de la Renta.

Olivier Theyskens and Zac Posen.

Neil Lane and Lorraine Schwartz.

They always lifted her spirits . . . made her feel successful, important, beautiful. Worth every penny.

But what to wear on the broadcast tonight?

She always aimed for conservative yet sexy. Pious but with an edge. After all, she had an audience to titillate. Research revealed that fourteen percent of the male viewers, especially the younger ones, tuned in chiefly to get a peek at her. Christians, maybe, but they appreciated a glimpse of cleavage or a flash of thigh as much as your average heathen. Like that impertinent toad Ted Finley. He'd had the gall to trash the Miracle Water concept while staring straight at her tits. Jerk.

A setback, yes, but more unsettling was the way Peter had spoken to her: harsh and condescending.

I think you should keep your mouth shut for ten damn seconds and let the poor man talk.

At that moment, every ounce of remorse she'd felt for her recent behavior had evaporated. Peter could be such an asshole at times. Didn't he realize that without her he'd be just another cheesy Bible thumper on cable TV? Didn't he understand that she was the one who'd helped reinvent the concept of what a minister could be? From a marketing perspective, it was genius.

She flipped through a rack of pantsuits.

Didn't he realize it was his own thankless attitude that had led her astray? She'd been considering apologizing—something she was admittedly not very good at—but not now. Everything that had happened was as much his fault as hers.

Right then, Peter surprised her by appearing in the doorway to the closet.

They made eye contact, and she started to speak but decided against it. Maybe he was here to make amends. That would explain why he was home at ten o'clock in the morning. Normally he'd be at the office, fine-tuning his sermon for that evening.

She went back to the task at hand, searching for the proper outfit, finding nothing she liked, while he simply stood there. Not watching her, really, just staring into space. Waiting for her to speak first, maybe, and hell if she would.

Finally, he broke the silence.

"What I don't understand," he said, "is how you lived with yourself. How you could sleep with Hollis Farley, then come home to me, and never seem to show a moment of guilt?"

Oh, so that's how he was going to play it. Blaming everything on her. She wouldn't give him the satisfaction of a response.

"For nearly a week now," he continued, "I've been battling my own conscience, trying to convince myself that we did the right thing. But I . . ."

He shook his head. There didn't seem to be any anger in his voice. Just remorse.

She didn't have time for this.

She was considering a strapless Christophe Decarnin number. Four thousand dollars, from a little boutique in Beverly Hills. Terribly hip. Designed for a waif of twenty, but Vanessa could pull it off. On the other hand, maybe it was a little *too* skimpy for the broadcast.

"It's time to tell the truth," he said.

She stopped what she was doing. "What?"

He didn't seem to hear her.

"Are you crazy? Tell the truth to whom?"

He turned to leave.

"Peter!"

He stopped and said something over his shoulder. "You might want to skip the show tonight." Then one last thing: "I'm sorry if I haven't been a good husband."

Red was wondering what to scrounge up for lunch when Billy Don bounced up the driveway in Red's truck, parked, and came through the trailer door carrying a six-pack of Keystone and a large sack from Sonic.

"You eat yet?" he asked.

"Was just fixin' to."

Billy Don placed the sack and a cold beer on the table beside Red's chair, then took his own position on the couch. He popped open a beer and took a long swig.

Red dug the contents out of the sack: a double-meat cheeseburger, no onions, and a large order of tots. What he always got. "Nothin' for you?"

"Already ate," Billy Don said.

At Betty Jean's, Red thought. *I'm officially pathetic, because Billy Don has a better social life than I do.*

Red bit into his burger, and Billy Don finally spilled his guts.

"I lied to you, Red. Well, not lied, but I didn't tell you everything, and I feel bad about it. What happened was, Betty Jean said she had a surprise for me—something Hollis had left behind. I figured it was the dinosaur fossil, just like you said, but I didn't wanna tell you about it 'cause I was afraid you'd try to trick it away from her. I didn't like to even think about that fossil when I was with her, so I told you she didn't have it. Then, last night, she showed me what the surprise was, and it wasn't the fossil at all, but one of them big TVs like you get at Wal-Mart. You mad at me?"

Red had quit chewing to listen to Billy Don's confession, and now he resumed, as he mulled it all over. He was relieved, frankly. Billy Don hadn't been trying to rip him off. He'd gotten his mind all twisted around because of a woman, and that was to be expected. Women screwed up your brain, that was a natural fact. Billy Don was just the latest in a long line of male victims throughout history. Red had been there himself, several times.

"I ain't mad," he said. "Just disappointed."

"Aw, hell, don't say that."

"Well, I wish you'd been straight with me."

"I know, and I'm awful sorry about it."

Red didn't say anything.

"We okay?" Billy Don asked.

Red munched on a tot and made Billy Don wait a few seconds for the answer. "Yeah, we're okay."

Billy Don grinned. "Then could I borrow your truck again later? Betty Jean's off today, and I promised to cut her grass."

Red shook his head in an older-brother sort of way. "Hell, boy, she's got you doing yard work? I hope you're getting something in return."

* * *

Sometime in the early afternoon—Jerry Strand knew it was after lunch, because Nadine had eaten a chicken salad sandwich and a cup of yogurt in his hospital room—a doctor stopped by.

"How are we today?" He sounded young. Strand risked a peek. He *was* young.

"Hanging in there," Nadine replied. She was using her poor-pitiful-me voice. They talked for a few minutes about Jerry's lung, and what kind of pulmonary function he could expect in the future, and how lucky he was that it hadn't been worse, then Nadine said, "Shouldn't he be awake by now?"

The doctor said that normally, yeah, they'd have expected him to regain consciousness by this time, but it wasn't anything to be overly concerned about. All vital signs were good.

Strand knew he'd have to face the music soon. He remembered everything that had happened, or at least the highlights. Getting kidnapped, smashing Butch with the toilet-tank lid, making that phony call to Nadine.

Feeling a bullet slam into his back.

Could he continue with the amnesia story? Could he fool the doctors? He might not have to, not if the cops had caught Butch. Maybe they'd already sorted this mess out and Strand was in the clear.

Then Nadine said in a low voice, "Doctor, why is that deputy still hanging around outside the door?"

On Snake's first pass, there'd been a truck in front of the house. Same thing on the second pass. So he came back two hours later and the truck was still there. He couldn't just keep driving back and forth, so he decided to take a break and go eat somewhere.

He sometimes forgot to eat. Or, the reverse, he'd eat and forget that he'd eaten, and eat again. He couldn't understand why his memory was so unreliable. He decided he wanted something nice. A steak, maybe. He could afford it.

Darwin Parker's tally was up to twenty-two thousand now, including the additional ten grand for the burglary Snake was preparing to commit. When the truck finally left the driveway. Or when darkness fell. Whichever came first. In the meantime, maybe he should go eat somewhere.

Events happened in rapid succession.

Marlin completed the affidavit, and the county judge signed off on it without a problem.

Garza then contacted the company that manufactured the Cadillac's navigation system; he spoke to a supervisor, who asked Garza to fax the court order, which he did.

Then they got on speakerphone with a man named Tim Cordes in the customer service department, who said in a friendly but professional tone, "Which do you want first—the vehicle's movements yesterday or its present location?"

"Let's start with yesterday," Garza said. "We're especially interested in the one o'clock to four o'clock time frame."

"P.M.?"

"Right."

Marlin could hear the tappity-tap of fingers on a keyboard. Scant seconds passed, but Marlin was impatient. Truth was, exploring new technologies—finding better ways to catch the bad guys—was one of the more exciting aspects of the job. Of course, nothing beat a good old-fashioned foot chase after a poacher in the woods, but this was a close second.

After a moment, Cordes said, "Okay . . . at one o'clock yesterday afternoon, the target vehicle was stationary at a location forty yards east of U.S. Highway 281, just north of the Blanco River. It didn't move until one fifty-four."

Hiding at the state park, Marlin thought.

Garza was jotting down notes. "Okay, good. Where'd it go?"

"North on U.S. Highway 281, arriving in Johnson City at two eleven. At two twelve, the vehicle stopped for four minutes at a location approximately twelve yards east-northeast of the intersection of U.S. 281 and U.S. 290."

Marlin was impressed by the precision. It was even a little creepy. Talk about Big Brother. "That's the liquor store on the corner," he said.

Garza nodded and said, "What next?"

"The vehicle then proceeded approximately three hundred and eighty yards south on U.S. 281, arriving at two seventeen. It remained in that location until three oh six."

The Super S parking lot. It all meshed with the video from the grocery store. But they'd learned something new: Strand and his accomplice had sat in the Super S parking lot for a little more than thirty minutes before placing the call to Nadine Strand. Probably getting boozed up. Courage from a bottle.

Cordes quickly rattled off the Cadillac's next movements: North on U.S. 281, east on State Road 2766 for six miles, south on County Road 202, also known as Yeager Creek Road. Straight to Jerry Strand's house, where the vehicle spent a total of three minutes and forty seconds. Then, at three nineteen, the Cadillac—sans Strand at this point—proceeded farther south on County Road 202.

Cordes said, "It stopped approximately one hundred and seventy yards south of the intersection of 202 and Nogales Road. About forty yards off the road, to the west side."

Marlin pictured that area in his mind. Mostly ranch land, plus the remains of an old homestead long since abandoned.

"How long did he stay there?" Marlin asked.

"He never left," Cordes said. "The target vehicle hasn't moved since then."

Marlin felt goose bumps rise on his arms. They had him.

"Can you give us the exact coordinates?" Garza asked.

Cordes did, and Garza hurriedly said, "Thanks for your help. We really appreciate it."

Talk about mind-numbing boredom, and now the barn was getting hot. Only mid-May, but the temperature was at least eighty-five. Even stuffier inside the Caddy. So Butch sat on the dirt floor, leaning against a tire, but there were ants crawling around, and his back started to hurt, not to mention his ear, and the top of his head, where Strand had whacked him with the toilet-tank lid.

He rose to his feet and stripped his shirt off. That helped a little. He peeked through a couple of cedar slats on the west side of the barn, away from the road. Nothing but open space for about fifty yards, then a bunch of cedars. No homes or anything back there. So he kicked a couple of the slats loose. That would let a little breeze in, maybe cool things down.

He opened the rear door of the car and gingerly lay down in the backseat. But now the dome light was on, and the car battery was already weak from listening to the radio. So he grabbed his Glock and used the butt to crack the plastic covering over the light. Then he smashed the bulb.

Now all he had to do was wait some more. Till the wee hours.

Butch was banking on the probability that a woman like Nadine Strand would spend the night in her husband's hospital room. Seemed likely, from what Strand had said. Not because she loved him, but because she wanted people to think she was a devoted wife, and that would give Butch the break he needed.

Because Butch had realized something. Somebody had probably boarded up the window he'd broken yesterday, but Strand's wife couldn't set the alarm system now, right? Not with a window missing. So . . . no alarm and nobody in the house. Shit, that was like an engraved invitation.

31

GARZA IMMEDIATELY DISPATCHED two deputies, one north and one south of the Cadillac's location on Yeager Creek Road. Whoever was in the car would be boxed in—assuming they hadn't left the vehicle.

Marlin said, "That whole southwest corner of Yeager Creek Road and Nogales—that's part of the old Tilford Ranch. Some investment firm in El Paso owns it now. Not much near that corner except the chimney of a farmhouse that burned years ago—but there is an old barn that's still standing."

Garza glanced at his notes. "Is it a hundred and seventy yards from the intersection?"

"That seems about right. That barn would be the perfect

place to hole up. I've run poachers out of there, and there's room for a Cadillac inside. No windows, either. He could stay there for weeks without anybody knowing."

Marlin quit talking and gave the sheriff time to think.

"I wish I knew how many people we're dealing with," Garza said.

Marlin sat silently.

"It might be just one, and he's wounded, and he might even be dead by now," Garza said.

"Could explain why he hasn't moved since yesterday."

"I'm gonna call Pringle," Garza said.

"Aren't you worried about tipping him off?"

"I've got something else in mind. A way to figure out where he is."

Alex Pringle's cell phone rang, and he checked the caller ID.

The Blanco County sheriff.

Pringle didn't want to take the call . . . but he was too curious. He answered, and the sheriff said, "Mr. Pringle, it's Bobby Garza. How ya doin'?"

"Just fine. What can I do for you?"

"I wanted to give you an update on the case. Could you stop by my office?"

"Well, I would, but I'm back in Dallas."

There was a pause for several beats. Then the sheriff said, "Did you say you're back in Dallas?"

"Yes, I returned yesterday afternoon."

"Hello?"

"I'm here."

"Mr. Pringle?"

"Yes, can you hear me?"

"Now I do, but this connection isn't very good. Can you call me back on a landline?"

* * *

Snake made another pass and the friggin' truck was still sitting there. *Go somewhere, dammit! Don't you have a job?* He was starting to get antsy. He'd wait for nightfall if he had to, but he wanted to get the job done and get back to Houston. And the money. So much money. He started saying to himself: *I will not piss it all away. I will not piss it all away.*

When Alex Pringle called back, Garza said, "Unfortunately, I don't have much to report yet, but I can tell you that I should be able to release the job site soon. Maybe a day or two."

"That's good to hear. But no developments on the case?"

"We're working on it. Nothing I can share yet."

"I understand. Any word on Jerry Strand?"

"You didn't hear? He was shot outside his home yesterday afternoon, but he's in stable condition. Should be okay."

"Oh, my Lord. Did he say who—"

"Look, I've got to take another call, but I if learn anything new I'll be in touch."

"I appreciate it."

Garza disconnected and buzzed the dispatcher. "Darrell, check the number of that last incoming call. Tell me if it's a cell phone or a landline."

Marlin was grinning. Slick move.

A moment later, Garza hung up and said, "He wasn't lying. He called back from the offices of Boothe Ministries."

"Which means it's probably just Theriot in the Cadillac."

"That's what I'd guess."

"Do we have enough for an arrest warrant?"

Garza shook his head. "I don't think so. But remember that speeding ticket? He already has a warrant out for that."

"Excellent," Marlin said. They could bring Theriot in on that charge, then question him about the Strand shooting. "You got a plan?" he asked.

"Not yet." Garza was tapping a pen on the desk, a habit of his when he got excited or anxious. "You know, we could call for a SWAT unit out of Austin. That's probably the way to go. We don't have to rush this thing. If Theriot is in the barn, we've got him bottled up."

"Unless he leaves on foot." Marlin could feel the pressure in the room. Garza had to make a decision. Now. "Is that what you want to do?" Marlin asked. "Call for SWAT?"

Garza took a deep breath, let it out slowly. "Hell, no. We've put a lot into this case. I think we should see it through to the end."

"Then let's do it."

He was shot outside his home yesterday afternoon.

Alex Pringle didn't know what to think. Had they caught Butch? Was Strand talking? Did the cops know Pringle was involved? Apparently not, based on the sheriff's comments. But how long would that last?

Jerry Strand opened his eyes—for real, this time, because he'd truly been sleeping—and Blanco County deputy Ernie Turpin was hovering over him.

Busted.

Turpin smiled and said, "Hey, Jerry. How you feeling?"

Strand looked around the room. Nadine's chair was empty, and for reasons he couldn't understand, that made him sad. "Where's my wife?" His voice was raspy. He was incredibly thirsty.

"She'll be back later. Ready to answer a few questions?"

Strand felt trapped, just like in the motel room. He swallowed hard. "About what?"

"About the shooting. About the two days before that."

It came to his lips, and he almost said it, *I don't remember anything. What happened?* It would've been so easy. But he couldn't stand it anymore. Was this who he was? A lying scumbag? What happened to the old Jerry Strand, an honest, hardworking, salt-of-the-earth type of fellow? He missed that guy. And there was only one way to get him back.

"If you'll get my lawyer up here," he said, "I'll tell you everything."

Sure, he wanted to come clean, but he wasn't a total idiot.

Marlin drove south on Yeager Creek Road on a reconnaissance mission. They'd decided that Theriot wouldn't be suspicious of a game-warden truck passing by out in the country.

Marlin passed Nogales Road, then slowed for a low-water crossing, and his pulse began to rise. The old barn was just around the next curve.

"Don't slow down," Garza had advised him. "Just cruise on past and check the coordinates."

Marlin's breath caught when he spotted a vehicle coming toward him. He grabbed his radio microphone. The vehicle was black, but he couldn't determine the make. Then he could. False alarm. A Suburban. The driver waved as he went by. Marlin lifted two fingers off the steering wheel in return.

Then he saw the barn through a grove of oak trees. Just a glimpse at first—old gray planking—then he passed the oaks and got a clear view. He'd been hoping to see some sort of indicator . . . he didn't know what. An open door. Muddy tire tracks. Something. But he didn't.

Now he was perpendicular to the barn, and he reached down to his own built-in GPS unit and punched a button. Then the barn was behind him.

A mile down the road, Garza was waiting, having driven up Yeager Creek Road from the south. Marlin pulled over to the opposite shoulder and checked the coordinates of the waypoint he had set as he passed the barn. He compared the numbers to the coordinates Tim Cordes had given them.

Then he stepped out of his truck, crossed the road, and climbed into Garza's cruiser.

"It's the barn," Marlin said. "No question about it."

The truck was finally gone. Snake couldn't believe it. He actually came to a stop—he knew he shouldn't, but he did—for a better look. Nope, no truck. He continued down the road.

It was four thirty. Should he wait until dark? It was a toss-up. He liked to move under cover of darkness, but he'd have to use a flashlight, and that was always risky. Plus, the truck might be back in the driveway by then.

But if he made his move now, he could get it done in a matter of seconds, or maybe a minute or two at the most.

Do it now, his instincts told him.

He started looking for a place to stash his car.

Marlin drew a square in the center of a piece of paper.

"This is the barn. It's all cedar, plenty of it rotten by now, so we won't want to use the walls for cover. But we've got a couple of options."

He drew a smaller square at the twelve o'clock position, to the north. "This is an old rock chimney—all that's left of the house. It's about seventy or eighty feet north of the barn. And down here"—he made a small circle in the five o'clock position—"is a concrete water storage tank. Maybe five feet high and a hundred twenty feet from the barn. He won't be able to watch us both at the same time, and I think there's enough angle that we won't create a crossfire. Either of these points has a clear line of sight. No obstructions."

"What if he runs out the back?"

"We'll see him."

"No trees?"

"Not right around the barn, no. There's a stand of oaks to the north, beyond the chimney, and a pretty good thicket of cedars to the west, but those are at least seventy yards away. He's got nowhere to go."

"Any fences to deal with?"

"Barbwire running parallel to the road, but there's an opening where a gate used to be. The only way in."

Garza nodded. "Okay, here's the deal. It's nearly five o'clock. We've got less than four hours of decent light. I want this wrapped up by sundown, but if Theriot doesn't respond, I'm putting a SWAT team on standby. Agreed?"

Marlin knew it was the smart thing to do. With Bill Tatum in Florida and Ernie Turpin posted at the hospital in Austin, they were short on manpower. As it stood, they'd be relying on two reserve deputies for backup. Good men, but their experience was generally limited to street patrol and accident response. Likewise, while Marlin and Garza had both trained for a situation like this, SWAT personnel lived and breathed it.

But all of those facts didn't make it any easier.

"Agreed," Marlin said.

Marlin had seen the lay of the land, so he led the way in his truck, and it brought back memories of spearheading his high school football team's charge onto the field, soaring on adrenaline.

Garza followed in his cruiser, trailed by Tim Delaney, one of the reserves, in another marked unit. The other reserve, Homer Griggs, was driving down from the north end of Yeager Creek Road.

Marlin drove slowly at first, keeping his engine quiet, then gunned it when he was one hundred yards from the gap in the fence, the point at which the barn first came into view.

At fifty yards, he spotted Griggs's cruiser approaching from the north. Perfect timing.

At twenty yards, Garza had closed up the space between them and was now right on the truck's bumper.

Then Marlin whipped a hard turn through the gap in the fence, and now he was tearing along the caliche road, small rocks pinging off his undercarriage, and the game was officially on.

32

BUTCH THERIOT WAS dozing in the Caddy, and he had an uneasy feeling that something wasn't quite right. What the hell was it? A sound . . . a sound was tugging at him, trying to wake him, and he resisted it, but then his eyes popped open and he sat up straight.

Oh, shit.

Multiple vehicles were approaching on the county road. He could plainly hear them now. Not plodding along, like the handful of vehicles that had rambled by in the past twenty-four hours. There was no mistaking it; these vehicles were driven by men on a mission.

He scrambled from the backseat and peeked through a knothole. And he saw them on the county road. A green truck.

Followed by a cop car. And another. And yet another coming from the opposite direction.

Go on past, you assholes. Don't turn. Don't turn.

The green truck turned, slinging gravel, engine racing, coming right at him.

Butch had the urge to run . . . but where? They'd be on him in seconds. Instead, he returned to the Cadillac, where both of his pistols lay on the floorboard.

Marlin broke to the left, toward the old water tank, and Garza split to the right, toward the chimney. The two reserves remained outside the fence, taking positions on either side of the gate entrance.

No activity at the barn. Nobody sprinting toward the trees.

Marlin plowed over a clump of prickly pear cactus, uprooted a cedar stump, slammed on the brakes, and came to a stop directly behind the water tank. He killed the engine and ducked out of the truck, carrying a Winchester .270 and a pair of binoculars.

He stopped briefly, half-squatting, his back against the tank. He was breathing heavily. The lacquered stock of the rifle felt slick in his hand.

Then he peered around the left side of the tank. Nothing. No movement.

He keyed the microphone attached to the breast of his shirt. "Bobby, I'm in position."

Ten-four.

Billy Don knew he'd have to make a couple of changes if this thing with Betty Jean turned into a long-term deal.

For starters, he'd have to get his own vehicle. He couldn't keep borrowing Red's truck all the time, and he really didn't

want to. It was an old junker, and there was usually animal blood
in the bed, so flies were always buzzing around, and that wasn't
the kind of situation that would impress a woman.

Secondly, he'd have to find steady work, maybe even a full-
time job—to pay for his new vehicle, not to mention the dates
they'd be going on. He wasn't complaining, but things got expensive real quick. Like right now, he was on his way over to
Betty Jean's to cut the grass, and he wanted to stop and get her a
box of chocolates. He'd already given her flowers, and that was a
nice touch, but he wanted to top that, and you couldn't pick
bonbons on the side of the highway.

He pulled into the Super S parking lot, wondering what kind
of candy he could get for four dollars and eighty-seven cents.

The bastards split up on him, and Butch followed the green
truck, which came to a stop behind an old concrete tank. All
Butch could see was the truck's rear bumper and the upper portion of the cab. For just an instant, he caught a glimpse of the
driver's head as he bolted from the truck.

Butch hurried to the other side of the barn. One of the cruisers
had taken a similar position behind a crumbling stone chimney.

How the hell did they find me?

It was eerily quiet, but that didn't last long.

Garza used a bullhorn.

"Butch Theriot . . . this is Sheriff Bobby Garza," he said.
"We have a warrant for your arrest. Come out of the barn immediately with your hands on top of your head."

Like that was going to happen. If Theriot was in there—and
who else could it be?—Garza didn't expect him to just give up at
the first sign of trouble. Not a man who'd hospitalized two Hells
Angels.

And Theriot didn't. There was no response from the barn. Garza gave it fifteen seconds, then repeated his message.

He was in the candy aisle when he heard, "Billy Don!" And here came Betty Jean, smiling, pushing a cart. "Fancy seeing you here," she said, being sort of silly, like they lived in some big city and the odds of running into each other were slim.

"I was just on my way to your place," he said. Should he give her a kiss? Right here in public? He didn't know. He decided to play it cool.

"And I was just picking some things up for supper," she said. "You *are* gonna let me cook you supper, ain't ya? A nice, thick steak? I got us some rib eyes."

Lord Almighty, he thought, *I've struck gold with this woman.*

Before he could say anything, she saw the bag of Baby Ruth miniatures in his hand and said, "But if you load up on those, you're gonna ruin your appetite."

He felt his face getting warm. "Well, these are, uh, sorta for you. I wanted to bring you something."

She flattened her hand over her heart, like she was touched. "You are so precious, but you don't have to do that. I'm making brownies! Come on, let's check out and you can follow me home."

Butch wondered where the other two cruisers were, and he finally spotted them out by the county road, flanking both sides of the gate entrance. But they weren't blocking it. That seemed stupid.

The sheriff was telling him to come out, and Butch was getting a charge out of it, to tell the truth. He'd always enjoyed confrontation, and this was like something out of a movie. Cagney, or one of those guys. He was tempted to yell, "You'll never take me alive, copper!" Just to fuck with them.

He knew he was safe for the time being. They wouldn't come in after him, not unless he fired a shot. But they wouldn't wait forever, either. And there might be more cops on the way.

The barn wasn't in falling-down condition, but some of the vertical planks had aged and contracted over the years, leaving gaps nearly an inch wide, like in a weathered picket fence. Looking through the binoculars, Marlin thought he saw movement at the near corner of the barn. Or was it his overeager imagination? He *wanted* Theriot to be in there. Alive.

And there it was again. Just a subtle shift, a dark shape moving across a darker background, but unmistakable.

He got on the radio. "Movement in the southeast corner."

"Ten-four," Garza replied. "Get ready. This is about to get interesting."

Garza grabbed a weapon that was leaning against the stone chimney. It looked like a single-shot breech-loading shotgun on steroids, but it was actually a thirty-eight-millimeter riot gun capable of firing a variety of projectiles, including rubber batons and buckshot, beanbag rounds, and smoke grenades. Garza was more interested right now in a ferret round—a specialized tear gas grenade designed to penetrate light barriers such as hollow-core doors, interior walls, and windows.

He figured old barn wood wouldn't be a problem.

"What do you like on your baked potato?" Betty Jean asked. "I've got butter and sour cream, of course—but what about grated cheddar cheese?"

They were in her kitchen, unloading the grocery bags. He

was handing her the items, and she was putting them in the refrigerator.

"Cheese is good," Billy Don said.

"Chives? Bacon bits?"

His mouth was watering. "Sure, throw 'em all on there."

"What about your salad?"

"We're having salad?"

She slapped him playfully on the arm. "Just like a man. If
you're gonna eat a big chunk of beef, you've gotta have some
salad, too. I've got some fresh tomatoes, straight from my garden. You like avocados? Carrots?"

"Sure." There wasn't much Billy Don didn't like.

"Croutons?"

"Sounds good."

"What kind of dressing? I've got ranch, Thousand Island,
Ital—"

Billy Don was holding a half gallon of milk, waiting for her to
take it from him, but she'd quit talking and had a strange expression on her face. She was looking past him, at something
behind him.

"That's weird," she said.

"What?" He turned to see what she was staring at, but the
only thing back there was the sink and a window above it.

And that's where she went—right to the window, which
overlooked her backyard. "The door to my shed is open," she
said. "It was closed this morning. And locked."

He set the milk down and joined her. "You sure?"

Butch was pacing the interior perimeter of the barn, keeping
an eye out on all sides, so those sneaky fuckers couldn't catch
him by surprise again. Meanwhile, the sheriff wouldn't quit
yammering.

Butch Theriot, you have one minute to exit the barn.

Yeah, right. He'd watched enough episodes of *Cops* to know they weren't going to come storming in here—at least not yet. Maybe right before dark. He'd start negotiating before then. Trying to arrange a deal. Because Butch had the information they were looking for. Surely they'd go easier on him when they learned he had the goods on a homicide. He had some leverage.

Do the smart thing, Butch. Come on out.

The smart thing? The smart thing would've been never getting mixed up with that dickhead Alex Pringle. The smart thing would've been refusing to abduct Jerry Strand, and watching out for toilet-tank lids, and getting the hell out of Dodge yesterday, after everything went south.

Thirty seconds, Butch. This is your last warning.

Had to be a bluff. They didn't have enough men out there to try rushing him. For all they knew, he had an Uzi waiting for them. He checked the green truck behind the water tank. Couldn't see anybody. Checked the sheriff behind the chimney. Same thing. The cruisers at the fence hadn't moved.

He figured he had about fifteen seconds now. He had his Glock in his right hand, his Ruger .22 in his left.

Ten seconds. If they wanted a blaze of fucking glory, well, that's what he'd give them. He was crouched low, his back against the passenger door, waiting.

Five seconds. He didn't hear any movement. No footsteps coming toward the barn.

Three, two, one, zero. And . . . nothing happened.

Yeah, a bluff. Typical bullshit that you'd expect from—

WOOMPF!

Butch flattened himself on the dirt floor as something ripped through the north wall of the barn and slammed into the Cadillac's front grille. Something began to hiss. Steam from the radiator? No, because the engine wasn't hot.

Then his eyes began to water.

Tear gas! Those assholes were using tear gas!

He jumped up, climbed into the Cadillac, and slammed the door—just as another round smashed through the cedar siding and ricocheted off a tire.

His throat was beginning to burn. All the windows were down, but he didn't bother raising them. He wouldn't be here long enough.

He twisted the key in the ignition, and—thank God—the engine roared to life. He wasted no time. He dropped it into drive and jammed the gas pedal to the floor. The Cadillac tore through the barn wall effortlessly, leaving nothing but kindling in its wake.

Just after Garza fired the second tear gas grenade, Marlin heard an engine inside the barn. He couldn't see what happened next, but he heard a crashing sound from the north side, and he knew exactly what it was. Hell, they'd planned on it.

He scooped up his gear and jumped into his truck, and by the time he got it started and wheeled around, Theriot had the Cadillac halfway to the gap in the fence. The reserve deputies had already pulled their cruisers onto Yeager Creek Road, one heading north and one heading south.

Theriot would have to make a choice, and by then, he'd have to do so with a disabled vehicle.

Billy Don opened the back door quietly and stepped into the yard. The garden shed was tucked in a corner, up against a wooden privacy fence.

Betty Jean had suggested calling the cops, but he'd talked her out of it. "It's probably nothing," he'd said. "Maybe some neighbor kids fooling around." Acting like it was no big thing. Wanting to impress her with his courage.

But now he wished he had a weapon. Red's handgun, maybe. Or even a baseball bat. After all, crime wasn't unheard-of in Johnson City. Like that Hollis Farley thing. Which made him think—what if the killer was in the shed?

He spotted a rake leaning against the side of the house, and he grabbed it. Better than nothing. Those metal teeth could do some serious damage.

He moved slowly toward the shed, wondering why anyone would bother breaking into it. What were they going to steal? An old lawn mower? A bag of fertilizer? Some hedge clip—

He stopped. He'd heard a noise. Somebody was definitely in there. Moving things around, sounded like. Looking for something. The door was on the side of the shed, so he couldn't see inside yet.

He raised the rake over his shoulder and took another step forward. He wanted to be ready. But he had to be careful. Maybe it *was* a neighbor kid. He didn't want to take some teenager's head off. He took another step. And another.

He could feel Betty Jean's eyes on his back, through the window. He was earning his dinner, that's for sure.

Butch gunned it hard for the gate—no cruisers there now— and he saw the green truck making a U, and the sheriff's car coming from his left. He was thinking how much fun it was going to be to get on the open road and outdrive these cocksuckers when he noticed something long and black, tucked in the grass, between the fence posts, and he realized they'd fucked him again.

A spike strip.

By the time he recognized it, he'd driven over it, and he knew that his tires would soon be flat. He gunned it onto the county road, fishtailing toward the north, and he could already feel a difference in the handling of the car. Like he was riding on putty. Well, shit. These fucking cops weren't playing fair. They were cheating!

I know a little something about that myself, boys. So cover your balls.

There was only one weakness to the plan.

To ensure that Theriot drove through the gate opening, rather than plowing through the barbed-wire fence, Garza had instructed the deputies to abandon the gate when they heard the Cadillac's engine. Which was good, because it meant there would be a car in front of Theriot no matter which direction he went. The drawback was that Marlin, reaching the fence first, had to jump out and move the spike strip.

He did, and Garza tore past him, wheeling left onto the paved surface, followed again by Tim Delaney. Seconds later, Marlin was back in his truck, goosing it hard, bringing up the rear.

The problem, as Snake saw it, was too many friggin' boxes. Hollis Farley's e-mail to his sister had said the fossil was "in a cardboard box in your garden shed," but which box? There had to be twenty or thirty of them in here, very few of them labeled, most of them full of junk, all of them taped up, and he was having to cut each one open and inspect the contents. It was taking too much time. Some of the boxes were pretty small, but Snake had to check them, too, because he had no idea what size the fossil was. He'd seen photos, sure, but they didn't give much sense of scale. For all Snake knew, the fossil could be the size of a poodle skull. Which is how small his own brain felt at the moment, for failing to ask the right questions.

Then he opened another box and he'd found it.

33

SO FAR, SO good. The tires were thumping, but Butch had the Cadillac up to forty, right on the bumper of the cruiser ahead of him. He passed a dirt road that branched to the left, but he didn't take it, because it was probably a dead end.

The deputy in front of him was getting cute, tapping his brakes, so Butch got close and shoved him with the Cadillac's bumper. The deputy sped up. *That's right. You don't fuck with Butch Theriot.*

Marlin couldn't see much of what was happening, but he heard Griggs on the radio: "He just made contact with my vehicle. Both front tires are flat."

Garza said, "His back tires are okay. I'm going to PIT him on the next straightaway. Delaney, don't run up my ass."

PIT. Precision immobilization technique. A tricky move that, if executed well, caused the fleeing car to spin out and stall, though there was a chance the suspect could flip and roll.

Bobby Garza didn't want Theriot to reach State Highway 2766, a much busier road. That's where things could get ugly. A greater danger to innocent motorists. So he waited patiently, around a curve, down a dip, over a hill, then he saw his chance. An open stretch of road about a quarter mile long. No oncoming vehicles.

He was right on Theriot's bumper, and now Garza suddenly broke to the left and came up alongside the rear of the Cadillac. Griggs was doing a good job in front, keeping the speed down.

Garza floated the right edge of his front bumper toward the Cadillac's left wheel well, behind the axle. He felt contact, just a bump at first, then steered firmly toward the right-hand shoulder of the road.

Butch was keeping an eye on the sheriff, who was trying to pull up beside him, but he had to watch out for the deputy ahead, too, in case he slammed on his brakes. Butch needed to get past the deputy, to the head of the pack, but the Caddy was driving for shit. He could hear pieces of tire whacking against the underside of the car.

Butch felt a light tap on the rear of his car.

Then he lost control, and he was sliding sideways, and there were terrible sounds of metal digging into asphalt. The skid continued, and now he was moving backward, off the road, over grass and rocks, and he finally came to a stop with his trunk against a small cedar tree. The other deputy and the green truck were coming this way, and he knew they'd try to box him in.

Another couple of steps, and now Billy Don was starting to see inside the shed. Just a little portion of it—the far wall—but not the intruder yet. Billy Don was glad he had an advantage. The element of surprise, they called it. He'd sneak right up on the sumbitch and—

A man stepped out of the shed holding a cardboard box. He saw Billy Don and froze, with his eyes bulging. "Hey," he said.

"The fuck're you doing?" Billy Don asked.

The man was tall, but not big, and he was shaped kind of funny. Like a bowling pin. Billy Don could take him, easy.

"I, uh, had to get some of my things."

"Your things? Who the hell are you?"

Billy Don was standing there like Sammy Sosa at home plate, ready to blast one out of the stadium, and the man was eyeing the rake. "Betty Jean had some of my things. She was keeping them for me. Go ask her."

Something wasn't right. The man seemed nervous.

"You know Betty Jean?"

The man smiled, but it seemed fake. " 'Course I do."

Then Billy Don heard Betty Jean behind him. "Should I call the police?"

And the man began to run.

Marlin knew this was their chance. They needed to surround Theriot now before he could get moving again. But the Cadillac began to roll forward on two exposed rims, moving surprisingly fast. Delaney didn't get there in time, and Theriot scooted past the deputy's car, back onto the pavement. He was coming right at Marlin, but then he swerved to the right, then back to the left, and the Cadillac zipped past Marlin's truck.

Marlin jerked the wheel to the left, leaving the road to make a wide U-turn, plowing over a cluster of saplings, then he was back on the road, heading south, and closing in on Theriot fast. Garza, Delaney, and Griggs were all behind Marlin now. Theriot had managed to get out in front of them all, the last place they wanted him to be. But the Cadillac was on its last legs, two tires gone, and Theriot would lose control if he pushed it too hard.

Marlin heard Garza: "PIT him again, John!"

The road was the problem. Too curvy, with a limited line of sight. He couldn't execute the PIT around a bend or over a hill, not without a good view of the road ahead. Too dangerous to any oncoming traffic.

So he simply followed the Cadillac, which was somehow clipping along at forty miles an hour. They passed Nogales Road again, then the old barn, and he knew he'd have to make his move soon. Farther ahead, on the right, was Majic Springs Road, then a couple of curves, then a fairly straight shot all the way to U.S. Highway 290. He couldn't allow Theriot to get there.

"Are you listening to me?" Annie Norris asked. "You should've turned back there, where I told you. There was a sign and everything."

Horace—Annie's husband of forty-nine years—grunted in reply. This was their second trip through Texas, and he was enjoying it as little as the first. Visiting some place called Pedernales Falls State Park, in his opinion, was an unnecessary delay on the road to New Mexico.

"Guess we'll have to skip it," Horace said.

"Horace! You promised."

"What, you want me to turn around?" Horace grumbled. It would be a headache in the big RV.

Annie was looking at a map. "No, you can take the next right. On Yeager Creek Road."

"Wonderful," Horace said.

They passed Majic Springs, and Marlin stepped on the gas. Theriot was cruising straight down the middle of the road, so Marlin had to hang his left tires onto the shoulder as he attempted to ease up next to the Cadillac. He glanced at his speedometer; they were up to fifty now. Theriot was increasing his speed, obviously wary of another PIT maneuver. Marlin finally gained on him, and his bumper was inches from the Cadillac's rear wheel well when Theriot applied his brakes. Suddenly they were side by side.

Marlin looked over and saw Theriot aiming a pistol at him. He hit his own brakes and dropped back, but then he saw something in the distance that gave him a chill—an RV, maybe a hundred yards away, coming this direction, and it wasn't slowing down.

He was out of time. He couldn't attempt the PIT. He made a snap decision.

Annie was still studying the map. Horace was looking at some strange deer behind a fence. Weird animals. Maybe they were imported. They had spots all over them, like fawns, but they were too big to be fawns, and their antlers were—

"HORACE!" Annie yelled.

The thief ran around the side of the house, still carrying the box, and Billy Don chased after him with the rake. The man had a strange way of running—like a chicken, or like his legs were too long for his body, and he couldn't seem to go in a straight

line. Billy Don had run like that a few times himself, when he'd
had too much tequila.

When he reached the street in front of Betty Jean's house,
the thief turned left, sort of, because he was veering all over the
road, and Billy Don was starting to gain on him. He was only
five yards back, but that was out of rake distance.

The goofy bastard made a turn and plowed straight through
some hedges at the house next door, and Billy Don had to go
around. He finally just tossed the rake, because he figured he
wouldn't need it, and it was slowing him down.

He'd lost some ground, but he was starting to make it up as
they crossed several front lawns and driveways. He was getting
winded, though. He had to catch this weirdo quick.

The thief stumbled on a sprinkler, almost falling, and now
Billy Don was right behind him.

Dogs were barking. An old lady yelled at them from her
front porch. A car honked.

Billy Don was almost out of gas. The thief glanced back over
his shoulder, which cost him a split second, and Billy Don made
his move. He sprang forward, launching himself as far as he
could, landing directly on the thief's back—a perfect flying
tackle. The thief collapsed and they crashed to the ground.

Unfortunately, Billy Don caught an elbow in the gut, and
now he was sucking for air. The thief was squirming to get
loose—kicking and thrashing—and Billy Don was having a
tough time hanging on. He couldn't breathe. His vision was
patchy.

The thief was almost loose now, and Billy Don had very little
strength left. He caught hold of the man's pants leg and held on
as tight as he could.

The thief was desperate. In the blink of an eye, he wriggled
sideways out of his pants and hopped up. He made one last grab
for the box, which was lying on the grass, but Billy Don put one
beefy paw on top of it and held it down. The thief turned and

ran, sprinting awkwardly down the street in his skivvies. Billy Don could only gasp, totally spent, watching him go.

He got away, Billy Don thought. *But I got the box back. Betty Jean will be proud of me. I got the box.*

The RV was closing fast.

Marlin surged forward again, beside the Cadillac, then a few feet ahead of it, and he took great pleasure in slamming his truck against the luxury car, momentarily engaging in a shoving match, feeling the resistance, until the big Dodge began to dominate, forcing the roadster to the right, off the pavement, and farther still, until they were both well off the shoulder, heading toward a massive oak tree, and Marlin finally stomped his brakes and came to a sliding stop.

Theriot had no control of the Cadillac at all, and it plowed into the tree trunk at fifty miles per hour.

Betty Jean was trundling down her driveway, coming toward Billy Don, with the cordless phone in her hand. "You okay?" she asked.

"Yeah, yeah, I'm fine."

"That was the strangest thing. Should I call somebody?"

He shrugged. "I got your stuff back." He grinned. "And I got his pants." The man's khakis were slung over Billy Don's shoulder.

"You're kidding. His *pants?*"

"He shucked 'em right off." They met by the mailbox, and she turned with him, heading toward the house. He was still breathing hard, and sweating heavily. "Did you recognize him?"

"Never seen him before. That was so amazing, the way you scared him off like that. I swear, I thought I was gonna have a coronary. Then you chased him down and got my property back. You're my hero." She gave him a kiss on the cheek.

He was blushing. "Billy Don Craddock, at your service."

They'd reached the porch, and they took a seat on the swing. Billy Don set the box on the railing.

"What on earth could he have wanted, anyway?" Betty Jean asked. "Ain't nothing but a bunch of junk in that shed. A few things for Goodwill, maybe, but that's about it. Here, let me see the pants. Maybe there's a wallet in there and we can figure out who he was."

Billy Don passed the khakis to her. She dug into the back pockets. Nothing. Then she reached into the right front pocket and came out with a folded piece of paper. She opened it up and began to read. Her face seemed to be getting pale. "I . . . this is odd, but it looks like an e-mail from Hollis."

"A what?"

"I don't . . . he sent me an e-mail. But he got my address wrong."

He kept silent and let her read, and just a moment later she said, "Oh, my Lord. Dear Lord." She kept reading.

"What?"

She didn't answer.

Billy Don looked over her shoulder. He'd only read a few sentences when the hair on his neck began to stand up.

Holy moly. Red was right all along.

Marlin, Garza, and the two deputies took positions behind their vehicles, with guns drawn. They could see movement inside the Cadillac, behind the deployed air bag, and the door slowly swung open with a squeal of stressed metal. Then they heard, "Don't friggin' shoot, okay? I'm getting out. Don't shoot."

"Let me see your hands!" Garza yelled.

Theriot complied. Leading with his empty hands, he emerged from the crumpled Cadillac, with blood smeared across his face.

He tried to stand, but his knees buckled and he fell backward onto the ground.

"Roll onto your stomach!" Garza said.

"Get me an ambulance."

"On your stomach!"

With obvious difficulty, Theriot rolled over. Garza and Marlin approached, weapons trained, and then Garza kneeled with one knee on Theriot's neck.

"Fuck, that hurts! I think I need to go to the hospital."

Garza holstered his revolver, wrenched Theriot's arms behind his back, and cuffed him.

"EMS on the way," Delaney called.

Garza stood. "Where's it hurt?"

"My head, my back. I think my leg's broken."

"Damn, what happened to your ear?"

Before Theriot could answer, Marlin heard, "Is everybody okay?" He turned and saw an elderly woman standing outside the RV, which had stopped in the middle of the road. Her husband was beside her, capturing the scene on a video camera. Griggs walked over to shoo them along.

Garza turned his attention back to Theriot. "I'm going to ask you what happened at Jerry Strand's house yesterday. But first I'm going to read you your rights."

Theriot coughed, and a small amount of blood came out of his mouth, but he was smirking at them. "Don't bother. I already know 'em."

From: H. Farley
To: bettyjeanfarley@momment.net
Subject: Whats been happening

Dear Sissy, first, promise that you won t read the rest of this unless something bad has happened to me. Just hang on to this message and read it ONLY if I die or something, because

I m suppose to keep my mouth shut. Promise? Okay, then I need to tell you about some things that have happened. It started when I found an old bone out on that preachers land where I been working. I was pig hunting and I found it in a small creek bed that runs to the Perdenales. It was so funny looking I figured it had to be a dinosaur skull and a geometrist at UT agreed that it was. Before that I told Jerry Strand about it and the preachers assistant a man named Alex Pringle wanted us to bury it but I thought that was wrong because of science. He even paid us some money, ten thousand dollars each to keep quiet but I learned that bones like that was worth a bunch of money. So we told Pringle and we all agreed to sell it and split the money three ways, not telling the preacher about it. I know it was wrong but Pringle said the preacher didn t want anything to do with the bone because of the Bible and everything. I found a buyer, a guy who collects these bones and we re fixing to sell it for two million dollars. Can you believe that? But I m not sure me and Jerry can trust Pringle. With so much money in the deal I m not even sure I can trust Jerry, because he kept asking me to let him keep the bone at his house. He thinks he has it, but I didn t really give it to him and thats the reason for this message, to let you know where it is. Its in your shed in a box on the second shelf above the lawn mower. We all promised not to tell anybody about the bone but I wnatd you to know in case something goes wrong, but I don t think it will. Porbably the next time I talk to you I ll be rich and I ll buy you a margaritta to selebrate.

                                                    Love, Hollis.

When Billy Don finished reading, he looked at Betty Jean, and she was staring wide-eyed at the box on the porch railing. Billy Don didn't know what to say. Should he tell her that he'd known about the fossil all along? He wanted to, because that was the truth, but then she might wonder why he'd been asking her out lately. She might think he was after the fossil, but deep in his heart, he knew that wasn't the case. He liked her. He didn't care about any damned old bone, even if it *was* worth two million dollars. So he kept quiet, which was the thing to do, because she still hadn't uttered a word.

Finally, after what seemed like an hour, she said, "Well, I guess we'd better have a look."

At six o'clock, Nicole called Michael Kishner's home number. He obviously had caller ID, because he answered by whispering, "Why are you calling me here?"

"It's the only number I've got," she said. "Relax, okay? This'll only take a minute."

She'd been thinking about Harry Grange's despicable scheme all day. She'd tried to convince herself to let it go, but she couldn't. Now she had a plan.

"What do you want?" Kishner asked.

"Two things. First I want Harry Grange's cell phone number. Then I need some help with my vocabulary."

34

LIKE ANY OTHER television program, *The Pastor Pete Hour* had a director, and his name was Walter Mimms. One hour before airtime, Mimms poked his head into Peter Boothe's dressing room and found the pastor sitting quietly, staring into space.

"I heard that Vanessa won't be joining us tonight," Mimms said. "That right?"

Boothe nodded but didn't look up.

"Who's going to handle the opening prayer?" Mimms knew from experience that last-minute changes on a live program could really cause headaches. He wished the Boothes had given him more notice, and it was irritating that he'd learned of Vanessa's absence from a production assistant.

Boothe didn't reply. Odd, because Peter Boothe was usually a bundle of energy before the broadcast—joking with crew members, rehearsing his sermon, greeting guests.

"Peter?"

Now Boothe made eye contact, and Mimms wondered if he was ill. Something wasn't right. "You feeling okay?"

"I'm fine."

"I was wondering who's going to deliver the opening prayer."

"There won't be one. We're going to do things a little differently tonight, Walter. Just bear with me, all right?"

Marlin was drinking coffee and flipping through a six-month-old copy of *Architectural Digest*. Garza was drinking a Coke and reading a *USA Today*.

It was seven forty, three hours since Garza had placed the cuffs on Butch Theriot. The EMTs had determined that Theriot's injuries were relatively minor—strains, contusions, a broken tooth, a fractured fibula—so the ambulance had taken him to Blanco County Hospital, rather than a trauma center in Austin or San Antonio. Theriot had indicated a willingness to talk—not just about the shooting of Jerry Strand, but about the Hollis Farley case—once he'd received medical care.

Now Marlin and Garza were sitting outside a patient bay in the emergency department, waiting for the doctor to finish wrapping Theriot's leg in a cast and to treat the wound to his ear. Marlin had left a message for Nicole, letting her know where he was.

Earlier, Garza had spent twenty minutes on the phone with Ernie Turpin, who'd relayed Jerry Strand's account of the past three days. Good stuff. Plenty to work with. Things were finally falling into place.

Garza folded the newspaper and placed it in his lap. He said, "In case I haven't mentioned this already, that was the ugliest bit of tactical driving I've ever seen in my life."

Marlin smiled. "You said that already. I'd agree with you,

except for that lame PIT maneuver you performed. What the hell was that? You're supposed to put the guy out of commission."

"Yeah, yeah, but at least I did okay with the tear gas. Give me points for that."

"Yeah, nice shooting. You hit the broad side of a barn."

Garza was chuckling when a nurse exited the bay and said, "We'll be taking him upstairs to a room now. He'll be a little groggy from pain medication."

Garza had anticipated Theriot's condition and spoken to the district attorney. The DA had assured him that any statements Theriot made would be admissible, so long as they were given voluntarily, knowingly, and intelligently. "Assuming he's not seeing purple elephants, you're fine," he'd said.

"You got any truth serum in there?" Marlin asked the nurse.

Billy Don couldn't quit staring at the skull. It was the freakiest, most wonderful thing he'd ever seen. Like something out of a sci-fi movie. No living creature had a head like that.

The skull was on the coffee table, Billy Don was on the couch, and Betty Jean was in the kitchen making dinner. She'd said she had some thinking to do.

He wanted Betty Jean to keep the skull for herself, or sell it if she wanted to, so that something good could come from Hollis's death. If anybody deserved two million bucks, she did, for all her pain and trouble. If he were in her shoes, he'd keep it for sure. No question about it.

She'd said it was evidence, and the e-mail from Hollis was, too. Those things might help catch his killer.

So Billy Don pointed out that she could give the cops the note and say the thief had gotten away with the skull. Who'd know any different?

"I would," she said.

What a woman.

* * *

Garza said, "Butch, I'm going to read your rights again, then I need you to sign a waiver."

"I know the drill," Theriot said. He was in a private room. His left arm was cuffed to the bed railing; his left leg was wrapped in plaster and elevated. His ear was covered with gauze.

Garza recited the Miranda warning, and Theriot freely signed the document with his right hand. Garza remained standing, bedside; Marlin was seated near the window.

"Okay," Garza said. "Earlier you indicated that you had some information regarding the murder of Hollis Farley."

"I do."

"What can you tell us about it?"

"Hold on, there, chief. First I want to know what you arrested me for."

Shrewd move on Theriot's part. Looking for a deal, no doubt, so he needed to know what charges he was facing.

"You failed to appear on a speeding ticket," Garza said.

Theriot's face broke into a wide grin. "Seriously? That's it? Shit, I—"

"Strand told us everything. He says you and Alex Pringle abducted him, tortured him, and then you shot him in the back."

Theriot's grin faded.

Garza waited. Marlin was enjoying the show.

Was Jerry Strand spilling his guts?

That question had been preying on Alex Pringle's mind all afternoon and into the evening, but he hadn't come up with a way to learn the answer. A call to the sheriff would be too obvious, and Garza would be too clever to show his hand. Then, finally, Pringle figured it out. There was a weak link. A way to gain some inside information. So simple.

He dialed a number, and Nadine Strand answered on the third ring. This was the moment of truth.

"Mrs. Strand, it's Alex Pringle. I heard about your husband, and I—"

"You sorry son of a bitch. I can't believe you have the gall to call here."

She slammed the phone down, and Pringle knew it was time to run. Immediately. Before the cops showed up with an arrest warrant. His heart was racing as he hurried to the closet in the master bedroom.

At eight o'clock, millions of viewers across America and around the world tuned in to the Wednesday evening broadcast of *The Pastor Pete Hour*.

The familiar theme music brought the church audience to their feet, applauding raucously, and Pastor Pete made his usual entrance from stage left. Vanessa Boothe, however, did not make an appearance from stage right. Apparently, the Boothes would not be joining hands at center stage; they would not be smiling and waving exuberantly at their adoring followers.

Instead, Peter Boothe stood solo and faced the crowd, looking grim. The audience, sensing that something was amiss, cut their applause short and took their seats. Peter Boothe closed his eyes, dropped his chin to his chest, and appeared to be praying silently.

This was something new. The congregants were puzzled and looked to one another for guidance.

Is his microphone broken?

Are we supposed to join in?

What, exactly, is happening?

Before they could come to any consensus, Pastor Pete lifted his head and spoke.

* * *

Theriot said, "I'm not saying any of that shit's true, but if it was, I want a deal. I give you Farley's killer and I walk on all those other charges."

"That's a lot to ask," Garza said.

"You know it's worth it," Theriot said.

"I can't promise anything. You have to tell us what you know before we can decide what it's worth."

Theriot breathed out heavily. "I can clear the Farley case for you, man. I guarantee it."

"You know who did it?"

"Not just *know*, I saw the whole thing happen."

"So you were involved."

"No, man, I wasn't. But I saw it, and I can serve the killer up on a platter."

"I hope so, Butch," Garza said. "But there's going to have to be some trust on your part. If your information proves valuable, you'll be in a good position to negotiate."

"We're negotiating now," Theriot said.

"Not until we hear your story."

"That sucks."

"It's the best I can do."

Theriot shook his head. "You fuck me over on this and I'll recant everything. I won't testify in court."

"Just tell us what you know, Butch. It's the only way to help yourself out."

Theriot leaned his head back on the pillow. Several seconds passed. Then he said, "Yeah, okay. What the fuck."

"My dear friends," Peter Boothe said, "I come to you with a heavy heart tonight, a humbled and remorseful man. It pains me to admit this, but I have not been a good Christian lately. I have brought shame upon myself, my wife, and this very church—and now it is time to confess my wrongdoings."

The audience was rapt, totally still.

"My biggest failing, sadly, has been in regard to my marriage. For several years now, I have not been a loving, nurturing, attentive husband, and because of that, my wife found comfort elsewhere."

The congregants emitted a collective gasp.

"This all started," Theriot said, "because Vanessa Boothe was banging Hollis Farley every chance she got. Pastor Pete found some sort of love note from Farley to Mrs. Boothe, and that really pissed him off. See, she'd been coming down here a lot lately, and now he knew why. You want my opinion, it wasn't the first time she screwed around, but a lady like that's got needs, you know? I'm only sorry I wasn't the lucky guy."

"How do you know all this?" Garza asked.

"Pringle told me."

Alex Pringle grabbed a single suitcase and began stuffing a few possessions into it. A couple of changes of clothes. His passport. He had to travel light. He needed more money. A lot more. And he knew where—

The phone rang and he nearly pissed himself. But it wasn't the cops, it was Vanessa Boothe. He couldn't resist.

"You watching this?" she asked.

"Watching what?"

"The fucking show!"

"Why? What's—"

"Turn it on!"

She hung up.

The audience was dumbstruck.

Peter Boothe said, "My reaction . . . well, it was sinful. Instead of speaking to God and asking for guidance, I followed my own flawed instincts. Instead of focusing on ways to heal my union with Vanessa, I sought vengeance."

"Pringle said Pastor Pete wanted to drive down here and kick the living shit out of Farley. That's why we went along. To make sure things didn't get out of hand. I mean, come on. Pastor Pete look like a fighter to you? Pringle was worried Farley might fuck him up."

"What happened next?"

"I traveled two hundred miles to confront the man who had turned me into a common cuckold. Then I had the temerity to invade the sanctity of his home. Was I thinking clearly? Of course not. Was I behaving like an adult? Sadly, no. The man wasn't home, so I contented myself, for the moment, by damaging some of his personal property."

"We shagged ass all the way down here, and Pastor Pete walked right into Farley's crummy old trailer. Shit, he was strutting like a banty rooster looking for a fight. Farley was nowhere to be seen, so Pastor Pete punched a hole in the wallboard."

"But I wasn't done yet. Despite wise counsel, I could not be appeased. Oh, how I wish Jesus had intervened at that moment and filled me with forgiveness! How I wish He had shown me the proper path. 'Save me from all my transgressions; do not make me the scorn of fools.' But my gravest sin was ahead of me. This man was a laborer, so I drove to the location where he was working."

*   *   *

Theriot chuckled.

"Pringle tried to talk some sense into him, but Pastor Pete was still mad as a hornet. So we get back in the car and go over to that new church he's building."

"When I arrived, the man was working far in the back of the property—on his backhoe."

There was a ripple of murmured disbelief as the congregants realized Peter Boothe was talking about Hollis Farley.

"The roads were impassable, so I hiked in on foot."

"We saw a car parked near the gate—Farley's car, we figured, because it was way too muddy to get in there without four-wheel drive. So Pastor Pete gets out and starts walking. Slipping all over the place in his wing-tip shoes. Pringle, too. I'm already thinking to myself, if the shit hits the fan, I'm gonna have to step in and take care of things, 'cause these two bozos won't be able to handle themselves. But it didn't come to that."

"Why not?"

"Something weird happened."

"It was a great distance—perhaps a mile or more. The terrain was rugged—rocky and hilly, with cactus and thorned under-brush blocking my way. But I was not deterred. Until . . ."

Boothe paused and began to smile. Two fat tears rolled down his cheeks.

"I could hear the backhoe to the north, like a siren's call. I was getting close now. I broke through a stand of cedar trees . . . and I found myself at the top of a great bluff, a hundred feet above the river. I could see the backhoe down below, and the man who was operating it . . . but I had no way down the sheer cliff. I stood at this wondrous vantage point, high on this hill, and it seemed I could see all of Creation. And it finally became obvious to me that God didn't intend for me to complete this journey. He placed this chasm here to make me stop and reflect upon my actions. It was a true epiphany, and I began to praise Him for His wisdom."

"We're looking down on Farley, and Pastor Pete suddenly starts bawling. I never seen nothing like it. Then he starts babbling about how God put this cliff here to stop him from doing something rash. Maybe he was pussying out or something. I figured there had to be a switchback trail or some other way down to the river, but I wasn't gonna say nothing. 'Specially when I look down again and see that Farley ain't alone."

"It was the most joyful moment of my life," Peter Boothe said wistfully, "but that changed in the blink of an eye."

Boothe paused again, and the audience members were like statues. The vast auditorium was dead silent.

"There was a second person on the riverbank that day."

"There was a woman down there," Theriot said.

The statement caught Marlin off guard. *A woman? We don't have any female suspects. Had it been an angry girlfriend all along? But no. There was someone else.*

Garza, to his credit, showed no surprise. "What was she doing?"

"She was behind the backhoe, and she had something in her arms, pointing at Farley. At first I thought it was a rifle, but then I realized it was a crossbow."

Damn, a crossbow. I never even considered a crossbow.

"And what happened?" Garza asked.

"What the hell do you think happened?" Theriot said. "She shot Farley in the back."

"And that person," Peter Boothe said, "was there to commit murder."

He pulled a handkerchief from his suit pocket and wiped his forehead. His hand was visibly trembling.

His voice was very low now, almost a whisper. "I saw it happen . . . and I did nothing. I chose to slink away like a serpent. I did not come forward to help the police. I did not bear witness to ensure that justice was done. For that, I can only ask for our Lord's forgiveness. I . . . I'm sorry."

He turned abruptly and walked off the stage.

"Oh my fucking God," said Alex Pringle. This was amazing. The Boothe Ministries empire would crumble. One more reason to leave. He actually laughed. Then he grabbed his suitcase and walked out the door.

"I need a drink of water," said Butch Theriot.

Garza found a pitcher on the nightstand and poured a glass. Theriot took it and sipped slowly. Marlin was ready to bounce off the walls, but he sat as quietly as he could. He'd picked up on something from Theriot's story, and he had a question, but he waited to see if Garza would get to it.

"Keep going," Garza said.

Theriot set the water glass down. "One of his tires ran up the side of this big boulder, and that caused it to flip."

"What did the woman do?"

"Don't know. We took off. Alex Pringle got all uptight and started saying we had to go. He said it would be bad publicity for Pastor Pete to be a witness to a crime, and that if we came forward, we'd have to explain why we were at the job site—and that meant everybody would find out about Mrs. Boothe's affair with Farley. So we split."

Oddly, Marlin was having no trouble believing what he was hearing about Peter Boothe.

"Did the woman ever see the three of you up there?"

"Nope."

"What did she look like?" Garza asked.

"Shit, hard to say. It was a long ways down there."

"Caucasian?"

"Yeah, a white gal. Light brown hair, I think. Past her shoulders."

"Height and build?"

"Short and thin."

"Age?"

"Not a clue."

Garza said, "You've got something better than a description, don't you, Butch?"

There you go, Marlin thought. *That's the question.*

Theriot grinned. "Damn right."

"Farley's truck was parked down near the river," Garza said. "He drove in through an entrance at the rear of the property. The same entrance he used for the backhoe. You spotted the truck down below, and you realized the car parked on the county road was the woman's."

"Bingo," Theriot said.

"So when you left . . ."

"I got her license plate number." Theriot tapped himself on the side of the head with a fingertip. "Got it filed away right in here. Think those other two pinheads even thought about getting that number?"

Marlin knew the answer to that.

"Maybe we should talk about my deal a little more," Theriot said. "Get the prosecutor involved. Otherwise, jeez, I might have a memory lapse."

"We will, but let's talk about Jerry Strand first."

"Hell, no. Not until I've got my deal."

Deputy Ernie Turpin climbed the folding stairs in the Strands' garage while Nadine and reserve deputy Homer Griggs waited below. According to Jerry Strand, the box was marked HUNTING STUFF. Turpin found it easily enough. He was tempted to cut the tape and take a peek, but he decided the sheriff might not be too thrilled about that.

Marlin and Garza waited in the hallway outside Butch Theriot's hospital room. The district attorney had been willing to drive down immediately from Llano, but it would take forty or fifty minutes. More waiting.

"You got an idea who that plate's gonna come back to?" Garza asked.

When Theriot had first started his tale, Marlin had expected him to say that Peter Boothe had killed Hollis Farley in a fit of rage. Or, possibly, Alex Pringle had stepped in and done it. Then, when Theriot mentioned the woman, Marlin thought, *Vanessa Boothe? Could she have done it? A lover's quarrel?* But no, Theriot would've recognized her, even from a distance. That left one plausible possibility.

"Yeah, I do," Marlin said.

Garza nodded. "So do I."

"The crossbow clinched it. If Farley already had it loaded, with the string pulled back, it wouldn't take much strength to pull the trigger."

A pair of nurses smiled as they passed by. Then the hallway was quiet again.

"Even someone as small as Kate Wallace could do it," Garza said softly.

35

ALEX PRINGLE WHEELED the rented Lincoln Town Car onto the highway and headed west. For all these years, as tempting as it might've been, he'd had a good reason not to pilfer cash from the mailroom. His salary was larger than any amount in the safe at any given time. He'd always thought, *Why screw up a good thing?* That's why he'd installed the video system. If he wasn't going to dip into the excess cash, he wanted to make damn sure nobody else could.

But things had changed, hadn't they? He couldn't run far without money. Besides, he deserved it, didn't he? He thought of the cash in the safe as a bonus for his years of good service. A golden parachute of sorts.

He found himself zipping along at eighty, and he eased off

the gas. Wouldn't do to get pulled over now. Traffic was fairly light, and he was making good time. He had a Volvo out in front of him, a Hummer well behind him. No cops anywhere.

He used his key card to enter the deserted parking garage, knowing his visit would be documented by the security system, but that was a moot point. Same thing when he used the card again to enter the building, and to ride the elevator to the darkened tenth floor. There was no reason to be stealthy.

The elevator opened, and there wasn't a soul in sight. Of course not; nobody worked late on show night.

He had to punch a five-digit code into a keypad to enter the mailroom, which was much larger than the name implied. It had to be. On average, the ministry received fifty-seven *pounds* of mail a day, six days a week. Nearly nine tons a year.

The safe was tucked in a rear corner of the room, in a small alcove. Only four people—the Boothes, T. Everett Farrell, and Alex Pringle—knew the combination.

Pringle had already realized his enormous good fortune. This Friday was the last business day of the month; thirty-six hours from now, an armed guard would tote the cash to the bank. Meaning the safe, right now, was as full as it ever got.

Pringle kept a rough total as he stuffed the cash into a plastic garbage bag, and when he was done, it contained somewhere in the neighborhood of eighty-two thousand dollars. Mostly fives, tens, and twenties, as he expected, so the bag was nearly full.

He headed for the door, then stopped and placed the bag on the floor. He found a pen, scribbled a single word on a piece of paper, and held it up to one of the video cameras.

Prosper.

*   *   *

The elevator seemed much slower on the way down.

He had no idea where he'd go now, and it was strangely liber-
ating. Staying in the States would be risky. Canada sounded
good, but it was cold as hell, and it was so far away. Mexico? He
wasn't thrilled with the idea, but it might be a good place to
start. Nuevo Laredo was a seven-hour drive. If he crossed on
foot, he probably wouldn't even have to show his passport. It
was people coming *into* the United States who had to jump
through hoops. After that, maybe rent another car and drive to
Belize. Or catch a flight to Argentina.

The elevator opened, and he crossed the deserted lobby.
Why was he so nervous now? He went to a set of double doors
and peered outside for several seconds. Nothing. He pushed
through them and followed the sidewalk around to the parking
garage. It was creepy in there without any cars—so quiet, like
Deep Throat might step out from behind a concrete pillar at
any moment.

Relax. You're home free.

He climbed into the Lincoln, tossed the bag of cash onto the
passenger-side floorboard, and started the engine. Backed out,
then headed for the exit. He had to stop at another kiosk and
insert his card, which raised the mechanical arm to let him out
of the garage. He pulled forward, and a Hummer came from
nowhere to block his path.

Billy Don was full to bursting, like a tick on a hound dog. He'd
eaten two rib-eye steaks, two baked potatoes, a big bowl of
pinto beans, and even a little bit of salad—smothered with
ranch dressing. Then they took a break for a while, and after
that, Betty Jean brought out the brownies, which were so good
they made Billy Don weak in the knees.

They hadn't mentioned the dinosaur skull in nearly three hours. Instead, they'd talked about other stuff, like it was just a normal night, while the bone sat on the coffee table.

Now Betty Jean was in the kitchen again, rinsing plates, sticking them in the dishwasher, humming while she did it. Then the water quit running, and a minute later Betty Jean came into the living room drying her hands with a dish towel.

"You want a beer or anything? Another brownie?" she asked.

"Naw, I don't think I have room for it. Maybe later."

"I'm going to call the sheriff in the morning. About the note. And the skull."

"Yeah, I figured you would."

"It's the right thing to do."

"I'm, uh, proud of you. I'm not sure that's what I'd do."

Pringle was staring straight through the passenger window of the Hummer, and he saw Omar smiling at him. Then Omar waggled a finger back and forth, like an adult scolding a child.

Pringle gave a friendly wave.

Omar opened his door and began to step out, and Pringle jammed the Lincoln into reverse. He floored it and shattered the mechanical arm, which had lowered behind him. Then he surprised himself with a very quick and nimble backward U-turn. Stomped the brakes, shoved it into drive, and gunned it again. Fuck Omar. Pringle wasn't giving up that easy. If he couldn't get out through the exit, then he'd leave through the entrance. He squealed around a corner, and another, and his heart sank.

A second vehicle, a Monte Carlo, was blocking the way.

He had no choice—no direction to go but up. He whipped it onto a ramp, tires squealing, and headed for the second floor. Headlights washed the interior of the Lincoln, and he sensed that the Hummer was coming up behind him now. If the Monte Carlo followed, too, he might have a chance. There were several different stairways in the garage; he could grab the bag of cash, bail out of the Lincoln, and make a run for it. Maybe beat them down to the street. He had no other options. But the Hummer was gaining. He crested the ramp to the second floor and continued up to the third, then the fourth. Where was the Monte Carlo? Was it behind the Hummer?

He rounded the ramp to the fifth and final floor—the top of the garage. The sky was full of stars, and it would've been a beautiful night, except for the Hummer on his tail. He raced to the far end of the wide-open surface, and that was it. End of the line. No stairwell. Nowhere to go. He hit the brakes and came to a stop inches from a four-foot concrete wall.

One last possibility came to mind. He leaped from the Lincoln with the garbage bag and raced to the concrete wall.

The Hummer slowly pulled up behind the Lincoln, and the driver shut off its headlights. The Monte Carlo was nowhere to be seen. Omar and a second man—much shorter and smaller—stepped languidly from the giant SUV.

"Alex Pringle!" Omar called, as if they were old friends. "You out for a drive on this fine evening?"

They came toward him. The driver had a gun in his hand.

Pringle held the bag up by the neck, showing it to them. "I have more than eighty grand in here."

They kept coming.

"But I'll dump it all!" He grabbed the bottom of the bag with his other hand and held it over the wall, poised to pour out the cash. A good breeze was blowing. They'd be chasing bills all night. They didn't know the money was banded.

They froze, fifteen feet away.

"Chill out," Omar said. "Don't do nothin' stupid."

"Here's the deal," Pringle said. "I got myself into a jam. I have to leave town. Tonight. But I need some money. So I'm willing to split this with you. I know I owe you more than that, and I'm sorry, but that's the best I can do."

"Shee-yit," Omar said. "You give me all that and you still come up light. What kinda businessman are you? Ain't you got no respect for the system?"

"I know, I know. But I have no choice. You take half of this now, let me keep the other half, and I'll send the rest later. I promise."

Omar chuckled. "Hear that, B-Dog? He send the rest later."

"Yeah, he funny."

Omar nodded toward the bag. "Eighty grand, huh?"

"About eighty-two, I think."

"Guess that'll do. B-Dog, shoot this dumb motherfucker in the face."

B-Dog instantly raised his gun.

"No!" Pringle yelled. He dropped the bag at his feet. "Take it all! It's yours! I don't want it!"

B-Dog looked at Omar, waiting for his orders.

Pringle had his hands in the air, and now he felt a warm trickle running down his leg.

Omar sauntered forward, shaking his head, and toed the bag with one foot. Then he bent down and opened it up. Pawed through it. He looked up at Pringle. "Where you get all this?"

"From the safe in my office. Pastor Pete."

"Pastor who?"

"Pastor Pete."

"They more in that safe?"

"No, that's it. I cleaned it out."

Omar nodded, apparently satisfied. Then he stood, and as he did so, he planted one hand on each side of Alex Pringle's rib cage and effortlessly tossed him over the concrete wall.

"This is Harry Grange."

Nicole was surprised that he answered, because she'd had to dial *67 to prevent her name and phone number from appearing on his caller ID. His tone was somewhat gruff, as if he expected her to be a telemarketer.

She was nervous, but giddy. She remembered Michael Kishner's advice. *Play it over the top. Flighty. Distracted. Full of yourself.* And . . . action!

"Harry, hi! This is Ashley Simon from ABC. You have a minute to talk?"

"Uh, I'm sorry, who?"

"Ashley Simon."

"With ABC?"

"Right, in the development department? I just came over from HBO a few weeks ago. Maybe you saw it in the trades?"

"I believe I did, yes."

Damned liar. She'd made the name up.

"Excellent. Look, Harry, I've only got a few minutes, so I'll get right to the point. I happened to see *Hell Hole* recently, and let me tell you, I instantly became a huge Harry Grange fan. I don't mean to gush, but that was really nice work! Not just the external struggles—what a great idea, that haunted cave—but, you know, the internal conflict each character deals with personally. It was like a thinking man's *Blair Witch,* know what I mean? Just a tight, dramatic story line from start to finish. Kudos, my friend."

As soon as she heard the tone of Grange's reply, she knew he had a shit-eating grin on his face. "Well, thank you. Thanks a lot. That really means—"

"So, what I was wondering—I'll just throw this against the wall and see if it sticks. Are you, like, married to this whole feature thing, or would you lower your standards and do some TV?" She laughed self-deprecatingly.

"Well, I—"

"Have you ever considered taking the characters from *Hell Hole* and adapting them for a series? Because if you have, I'd really love to talk. Forgive me if I'm getting ahead of myself, but I'm thinking one-hour prime-time drama, okay? About a team of professional spelunkers. Yes, there really is such a thing, I've checked. Does that sound interesting to you? Does that concept have legs? That's the question I have right now."

"I think it does, yes. In fact, I've even—"

"Oh crap, Harry, I just got to the restaurant and I really need to get inside. Jennifer gets so bitchy if she has to wait. So let me run this past you. What's this, Wednesday? Yeah, okay, I have a meeting tomorrow afternoon at three o'clock. Just a brainstorming session for next year's lineup. I know this is short notice, but could we sit down before then? Maybe an early lunch? Say eleven-thirty at the Ivy?"

Harry Grange would cut off his left nut for an opportunity like that, Kishner had said. *He'd hop a flight for sure.*

And Kishner was right.

"That sounds great," Grange said.

"Good, then I look forward to meeting you," Nicole said. *You prick.*

By two in the morning, after a prolonged interview by the prosecutor, Butch Theriot had his deal. Instead of assault with a deadly weapon, he agreed to one count of reckless discharge of a firearm. The prosecutor told Garza and Marlin that the kidnapping charge was a no-win situation, since Jerry Strand had, by his own admission, ultimately teamed up with Theriot. A grand jury would punt it in a heartbeat. That sleazeball Alex Pringle didn't know it yet, but he'd skate on all charges, too. Garza had been trying to call him, to arrange an interview with him and Pastor Boothe, but all he got was voice mail.

Now Marlin and Garza were back at the sheriff's office, with the license plate number written on a scrap of paper.

Garza was sitting at his computer, Marlin watching over his

shoulder as the sheriff typed the number into the database. The computer clicked and hummed, then delivered the results. Marlin stared at the screen, wishing it said something different.

"We'll go talk to her in the morning," Garza said.

Marlin nodded. He was ready to go home and get some sleep.

But Garza said, "So, you want to see this infamous fossil?"

A locking metal cabinet behind the dispatcher's desk served as an evidence locker for the sheriff's department. Garza turned the key and swung the door open. Inside was the large cardboard box Ernie Turpin had retrieved from the crawl space over Jerry Strand's garage. Garza carried it to the conference room and placed it on the table. He slit the duct tape, then lifted the flaps. The object inside was wrapped in newspaper. Garza removed the sheets, carefully, one by one, and Marlin began to see bone.

Then he saw a tusk.

He hadn't expected to see a tusk. Scott Underwood's drawing of the *Alamosaurus* hadn't shown it as a tusked animal.

Because it wasn't.

Garza finished with the unwrapping. He said, "Well, crap."

Marlin couldn't help stating the obvious. "That's a hog skull."

36

IN THE MORNING , Bobby Garza tried Alex Pringle's cell phone again. This time, a man said, "Hello?"

"Mr. Pringle?"

"Who'm I talking to?" It clearly wasn't Pringle.

"Bobby Garza, sheriff of Blanco County."

"Sheriff, this is Sergeant Andy Cox with Dallas PD. Can you tell me, uh, why you're looking for Alex Pringle?"

"Yeah, he's a possible witness in a case down here. What's going on? You got him for something?"

"No, it's not that. Right now, I'm standing about ten feet away from his body. He took a header off a parking garage sometime last night. His cell phone survived the fall, but he didn't."

Marlin appeared in his doorway, and Garza held up his hand in a just-a-minute gesture.

"Suicide?" Garza asked.

"Well, we're just getting started, but it wouldn't surprise me. Might have something to do with his boss's meltdown on TV last night."

"Pardon me?"

"You get *Pastor Pete* down there? From what I've heard, last night he put on quite a show."

Billy Don woke up naked this time. Finally. He and Betty Jean had chatted well into the night again, and they'd begun to hold hands, and before he knew it, she'd led him into her bedroom and turned off the lights. After that, well . . .

A big grin broke across his face.

He figured things had gone pretty smoothly. Sure, there'd been a couple of clumsy moments, but they'd gotten everything sorted out. And, unlike some previous encounters he'd had, Billy Don hadn't wanted to get up and leave afterward.

He heard a voice. Betty Jean on the phone. He stayed right where he was, enjoying the just-washed smell of her bed linens. He wondered what time it was, then realized it didn't matter. A few minutes later, Betty Jean came into the bedroom wearing a flowered muumuu and fuzzy slippers. She smiled at him and slipped under the covers.

"Hey, there," he said.

"Hey, yourself. You sleep all right?"

"Like a baby."

"Oh, Billy Don! Does that mean you wet the bed?"

He chuckled. He liked a woman with a sense of humor.

She snuggled up beside him and said, "Bobby Garza isn't in right now. I'll have to go see him later."

So that's who she'd been talking to. Someone at the sheriff's department.

"You know what that means?" she asked.

"What?"

She rubbed a palm across his chest. "We have some time on our hands. Got any ideas what we might do with it?"

When Kate Wallace opened her apartment door, Marlin could tell that she knew. It was written on her face, in her eyes. Garza had been vague on the phone: *We have a few follow-up questions about Hollis Farley.*

But she knew.

She invited them in, forcing a smile, probably hoping her intuition was wrong. She asked if they wanted something to drink, and they both declined.

Then they sat—Kate in an upholstered chair, Marlin and Garza on a cheap couch with a Mexican blanket thrown over it. Her hair was pulled back, and she was wearing sweats and a T-shirt: the laid-back doctoral student, with time on her hands because the semester was over.

"Okay," she said, raising her eyebrows. *What now?*

"Miss Wallace," Garza said, "I'm going to be straightforward with you. We've gathered some evidence that indicates you were involved with the death of Hollis Farley."

She didn't react other than to frown slightly and glance at the floor.

Garza continued. "We'd like to ask you some questions in the hope that we might be mistaken. If we're wrong, you can set us straight. Standard procedure, I'm going to read you your rights."

He did, and she acknowledged that she understood them.

Then Garza said, "Did you ever have contact with Hollis Farley other than his one visit to Dr. Underwood's office?"

She shook her head.

"You never went to his home?"

"No."

"Never visited him on the job site?"

"No."

"So you've never been on or near his backhoe?"

"Of course not."

"Do you still own a 2003 Nissan Maxima, red in color?"

They knew she did. They'd seen it in the parking lot.

"I do, yes."

"Have you let anyone borrow it recently?"

She paused. "Not that I can remember."

"To be more specific, did you let anyone borrow it one week ago today, on the day Hollis Farley was killed?"

"I . . . I'm not sure."

"You can't remember if you loaned anyone your car?"

It was painful to watch. She was trapped.

"I don't think I did," she said.

"Did you work that day? One week ago."

"Half a day. I left after lunch with a sore throat."

"Did you go to the doctor?"

"It wasn't that bad."

"Did you go straight home?"

"Yes."

"Did you go anywhere later that afternoon? To the store for medicine? Anything like that?"

"I didn't. I stayed here."

Garza nodded. "I can't stress how important that fact is. You're absolutely certain you didn't go anywhere?"

He was locking her in to her story. Naturally, she concluded it was best to claim she'd been home all day.

"I got home at about two o'clock," she said, "and didn't leave again until the next morning. I'm positive of that."

"Okay, then," Garza said, and he paused for a moment. The questions were over. Now the hard part. "Miss Wallace, we have an eyewitness who saw a woman matching your description kill Hollis Farley. He also gave us a description of a car at the scene—a red 2003 Nissan Maxima—and he gave us the license plate number, which matched the plate on your car."

Garza pulled a folded sheet of paper from his breast pocket. "I have a warrant to search your apartment. What we'll be looking for is a particular pair of jeans with a black stain on the left inside cuff. If that stain came from oil or grease on Hollis Farley's backhoe, our forensic technician will be able to confirm a match. We think you got that stain after the backhoe flipped. You were checking on Hollis to see if he was dead."

Kate Wallace was tearing up. Her face was beginning to contort. She didn't look like a killer.

But Garza had one last thing. The same technology that had helped catch Butch Theriot was going to put the nail in Kate Wallace's coffin.

"There are security cameras everywhere nowadays," Garza said. "Banks and grocery stores. Even this apartment complex. If you went anywhere on Thursday . . ."

He didn't have to finish the sentence.

Kate Wallace covered her face with her hands. Then she began to talk.

She told it all. How she followed Hollis Farley to his truck and copied his license plate number. Got on the Internet and paid a fee for his name and address. Drove out to his trailer the next day, a Saturday, to reason with him. Surely he could understand what was at stake here. A piece of scientific history. At first he was angry that she'd tracked him down, but then something unexpected happened. Despite their enormous differences, they hit it off. They talked for hours, and by that evening, she had a proposition for him.

"I could tell he wanted to do the right thing—to tell me

where the fossil was. So I . . ." She shook her head, embarrassed. "We'd been drinking, flirting with each other, and I suggested a trade. Sex for the fossil. It was sort of a joke, really, even though I meant it. He was so close to giving in, and I needed to put him over the edge. I should've known better."

"So you slept with him?"

She nodded, clearly full of regret.

"Then what happened?"

"The next morning, he started waffling, saying he needed time to think. I told him that wasn't fair . . . but what could I do? I called him on Monday but got no answer. Same thing on Tuesday, but on Wednesday an old woman answered. She'd never heard of Hollis Farley. He'd given me a wrong number."

She stopped talking, and Garza gave her some time. Then he said, "On Saturday, at his place, he told you where he found the fossil, didn't he?"

She nodded.

Garza said, "And it wasn't very difficult to figure out how to get to the job site."

She didn't reply.

"Go ahead," Garza said. "Tell the rest of it."

She folded her hands in her lap. "I drove out there on Thursday afternoon. It was muddy, so I parked on the county road and walked in. I didn't know exactly where I was going, but I could hear his backhoe in the distance, and that led me to him. I had to follow a trail down a steep hill. By the time I got there, he was taking a break. Sitting in his truck, drinking some water. When he saw me, he . . . it didn't go well."

"How so?"

"He was mad that I'd come out to the site. He told me to leave. I asked him if he'd made up his mind about the fossil, and he said he was going to sell it. I reminded him that we'd made a deal, and he said, quote, 'Sorry, but I ain't gonna pass up a fortune for a piece of ass.'"

She took a deep breath, trying to control her emotions. "He just . . . dismissed me. Said he had work to do and got back on his backhoe. I was so angry for letting him take advantage of me. So I did something . . . oh, Jesus, I did something so stupid. He had a crossbow in his truck. My uncle used to hunt with one, and I'd watched him shoot it. So I went and grabbed it. I wanted to freak him out, you know? Do something dramatic. Surprise him." She was sobbing now, but Marlin could understand her next statement: "I was trying to shoot his tire. That's all I wanted to do."

37

"DO YOU BELIEVE her?" Nicole asked.

"Maybe I shouldn't, but I do," Marlin said. "She was a wreck."

It was past one, and they were having lunch at Ronnie's. There weren't any sultry blondes casting glances his way, and for that, he was genuinely grateful.

"Maybe she was acting," Nicole said. "Some people are pretty good actors."

"It seemed genuine. I think it was an accident, and she panicked afterward."

"Doesn't help that she didn't come forward and admit what happened. What'd she do with the crossbow and the arrow?"

"It's a *bolt*."

"What is?"

"The arrow you shoot from a crossbow. It's called a bolt."

"I'll remember that the next time I'm shopping for crossbow supplies."

He smiled. "She took the crossbow and the bolt, and the other bolts from his truck, and tossed them all into a Dumpster on campus."

"What about the fossil? Any idea where it went?"

Betty Jean Farley stepped into Bobby Garza's office carrying a cardboard box. He'd returned her call earlier, telling her they'd made an arrest in the case and asking her to come see him.

And here she was. With a large box. He had to wonder about that box.

"Thanks for coming by," he said as they sat.

"You've made an arrest?"

She had an expression on her face he'd seen dozens of times on other survivors. Hopeful. Anxious. Maybe a little over-whelmed. *Tell me what happened. I need to know.*

She deserved the full story, so he gave it to her, which took twenty minutes. He told her about the dinosaur fossil, Hollis's partnership with Alex Pringle and Jerry Strand, and their intention to sell it. He went into detail about Strand's abduction, and the car chase with Butch Theriot, and how both events tied into the case. He told her about Scott Underwood, and his assistant, Kate Wallace, and the confession she'd made just hours ago. "She claims she was aiming for the backhoe's tire. We have no way of knowing if that's true or not."

Finally, he told her about the three witnesses—Pringle, Theriot, and Boothe—and why they hadn't come forward on their own. They'd use Boothe's statement to bolster the case—as soon as they heard back from him. So far, he hadn't returned calls, but it was obvious from Sergeant Cox's description of Boothe's show the previous evening that the pastor was ready to talk.

As Garza told the tale, Betty Jean's expression ranged from surprise to anger to disbelief. But when he was done, all she showed was disappointment. He'd seen that before, too. If she'd been hoping the truth would ease her pain, well, like so many others, she was learning that it didn't help much.

Garza was still wondering about the box. "The only thing we haven't been able to figure out," he said slowly, "is the location of the fossil. Jerry Strand thought he had it, but he was wrong."

Betty Jean opened her mouth, and Garza held up a hand to stop her from speaking.

"What pisses me off," he said, "excuse my language, is that Peter Boothe still owns it, legally, since it was found on his property. Now, I have no idea whether he'd want to lay claim to it or not, but he might. I think that sucks, considering how he behaved. He saw Hollis get killed, but he didn't report it. That's one of the least Christian things I've ever heard. I'm kind of hoping the fossil never turns up."

Betty Jean looked at the box. Then she looked at Garza. "Won't you need the fossil for evidence?"

"At this point, no. We have a confession."

"What if this Kate Wallace changes her mind?"

"She could recant, but having the fossil in our possession wouldn't change anything. Even if we can't prove it really existed, believe me, we *can* prove that Kate Wallace is guilty."

Betty Jean sat still for the longest time. Finally, she said, "I miss Hollis a lot. He was a good brother."

"I'm sure he was," Garza said. "And I bet I know what he'd want you to do right now."

She smiled. "Yeah, me, too." She stood up and said, "Thank you, Sheriff. For figuring out what happened."

"I had a lot of help," Garza said.

"Will you thank everyone for me?"

"I will."

Betty Jean reached out and clasped his hand for a few moments. Then she left. She took the box with her.

Harry Grange had been to the Ivy before, but just to make the scene, never to discuss a potential television deal with a network exec. It added a certain swagger to his stride, a cockiness to his smile. He was a player! He'd made it!

He'd carefully considered what to wear (his best Armani suit), what kind of car to rent (a Mercedes coupe), and what time to make his entrance (he didn't want to appear too eager, but he knew Ashley Simon had a busy day ahead, so he handed his keys to the valet at eleven forty, just a tad late).

He strutted up the sidewalk, checking out the crowd on the patio—was that Kiefer Sutherland at table 41? As Harry Grange stepped through the front door, he tried to remove his sunglasses with as much elegance and panache as possible.

There was one couple waiting ahead of him—losers, from the looks of it, from someplace like Iowa, probably. Tourists. Nobodies.

Then, finally, the hostess—a cute young brunette—turned her attention to him.

"I'll be joining Ashley Simon," he said. "Has she arrived?"

The girl smiled broadly. "Are you, uh, Harry Grange?"

"I am."

Now the girl wasn't just smiling, she was actually stifling a giggle. What was up with that? She reached into a cubbyhole in the hostess stand and came out with a folded piece of paper. "Miss Simon phoned and asked me to give you this message." She handed it over with another giggle.

What the hell was going on? Grange unfolded the paper and read:

Dear Harry,

I'm sorry, but I could never do business with anyone who has a penis as small as yours. I hope you understand.

Best regards,
Ashley Simon (a.k.a. Nicole Brooks)

Marlin and Nicole walked out the door into a beautiful day, with clouds as wispy as cotton candy floating in from the south.

Her car was parked next to his truck, and he opened her door for her. The way the sunlight bounced off her hair made his heart flutter. They lingered for a moment, enjoying . . . everything.

"Six weeks and two days," he said.

"I'm impressed. Come to your senses yet?"

"About what?"

"About marrying me."

"Yeah, I think I'm crazy enough to do it."

He stuck out his tongue and crossed his eyes. She poked him in the ribs with an elbow.

"You gonna tell me what was bothering you earlier this week?" he asked.

She was playful. "Who, me? You think something was bothering me?"

"Well, something wasn't quite right. But if it was wedding stuff, I understand."

"Yes," she said, "in a way, that's exactly what it was. Wedding stuff."

"Everything okay now?"

"Marvelous. I won't bore you with the details, but there was a problem, and I took care of it."

"We need to talk about it?"

"Not particularly, no."

"You're being very mysterious."

She grabbed his collar, pulled him close, and gave him a kiss that made his knees weak. Then she whispered in his ear: "If you want mysterious, just try to figure out what I'm gonna do to you tonight."

She patted him twice on the chest, then ducked into her car. The window was down, and he said, "I'm a lucky man."

"Who am I to argue?" she said.

EPILOGUE

TWO DAYS AFTER Pastor Peter Boothe's tearful confession on worldwide television, he arrived unannounced at the Blanco County Sheriff's Office, gave a statement that matched Butch Theriot's version of events, and then vanished from the public eye. (Rumors spread in the following months that he had renounced the prosperity gospel and was now working as a deckhand on a Mexican fishing trawler.)

That same afternoon, Vanessa Boothe called a press conference to announce that she had begun divorce proceedings. "I've been totally humiliated," she said. "Further, I deny all of Peter's accusations regarding my fidelity, and I challenge anyone to produce one shred of evidence to the contrary." To present her side of the story, she said, she had signed a contract with a major

New York City publisher. The forthcoming book—to be titled *As God Is My Witness*—would be released in hardback for the low price of $34.95. Appearance on the *Oprah Winfrey Show* to follow.

In the confusion following the ministry's collapse, the CFO, T. Everett Farrell, discovered that a large sum of cash was missing from the safe in the mailroom. Security video implicated the deceased Alex Pringle in the theft. Farrell alerted the Dallas police, who reclassified the Pringle case as a homicide. An alleged bookmaker named Omar Swann is the chief suspect at this time, but detectives admit that an arrest is unlikely.

Jerry Strand was not charged with any crime, and upon his release from the hospital, he returned to live with his wife, Nadine. His first day home, he "accidentally" broke the Yogi Bear sugar bowl. A week later, he broke the bear-shaped cookie jar. He blamed both incidents—and the many to come—on his injured right hand.

The evening after the break-in at Betty Jean Farley's shed, Darwin Parker tried to phone Kevin "Snake" Sawyer, but the pothead didn't answer. Nor did he answer any of the other thirty-seven calls Parker placed in the following week. Parker began to suspect that Sawyer had absconded with the fossil—until a bit of stunning news appeared on the *Paleontology Quarterly* Web site. The Smithsonian Institution had received an anonymous donation—an *Alamosaurus* skull packed skillfully in a cardboard box. "It's a one-of-a-kind specimen," a curator said. "A little worse for the wear after its unusual journey here, but still truly breathtaking. We're proud to add it to our collection, and we only wish we could thank the generous donor in person."

Kate Wallace avoided a charge of second-degree murder by pleading guilty to criminally negligent homicide, which earned her a two-year stint in state jail. In her second month, while working on a crew collecting trash on a rural highway, she made national headlines by finding the remains of a *Chasmosaurus,* a ceratopsid from the Upper Cretaceous period.

Later that summer, Perry Grange agreed to DNA testing on all of his white-tailed deer. The test results indicated that Hollis Farley's accusations against Grange were unsubstantiated. Grange filed a lawsuit against the Texas Parks and Wildlife Department that was later dismissed.

On the second Saturday in July, in a small evening ceremony on Phil Colby's ranch, John Marlin and Nicole Brooks were married. The bride wore a strapless drop-waist organza ballgown with alençon lace appliqué. The groom wore a black three-button notch tuxedo over snakeskin boots. The videographer was right on time.